"Nurse Lawrence, see what you can do for this Marine."

Maggie straightened automatically at the order. Since the attack began, she had been working frantically. The stream of casualties seemed endless. Added to the lack of water and electricity, it made the medical team's task all but impossible.

Yet somehow they were carrying on. Hurrying toward the doctor, she was thinking only of the next patient, the next wound, the next life saved or lost. Until she saw Anthony.

The sight of him standing bare-chested and bloodstained in the gloom of the tunnel, surrounded by the moans and screams of dying men, took her aback. For an instant, she thought he was an illusion. Then, realizing that he was real, she feared he had been wounded.

"What happened? Are you all right?"

He nodded swiftly, not questioning the brief glimpse of gut-wrenching distress he had seen in her eyes. It seemed incredible that in the midst of such devastation a single man and woman could reach out to each other.

"One of my men's been hurt," he explained quietly. "He's over here."

Together they knelt beside the boy.

EYE OF THE STORM

MAURA SEGER

WORLDWIDE

TORONTO • NEW YORK • LONDON • PARIS
AMSTERDAM • STOCKHOLM • HAMBURG
ATHENS • MILAN • TOKYO • SYDNEY

First published April 1985

ISBN 0-373-97013-7

With special thanks
to Major Donald S. McQuinn, U.S.M.C., Ret.,
and Lieutenant Colonel Henry W. Stankus, U.S.M.C., Ret.,
for their very generous assistance.

U.S.S.R.

China

Japan

Philippines

New
Guinea

Indian
Ocean

south
pacific

Australia

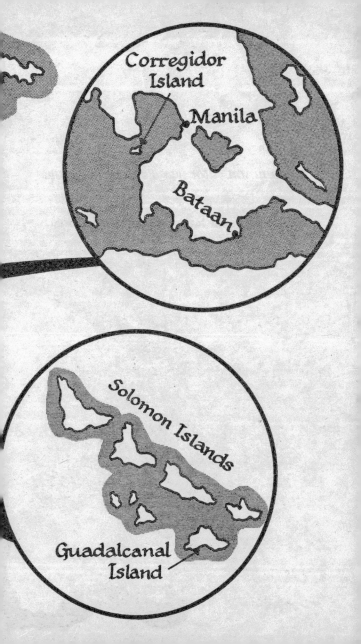

Uncommon valor was a common virtue.

Inscription on the Marine Corps War Memorial,
Arlington National Cemetery

December 1941–May 1942
THE ROCK

Chapter One

Major Kay Broderick had recently taken to keeping one of her late father's medals in the pocket of her white nurse's uniform. He had been awarded it for his service as a doctor during World War I. The medal was about two inches in diameter, its raised surface cool and slightly rough to the touch. Her thumb and index finger rubbed over it absently as she gathered herself together to carry out what might well be her last official act as an Army nurse.

It was ominously quiet in the ward. Most of the men packed closely together on narrow cots were too severely wounded to cry out. Only a few moaned fitfully.

Normally, sounds of traffic from the surrounding city would have undercut the stillness. But that morning nothing was normal in Manila, despite the valiant efforts to carry on as usual.

The louvered windows were open as wide as possible but still admitted only a grudging breeze through their thick screens. Ceiling fans struggled to stir air heavy with the pungent scent of ether and antiseptic, the iron tang of blood and the fetid reek of putrefaction. A handful of nurses and orderlies moved amid the rows of cots, giving what comfort they could.

The major took a deep breath, barely noticing the smell that had become so familiar as to be innocuous.

She was weary to the point of collapse, yet she was determined not to let that affect her.

Of the hundred or so nurses who had been in her command, only half a dozen remained. The greatly shrunken number did not change the fact that she keenly felt her responsibility to each and every one.

Her presence in the ward had not gone unnoticed, but work went on without a ripple. She paused for a moment, proud of the dedication and discipline of her staff, then approached the nurse closest to her and spoke a few quiet words.

The young woman swallowed tightly and nodded. She finished what she was doing and left the ward. Although all the nurses were being given the same orders, Major Broderick had decided to inform each one separately. A general announcement was not only unnecessary, it would intrude on the hushed, almost reverent atmosphere of this place where lives were slowly flickering out.

She came at length to the end of a long row of cots. The boy lying there, his chest and abdomen heavily swathed in bandages, gazed up at the slender young woman bending over him. Her heart-shaped face still bore a slight tan undercut by the pallor of weeks on round-the-clock duty. A wisp of thick chestnut hair had escaped from beneath her nurse's cap. She bit her lower lip unconsciously as she took a blood-pressure reading.

The major hesitated a moment before approaching her. The evacuation was hard enough on all the medical personnel, but she knew that for Maggie Lawrence it was particularly difficult.

The young woman came from an old Army family

in which the traditions of duty and self-sacrifice were deeply imbued. Kay Broderick had been her superior officer ever since Maggie's arrival in Manila the year before, and had found her to be an exemplary nurse, one of those rare individuals with the capacity to give far beyond ordinary limits. For Maggie to have to leave her patients would be heart-wrenching.

Yet there was no acceptable alternative. Waiting until Maggie had unwrapped the blood-pressure cuff and returned it to the instruments tray, the major said crisply, "Finish up here, Lieutenant. It's time to move out."

Maggie's hand froze in the act of reaching for a syringe. She had known as soon as Broderick appeared on the ward what was about to happen, but that was not the same as hearing it. Until the order was given, some faint hope had remained that perhaps she would be allowed to stay after all. Now that hope was gone.

Her mouth trembled slightly as she acknowledged the order with a stiff nod, then concentrated all her attention on filling the syringe and injecting its contents of morphine into the young private. Through the merciful haze of the medication, he managed to give her a faint smile.

Maggie returned it bravely, hoping he could not see how her composure had begun to crack. She arranged the sheet more comfortably around him and touched a cool hand to his damp, feverish brow before straightening up reluctantly.

As she did so, her gaze locked with the major's. All that she could not say out loud was vividly expressed in the misery of her large blue eyes.

The older woman's stern features softened slightly. Huskily, she said, "Go on now. The truck's waiting."

The other nurses had already left the ward; only the orderlies remained. They were all men, members of either the American or the Filipino medical corps, and each had volunteered to stay at his post. The need to do the same stabbed through Maggie.

She had no illusions about what would happen to those who were remaining. Many, if not all, might well die once the Japanese took the city. Life was precious to her—all life, including her own—but she still found it impossible to welcome the chance to escape. Were it not for the knowledge that she was being sent where her superior officers believed she could do the most good, she didn't think she would have found the strength to obey.

Her eyes were blurred by tears as she tore her gaze from the major and turned away. Holding herself rigidly erect, she walked down the long row of cots. At the double doors leading from the ward, she hesitated for a moment, then pushed them open and went through quickly. She did not look back.

Kay Broderick watched Maggie go, her fingers tightening around the medal in her pocket. The incised surface dug into her palm. She didn't mind the small discomfort. It helped to keep at bay the terrible sorrow and dread flickering at the edges of her mind.

Her knees trembled slightly as she sat down beside the young private and with her free hand took hold of his. The gesture was all she had left to offer.

ONLY ONE DUFFEL BAG remained in the corridor. Maggie picked it up numbly and moved on. The hall was cool and shadowy. At its end, where the main doors to the hospital stood open, the glare of light was almost blinding. A dull pain began to pound behind her eyes.

The truck was parked on the far side of the walled garden that surrounded the hospital. Fat lizards dozed in the morning sun, and blooming jacaranda and bougainvillea bushes waved lazily in the desultory breeze. Maggie walked past them dazedly, trying not to think of what lay beyond.

The iron gate creaked as she let herself out. She turned to close it behind her, knowing even as she did so that those who came after her would have no reason to show such care.

A quick flurry of feminine voices greeted her.

"Here's Maggie. . . . Come on, hon, we've got to get moving."

"Toss me your bag. I'll put it with the rest."

"We were getting worried about you."

Willing hands reached down to help her climb into the truck. She murmured her thanks but kept her eyes averted as she took her place on the narrow bench.

"Are we all set?" the Army driver called from behind the wheel. His voice was tightly controlled, yet unmistakably anxious.

"That's the last," one of the nurses briskly confirmed. "Let's roll."

The engine gunned, and the truck lurched forward. A goat scampered out of the way. Dust churned beneath the wheels as the vehicle picked up speed.

They had gone a little distance along the bumpy cobblestone street when the slender, blond-haired girl seated next to Maggie murmured, "Are you okay?"

Maggie nodded jerkily. "I couldn't seem to get my legs to move very fast." Her voice was low and ragged with the tears she had not quite managed to suppress.

Sheila Kilpatrick smiled gently. She and Maggie had been good friends since shortly after their arrival in Manila the year before. Both were twenty-three, former Army brats and dedicated nurses. But there the similarity ended. Maggie was tall and slender with shoulder-length chestnut hair and large blue eyes. Sheila was a petite, curvaceous blonde, whose tour of duty had so far consisted mainly of turning down proposals from smitten soldiers and sailors. She was deeply in love with a young lieutenant assigned to the battleship *Arizona*, which had been sunk during the Japanese attack on Pearl Harbor a little less than three weeks before. News of Charlie Fletcher's fate had yet to reach her, but she refused to believe that he might be among the casualties.

Seated in the back of the rickety truck usually used for hauling supplies, the nurses held on tightly as the driver sped toward the docks. There were rumors that the Japanese might strafe the city, and no one wanted to risk being caught out in the open.

None of the women was disposed to talk; each sat in silence, staring out. Maggie's gaze was remote and unfocused at first. She was still seeing in her mind's eye the face of Major Broderick as she had given the order to leave, interposed with the face of the young private who was dying of chest and stomach wounds.

Both images were part of a world suddenly collapsing in on itself like a smashed seedpod that had turned out to be surprisingly empty.

Rather than fall into that anguished vision, Maggie forced herself to concentrate on her immediate surroundings. The civilians who had still remained as of that morning seemed to have vanished. Shopwindows were boarded up, debris littered the streets, and only a few scraggly dogs moved through the heat of midday. Here and there, Christmas decorations fluttered morosely, silent reminders that this year the birth of the Saviour was being observed with death and destruction.

In the shantytown barrio surrounding the seedy dock area, there were more signs of life. People here had no way of leaving. Naked brown-skinned children stood at the doors of the thatched huts, staring mutely at the activity swirling around them. Men and women talked quietly among themselves in the rhythmic native dialect of Tagalog. What they thought of the coming change, no one knew. Perhaps one conqueror was the same to them as another.

"Sweet Lord, would you look at that!" Sheila exclaimed as the truck careened to a stop at the edge of a pier. Before them was the interisland steamer *Don Esteban*, a picturesque relic of the era that had ended short weeks before. "There's not an antiaircraft gun on the thing."

"'Fraid not," Maggie agreed. She hopped down from the truck and joined her friend.

"I hope the Japs are taking time out for tea," Sheila muttered, continuing to survey the steamer dubiously. People were hurrying on board, but she showed no eagerness to join them.

"At least it floats," Maggie pointed out sensibly. Considering the wreckage of boats lying all around, that was a definite plus. "Come on, let's get going."

"Wait a minute. I've got to find some way to mail my letters. Charlie hasn't heard from me in weeks, and he'll be worried."

Maggie sighed resignedly. There was nothing to be gained by pointing out that all mail service had ceased. Sheila wasn't about to let that deter her, any more than she was willing to consider the possibility that Charlie might no longer be alive.

"I'm not letting him think something's happened to me," she went on stubbornly. "Here, take my bag and go on board. I'll be right behind you."

"Sure you will. You'll be standing here when Tojo arrives—and believe me, *he* won't take your mail."

Casting around for some way to get rid of the letters fast, Maggie spied a young officer standing on the next pier where a submarine was completing its loading. He was scanning the sky anxiously.

"Over there. I heard all the subs that are left are heading for Australia. Maybe he can get the letters through."

Sheila quickly dug in her bag, pulled out the packet and was about to scramble over to the other pier when she paused for a moment. "Don't you have anything to go?"

Maggie hesitated. She did have a letter to her parents in Virginia but wasn't sure about sending it. While she wanted them to know she had come through okay so far, she didn't think for a moment that they would be fooled by her deliberately optimistic tone.

Still, some word from her would undoubtedly be better than none. Pulling the envelope out, she handed it to Sheila and watched as her friend hurried up to the young captain, flashed him her sweetest smile, and briefly explained what she wanted.

He was nodding before she had finished, holding out a hand for the precious letters. They chatted a few minutes more, until the shrieking whistle of the *Don Esteban* warned that time was up.

Even so, Sheila only just made it back as the ropes were being untied and the steamer prepared to depart. She and Maggie had to run for it, jumping the last few feet to the deck.

Maggie stumbled slightly and would have fallen had not strong hands grasped her waist and pulled her upright. Momentarily winded, she had to catch her breath before thanking the man who had helped her.

"My pleasure, ma'am," a deep voice intoned.

Something in it, some note of amusement utterly out of keeping with the seriousness of the moment, piqued her curiosity. She looked up, into hard black eyes that seemed to see straight through her. He was, she noted almost absently, very big and heavily muscled. But then, most Marines were. Her father had always said that the Corps attracted men who were somehow larger than life.

He hadn't meant that admiringly. In the view of Colonel Lawrence, the leathernecks were a bunch of foul-mouthed, trigger-tempered braggarts who weren't good for anything more than getting into bar fights. Maggie had absorbed a great deal of his attitude.

She nodded at the Marine coolly, noting in passing that his khakis were encrusted with mud and grime, he obviously had not shaved in several days, and his eyes for all their intensity were red-rimmed from lack of sleep. In short, he was in the same shape as every other man on board the steamer, yet he somehow managed to look considerably better.

His thick ebony hair, dark gaze and swarthy skin suggested an Italian heritage, as did his finely chiseled mouth and a nose that could most graciously be called Roman. She guessed him to be about twenty-six, but with none of the immaturity that still clung to some men at that age. On the contrary, an air of quiet competency hung about him, in keeping with the sergeant's stripes he wore.

Abruptly recalled to her surroundings by the lazy but purposeful way his eyes were roaming over her, Maggie flushed. She turned away quickly, joining Sheila under a canvas shelter near the prow.

Her friend grinned at her knowingly. "Whoo-ee! Was that one ever putting the eye on you!"

"Don't be silly," Maggie muttered tartly. "He just helped me when I started to fall."

"Honey, if there's one thing I know, it's how a man looks when he's interested. And believe me, he is."

"Sheila, in case you haven't noticed, we're at war. There's no time for anything like that."

Her friend's hazel eyes lit up with mischief. "Don't kid yourself. The more shots get fired, the more people are going to want to do you-know-what."

Maggie gave up trying to argue. Sheila was in love

and thought everybody else should be in the same condition. She had tried several times to play matchmaker. The men she'd come up with were always very pleasant and attractive. Maggie had enjoyed herself, but that was all. She wasn't ready for any sort of commitment and had told her friend as much.

Repeating herself now wouldn't serve much purpose, especially since they had rather more serious things to be concerned about. The waters of Manila Bay were choppy and the sky above was ominously clear. The *Don Esteban* was making slow progress, a sitting duck for any enemy pilot in the mood for a little shooting.

Glumly Maggie settled down on top of her duffel bag, trying to get comfortable despite the swaying deck, the press of people and the uncanny sensation that she was being watched.

Telling herself it was just her imagination, she kept her eyes straight ahead and refused to glance over at the cluster of Marines standing out in the open, smoking and laughing among themselves as though they didn't have a care in the world.

Anthony Gargano listened absently to the comments of his men. He was tired, hungry and pretty much fed up. The Fourth Marines had been in the Philippines barely a few weeks and had hardly had a chance to set up their base at Subic Bay when they were surprised by a Japanese air attack that took a heavy toll of both men and equipment.

The attack had come several hours after the assault on Pearl Harbor, yet the commanding officer of the combined American and Filipino forces—General Douglas MacArthur—had not seen fit to put his men on alert.

To Anthony's way of thinking, this only confirmed his belief that Marines had no business being led by an Army general. In fact, he suspected they would be better off with no officers at all, for whom he felt only disdain.

As though to justify all their worst thoughts about him, MacArthur was now adding insult to injury by denying the Marines an opportunity to fight back. Instead, they were being withdrawn to Corregidor, some five miles off the mainland, where they would have the dubious honor of guarding the great man in his new headquarters.

What a damn stupid way to run a war, Anthony thought morosely. He was a member of an elite fighting force, not some glorified baby-sitter. After weeks of seeing planes blown out of the air, ships destroyed and men killed, he ached to get a little of his own back. Instead, he found himself assigned to a hunk of rock out in a bay, told to sit and wait like a good boy while the rescue force steamed toward them.

That was all right for regular Army types like MacArthur, but it sure didn't sit well with Marines. About the only good thing that had happened to him since rolling into these godforsaken islands was that little encounter with the nurse a few minutes earlier.

His reaction to her surprised him. Generally speaking, he went for nicely stacked blondes like her friend. But something in those wide blue eyes and defiant chin had egged him on.

He didn't have to be able to read minds to know what she thought of him. He was a big, tough, rough Marine sergeant in need of a shave, not to mention a bath, and she was a white-clad angel of mercy with lieutenant's bars who somehow managed to look fresh as a daisy, despite the chaos all around her.

Maybe it was just that he was worn out, or that he'd seen too much of death in the past few days, but he definitely liked looking at her. She made him think of better times—strolling through the old neighborhood in Brooklyn on Sunday afternoon, watching the girls go by, maybe taking one of them out for a movie and later, in the backseat of his Buick...

He grinned wryly to himself. He'd learned a thing or two since then. Much good it would do him. The days of easy living were gone, and it didn't look as though he'd have any chance to verify the claim that the Filipino women were the loveliest on earth.

If they were, that feisty lieutenant gave them a run for their money. Seated on the duffel bag, with the skirt of her white uniform riding up to expose long, shapely legs that were lightly tanned, she made him feel decidedly less glum.

Until his corporal tapped him on the shoulder and said nonchalantly, "Uh, Sarge, I don't suppose that's one of ours?"

Anthony shifted his gaze from Maggie and glanced up. A snub-nosed Zero emblazoned with the emblem of the Rising Sun was coming at them out of the west.

Even as he watched, bursts of fire began to pour from machine guns mounted beneath the wings. He barely had a chance to yell "Hit the deck!" before the first splatter of bullets carved its jagged pattern right next to him.

On his belly, cursing mightily, he crawled toward the prow. There was room there to set up a machine gun. With a little luck, they could get the son of a bitch. But first he had to survive the lethal strafing fire falling like deadly hail all around him.

Maggie had gone down on her face at the first shots. It had been a purely instinctive reaction, but now another was taking its place. Glancing up, she saw a Filipino civilian slumped nearby, blood gushing from a wound to his throat. Automatically, she started to rise, at the same moment reaching for her bag with the first-aid kit she had carefully packed.

Anthony was thinking only of getting the gun into place when, from the corner of his eye, he saw the pretty lieutenant about to stand up. Reacting like a stone shot from a catapult, he hurled himself at her, bringing her down with a tackle that would have had the football fans back at St. Ignatius High on their feet, cheering wildly.

Maggie was doing anything but. Facedown on the deck, unable to see her gallant rescuer, she still knew who it was. Anger roared through her. "What the hell are you doing?"

"*Me?* Are you out of your mind? You can't do that guy any good, but you sure as hell can get yourself blown to bits!"

His patronizing tone was bad enough, but there were other ramifications of their little encounter that were rapidly disturbing her. The weight of his body pressing her onto the deck made her vividly aware of her own comparative frailty. The warmth of his burnished skin seemed to engulf her. A musky aroma of sweat and virility made her senses swim.

In her best officer's voice, she snapped, "Get off me, Sergeant. That's an order."

Dead silence for a moment; then Anthony muttered, "Yes, ma'am, right away, ma'am. You want to get yourself killed, don't let me get in your way."

Rolling onto the deck, he glanced quickly at the sky and spotted the Zero turning at the far end of its approach. There was barely time to get the machine gun in position before the pilot began another deadly run.

Anthony took a deep breath as he propped himself up against the railing. His hands grasped the trigger. Crouched low on the deck, he automatically gauged the rapidly diminishing distance, waiting for his moment.

Five hundred feet. . . check the ammo belt. . . Hail Mary. . . correct for angle of approach. . . full of grace. . . two hundred. . . Hail Mary. . . God, that bastard's coming in low! He thinks he's got us. . . full of grace. . . he's wrong. . . please, God, let him be wrong. . . Hail Mary. . . now!

He fired in steady, perfectly aimed bursts, controlling the heavy weight and thrust of the gun with apparent effortlessness. As the Zero screamed overhead, he turned to follow it.

The pilot banked sharply and began to return, clearly intending to get rid of whoever was troubling him down below. Anthony surveyed the angle, knew he had no choice and rose. Fully exposed to the strafing, he continued to fire.

The Zero arched downward, gushing a stream of black smoke. It hung for a seemingly endless instant against the sky, then nose-dived straight into the sea. Plumes of spray shot up all around it, high enough to wash over the *Don Esteban*. Even before the water could recede, the plane had begun to sink.

Anthony lowered the machine gun slowly to the deck. The metal was very hot and his hands were burned. He stared at them absently, oblivious to the wild cheers rising on all sides.

Compared with the horror of the past couple of weeks, it was a very tiny victory. But it gave the beleaguered men and women some sense of hope. They surrounded him joyfully, pounding him on the back and all but drowning him in thanks until his corporal was finally able to push through the crowd and rescue him.

"Let the sarge catch his breath, folks." Turning to Anthony, he grinned. "Felt like a little target practice?"

"You might say that," Anthony muttered dryly. He understood everyone's appreciation, but enough was enough. He hadn't done anything except his job.

"Why don't you sit down, Sarge?" the corporal suggested tactfully. "Those hands of yours could use a little salve. I'll see if I can find some."

"Never mind," a soft but firm voice said. "I'll take care of it."

Anthony looked up to find the pretty lieutenant gazing at him, a startled, somewhat contrite look on her face. Though he was still chafing at her angry rejection of his help, he thought he might be talked into forgiving her. Sitting back against the railing, he watched through half-hooded eyes as she approached.

"Your hands..." She held out her own, and instinctively he placed his in them, palms up. Her touch was infinitely gentle as she assessed the damage done by the hot metal of the machine gun.

"Does that hurt?" she asked softly.

"No," he lied, "not a bit."

Maggie shook her head wryly. "What is it with you Marines? I've never met one who didn't think he was some kind of superman."

He laughed softly, his breath stirring the wispy tendrils of hair drifting over her brow. "Have you met many?"

She looked up, straight into his taunting gaze. "Enough."

His smile deepened, a white slash against burnished skin. "Funny thing about Marines—you can never have too much of us, but one's always plenty."

As he spoke, his voice dropped slightly, becoming low and caressing. Maggie flushed, feeling somehow flustered. She was no stranger to sexual innuendo and generally had no trouble ignoring it. But this man was different; he got to her in some way she hadn't expected and didn't understand.

Quickly uncapping the tube of salve, she spread a thin coating on the burns, then reached for a roll of bandages. "The dressing will have to be changed daily for a week. After that, leave your hands open to the air, but try not to pick up anything rough or heavy."

His ebony eyes gleamed ironically. "I wouldn't dream of it."

Her mouth tightened, giving her the look of an annoyed kitten. He grinned to himself, sure she wouldn't care for that comparison. But he thought it accurate nonetheless.

Her bone structure was delicate, her face heart-shaped. There was a smattering of freckles across her upturned nose. Her eyes were a dark shade of blue that reminded him of the hyacinths his mother had grown each spring in the backyard of their house in Brooklyn.

Leaning forward slightly, he breathed in the scent of her sun-washed hair. Her cap had fallen off when he grabbed her, allowing the waves of gleaming chestnut silk to tumble about her shoulders, not unlike the pinup he'd seen of Rita Hayworth.

"You sure are pretty, ma'am."

Maggie looked up sharply, her eyes clashing with his. She was torn between feminine pleasure and professional discipline. Discipline won—sort of. More gently than she should have, she said, "You know you're not supposed to talk to officers like that."

He sighed eloquently, as though the vagaries of military law baffled him. "I suppose, but sometimes a man just can't help himself."

Sensing the playfulness beneath his plaintive facade, she laughed. "It seems to me that you manage just fine." In a more serious tone, she added, "That was spectacular shooting, and you were incredibly brave."

Not even the shadow of several days' growth of beard could hide his blush. He cursed himself inwardly, wondering what on earth was happening to make him feel like a fifteen-year-old confronted by his first pretty girl.

"It was nothing," he said flatly. "I just didn't happen to feel like getting killed today."

Maggie understood his embarrassment; she had grown up with military men who wore their courage like a second skin and didn't care to have it commented on. Respecting his wishes, she changed the subject. "I'm sorry I was rude before. Thank you for what you did."

He looked at her carefully, gauging her sincerity. The Filipino she had been trying to help was dead; they could both see that. The man had been shot through an artery in the throat and had had no chance of being saved, but she would have risked her life to try. She had guts, Anthony gave her that. And she would need them where they were going.

"If you wouldn't mind a little advice," he said, "you're going to have to be more careful. Corregidor's not exactly a picnic."

The softness she had been feeling toward him vanished. He was a good one to be giving advice after the way he'd stood up and exposed himself to gunfire! "I'm sure I'll manage," she replied stiffly.

Anthony took in the sparks flaring in her lovely eyes and chuckled. "Now don't get your fur ruffled. All I meant was that you've got to stop and think before you do something."

That was too much for Maggie. She was feeling very self-conscious about her reaction to him and didn't need to be pushed any further than she already had been. "What I think," she said sharply, "is that I've heard enough. You seem to have a continual problem figuring out what these bars on my shoulders mean. I have been through officers' training, you know."

Anthony tried hard to keep from laughing but failed. His deep, rich chuckle brought surprised looks from the other passengers. "Pardon me, ma'am, I should have realized I was talking to a veteran."

After the torturous weeks in Manila, Maggie felt

exactly like that, and she didn't appreciate any suggestion to the contrary. "I'm glad you're finding this all so amusing, Sergeant," she said coldly. "But my experience has been a little different."

That was all she had meant to say, but somehow it didn't stop there. Instead, she heard herself adding, "This morning I had to leave the side of an eighteen-year-old boy who isn't going to live much longer. At least he won't have to worry about being taken prisoner like my chief nurse, who volunteered to stay behind."

Despite herself, her voice cracked. She was so damn tired, so frightened and so sick to death of death itself. A few weeks before, she had been a happy young woman enjoying the first great adventure of her life. Now she was weighed down by a burden of maturity that had been gained in the harshest way possible—by watching people die.

How had they come to be in the midst of such insanity? What hellish turn was the world taking?

Anthony saw the play of emotions across her face and understood instantly what they meant. He had been asking himself the same questions and was no closer to the answers.

Not having intended to push her so hard, he felt genuinely contrite. All he really wanted to do was protect her. That surprised him. He was used to caring for his men, but it was different with her. How exactly, he wasn't sure; he was groping toward something he couldn't recognize and felt clumsy doing it.

"Hey," he said gently, "I'm sorry. I was out of line. Forget what I said." Holding up his bandaged hands, he smiled, with no awareness of how that smile transformed the harsh lines of his face. "You're a terrific nurse, you know that? I feel better already."

Maggie hesitated, then returned his smile reluctantly. She would have preferred to stay angry at him—some instinct warned her she was safer that way—but she couldn't seem to manage it. He looked so little-boy endearing, not unlike her younger brother, Tad.

"You should probably get a medal for what you did," she said softly. "Your family would be proud."

He shrugged and looked away, embarrassed. "I'd just as soon they didn't know. They worry enough as it is."

"Mine, too." Almost to herself, she mused, "You'd think they'd be used to it by now."

"What do you mean?"

"Just that my family's always been in the service." When he continued to look curious, she said, "Dad's with the War Department. He'll be going crazy trying to get a combat assignment. And Tad—he's my brother—I guess he'll be in uniform, too, by now."

"And you're over here. That makes things kind of rough on your mom."

Maggie nodded somberly. "But she'll never complain. She's the granddaughter, daughter, wife and mother of soldiers. She used to say that at her wedding she was the only person out of uniform."

"Your family sounds a little different from mine," Anthony commented dryly.

"Are they civilians?"

He nearly choked on that. His family was about as civilian as any could get. "You might say so. Pop doesn't think much of armies. Saw enough of them in

Europe when he was a kid. He's probably going
around telling everyone this is just a flash in the pan
and not to get excited. Meanwhile, Ma will be cooking anything that doesn't move, stocking up the pan-
try in case they run short. And Dominick—"

"Who's he?"

"My kid brother." He chuckled affectionately.
"Dom's a real smart aleck. Thinks he knows it all.
Jeez, maybe he's been drafted by now. That could ex-
plain a lot."

"Like what?" Maggie asked, settling back against
the railing beside him. A quick glance around had
reassured her that there were no other casualties. She
was free to remain where she was, at least as long as
she didn't examine too closely her reasons for wanting to do so.

"Like why we're losing, which we are, in case you
haven't noticed. Dom could screw up the greatest
army in the world."

She laughed. "I think you may be giving him a little too much credit. Guys like my dad will whip him
into shape in no time."

He cast her a frankly skeptical look. "Don't bet on
it. Even Salvatore never managed to beat any sense
into Dom."

"Who's he?"

"My eldest sister's husband. He and Vita got married five, six years ago. They've got a couple of nice
kids."

"So you're an uncle. That's great."

Anthony flashed her a smile that stripped years off
his age and made him look almost carefree. "The
first time it happened it was great. Now it's a habit."

"All right, I'll bite. How many nieces and/or nephews do you have?"

"I never heard anyone do that before." At her quizzical look, he explained. "Say that 'and/or' business. I thought you could only write that."

It was Maggie's turn to look skeptical. She had no idea how much formal schooling he'd had, but she wasn't about to accept the idea that he was uneducated. He struck her as the sort of man who had crammed a great deal of learning into his life.

Seeing her disbelief, Anthony grinned and relented slightly. "I've got four—Vita's two, plus my second sister, Lucia—the one who lives in Chicago—has a boy and a girl. That's pretty good, considering that Dom, Paulo—he's my middle brother—me, and Sophia—the baby in the family—aren't married yet."

Coming as she did from a fairly small family, Maggie was a bit stunned by the complexity of his. "How do you keep them all straight?"

"It's not easy," he admitted, enjoying her surprise. He was telling her far more about himself than was usual for him, but he didn't question why. Something about her made him feel both comfortable and excited. It was a heady sensation.

"There are also a couple of dozen aunts, uncles and cousins," he added absently, caught up in watching the play of sunlight on her hair, "not to mention my father's parents, my mother's parents, my mother's grandmother—"

"You don't all live together, do you?"

"Pretty much, except for Lucia and me. As soon as Pop could afford it, he bought a row house in Brooklyn. Other members of the family bought houses on the same block or right nearby."

The thought of his family sobered him. Throughout the past few weeks, they had often been on his mind. He had taken comfort from picturing all of them in the big living room of his parents' home, with the Christmas decorations up and the smells of the traditional "seven fishes" dinner wafting from the kitchen. It made his mouth water to remember the lobster, mussels, squid, shrimp and so on that his mother prepared so spectacularly.

But now it occurred to him that his mental image was out of kilter. His family would be caught up in the war, worrying about what was going to happen to him and his brothers, worrying perhaps about whether or not he was still alive.

A terrible sense of futility tore through him. He had left home at eighteen because he'd found it too confining; if he'd stayed, he'd be married with a couple of kids, and working in the factory, and maybe another child would be on the way. Not a bad life, but something deep inside him had always insisted there was more.

So he'd signed on with the Navy and, after a stint with them, joined the Marines, drawn by the lure of adventure. He'd been to most parts of the world, including several so alien as to be almost on other planets. He'd fought, drunk and done a few other things to a degree other men only fantasized about.

He was twenty-six years old, at the peak of his physical and mental powers. And he'd just killed a man whose family was undoubtedly wondering about his fate.

It was dangerous for him to think of the enemy in such terms. Better to concentrate strictly on his own men. Once they reached Corregidor, he'd have them to think of. But that didn't mean he wanted to lose touch with the pretty lieutenant whose eyes saw — and understood — so much.

He glanced at her obliquely. There was a smudge of dirt on her cheek and a rip in one sleeve of her uniform. Her mouth was soft and looked very sweet. That gorgeous hair shone brightly in the sun.

Jeez, he was getting downright poetic, he thought. It must have something to do with the stench of sweat, blood and simple fear wafting over the deck. Still, there was no sense in letting a good thing go by.

"If you don't mind my asking, ma'am," he said softly, "what's your name?"

She started, surprised by the realization that, after all they had shared in the past few minutes, they were still strangers to each other. On impulse, she held out her hand, pleased when his swallowed it up without apparent discomfort.

Looking directly at him, she said, "I'm Maggie Lawrence. And you're...?"

"Anthony Gargano. Nice to meet you."

His gaze was so intense that after a moment she dropped her eyes and laughed a little nervously. "Not exactly a proper introduction, but I guess it will do."

He nodded slowly, bemused by what was happening to them. Several moments later, he said, "I guess it will have to."

Something in his voice made Maggie look up. He was staring out over the bow, and she followed his gaze. Dead ahead loomed the purple mass of Corregidor, rising ominously out of the water.

The final stronghold of the American forces was expected to endure even if Bataan — their last remaining fortress on the Philippine mainland — fell. The military leaders seemed absolutely certain that the citadel would protect them until the rescue force could arrive.

The tunnel-gouged rock glinted darkly in the sun, looking for all the world like an immense, elongated tombstone.

Chapter Two

"PICK OUT BUNKS and get your gear stowed," Captain Jean Davies instructed. "Then we'll meet for orientation and a tour of the medical facilities."

Smiling slightly, she added, "I think you'll be surprised at how quickly you'll get used to this place. It's really not as bad as it looks at first glance."

Maggie had some difficulty believing that. The Malinta Tunnel, where she and the other new arrivals had been met by their commanding officer, was one of several running through Corregidor. It had originally been intended to store supplies, not people. Crowded as it was now with all manner of refugees from the mainland, it swiftly threatened to become a claustrophobic prison.

Maggie followed Sheila down a branching tunnel to the nurses' quarters. There they picked out adjacent cots and unpacked. Extra clothes and toiletries, what few there were, went into the footlockers. Maggie put a group picture of her family on the table between the beds, and Sheila added a picture of Charlie.

Finished, they surveyed their surroundings. They were in a lateral tunnel beneath "Bottomside," the third and lowest of the three crests that made up the Rock. This was the one closest to Bataan and had the best beaches, over which the Japanese were expected to come if and when they invaded.

To reach the lateral, Maggie and Sheila had walked through the main tunnel, some twenty feet high and thirty feet wide, crowded with officers and civilians alike. The people they'd passed were earnestly going about their duties, but all had blank expressions on their faces. It was as if they had deliberately chosen to absent themselves mentally from their surroundings.

Not that anyone could blame them. Even on such short acquaintance, the problems with "Fortress Corregidor" were obvious. To begin with, there was the heat. It was at least ninety-five degrees in the tunnel.

What little ventilation there was labored inadequately. The smell of closely packed humanity mingled with the odors of foodstuffs shipped from the mainland, diesel fuel, creosote, cordite and oiled metal. Dust fell constantly from the walls and ceilings. Maggie thought of what it would be like in surgery and grimaced.

"It's not the Waldorf," Sheila admitted, "but I suppose it could be worse."

Tempted to ask how, Maggie stopped herself. Morale was going to be critically important as the days wore on. She would do her part to uphold it. Instead, she said lightly, "It's enough to make a girl long for her bubble bath."

"Speaking of which, do you have any idea how we're going to keep clean around here?"

"Not off the top of my head. It looks as though that's going to be a real problem."

"I'll say! If they expect us to stay in regulation whites, they've got another think coming!"

What "they" expected was spelled out a short time

later at orientation. Captain Davies stood up in front, next to a map pinned to the wall. As she spoke in her tired, slightly husky voice, she pointed to a spot on the map.

"This, for those of you who don't know, is Corregidor, otherwise called the Singapore of the Pacific. The island guards the mouth of Manila Bay, which is strategically vital to anyone attempting to take the Philippines. The military viewpoint is that this is an impregnable fortress.

"The southern tip of the island, where we are, is crisscrossed by a maze of tunnels and guarded by regular Army troops and the Fourth Marines. At least six months' worth of supplies is on hand. In short, there is every reason to believe we will be able to hold out until help arrives."

She paused for a moment, letting her words sink in. None of the nurses misunderstood what she was telling them. In their contact with the men, they were not to suggest by word or deed that they feared for the outcome of the struggle.

That made sense to Maggie. Whatever the reality of the situation, they were all stuck there, so they might as well make the best of it. At least they were better off than those still on the mainland.

Captain Davies pulled down another map and continued her talk. "This is the medical lateral, where you will be living and working. It includes the hospital, mess hall, surgery and accommodations for about one hundred doctors, nurses and orderlies. Besides the entrance you came through to the south, there is another that opens onto the north road. During your off hours, you may go aboveground unless otherwise informed, but keep in mind that it could be necessary to seek shelter suddenly."

That was hardly news. With the Japanese in control of what had been Cavite Naval Base a few miles across the bay, Corregidor could be easily shelled. Air attacks also had to be anticipated, but at least there would be some warning of those.

"Any questions?" Captain Davies asked.

There were none. Everyone needed time to assimilate what she had learned.

"All right, then," Captain Davies said. "You're all on the next shift, which reports in thirty minutes, so get moving."

The following hours passed in a blur for Maggie. She scrubbed for surgery, then assisted a young Army doctor in removing shell fragments from a gunnery officer and repairing an abdominal wound suffered by a civilian. She gave out medication, smiled, joked and talked of home. She admired pictures of girl friends, read letters for men too injured to do it themselves, and changed dressings. Late in her shift, she was called back into surgery and watched helplessly while, despite their best efforts, a young private died on the table.

By the end of the day, she was dirty, exhausted and too tired to do more than put one foot in front of another. Manila seemed a lifetime ago, tomorrow a dream that would never come. There was only the stale air, the pain and the dank tunnel.

Sheila had to coax her to eat. "Isn't this about the best canned salmon you've ever had? Come on, take another bite."

"How come you still have so much energy?" Maggie inquired wearily. "I'm wiped out."

"You pulled tougher duty than I did," her friend admitted frankly. "The word is already out that you're a fantastic scrub nurse."

"Lucky me."

"Bet you see some terrific surgery here."

Maggie thought of the private who had died, and didn't respond. Instead, she said, "Want to go topside and take a look around?"

"Sure you aren't too tired?"

"Probably, but I'm too wound up to sleep. Besides, if I don't get some fresh air soon, I'll pass out."

"You've convinced me. Let's go."

This was easier said than done. First they had to make their way through the medical lateral to the main tunnel, then along it to the north exit. Once there, they had an unrestricted view of barbed-wire beaches, concrete trenches, foxholes and tank traps.

"So much for paradise." Sheila sighed. "And here I was hoping for a swim."

"Not in these waters. They're shark-infested."

"Hmm...maybe you've got a point. Better the wolves than the sharks." Grinning, she indicated the cluster of Marines hard at work maneuvering an anti-aircraft gun into place.

The men were all stripped to the waist, wearing khakis cut off at the knees, dog tags and very little else. One glanced up, spotted the nurses and called an impromptu break.

"How-do, ladies," the corporal in charge of the operation greeted them genially. "Just shipped in?"

"As a matter of fact, yes," Maggie said as she and Sheila went over to join the men. "What tipped you off?"

Another Marine laughed. "You looked curious. A few days here will cure you of that."

"I guess so. . . . Have you been here long?"

"About a week. We came over with the first group to set up our barracks north of here at Middleside."

"What's it like there?" Sheila asked, accepting a Lucky Strike from a private. The smile she gave him by way of thanks left the young man dazed.

"Not too bad," he murmured. "We brought all our own food and ammo, even a mobile hospital. None of us wants to go down into that tunnel any sooner than we have to."

Sheila and Maggie glanced at each other. If the Marines were even entertaining the possibility of redeploying into the tunnel at some date, things were worse than they had thought.

Gingerly, Maggie asked, "Do you think it will come to that?"

The young man shrugged. "Marines don't surrender, ma'am. Given half a chance, we'll fight to the last man, and that tunnel's the place to do it."

"That's enough," the corporal snapped. "You know damn well the relief force will be here in no time."

"That's right," said another. "Scuttlebutt is, there's a mile-long convoy steaming at top speed straight for us. We'll barely have a chance to get settled in before it arrives."

Maggie wasn't so sure. Every time she heard about the rumored relief force, it seemed to get bigger in size and closer to the Philippines. The only trouble was, it showed no sign of arriving.

Despite her close resemblance to her mother, she was in many ways her father's daughter. Colonel Lawrence had taught her to read between the lines of official military pronouncements to get to whatever scrap of reality they might contain. And so far, whenever the subject of the rescue fleet came up, all she could discern was a desperate hope based on nothing more than a beleaguered president's assurances that they would not be forgotten.

Unfortunately, there were a lot of ways to be remembered—as martyrs, for instance.

As the sun sank toward the west, the Marines headed back to their barracks at Middleside, and Maggie and Sheila reluctantly reentered the tunnel. They took their turns in the single shower that had to serve some two dozen nurses, then slipped into their pajamas and lay down on their cots. To get beneath the covers was unbearable.

Long after the lights were turned off, the strange sounds and smells of the tunnel kept Maggie awake. She dozed only fitfully, dreaming of young men dying and of a dark-eyed Marine who had, for a brief time, made her forget.

MORNING CAME too soon, and with it another meal of canned salmon and rice. Word was out that fresh food was in extremely short supply. They could expect little variety in a diet that would, over time, lead inevitably to severe nutritional deficiencies and weight loss.

The routine of the day was broken by news that the

commander of the naval forces, Admiral Hart, had sailed from Manila Bay in the submarine *Shark*, bound for refuge in Australia. With his departure, the Navy's presence in the Philippines ended. They were now truly on their own.

That evening, neither Maggie nor Sheila had the energy to leave the tunnel. Instead, after more salmon and rice, they joined most of the other inhabitants around the shortwave radio to listen to the news broadcast from San Francisco.

The report wasn't good. Manila was now officially an open city, and the Japanese were expected to enter at any moment. How they would treat the civilians and military personnel they found there remained to be discovered.

Hong Kong had fallen to the emperor's forces. It seemed that the British were no more successful at stopping them than the Americans. Pearl Harbor continued to dominate attention.

It was almost three weeks after the attack, but the commentator's voice still shook as he read again the list of mighty ships destroyed by the assault. The number of dead grew with each passing day. Sheila's hands were clenched in her lap, her mind clearly on Charlie and his fate.

A wave of depression washed over Maggie. She had no way of reassuring her friend—or, for that matter, herself. Almost the entire United States fleet in the Pacific had been wiped out. Without any ships, how were they supposed to be rescued?

Yet how could they not be? There were some thirty thousand American troops and civilians in the Philippines. Surely no government would abandon them to their fate.

LYING IN HIS BUNK at the Marine barracks, Anthony was thinking the same thing. He had spent the day supervising gun emplacements, which had given him the chance to move around the island a bit and get the lay of the land.

What he had seen worried him. To begin with, there was an unrestricted flow of Filipino civilians onto the island. He could hardly blame them for wanting to escape the approaching enemy, but he knew that their presence would inevitably weaken the fighting capability of the fortress.

And if that wasn't bad enough, they were top-heavy with brass. There seemed to be at least two officers for every enlisted man. So who the hell was going to do all the work?

Thinking of the brass reminded him of MacArthur. Anthony felt a grudging admiration for the general, but still thought he had to be crazy. It was bad enough that he had his wife and little boy with him weeks after they should have been evacuated, but he had refused to live in the tunnels, insisting instead on taking over a house that had to be on the most exposed point of Corregidor.

The Japanese had already flown a few strafing runs over it, and each time MacArthur had gone outside to walk around, puffing on his corncob pipe and looking as though he didn't give a damn about anything while his aides scrambled around frantically, trying to protect him.

If the general had thought to make a demonstration of his courage, he had succeeded. But there was more to winning battles than sheer guts. Strategy counted for something, and MacArthur's strategy, whatever it might be, continued to elude Anthony. He fell asleep wondering if the great general wasn't deliberately challenging the Japanese to come and get him.

Two days later they took him up on the offer.

The bulk of the Fourth Marine Division had just completed the journey over from Bataan and was settling into the barracks when the air-raid siren went off.

"Another friggin' drill," one of Anthony's men groaned as they grabbed their World War I–vintage helmets and raced for their gun emplacement.

Anthony didn't think so. He looked up at the heat-hazed sky and saw the twin-engine Mitsubishis coming in from the north. Quickly he rapped out orders, giving his men no time to think of their danger.

The air screamed with a deluge of .50-caliber tracers rocketing up from their gun emplacement and the others surrounding it. But the bombers seemed impervious. They were flying above eighteen thousand feet—outside of range—when their bellies opened and the bombs began to fall.

Several scored direct hits on the barracks building. It trembled convulsively, like a house of cards struck by a careless hand. Thick black smoke and tongues of flame roared upward.

Anthony watched in helpless fascination as cracks opened up near the roof, widening swiftly to reveal the inferno rapidly devouring the inside. Dust and bits of concrete began to pour out from between the fissures until entire chunks of wall crumbled away, falling inward to crush anyone unlucky enough to be still alive.

There was a moment of stunned silence in the trench before one of the men screamed, "We've got to get them out!" He was halfway over the sandbags when Anthony grabbed hold of his belt and dragged him back.

"Don't be a jackass! You wouldn't get ten feet without being killed!"

The private, a seventeen-year-old former farm boy from Nebraska on his first tour of duty as a Marine, stared back at Anthony in anguish. His face was gray, and his big, rangy body shook with the denial of what was happening. "Th-they're our buddies.... We gotta help 'em."

Anthony's face softened slightly. Still keeping a firm hold on the boy, he said quietly, "They're dead, Johnny. We can't do them any good."

A child's eyes met his, full of pleading to say it wasn't so and make the pain go away. Anthony gazed back unrelentingly. The best favor he could do for Johnny was to force him to face the truth. He held on to him tightly, until the wide, horror-filled eyes gradually dulled as numb acceptance seeped through.

Anthony gave him a last careful look before he stepped back and gestured to the gun. "Get back to work, Private."

Silently, Johnny did as he was told. The whole encounter had taken less than a minute, but already the pace of the battle was speeding up.

The destruction of the barracks had been the signal for a new wave of bombs that impacted all around them, throwing up great clumps of the volcanic dirt and rock that made up the island. It seemed as if Corregidor were vomiting itself into the sky, along with the broken bodies of the dead and wounded.

The Mitsubishis were followed swiftly by divebombers, which were capable of pinpoint targeting but were also more susceptible to the antiaircraft fire because they had to fly much lower. Several went down in wreaths of smoke, but many remained to wreak havoc on the island.

Through it all, Anthony concentrated on keeping his men steady and trying to limit as much as possible the extent of their exposure. His bandaged hands, still covered to protect the burns, might have held him back had he deigned to take any notice of them.

The task they had to perform was fairly simple: load and fire the gun, getting off six rounds of ammo at each target, then swiftly reload and take aim again. Their greatest danger would come if and when they were in the direct line of attack, the deadly zero-zero approach every gunner dreaded.

The assault was well under way before that happened. Sighting along the line of the gun barrel, Anthony saw the dive-bomber approaching on a steady course, not rolling to the left or right. That could mean only one thing: he and his men were the target.

Anthony waited only long enough for the six rounds to be fired, then yelled, "Take cover!"

The Marines scrambled to obey, flinging themselves out of the trench and crawling as far away as they could in the seconds before the bomb hit. Flat on his belly in the dirt, Anthony kept his arms over his head while the ground bucked and heaved beneath him.

Falling rock and debris pounded down on his bare back. Hard on the first explosion came a series of others as the ammunition exploded. The last convulsion had barely subsided when he was on his feet, heading toward the emplacement.

The bomber had scored a direct hit. The gun lay in smoldering fragments, beyond any hope of repair. That was bad, but not nearly as devastating as the sight of Johnny lying nearby, crumpled and bleeding.

Anthony was at his side instantly to take in the extent of his injuries. They looked very severe. He patted Johnny's face gently while frustration and anguish welled up inside him.

The only first-aid kit available dated from the last war and held bandages that were useless against the shrapnel wounds the boy had suffered. The Marine hospital near the barracks was already overflowing with casualties. There was nothing for it except to take Johnny to the Malinta Tunnel.

"Get me a jeep," Anthony told his corporal. As the man hastened to obey, Anthony lifted the boy's shattered body and stood up. The rest of the gun crew stood somberly by. Each knew that, but for a fluke of fate, it could easily have been he instead of Johnny.

With the wounded Marine in the backseat, Anthony took the steep road down to the tunnel in record time. All around him was the evidence of battle, if such a one-sided encounter could be called that. Lacking all air cover, the dive-bombers had been able to raid at will. He did not doubt that they would be back.

Outside the Malinta Tunnel, there was chaos. The water and electrical systems had both taken direct hits. People were running around frantically, trying to assess the damage. With no one to hinder him, Anthony carried Johnny into the lateral.

Barely had he stepped inside when he was struck by a wave of heat, smells and noise that was all but intolerable. Worse yet was the palpable sense of fear that seemed to seep from the very walls. Stark raw terror was etched on the faces of the civilians and military personnel who had taken shelter in the tunnel.

The behavior of the civilians he could understand, but that of the soldiers dismayed him. Until he realized that most of them had never been under direct fire before and were totally unprepared for its consequences.

The darkness fed everyone's horror. Only a few flashlights sent wavering beams up and down the tunnel, enabling Anthony to find his way at last to the medical lateral.

Conditions there were just as bad, yet completely different. Instead of chaos, there was a disciplined sense of order and purpose. Emergency lights were already in place, illuminating the doctors, nurses and orderlies who hurried about their duties, grim-faced but calm.

Treading among them, Anthony found the area where casualties were being received and gently laid Johnny down before going in search of a doctor. The white-coated man he approached was rattling off instructions to a nurse.

Anthony waited until the doctor had finished before he said, "Excuse me, sir, I'd like you to take a look at one of my men. He's over there."

The doctor glanced up, first at Anthony, then at the wounded boy. He shook his head. "He'll have to wait his turn."

As calmly as he could, Anthony said, "He'll die if he has to wait."

The doctor hesitated, but only for a moment. "I'm sorry." He turned to walk away, only to be stopped by Anthony's iron grip on his arm.

The two men—one an officer, the other a noncom—stared at each other. There was no question that Anthony was out of line. His only hope was that the exhausted, harassed doctor would somehow summon up an extra measure of compassion.

The officer glanced down at Anthony's hand still gripping his arm, then back into the onyx eyes burning with anguish. A long moment passed before he sighed deeply and called to a woman bent over a nearby bed. "Nurse Lawrence, see what you can do for this Marine."

Maggie straightened automatically at the order. Since the attack began, she had been working frantically. The stream of casualties was endless, and with the lack of water and electricity, the medical team's task was made all but impossible.

Yet somehow they were carrying on. Hurrying toward the doctor, she was thinking only of the next patient, the next wound, the next life saved or lost. Until she saw Anthony.

The sight of him standing there in the gloom of the tunnel, bare-chested and bloodstained, surrounded by the moans and screams of dying men, took her breath away. For an instant, she thought he was an illusion. Then, realizing that he was real, she feared he had been wounded.

"What happened? Are you all right?"

He nodded swiftly, not questioning the brief glimpse of gut-wrenching distress he had seen in her eyes. The knowledge that she cared enough for him to experience such fear sent a wave of pleasure through him that was in sharp contrast to the horror all around.

It seemed incredible that in the midst of such devastation a man and a woman could reach out to each other. Yet perhaps it was also inevitable. Something very important was taking root between them, strengthening him just when he needed it most.

"One of my men's been hurt," he explained quietly. "He's over there."

Together they knelt beside the boy. Anthony watched intently as Maggie's hands moved over Johnny, seeking out the extent of damage, telling her of his chances.

Her hands were slender and graceful, like all the rest of her. The nails were cut short and neatly manicured. She wore no rings. Noticing this, Anthony marveled at the fact that he had somehow taken it for granted that she wasn't married. Now that his assumption was confirmed, he could admit how much it mattered to him.

"Will Johnny make it?" he asked gruffly.

"I don't know yet. He's. . . very bad. . . ." Her voice trailed off as she continued to work on the young private. All her attention was focused on him. Even her awareness of Anthony faded as she quickly and efficiently went about the task of stabilizing her patient's condition.

It was an uphill struggle. Johnny had suffered massive internal injuries, the extent of which she could only guess at. Surgery was vital, yet there was no guarantee that he would be treated in time to save his life.

Spotting Sheila hurrying by with a tray of bandages, Maggie called, "Any chance of a free table in OR?"

Sheila glanced at Anthony and the patient as she shook her head. "They're backed up three deep, and more are coming in. He'll have to wait."

"Wait?" Anthony repeated. "What the hell kind of thing is that to say?"

"It's not Sheila's fault," Maggie pointed out reasonably. "We're operating on a triage system. The wounded who have the best chance of survival if they get prompt care go in first. Those who will live without immediate attention wait. So do those who—"

"Who have bought it," Anthony finished grimly. "Let me tell you something—nobody writes off one of my men just because he's hurt bad! He'll live, if he gets the chance. Dammit, he's a Marine!" He thought of Johnny wanting to try to help the men in the barracks who were beyond help, and he swore he wasn't going to let him perish as they had.

"He's bleeding internally and he's deeply in shock," Maggie said quietly. She didn't resent Anthony's attitude; on the contrary, she understood and shared it. But she also understood the realities of their medical situation. Resources were in extremely short supply and had to be concentrated on those who would benefit the most from them.

And yet. . . this was a life they were talking about. A human being who only a short time before had been full of youth and vigor and dreams. Somebody's child, friend, brother, perhaps lover—if he'd even had a chance for that. Somebody who, like all the other somebodies littering the floor around them, mattered a great deal.

"Look, I'll see what I can do. Maybe we can slip him in. But it won't be for a while yet. You'll have to stay with him."

Anthony nodded curtly. He was ashamed of his outburst and grateful for the way she had responded. If she'd gotten mad, he couldn't have blamed her. She had it tough enough without his barging in and making trouble.

As he muttered his thanks, Maggie squeezed his hand gently, then hurried off.

She worked through the rest of the day and into the night without pause. Johnny was taken to surgery about an hour after he arrived. Against all odds, he survived and was removed to the ward, where he would have as good a chance as any of recovering.

Anthony stayed with him for a few minutes, then left to return to Middleside and whatever remained of the Marine barracks. He was on his way out of the tunnel when a captain stopped him.

"We're getting up a team to lay in emergency wiring and pipes. You're on it."

"Sorry, sir. I've got to get back to my men."

The captain shrugged, uninterested in Anthony's

priorities. "You're a Marine, right? You guys took a hell of a beating. Middleside's being all but abandoned. They'll be redeploying to the Navy tunnel, so you may as well stay here and join them later."

It didn't seem as if he had any other choice. At least the work was useful. Throughout the night he strung wire and put down pipe in the company of other men who, like him, were numbly unaware of the exhaustion of their minds and bodies.

Dawn found him asleep on the floor of one of the laterals, not far from where Maggie still labored against the remorseless tide of death that threatened to engulf them all.

Chapter Three

JOSEPH GARGANO LIKED to think of himself as a simple man. Since coming to America more than thirty years before, he had worked hard, saved his money, and done better than a lot of other people he knew.

Things had been tough during the Depression, but he had managed to hold on. He'd raised his children, tended his garden on the long summer evenings, and taken part in the occasional boccie game with his friends from the old country.

He believed in God, the Constitution and Franklin Delano Roosevelt, not necessarily in that order.

Three times he had voted for the genial patrician with the common touch. The president's picture hung on the living room wall, next to those of Jesus Christ and the Virgin Mary. Roosevelt's name was spoken in the Gargano home with reverence, all the more so lately, when they had realized that it would be up to the president to save Anthony.

"I told that boy," Joseph said over dinner the night they learned that the Marines had withdrawn to Corregidor, "I told him, 'Come into the factory with me. You'll have a good job, decent pay, a future.' But no, that wasn't enough for him. He had to put on a uniform and get shot at."

Joseph sat back in his chair with a sigh, his hands clasped over his flat stomach, his rough-hewn face grim. The large table was cluttered with half-empty platters of antipastos, chicken roasted with rosemary, spaghetti in his wife's special herb sauce and fresh-baked Italian bread.

In the background, the radio was on, just in case there was a bulletin. Kate Smith was singing "God Bless America"; it was a nice song, but he was getting a little tired of hearing it night and day.

Although he would never admit it, Anthony was the most dearly loved of his children, the one most like him and for whom he had the greatest hopes. They were very similar in appearance and attitude, both driven to achieve a better life. But they disagreed completely on how to do that.

For Joseph, a good life meant home, family and security. For Anthony, it seemed to mean adventure and a lack of responsibility to anything except himself and the traditions of the Corps — traditions Joseph did not pretend to understand.

Maria Gargano watched her husband sympathetically. She was a slender, small-boned woman of Northern Italian origin, with ivory skin, pale blond hair and soft gray eyes. Next to her husband and children, she looked frail. But her backbone was pure steel.

From the first moment she met Joseph Gargano, just a few months after he got off the boat, she had known she was going to marry him. It had taken Joseph a little while longer to figure it out. Later he confessed that he hadn't expected the beautiful daughter of a prosperous grocer to agree so readily to become his wife.

But she had, and she never regretted it. She loved him with a fierce passion that belied her cool, aloof looks. And she hated anything that troubled him.

He had barely touched his dinner, which was unusual for him, since he worked hard and had a robust appetite. Only the fragrant chicken had piqued his interest, but barely, despite the fact that it was one of his favorites.

The previous night, they had lain awake side by side after making love, not talking, just holding hands and trying to draw some comfort from each other's nearness. Briefly, he had seemed a little more optimistic, but the burden of not knowing what was happening to their eldest son proved unrelenting for them both.

As the news came in from the Philippines, Maria told herself over and over that Anthony was a smart boy and could take care of himself. Wasn't he the one who had a paper route when he was only nine and earned enough money to take all his brothers and sisters to the movies? Hadn't he gone out for the football and basketball teams at St. Ignatius High and made both while maintaining a B + average?

He was smart, strong, clever. Surely it wasn't beyond him to stay alive long enough to be rescued.

Across the table from her, Vita, the oldest offspring and the one most sensitive to her mother's moods, swallowed a bite of marinated artichoke and said gently, "Take it easy, Ma. He'll be fine."

Her husband, Sal, took a sip of wine and nodded. "Heck, Tonio's got it good. Me and Dom and Paulo will be in uniform any day now and shipping out for who knows where. Meanwhile, all he's got to do is stay out of trouble for a few more weeks."

Maria nodded but remained unconvinced. She liked President Roosevelt all right, but she didn't have the same fervent trust in him that her husband did. Her faith was reserved for her church and her family. It did not extend to strangers, no matter how well-intentioned they might be.

"Look at the bright side, Ma," Dom teased. "At least you know where he is and what he's doing. That's more than you could say when he was home."

"That's more than I can say about you," she shot back tartly.

"Not for long." He glanced around the table before he added quietly, "I joined the Marines today."

There was an instant of stunned silence before Joseph slammed his large fist down on the table and roared. "The Marines! What did you go and do a stupid thing like that for?"

"It's not stupid!" Dom protested. "The Marines are the best. Tonio said so."

"What does Tonio know? He's stuck on some god-forsaken rock at the ends of the earth. You couldn't settle for the Army? You want to be the first to die on some damn beach?"

"Joseph, stop that!" Maria demanded. She shared his shock, but there would be no talk of dying in her home.

"You really joined the Marines?" Paulo asked, clearly impressed. He was the middle son, quieter and less assertive than his brothers. Yet in his own way he was just as determined. When Dom nodded, he said, "That's great. Maybe we'll see duty together."

"*What are you talking about?*" Joseph bellowed. He'd had enough surprises. He didn't need another from the one son who had never before given him any trouble.

But those days were apparently over. Paulo said, "I enlisted in the Navy, Pop. You know I always liked ships. They're going to see about getting me trained as a radio operator."

That left only Sal, and instinctively all eyes shifted to him. He swallowed a forkful of spaghetti and shrugged. "I guess there's no reason not to tell you now. I figured I'd get drafted in a few weeks anyway, so I signed on with the Army." He grinned genially. "Told 'em I wanted to be a cook. That should keep me out of the front lines."

Vita uttered a little moan and slumped in her seat. Sophia, the youngest in the family, jumped up to get a wet washcloth for her sister's head. Sal hovered over Vita, struggling to explain his reasons for joining up rather than waiting to be called.

Dom and Paulo were arguing about the relative merits of the Marines and the Navy. The children, who had been fed earlier and were supposed to play quietly in the front room while the adults ate, ran in to see what all the excitement was about.

"Uncle Anthony's going to beat the Japs," little Sal, Jr., hollered, racing around on his short, plump legs.

"Uncle Anthony's going to be a hero," his sister, Philomena, chimed in.

Dom broke off his argument with Paulo and scooped her into his arms. "We're all going to be heroes! The Japs'll be sorry they ever came near us. And as for the Germans—"

"We're not talking about the Germans," Joseph exclaimed. "There's enough trouble without throwing them in, too."

"Face it, Pop," Paulo said gently, "we're at war on two fronts. It's going to be tough for a while."

Joseph pointed toward the picture of the president on the wall. "He can handle it. Remember what he said. 'The only thing we have to fear is fear itself.' Smart man."

"Yes, he is," Paulo agreed. Smart enough, he added silently, to use his strength where it would do the most good. He thought of his brother trapped on the rock thousands of miles from nowhere, and his throat tightened. Maybe there really was a rescue fleet, but somehow he doubted it.

So DID ANTHONY. With each passing day, he had become more convinced that the fleet was a myth. But he said nothing of his suspicions. Things were bad enough without adding to them.

In the aftermath of the attack on Middleside, his battalion had drawn the assignment of protecting the beaches immediately in front of the Malinta Tunnel. The men set up their guns, dug in and prepared to hold their ground, come what may.

The Japanese could be counted on to shell the Rock for several hours each morning, and there were sporadic bombing runs whenever the weather permitted. The gunners fired at any likely target, but their accuracy was steadily diminishing as they struggled to survive on a subsistence diet so low in Vitamin A that their eyesight was weakened. Rations consisted of a cup of cracked wheat for breakfast and a scoop of rice with a little corned-beef gravy for dinner, alternated sometimes with the canned salmon everyone had come to loathe.

Their only consolation was that they had it better than the people in the tunnel. Anthony went down there to visit Maggie and the injured men from his squadron, and each time he wondered how anyone could stand it.

The air was damp, foul and unmoving. With so many people packed closely together, the noise was deafening. Every available inch of wall space was stacked high with supplies and personal belongings. Just finding a place to sleep was a challenge.

At least Maggie had a cot. Not that he thought she used it much. He was getting more worried about her by the day. They were all losing weight, thanks to the poor diet, the constant work and the tension. But Maggie seemed to be losing more than most people. He'd mentioned that to her friend Sheila, who had come up with a reasonable explanation.

"Maggie keeps pulling extra OR duty. Every surgeon here wants her on his team."

"That's crazy. Don't they know she has to rest sometime?"

"Tell that to the brass. Not that it would do any good. Maggie's. . ." Sheila had groped for the right word—"dedicated."

He supposed her military background had something to do with it. No matter how tired or frightened she was, she kept on going. Of course, he did the same, but that was different. He was a man, and a Marine.

And that meant, among other things, that he wasn't just going to sit and take whatever the enemy felt like dishing out when he could do something— however slight—to help himself and others.

The daily shellings were taking a toll on the local sea life. After each pounding, the bodies of fish could be seen floating belly up. He found it simple enough to dive in after them, sometimes gathering as much as a sackful despite the danger from Japanese Zeros and sharks.

The fish gave him another excuse to visit Maggie. Watching him choose a dozen of the plumpest, his men nudged each other and grinned. "Going somewhere, Sarge?" one asked innocently.

They knew damn well he was, just as they knew whom he was going to see. It was impossible to keep any secrets when everybody was living on top of everybody else.

Casually, he said, "Thought I'd take a stroll through the tunnel, see how things are going."

"Probably the same as they were yesterday," a would-be wit suggested. Anthony shot him a glare that caused a hasty retreat. "Not that there's anything wrong with taking a look, Sarge."

"Glad you approve," he muttered dryly as he fastened his least filthy pair of khakis and ran a hand through his thick black hair, grown out almost to the nape of his neck. If he'd been wearing a shirt, his hair would have brushed the collar.

He grinned as he imagined what his father would say if he could see him. Probably try to drag him off to the nearest barbershop while yelling at him to stop walking around half-naked. Not that everyone on the Rock wasn't doing the same thing. The constant, unrelenting heat made anything but the bare minimum intolerable.

Gathering up the fish, Anthony turned command

of the battery over to his corporal and headed for the tunnel. It was late enough in the day that the shooting wouldn't start up again before morning. For a few hours at least, his men would be able to relax, which was exactly what he intended to do.

Maggie was coming off duty as he arrived at the medical lateral. She had pulled a double shift, spent mostly in the operating theater, and was bone-tired. Yet the sight of him was enough to wring at least a wan smile from her.

"Hi," she said softly. "Been fishing again?"

He gestured to the sack and nodded. "Sure. What else is there to do around here?" His eyes wandered over her, taking in her pale face, the slight slump to her shoulders and the almost painful slimness of her body. His throat tightened as he asked, "How are you doing?"

She grimaced slightly. "We're so busy I'm not sure I know. The casualties just keep coming and coming as though there will never be any end to them."

Words of comfort sprang to his lips, but he bit them back. Maggie was far too intelligent to be fooled by false reassurances. She knew nothing was going to change until they were either rescued or crushed.

An Army captain passed them, slowing down as he noted the pretty young nurse talking with a noncom. Mindful of the regulations that were supposed to limit such contacts to strictly official matters, Anthony quickly shifted gears.

"Is Johnny coming along okay?"

Maggie pretended not to notice the captain, but wasted no time saying, "He's doing quite well, Sergeant. In fact, just this morning he tried to convince me that he was ready to go back on duty. I explained to him that we weren't ready to part with his company."

Anthony laughed softly, pleased by the understanding he saw in her eyes. Though they hadn't spoken of it, both knew that their meetings came perilously close to violating the rules. The regulations didn't matter much to him. But for Maggie, raised with respect for military authority, the situation had to be handled delicately, if only so that she could go on seeing him.

His visits had come to mean more to her than she wanted to admit even to herself. They were a ray of light in what was otherwise perpetual darkness. After three weeks in the tunnel, she had begun to wonder if there really was a world beyond the Rock and, if so, if she had ever been part of it.

Her days were a constant struggle to provide even the most minimal medical care for the wounded and sick. Supplies of all types were beginning to run short, just as the full effects of the siege were starting to be felt. At least half of those admitted to the hospital were suffering, not from wounds, but from virulent respiratory infections that, in the dampness of the tunnel, spread like wildfire.

Still, amid all the horror, there was a flicker of hope. Excitedly, Maggie held out a slip of paper to Anthony. "Have you seen this?"

"What is it?" he asked, taking it from her.

"A statement from General MacArthur. I copied it down so you wouldn't miss it. He's heard from the top brass, and they absolutely confirm that the relief force is on the way."

Though his eyebrows rose skeptically, Anthony read the message MacArthur had ordered circulated among his troops:

HELP IS ON THE WAY FROM THE UNITED STATES. THOUSANDS OF TROOPS AND HUNDREDS OF PLANES ARE BEING DISPATCHED. THE EXACT TIME OF AR- RIVAL OF REINFORCEMENTS IS UNKNOWN, AS THEY HAVE TO FIGHT THROUGH JAPANESE LINES. IT IS IM- PERATIVE THAT OUR TROOPS HOLD UNTIL THESE RE- INFORCEMENTS ARRIVE.

Despite himself, he was impressed. MacArthur ob- viously believed the rescue force was coming. Hand- ing the message back to Maggie, he said, "Pop will be going around telling everyone that Roosevelt came through again."

"Maybe he has." A bit tentatively, she asked, "You think it's true, don't you? I mean, no one would tell a lie this big."

"Maybe not. . . but. . . ."

"But what?"

"If people want something badly enough, they're liable to talk about it as though it's already happened even when it hasn't. I'm not suggesting that's the case here, but the best intentions in the world aren't going to help us much unless they can really be carried out."

The brief euphoria Maggie had been feeling evap- orated as she recognized the truth of what he was say- ing. Her face, animated a moment before, turned somber. "You're right. For a while there I lost sight of the immense difficulties of getting any help to us."

Anthony regretted having punctured her happiness. "Don't worry," he said gently. "Things are bound to get better. We're dug in real well. Sooner or later, the Japs may just get tired and go home."

Maggie didn't believe him for a moment, and she knew he didn't expect her to. But she was gratified by his moral support.

Handing her the sack, he said more sternly, "I hope you're actually eating some of this stuff and not giving it all away."

In the khaki skirt and shirt that had long since replaced her white uniform, she looked increasingly small and slight. His throat tightened as he considered the differences between them. He'd lost some flesh in the past few weeks, but he was still rock-hard and muscular. She, on the other hand, looked as though a puff of wind might blow her away.

If it really came down to it, he thought, he would at least have the satisfaction of going out fighting. She would be helpless prey for an enemy that had given no indication of respecting the conventions of war.

The more he thought about it, the more sickened he felt. She just didn't belong there. No woman did. She ought to be safe at home like his mother and sisters.

Wondering what was responsible for his sudden scowl, Maggie said, "Of course I eat some of it. So do the other nurses, and we appreciate it very much." She didn't add, because she couldn't bear to, that they all knew he risked his life to get the fish.

If she thought it would have done any good, she would have asked him to stop. But she had learned to know him well enough to realize her words would fall on deaf ears.

Sergeant Anthony Gargano was many things: intelligent, courageous, and—much as she tried not to think about it—sexy. But above all she sensed in him great pride, a trait he shared with all his fellow Marines. None of them took kindly to suggestions that they give more than the most passing attention to their own safety.

Knowing how much he hated being down in the tunnel, she decided to put her qualms about the regulations aside for the moment and suggested they go topside. It was a little cooler up there—not much, but at least there was a slight onshore breeze.

Dusk was settling over the island. To the west, the sky was shading from fiery orange to lavender to mauve in the dying rays of the sun. A few stars were already twinkling in the cloudless sky. Since their arrival on Corregidor, the weather had been unrelentingly lovely, in sharp contrast to the horror all around them.

Seated behind a wall of sandbags, they shared a Lucky Strike, rationed like everything else, and talked quietly.

"How are your men holding up?" Maggie asked.

"Okay. It's hard for them just to sit here getting shot at day after day. They'd rather be over on the mainland, where the action is."

"I've heard things are bad at Bataan."

Anthony nodded. "They're on even shorter rations than we are, and taking a hell of a beating." He was silent for a moment, looking up at the darkening sky, before he asked, "Do you ever think about what you'd be doing right now if there wasn't a war?"

"Sometimes. . ." A little abashed, she added, "Life in Manila was like a dream—dances at the officers' club, golf matches at the course that overlooked the bay, dinners in those wonderful red-tiled mansions in the Old Quarter. If I close my eyes, I can still see the incredible blue light that settled over the city at the end of every day. . . . I guess that part at least is still true. I wonder if the rest ever will be again."

"I wonder the same thing," Anthony murmured. "It seems as though everything we knew has vanished, even the most simple things. You know what I keep thinking about? Sitting around the dinner table, stuffing myself on Ma's lasagna and listening to Dom tell me how smart he is." Anthony chuckled indulgently. "He's a good kid, just a little too big for his britches."

Maggie settled more comfortably against the sandbags and nodded. "I know what you mean. My brother, Tad, is like that. He always jumps in headfirst, but somehow manages to come up with an excuse for whatever trouble he lands in."

"Do you have any other brothers or sisters?"

"No, there's just Tad and me. Mom had us only a couple of years apart, so we've always been close."

He drew a puff on the cigarette. "You miss your family a lot, don't you?"

"Yes, and I wish there was some way to let them know I'm all right."

"Your dad's regular Army, right? Maybe he can find out."

"I hope so. It's got to be rough enough on them as it is without their worrying about me." Her voice broke slightly as she considered what it must be like in the big white house in Virginia. Tad would be gone by now, and perhaps her father as well. It would be very lonely there.

Not unlike the Rock. Incredibly, in the midst of so many people, she often felt a deadening sense of isolation. It was as though they were all drifting farther and farther away from one another, retreating into hidden corners of their souls.

Simple human communication was breaking down. People spoke only to give orders or relay vital information. Lately she hadn't even had Sheila to talk to. They were on different shifts now and rarely saw each other.

Only Anthony remained an enclave of warmth and gentleness in the gathering dark. Instinctively, she reached out to him, her hand touching his. He hesitated for barely an instant before his fingers closed around hers in a firm, reassuring grip.

He hadn't expected her to touch him. It wasn't because he didn't think she found him attractive — he'd been with her enough to know that she returned his interest on all levels. Rather, it was because he sensed a shyness in her that, coupled with the regulations against fraternization, would hold her back from taking the initiative.

Yet she had done exactly that. He suddenly felt as though he were fifteen again, holding hands with Mary Clare in the schoolyard, his palm sweating and his heart beating hard.

As for Maggie, she was surprised at her daring. She had always been reticent with men, partly because of her upbringing and partly because she was uncertain of her own attractiveness. But with Anthony everything was different. Maybe it was the circumstances in which they were caught, or he himself, or some combination of both. Whatever the reason, she felt at once relaxed and excited with him.

The irony of what was happening did not escape her. Her mother had said that one day she would meet a man who would make her feel like that. But what Elizabeth Lawrence could not have anticipated was that it would happen amid the hell of Corregidor, where life itself seemed to be slipping away like the last dying glow of the sun.

ANTHONY HAD ESCORTED Maggie back to the medical lateral and was returning to his post when he noticed activity around the south dock. The submarine *Trout* had come in earlier, bringing fresh supplies of three-inch shells, which the men had received joyfully. It meant they could finally shoot at the high-flying bombers that rained down such deadly terror on them.

The *Trout* had been scheduled to sail several hours earlier. Anthony wondered what it was still doing in port. Since he was off duty, he headed down to the dock to see what was going on.

It didn't take long to find a supply sergeant he remembered from his days at the Marine training base on Parris Island. They squatted down in a shed, sharing a precious bottle of whiskey, while the older man brought him up to date.

"No ballast," the sergeant explained. He belched fragrantly. "Friggin' idiots thought they could use sandbags, but no one here's about to part with them."

"Hell, no," Anthony agreed, taking a long pull on the bottle. "They're worth more than gold."

"You guessed it."

"Guessed what?"

"What they're gonna use instead."

Anthony shook his head, perplexed. He could usually hold his booze, but this stuff must really be getting to him. "What're you talking about?"

"Gold. They're gonna fill the hold with gold."

"Yeah, sure, and I'm gonna grow wings and fly out of here."

"Better watch out for Zeros if you do." The sergeant laughed. "I'm not kidding. All the gold in the Philippine Treasury was moved over here before the siege started. Now it's going into the holds of the *Trout.* Next stop, Australia."

They talked awhile longer, in between finishing the bottle. Anthony gave the sergeant a letter to mail to his parents. It wasn't much, but at least it would let them know he was alive.

Making his way back to his post, he wondered how much longer that would be true. If there was any truth at all to that story about the rescue fleet, it didn't make much sense to go to all the trouble of moving the Philippine Treasury. No matter how he cut it, he kept coming up with the same suspicion: If they were shipping out the gold, chances were the brass wouldn't be far behind.

During the next few weeks, the already grim situation worsened steadily. Anthony watched his men for signs of despair or rebellion—which he thought would have been understandable under the circumstances, even for Marines. But he found only steadfast determination. Few spoke any longer of the rescue fleet. Everyone seemed to accept that it was not coming.

That conviction was strengthened when President

Quezon, despite his debilitating illness, suggested that the Americans could best save the Philippines by freeing it from their control and allowing it to make a separate peace.

The response he received directly from President Roosevelt did not remain confidential for very long. Soon every man on both Bataan and Corregidor knew that he was pledged by his commander in chief to fight to the death. The only consolation Roosevelt offered was that United States forces would ultimately return and drive the invader out.

A biting bit of doggerel quickly became popular: "We are the battling bastards of Bataan/No momma, no poppa, no Uncle Sam/No aunts, no uncles, no nephews, no nieces/And nobody gives a damn!"

The men sang it in the trenches and the foxholes, behind the sandbags and the barbed wire, over the dismal meals and the diminishing stores of ammunition. They sang it softly, yet their voices carried a note of deadly conviction. Slowly, each in his own individual way, they began to prepare themselves for the end.

Anthony had never been particularly religious, but now he found himself dropping by the tunnel to attend mass. He went as much to see Maggie, who also attended, as for whatever comfort that thoughts of God and the hereafter might offer.

They usually managed to get a few minutes together afterward. He continued to bring her fish; she gave him advice for his men on how to preserve their diminishing strength and cope with the increasing problems of dysentery and skin rashes brought on by the heat.

They rarely spoke of more personal things, and they did not touch again. But between them there was a poignant sense of what might have been. If only the time and place were different...if only the world was at peace...if only they were not surrounded by the slowly closing vise of death.

Around the middle of March, after they had been on the Rock almost three months, they learned that General MacArthur, President Quezon and their respective families had left during the night for sanctuary in Australia. With them had gone as much of the brass as could fit on the ship.

General Jonathan Wainwright, U.S. Army, was left in command. He was a highly respected and able officer; even Anthony thought well of him. But he was not a miracle worker. It was his fate to preside over a debacle, and every man and woman in his command knew it.

The only question remaining now was when the end would come.

Chapter Four

SEATED ON A SMALL, silk-covered couch near the windows that overlooked her garden, Elizabeth Lawrence read the letter from her daughter yet again.

Dear Mom, Dad and Tad,

I hope this finds you all well. It's Christmas Eve here and relatively quiet, for a change. There's no telling how long that will last, so I thought I would take the opportunity to get a few words off to you.

Your presents were all very much appreciated. The lingerie may not be quite regulation, but I love it, and the lipstick and rouge definitely boosted my morale. The copy of *Lost Horizon* was particularly welcome, although I was surprised to see how it was printed. I think "paperbacks" might catch on.

I know I don't have to tell you how things are here. We're holding on as well as we can, but no one is too sure what will happen. I guess by the time you get this, you'll know. Don't worry about me. I'm fine and expect to stay that way.

There was a break in the letter, and where it started up again, the handwriting was fainter and a little shaky.

I had to stop for a while—some new wounded came in. Looks as though the lull is over. Must go. My love to you all, and may the new year be better.

Maggie

Elizabeth put the letter down slowly. It had arrived that morning from Australia, posted by an obliging submarine captain. She had been poring over it ever since, listening to the faraway voice of her daughter in her mind, trying to imagine how Maggie was now.

Outside, the garden was in full bloom. Her prize azaleas were doing well, as were the tulips and irises. A robin perched on the lush green lawn, eyeing her for a moment before darting away toward the copse of willow trees that bordered one end of the property.

Four months had passed since Maggie had penned those words—four months of terrible fighting, culminating almost always in defeat. Bataan had fallen a few weeks earlier. Some twelve thousand Americans and sixty-four thousand Filipinos had surrendered.

Corregidor's turn was next.

Carefully folding the letter, Elizabeth placed it in the pocket of her silk day dress and rose. She had heard a car pulling up and guessed that Will must be home. His work at the War Department kept him at his desk for long hours, but whenever he could, he tried to steal a few minutes for them to be together. With Tad at sea on the carrier *Hornet*, the house seemed very empty.

Colonel Wilson Maddox Lawrence strode into the house with the erect bearing of a man who wore his military vocation naturally. His perfectly tailored uniform still looked as pristine as when he had put it on the previous day. His regulation tie was properly knotted at the throat, and the visor of the hat he carried in his hand glistened in the sun.

At forty-nine, he looked far younger than the out-of-condition businessmen he had occasionally shared the golf course with in prewar days. His dark blond hair showed only a few strands of silver, his gray eyes were clear and steady, and his patrician features appeared as imperturbable as ever.

But Elizabeth was not fooled. She came down the stairs of their graceful antebellum house and held out her arms to him. "Welcome home, dear. I'd begun to think you might have forgotten the way."

Her gentle teasing wrung a smile from him. Once they were inside the vestibule, away from the eyes of his military chauffeur, he dropped a lingering kiss on her mouth. "I'm sorry, sweetheart. The meetings ran longer than I'd expected."

She didn't press him for any more of an explanation. Will talked about his work when he could, but more and more often the matters that crossed his desk were so confidential that he could not discuss them even with her.

Elizabeth had no trouble accepting that. Like her husband, she had been raised in the military tradition and knew the demands of his calling.

"You must be tired," she said softly. "Do you want to lie down for a while before eating?"

He shook his head, smiling down at her. She came barely to his shoulder and was still almost as slender as on the day they were married. Her chestnut hair, sprinkled with silver, was worn in short curls, and her large blue eyes were warm and loving.

They had been together a quarter century, but not a day went by that he didn't marvel at his luck in having her as his wife. He knew that, should he accept her suggestion that he rest, she would hold dinner until he awoke, no matter how late that might be.

It would not occur to her to do otherwise, any more than she could resent the long hours he spent away from her or the frequent upheavals in their lives when the Army transferred him to one post or another.

But he could not help but wonder if somewhere in the back of her mind she did not regret the part he had played in raising their children, especially Maggie. It was he who had encouraged her decision to become an Army nurse and to apply for a posting overseas. At the time, he had thought only of the excellent experience she would gain. Now he had to face the chilling possibility that he might be an accessory to his only daughter's death.

His quiet inquiries in recent days had failed to turn up any information about her well-being, but he knew that even if she was all right at the moment, she might not be that way much longer.

The Japanese were at the very doors of Corregidor. That the fortress had held out this long was a testament to the strength and fortitude of its men. But the end was inevitable—had been, in fact, since the moment early in the war when the United States had agreed to give priority to the fighting in Europe, even though that meant sacrificing some of its forces in the Pacific.

From a purely military point of view, the decision made perfect sense. But to the father of one of those about to be sacrificed, it was anguishing in the extreme.

Joining Elizabeth in the sitting room, Will accepted the very light highball she prepared for him and sat down next to her on the couch. She waited until he had taken several sips before she said, "We had a letter today from Maggie."

The color faded from his face, only to come rushing back more vividly. For one incandescent moment, before reason reasserted itself, he thought the letter might have been written recently. Then he realized the impossibility of that and reached out a hand that shook slightly. He scanned the words Maggie had written, reading more into them even than Elizabeth had.

Far in the back of his mind, a memory began to surface. It was of a field hospital near the Somme in France, during the brutal trench battles of World War I. He had been a very young lieutenant fresh out of West Point, thrown into combat with no clear idea of what it would mean.

But he had learned fast; learned to endure the cries of men and the stench of blood, the deadly hopelessness and fear, the terrible sense of abandonment and approaching doom. He had learned because, in the end, there was really very little else he could do. Lives hung each day by thin wires, and many snapped.

His did not. He came home strong and whole to marry the woman he loved and to sire a daughter who would follow in his footsteps. God help her.

For all that she had been suffering when she wrote the letter, she sounded strong and resolute. He prayed that she had remained so, to endure what was coming.

Putting the letter down, he said softly, "It seems like such a short time ago that she was still in college, without a care in the world."

Together they glanced at the framed photo on the mantel. There was Maggie as she had been, gay and laughing, wearing bobby socks, a plaid skirt and a sweater draped with a strand of pearls, the "uniform" of the smart college set.

Maggie, smiling into the camera, the sun dancing through her hair and all of life stretched out before her.

Maggie, as she had been but was no longer.

THE WOMAN CROUCHING beside the dying soldier was pale and drawn. She had been on duty for thirty-six hours and should have been blessedly numb. But instead she was painfully aware of everything going on around her.

They were very, very close to the end. The Japanese bombardment was constant now. Even this far underground, she could hear it. Incessant tremors racked the tunnel, sending down showers of dust and gravel.

The American batteries on Bataan had been turned against them several weeks before, when the peninsula fell to the enemy. Since then, they had learned the true meaning of hell on earth.

The constant shelling and bombing runs by the Mitsubishis had wiped out their own antiaircraft batteries one by one. She had lived in dread that the next man carried into the medical lateral would be Anthony. That she might find him among the dead had been too intolerable a possibility even to consider.

But as of that morning, when an obliging Marine had brought her a message from him, he was still alive and unharmed, holding out in his foxhole with his men, waiting for the Japanese to come ashore.

No one doubted that they would come. The softening-up process that preceded a landing was almost over. Soon the amphibious forces would set out across the bay to deliver the last hammer blows of defeat.

Maggie kept her fingers on the pulse of the young soldier as it slowed and finally stopped. She put his arm down gently and drew the rough blanket over his face, then rose and walked stumblingly to the desk at the front of the ward.

At least this death had been relatively easy. The soldier had been brought in unconscious from massive head wounds and remained that way as his life ebbed. Considering that they were almost out of morphine, that was a mercy.

Meticulously she noted the name, rank, serial number and time of death in the log, then instructed an orderly to remove the body. Barely had he done so than the bunk was taken by one of the many wounded lying outside in the tunnel.

She was starting back to work when Sheila came by with the medical tray and said softly, "You should try to get some rest."

Maggie smiled but shook her head. "I can't sleep even when I try, so there's no point."

As she spoke, it occurred to her that Sheila was looking worn out. The khaki overalls hung on her. Her once gleaming blond hair was dry and limp. Her face was ashen, and even her hazel eyes seemed dimmed.

Glancing down at herself, Maggie said, "We're both a sight, you know that?"

Sheila grinned weakly. "For sore eyes?"

"They'd be sore, all right. Oh, what I'd give for a bath!"

"And a bed with clean sheets," Sheila murmured.

"And steak with a big salad. . ."

"An ice cream soda."

"A slice of my mother's chocolate layer cake."

They broke off, giggling. "Listen to us," Maggie said. "Here we're finally starting to look like a couple of Paris models and we're all set to ruin it."

"Given half a chance, I promise to eat my way into a size sixteen," Sheila vowed solemnly.

"Me, too. I will never turn down another forkful as long as I live."

A poor choice of words. The two young women stared at each other for a long moment. At length, Sheila sighed. "I'd better get on with it."

Maggie watched her go, wondering at the unfathomable injustice that was controlling their lives. A few days before, they had known a brief moment of hope when word got around that most of the nurses would be leaving on two Navy flying boats that had dared the Japanese antiaircraft guns to come in for them.

Most, but not all. Neither Sheila nor Maggie was among the thirty nurses chosen to go. Captain Davies had made the selection on a purely pragmatic basis. The nurses she could spare went. Those most vital to the care of the wounded remained. In an odd sort of way, it was a compliment.

The women who were staying had written final letters to their families. In hers, Maggie said only that she was expecting to be taken prisoner shortly and would look forward to the reunion they would have at the end of the war. In particular, she asked her mother to plan on making her famous sweet potato pie, which, as they all knew, was Maggie's favorite.

Of the possibility that she might not survive, she said nothing. Everyone on Corregidor had heard the terrible stories of atrocities taking place throughout the Philippines. Maggie knew what might await her in captivity.

Yet she had also heard that other prisoners were being treated decently, with proper food and medical care, and that non-Filipino civilians, though interned, were not being killed.

Experiences seemed to vary enormously, depending on the individual Japanese responsible. Maggie could only hope that, as was the case with most peoples, the good would outweigh the bad.

For the moment, she could only go on as before and pray that it would be over soon.

IN HIS FOXHOLE overlooking the beach, Anthony was getting in a quick nap. He slept little, usually only a few minutes at a time. The slightest change was enough to wake him.

A week's growth of beard darkened his strained features. The bared chest above his torn and tattered khakis was still heavily muscled, but the ribs showed clearly, and his stomach was now concave rather than simply flat. He estimated he had lost about thirty pounds, and could not lose much more without suffering severe weakness.

As he slept, he clutched his rifle in his arms. He intended to die with it in his hands, having made up his mind that he would not be taken prisoner.

Around him, some of his men slept while others kept watch. As the final battle approached, there had been a few desertions among the American and Filipino forces, but none from Sergeant Gargano's squad.

He didn't go in for a lot of morale boosting and he certainly never lied, but he nonetheless managed to maintain the pride and determination of his men. There was no great secret to that accomplishment; he did it the only way he knew how—by example.

No matter how weary or frightened he felt, he ignored it and got on with the job. His men, drawing on the powerful sense of personal honor that had first attracted them to the Corps, followed his lead. They knew that the eyes of the world were on the fortress of Corregidor—and they were damned if they weren't going to look good.

Across the bay, along the lush green curve of the Bataan peninsula, other men scanned the sea and waited. The Japanese were eager for an end to the fighting. They had never expected the Americans to hold out so long.

Many more troops and equipment had had to be committed to the area by the Japanese than they had anticipated. Resources that might have been hurled into the attack against Australia and New Zealand had instead ended up in the Philippines.

To that extent, the Americans had won. As the man in the White House had hoped, they had earned with their blood the precious time needed to rebuild the forces shattered at Pearl Harbor and begin to turn the tide of battle.

It would be months before anyone would know for sure if the decision not to reinforce Bataan and Corregidor had been correct. But at least it had opened the way for eventual victory, where before there had been none.

Anthony stirred restlessly in his sleep. He was dreaming of Maggie, imagining her running along a beach somewhere, her gleaming chestnut hair streaming out behind her, slender legs flashing in the sun. She turned to him and laughed happily, sending music rippling through his soul. He groaned and tried to reach out for her. But his hands grasped only air.

A sound—far off and high-pitched—penetrated his dream. His eyes shot open. He remained frozen through the space of a heartbeat, all his attention focused on the sound. Then he straightened up and yelled at the top of his lungs, "Incoming fire! Get down!"

His men obeyed reflexively, throwing themselves flat on their faces and clawing into the dirt—but not for long. Seconds later the earth began to shake in long, convulsive tremors. Startled, Anthony glanced up. What he saw turned his blood cold.

At Battery Geary to the north, where the most powerful guns left on Corregidor were stationed, smoke and debris shot up into the air. As he watched, spellbound, a long black tube of a mortar spun against the sky, followed by the gigantic slabs of concrete in which it had been set.

Anthony shook his head dazedly. The mortars

weighed more than ten tons each. Any explosion that could do that to them must be . . .

Even as the realization of what was happening tore through his brain, he threw his head back down to the ground and clamped his hands over his ears. Around him, his men were doing the same, correctly anticipating what was coming.

The wall of sound that rolled toward and over them shattered the eardrums of those less aware. With it came the splintered trunks of gigantic teak and mahogany trees, spinning through the air as though they were toothpicks, but crashing down on top of men with a deadly force.

Burrowed deep within its foxholes, Anthony's squad survived the blast without injury. But few others were as fortunate. The already overcrowded hospital was quickly swamped by new casualties.

Maggie and Sheila were run off their feet trying to care for the injured. Not until well past midnight were they at last able to get a few minutes' rest.

Slumped in a chair near the wardroom, Maggie was at first unaware of Captain Davies's presence. Not until a cup of precious coffee appeared on the table in front of her did she look up.

The chief nurse smiled gently. Like all the rest of them, she was dressed in very loose khakis and showed the evidence of severe weight loss. But she still retained the calm competency so essential in a commanding officer.

Quietly, she said, "We haven't had any chance to talk lately, so I want you to know how much I appreciate the job you've done."

Surprised, Maggie flushed. "It's no more than what should be expected."

"Yes," Captain Davies agreed, "but under these circumstances, that's quite a lot." She paused a moment. "You're an extremely gifted surgical nurse. Your skills are going to be even more essential in the coming months. It would be a shame to lose you."

Puzzled, Maggie did not respond. She knew Jean Davies well enough to understand that she did not talk just for the sake of hearing her own voice. There had to be some point to what she was saying, but Maggie couldn't begin to guess what it might be.

The chief nurse glanced around the wardroom for a moment, then lowered her voice. "The submarine *Starfish* will leave here in approximately eighteen hours. Its destination is Australia. You will be aboard."

Maggie's mouth opened soundlessly. Her first thought was that she had fallen asleep in her chair and was dreaming. Only gradually did she understand that what was happening was real. "Y-you mean I'm...getting out...?"

"That's right. There will be a few others going with you, but not many. There simply isn't room."

"Sheila?"

Captain Davies shook her head. Her eyes were full of sympathy as she said, "I'm sorry. Sheila is an excellent nurse, but all those who are going have some special skill in addition to that which is vital to the war effort."

"A-are you...?"

"Me?" The question clearly surprised the older

woman. "No, of course not. I'll stay with my nurses and the wounded."

Maggie stared at her for a long moment, taking in the matter-of-fact acceptance of what was to be and marveling at the discipline and courage that made such acceptance possible. Captain Davies was every bit as skilled a surgical nurse as Maggie, yet she would not consider leaving those in her care to face their fate alone.

This was, in the final analysis, what command was supposed to be all about. It wasn't privilege, or authority, but responsibility—to oneself, to others and to the flag.

In the fat, lush days of peacetime, this point of view had sounded a little hokey. But in the midst of a war that would decide whether men and women lived in freedom or tyranny, it was nothing short of admirable.

Maggie had witnessed such sacrifice twice within the past few months, once with Major Broderick and now with Captain Davies. Far in the back of her mind flared the hope that, if the time ever came for her to do the same thing, she would be worthy of the example they had set.

"Get some sleep," the captain said gently. "You'll do one more shift. Then be ready to leave by eighteen hundred hours."

Maggie nodded silently. She went off to her cot and lay there staring up at the ceiling, thinking of the vagaries of fate that had decreed she would have a special talent for surgery at a time when it was most needed.

Sheila came in a few minutes later and sat down on

her bunk. Neither woman spoke for a long time. At last Maggie turned her head toward her friend and asked, "Have you heard?"

"Yes," Sheila said softly. She reached across the distance separating them and touched her hand. "I'm glad."

A choked sob broke from Maggie. "I'm not. It isn't right."

"It most certainly is! You're too good a nurse to be stuck here." A winsome smile curved Sheila's mouth. "Look at it this way, kid. I get to sit out the rest of the war in a tropical paradise, while you get all the dirty work."

Tears burned the back of Maggie's eyes. She sat up shakily. "You're the best friend I've ever had. I don't want to lose you."

"You won't," Sheila promised. "We'll meet again, you'll see. But in the meantime, would you do me a favor?"

Maggie nodded. With a rueful grin, Sheila reached under her bunk, pulled out a sheaf of letters and handed them to Maggie. "For Charlie."

The two friends embraced silently. Sheila pretended not to notice that Maggie was crying. She gave her a quick kiss on the cheek and hurried away before her own tears could begin to flow.

BY 1700, MAY 3, 1942, MAGGIE was ready to leave Corregidor. She had packed her few belongings in her duffel bag, but slipped Sheila's letters inside the pocket of her skirt and stitched it shut just to be safe.

Word had finally reached them that Charlie had survived the sinking of the *Arizona* at Pearl Harbor and been reassigned to the heavy cruiser *Nashville*. Maggie was sure he was worried sick about Sheila and would be overjoyed to hear from her.

With the other nurses and a few officers who were leaving, she stood on the dock and waited for the launch that would take them out through the mine field to the submarine. As she looked out over the open sea, she tried hard not to think of all that she was leaving. The slightly more than four months that she had been on Corregidor were the equivalent of a lifetime. She had come there a young, relatively unaware girl. She was departing a woman, fully conscious of both the brutality and the preciousness of life.

Most importantly, she was leaving Anthony.

That thought twisted through her, making her throat tighten painfully. They had last seen each other several days before, when he'd dropped by on one of his usual fish deliveries.

As always, he had been gentle and reassuring, never pretending that things were better than they were, but still trying to ease at least a little of the sadness and fear he knew she felt. Maggie had done the same for him, and together they had managed to find some comfort in simply being together. Now she had to wonder how they would manage apart.

For herself, she didn't mind that much. She would, after all, be alive and free, while Anthony. . .

Visions of his captivity or death rose to torment her. Stifling a sob, she fought down her tears and went in search of a Marine to carry her last message to him. There was so much she wished she had said to him, so much she wished they could have shared. And now, suddenly, there was no more time.

IN HIS FOXHOLE overlooking the beach, Anthony listened to the message the young private delivered, then hollered for his corporal. "Take over for a while. I'm going down to the docks."

He was off and running before the man could reply. What he was doing was crazy; Maggie might already be gone or he might not be able to find her. But he had to try, had to tell her what he felt. . . .

When he reached the south harbor, he was covered with sweat and panting. In the chaos of charred piers, shouting men and careening vehicles, he thought for a moment that he was too late. Then he spotted a flash of chestnut hair and saw her standing on a dock nearby.

Maggie saw him at the same time. She dropped her bag and, heedless of curious stares, ran toward him. They met halfway, his arms flung wide to receive her as she darted into them.

It was the first time they had touched since that evening outside the tunnel, and the effect on them both was electric. The care they had taken to avoid speaking of their feelings in order not to put too great a burden on each other was abruptly shattered.

"Oh, God," Anthony groaned, his embrace tightening convulsively, "I thought I might be too late."

"I don't want to go," she cried against his chest. "I don't want to leave you."

His hands tightened on her shoulders, pulling her back so that she had to look at him. "You *have* to go. You have to live, for both our sakes!"

Maggie could not argue with that. She could only cry soundlessly as he drew her once again into his arms and rocked her gently. They were standing like that when a deep voice suddenly interrupted them.

"Hey, Gargano! Is that you?"

Anthony looked up reluctantly, surprise widening his eyes when he spotted a buddy from his Navy days. "Ferguson," he murmured huskily, "don't tell me you haven't been court-martialed yet."

The slender, sharp-faced young man laughed. "They'll never catch me. Still a leatherneck?"

"Of course. I got tired of playing kiddy games." Keeping an arm around Maggie's waist, he introduced her to his friend. "This is Radio Operator First Class Mac Ferguson. He's rotten through and through, so don't believe a word he says."

The young man groaned in mock dismay. "Ma'am, he's the one you shouldn't believe. Why, I could tell you stories—"

"Never mind about that," Anthony said hastily. "Maggie's going with you guys on board the *Starfish*. Do me a favor and watch out for her."

She was about to protest that she didn't need anyone looking out for her when the sudden shriek of the air-raid siren sent them hurtling to the ground. Anthony dragged her under him, shielding her with his body as a Japanese Zero came in low, spraying the dock and the surrounding area with machine-gun fire.

The plane made three passes before the pilot apparently decided he had inflicted enough damage and, wiggling the wings in mock salute, took himself off. Anthony stood up slowly, helping Maggie to her feet.

"Jeez, that was close!" he exclaimed. "Come on,

there's no more time to waste. You've got to get out of here."

Maggie wasn't listening to him. Her attention was on the crumpled body of Radio Operator First Class Mac Ferguson. He lay facedown in the dirt with his arms and legs spread out, as though he had fallen into an exhausted sleep.

But he had not. A quick check of his pulse told her that.

Anthony stared at him in shocked disbelief. He had seen death over and over on the Rock, but he was still not inured to it. The idea that life could be torn from his friend so abruptly struck him as obscene.

Maggie gave quick instructions to a private to notify the captain of the *Starfish* that he had just lost a member of his crew. Then she took Anthony's hand and urged him away. He followed her obediently, and she guessed that he had no idea of what he was doing.

Beneath the sweat and grime that stained his tanned skin, he was ashen. His entire body felt cold and clammy. She knew he was deeply in shock and wondered desperately how she could possibly leave him in this condition.

The submarine captain marched down the dock, stared at the body of his radio operator, and cursed mightily. After removing Mac's dog tags and personal papers, he ordered the private to have the body taken on board for burial at sea.

As he headed back toward the launch, which had escaped the Zero's strafing, he shook his head and muttered glumly, "How the hell am I supposed to get all the way to Australia without a radioman?" His brow furrowed as he spotted Anthony. "Don't I know you?" Not waiting for a reply, he said, "You're Gargano. I remember you. You and Ferguson trained together."

"Yes, sir," Anthony murmured. "He was a good man."

The captain nodded somberly. "And a damn fine radio operator." He thought for a moment, then said suddenly, "You studied radio, too, didn't you?"

"Yes. . .sir. . .but that was several years ago. I'm a Marine now."

"Bully for you. Get in the launch."

"Wh-what?"

"You heard me. There's no way I'll be able to get the *Starfish* back to port without a radioman. The Japs just killed mine, so you're his replacement. Get in the launch."

"Sir. . .maybe you didn't hear me. I'm in the Marines now."

"Son, I don't care if you're one of the Twelve Disciples. You're going to Australia. Now get in the friggin' launch." Abruptly becoming aware of Maggie, the captain murmured, "Beggin' your pardon, ma'am."

"Th-that's all right." Could this possibly be happening? Was there really a chance that a man's death might buy Anthony his life?

"I've got men up on that hill," Anthony was saying angrily. "You're not seriously suggesting I go off and leave them?"

"I'm not suggesting anything," the captain said with dangerous softness. "I'm telling you, you're my new radioman." Before Anthony could respond, he motioned to two burly sailors standing nearby. "This

Marine is having a little trouble getting into the launch. Help him out."

It took the efforts of both sailors, the captain and two other officers, but eventually Anthony was hoisted and tugged into the boat. Maggie, the nurses and the rest of those chosen to leave jumped in after them.

Night was falling as they pulled away from the dock. The sticklike figures of the men and the few remaining nurses who had come to see them off receded slowly into the shadows. Looming above, the pitted, gouged slab of Corregidor stood out in stark relief.

To Maggie, it was no longer the purple isle she had first glimpsed from the deck of the *Don Esteban*. Instead, its twisted, broken sides seemed to be stained red against the cloud-draped sky.

Anthony was silent now, no longer fighting. If he had learned anything on the Rock, it was to accept the remorselessness of fate. For some unknown reason, he had been chosen to live, at least for a little while longer.

His hand reached out for Maggie's. Side by side, they watched as the island faded away into the darkness.

May 1942–July 1942
AUSTRALIA

Chapter Five

"HAVE A SEAT, MA'AM," the warrant officer said. "It'll just take me a minute to get your papers together."

Maggie nodded and sat down on the straight wooden chair in front of his desk. She smoothed the slim white uniform that was part of her new wardrobe and glanced around curiously.

The Quonset hut that was serving as part of General MacArthur's new command headquarters in Brisbane, Australia, was crowded to bursting. Telephones shrilled constantly, men bustled in and out, and there was a general air of important business.

To her still weary mind, it was hard to take everything in all at once. The *Starfish* had docked a week before, after a long, arduous journey during which they learned of the fall of Corregidor.

Barely seventy-two hours after their departure, the end had come. General Wainwright, acknowledging that his embattled men had given to the utmost of their abilities and beyond, had sorrowfully ordered the white flag raised.

Before the Japanese had set foot on the island, the Fourth Marines—what was left of them—had gathered together and burned their divisional colors. These, at least, would not fall into the hands of the enemy.

Since arriving in Australia, Maggie and the other survivors of the Rock had been in the hospital, being—as one doctor put it—"fattened up in a hurry." Rest, freedom from fear and nutritious food were having the desired effects.

Though she had a long way to go to regain all the weight she had lost, some color had returned to her cheeks, her eyes were brighter, and she moved more energetically. At night, she slept unexpectedly well, despite her dreams of Sheila, Major Broderick, Captain Davies and all the other people left behind.

She and Anthony had managed to meet occasionally near the hospital. Strolling unnoticed through Brisbane's busy streets, talking quietly among themselves, they began to take the first tentative steps toward both an emotional and a physical recovery from the horrors they had lived through.

This, in defiance of the fact that reminders of the war were everywhere. The Australians were in a state of high alert. With their most experienced soldiers fighting in the North African desert and with the British unable to provide them with the protection they had counted on, the people felt as though they were ducks in a shooting gallery, waiting to be picked off by the victorious Japanese.

Word had it that some of their leaders had wanted to establish a defensive line that would have effectively sacrificed half the country to the onrushing foe. MacArthur—with the full support of many Australians—had other ideas. Having been appointed Commander in Chief of the Southwest Pacific Area, he was determined to go on the offensive.

Maggie was in full sympathy with that. She had seen firsthand the ravages of being under siege and felt that combat had to be preferable.

"Thanks for waiting, ma'am," the warrant officer said as he at last unearthed the appropriate papers from the precarious piles on his desk. "Let's see, now. . . You've been reassigned to the Army hospital here in Brisbane, where you'll be in charge of the surgery ward, Captain. If you'll report to—"

"Captain?" Maggie repeated blankly. "There's been some mistake. I'm only a lieutenant."

The officer glanced back down at her papers and shrugged. "You're a captain now."

"H-how—"

"A Captain Davies recommended your promotion early this month. It was acted on a few days ago. Congratulations."

A short time later, a rather dazed Maggie was back out in the fierce sunlight, swatting automatically at the ubiquitous black bugs while she tried to come to terms with her new status.

Captain? She was still only twenty-three years old; how could she possibly have reached that rank already?

Distantly, she remembered her father talking about the speed with which promotions occurred during wartime. Apparently he was right, but even so, this was a bit ridiculous. How was she supposed to lead nurses much older and more experienced than she?

Deep in thought, she crossed the street toward the motor pool, where her jeep waited. A familiar voice brought her up short. Turning, she spied a short, stolid figure she knew well. Colonel Rusty Osborne was a West Point classmate of her father's and a close family friend.

"Little Maggie Lawrence!" he exclaimed as they

greeted each other. "I couldn't believe it was you. Lord, but you've grown up!"

She smiled warmly, delighted to see him. He looked much the same as she'd remembered, with a round, flushed face and a balding scalp liberally sprinkled with freckles. His dark brown eyes were alert and intelligent. He missed little, despite his benign appearance.

"I guess it happens to the best of us," she responded. "You're looking pretty fine yourself, Colonel, if you don't mind my saying so."

He chuckled and offered her his arm. "Never let it be said that I turned down a compliment from a lovely woman. You've inherited all your mother's charm. By the way, how are your folks?"

"I don't know...I haven't heard from them in months."

Colonel Osborne paused and looked at her, perplexed. "Why not?"

Maggie hesitated. She hadn't talked very much about her experiences and was reluctant to start now. But Rusty was a gentle, genial man who deserved an explanation. Quietly, she said, "I've been on Corregidor."

His face paled, and the hand resting on hers tightened. "My God...I should have realized...you're so slender and pale...."

Determined to lighten the mood, she said, "Don't let the folks at the hospital hear you say that. They're very proud of the care they've given me."

Still deeply shaken, the colonel asked, "How long have you been here?"

"A little over a week. I came on the *Starfish*."

"Then you were part of the last group that got out. I suppose. . .you've heard what's happened."

"I know the Rock fell."

Rusty hesitated a moment, studying her compassionately. "Come over to the club with me and we'll have a drink. You shouldn't be standing out in the sun."

Since Maggie had not yet been assigned regular duty hours, she agreed. It would be nice to catch up on old times, but she suspected that wasn't all the colonel wanted to talk about. He had something to tell her and was trying to do it gently.

Still, there was really no way to soften what he had to say. After they were seated at a round mahogany table on the veranda overlooking the harbor, with a ceiling fan turning lazily above them and potted palms waving gently in the breeze, he described what had happened after Corregidor's surrender.

"You're going to hear this sooner or later," he began quietly, "so it may as well be now. The men on Corregidor were shipped over to Bataan, where the rest of our forces were being held. Once they were all together, they were marched to the POW camps."

"Marched? But they were all in very poor condition, and with the heat. . ."

Rusty nodded somberly. "As nearly as we can figure out, the Japanese just weren't adequately prepared. They thought there'd be far fewer prisoners for them to cope with."

"But why? They must have had some idea of how many men we had."

"Sure they did, but they think that surrendering is so dishonorable that they'd rather kill themselves. I guess they expected our men to do the same." Grimly, Rusty added, "I'm afraid a lot of them may wish by now that they had."

Maggie set her glass of iced tea down. Tormenting visions of Sheila filled her mind. Her hands shook, and she clasped them tightly in her lap. "W-what happened to the nurses?"

"They went into a civilian internment camp, where conditions seem to be a little better. As far as we know, there were no...atrocities committed against them. Although there have been attacks against Filipino civilians."

She shook her head blankly, fighting the rising sense of nausea that threatened to grip her. She knew it was pointless to ask how or why this had happened. They were dealing with people from a culture completely alien to their own, one founded on traditions of honor and duty that were, unfortunately, incomprehensible.

"Will it go on like this?" she asked at length, so softly that the colonel had to lean forward to hear her.

"For a while. They caught us with our pants down—if you don't mind my saying so—and we've got a lot of lost time to make up for. But already there are some signs that the tide is beginning to turn in our favor."

Maggie knew what he was referring to. Within two days of Corregidor's fall, the United States Navy had challenged the southward push of the Japanese toward New Guinea and, ultimately, Australia. The opposing forces had met in the Coral Sea, where the Americans had won a decisive victory. Again time had been bought, but it remained to be seen how much could be done with it.

"I'm going back to Washington in a couple of days," Rusty told her. "I'll report to the War Department on the situation here and then, I hope, draw a combat assignment. Would you like me to take a letter to your folks?"

"Oh, yes, please. I know they must be terribly worried."

While he waited, she used a desk in the club lobby to scribble a quick note. Since the colonel was traveling on vital military business, he had a seat on one of the few aircraft flying the route home. The letter would be in her parents' hands within days.

"Now you take good care of yourself," Rusty admonished as he dropped her off at the hospital. "When I get back here, I want to see you looking fat and sassy."

"I'll do my best," she promised, laughing. Then she remembered something she had forgotten to put in her letter. "Colonel, please tell my dad I made captain!"

Rusty grinned and flashed her a thumbs-up signal. "I sure will. He'll about burst with pride!"

Maggie stood on the steps of the hospital for a while after Rusty had driven off, thinking about that. Her father *would* be proud, as would her mother and brother. They would all—like Captain Davies—believe that she could do the job.

Which meant, Maggie told herself firmly, that she had better get on with it. Squaring her shoulders, she headed through the door to begin her new assignment.

SEVERAL MILES AWAY, Anthony was having less success getting himself back in the war. The captain he approached on the matter was not particularly helpful.

"You did a good job on the *Starfish*," the man pointed out. "They'd like to keep you on as their radio operator."

Patiently, as though speaking to a child—which was pretty much how he regarded all officers, anyway—Anthony said, "I'm a Marine, sir."

"You used to be in the Navy."

"Not anymore, sir."

"Hmm...no, I guess not. In that case, you'll have to wait until the First Marine Division gets here. It's on the way from the States and should arrive in New Zealand around mid-June. You'll be assigned to it."

Anthony nodded glumly. The First Marines had been an understaffed division stationed on the East Coast. Most of its men were bound to be raw recruits, too green to know how to lace their boots up.

He thought of the experienced fighters he had left on the Rock and cursed inwardly. Haunted by thoughts of them, he stumped out of the hut and stood for several minutes struggling against the anger and guilt that threatened to overcome him.

His survival—miraculous as it was—continued to be a source of both joy and pain. He was glad to be alive, but he could not shake the burden of knowing that the men he had left behind, however inadvertently, were suffering a fate he believed he should have shared.

Without Maggie, he didn't know how he would have made it through the past few days. The mere thought of her was enough to ease his anguish. He even managed to smile slightly as he considered how very well she was learning to ignore the nonfraternization regulations. His Maggie—as he had come to think of her—had the definite makings of a rebel beneath that proper but nonetheless delectable surface.

Heading in the direction of the motor pool, he pushed his cap forward at a determined angle. The gnawing guilt he felt for still being alive and free would do no one, including himself, any good. Worse yet, it came perilously close to self-pity, something he abhorred. Better to concentrate on making the most of the time he had so unexpectedly been given.

A brief chat with an understanding sergeant secured him a jeep. Moments later, he had left the dusty camp behind him and was speeding along the road to central Brisbane.

With several hours to kill before Maggie was due to meet him, he amused himself by wandering around, looking in the store windows and watching the pretty girls go by. There was very little in the former—thanks to strict rationing—but no shortage of the latter.

Despite the pain and anguish of war, the Australian women were remarkably lovely. Their slender bodies, clad in thin cotton dresses, moved with a grace and vivaciousness he could not help but appreciate. He began comparing each woman he saw with Maggie, deliberately trying to see if he would find any of them as attractive as he found her.

That he did not was a source of mild chagrin, coupled with a surprising sense of satisfaction. For days he had been wondering in the back of his mind if his desire for her was no more than the expected aftereffect of their having shared a brutal and terrifying experience. Away from the tragedy of Corregidor, with their lives miraculously intact, might they not drift their separate ways?

During the little walks they had taken through Brisbane, he had felt the same question in her, even though neither had mentioned it. Unspoken between them was the knowledge that they were at a turning point in their relationship, one that would decide whether they were ever to be more than simply friends bound by a common memory of defiance and defeat.

He leaned back against a stone wall warm from the late-afternoon sun and sighed deeply. It was in his nature always to look for options that would keep him from getting pinned down too tightly. That was why he had never made any commitments except to the Corps, and why he was so effective in battle.

Women knew what to expect from him; he never misrepresented himself and despised men who did. But neither had he ever experienced anything like the feelings Maggie set off in him. Even as he half resented her for the unaccustomed sense of vulnerability she provoked in him, he was also excited by the prospect of what might lie ahead for them.

That excitement shone clearly in his dark eyes as he made his way to their prearranged meeting place and watched her come toward him along the sidewalk crowded with soldiers and civilians in search of an evening's amusement.

His gaze narrowed slightly as he studied her. She was wearing a simple blue cotton wraparound skirt and a white short-sleeved blouse. Her slender legs were bare, her skin was lightly tanned, and her glorious hair was restored to a healthy shine.

Everything about her was pleasantly familiar to him, yet something had changed. Her shoulders were a little straighter, her step was a little quicker, and the set of her lovely mouth was a little more confident. She radiated a barely contained sense of happiness that made more than a few men look at her longer than they should have.

Despite his annoyance at the admiring stares she was receiving, Anthony couldn't help but smile. He had no difficulty guessing the source of her pleasure. Abandoning his leisurely posture, he moved into the stream of pedestrian traffic.

Maggie stopped when she saw him heading toward her. For an instant, surrounded by the people hurrying by, she looked uncertain. Then the doubt fled as he came up to her and said softly. "You got your new assignment."

The brightness of her hyacinth-blue eyes deepened, as did the warm flush of her cheeks. His immediate understanding only reaffirmed her eagerness to share her news. "I did, as chief nurse on the surgery ward." A very unmilitary grin wreathed her heart-shaped face. "Can you imagine, they even made me a captain!"

Anthony's smile did not fade, despite the sudden twinge he felt. He was glad for her promotion, because it meant she would be doing the work she loved best, but it also broadened the gap between them just when he was most determined to eliminate it entirely.

But, like any good Marine, he was more than prepared to rise to the challenge. Taking her arm, he steered her through the crowd to a quieter side street where they could talk more easily. They walked in silence past shops shaded by awnings, amid the drowsy hum of flies and the increasingly distant sounds of rumbling traffic and rushing humanity.

As they did so, Maggie cast him several swift glances. As a nurse, she automatically took in the signs of his ever-improving health, but it was as a woman that she was most seriously affected. The broad sweep of his chest and shoulders beneath the khaki shirt, his trim waist and hips, and the long expanse of his legs in sharply pleated trousers made her acutely aware of him as a man restored to the peak of his strength and virility.

Yet another sidelong look confirmed for her that he was unusually serious. His ebony eyes were hooded, his mouth was tautly drawn and his square jaw jutted out slightly. Her throat tightened as she wondered if he was upset by what she had told him.

Suddenly, not having him angry at her—even if unfairly—was the most important thing in the world. She didn't pause to question why that should be or what the implications of admitting it might mean.

"Anthony...my new job...it doesn't have to make any difference to us."

He stopped and turned to her, his steady gaze searching hers, allowing for no dissembling. "Because you were already an officer?" His voice was low and slightly gruff.

She didn't pretend to misunderstand what he was saying. If she truly meant to respect the nonfraternization regulations—even belatedly—now was the time to tell him so.

For a moment she was tempted. That way lay safety, an end to the challenges he posed. She could retreat back into the protected cocoon of her military identity, back into the neat, ordered world that had been hers since childhood. She could forget that she had ever known a strong, tender, fiercely proud man who made her feel almost more of a woman than she was ready to be.

Almost, but not quite. Courage—and her own pride—demanded that she deal with him honestly.

They had stopped in front of a fruit-and-vegetable store whose broad glass window was all but empty. Maggie stared into it, finding it easier to look at his reflection than at the man himself.

"No," she said softly, "that's not what I meant." When he still did not move or speak, she took a deep breath and voiced the conviction that had been growing in her ever since those agonizing days on Corregidor. "As far as I'm concerned, life is too short and too precious to run away from. Our...feelings for each other have nothing to do with the military or our ranks or anything like that—and they certainly won't affect our ability to do our jobs properly—so I don't see why we should worry about senseless regulations."

Anthony could not have asked for more reassuring words, but he still had to be sure that she fully understood what she was promising. "Other people wouldn't see it that way."

"I know," she agreed unhesitantly. "So we'll have to be discreet."

Discreet. He turned that word over in his mind, savoring it. It sounded very...proper, carrying with it no admission of wrongdoing, but simply a mature acceptance of their situation and the best way to cope with it.

His hand reached out, his fingers curling around hers. They smiled at each other in the shopwindow. A moment passed, during which he struggled to come to terms with the powerful emotions welling up inside him.

He was at once infinitely grateful for the risk she was willing to take, and determined that she would never regret it. "Will you spend the evening with me?" he murmured. "Discreetly, of course."

She smiled her acceptance. Taking advantage of the empty street, they continued walking hand in hand until they reached the avenue; then they separated a few inches, sharing a quick grin as they did so. They had gone another half block before Anthony said, "There's a movie playing that you might like to see—Hitchcock's *Rebecca*."

Maggie nodded eagerly. "I'd hoped to catch that before I shipped out for Manila, but I missed it by a few weeks."

Either quite a few other people shared her enthusiasm or dark, relatively private places were simply in great demand. Whatever the reason, the theater was crowded, mostly with servicemen and their dates. Heads were bent close together and voices were no more than soft murmurs as everyone waited for the movie to start.

"Hitchcock's good," Anthony said, taking advantage of the darkness to slip Maggie's arm through his and lay his hand over hers. "I really liked *The Man Who Knew Too Much*."

She laughed softly, a sound he had heard too rarely but had already come to love. The simple, ordinary fact of being on a date with him delighted her. In the face of what they had so recently endured, it seemed nothing short of miraculous that they should both be there, safe and whole and together. The terror and turmoil of the outside world faded away as she determined to savor every moment of whatever time they had.

"I think," she murmured teasingly, "that you'll find this a little different."

"Oh, yeah? How come?"

"*Rebecca* is a romance."

"You sure?"

"I read the book," she informed him gravely. "Daphne du Maurier is one of my favorite writers. My mother's, too."

"Oh. . . well, that's okay. I guess it won't kill me to sit through."

He sounded so resigned that she had to stifle a laugh. Then the curtain opened and the credits began to roll. Soon she was caught up in the enthralling story of an innocent young wife, an inscrutable husband and a hauntingly beautiful house called Manderley. The stillness of Anthony's big body was enough to tell her that, despite his reservations, he was also engulfed in the unfolding drama.

They emerged much later into the gathering twilight. The city was even more crowded and fast-paced than it had been earlier. "I know a good place for dinner," Anthony said as they waited on the curb for a convoy of supply trucks to pass. "Are you hungry?"

"Famished," Maggie admitted with a grin. "There's no doubt that my appetite has returned in full."

"Good, then Digger Sam's will be perfect." The provocative glance he shot her made it clear he was well aware that establishments with such inelegant names were not within her experience. But Maggie was more than willing to give it a try, especially since all the grander Brisbane dining spots were strictly off limits to noncoms.

"It sounds very discreet," she assured him, earning a tender grin that made her heart race.

Whatever else it might be, the combination pub and restaurant was certainly popular. Maggie got a quick glimpse of the bar as they entered, enough to see that the patrons were five and six deep. The crowd was about evenly divided between soldiers and sailors vying for the attention of the greatly outnumbered young women who seemed well adept at sharing their favors.

The restaurant was a little more sedate, although almost all the three dozen tables were already occupied. Anthony had called ahead, so there was no trouble getting seated. The friendly, gum-chewing waitress handed them menus before going off to fill their drink orders.

"What did you think of the movie?" Maggie asked as she sat back in her chair, looking at him with unabashed pleasure. He was easily the most attractive man in the room, a fact that had not gone unnoticed by the other women there. She tore her eyes away long enough to shoot a speaking glance at a well-endowed blonde at the next table whose attention had wandered from her sailor date.

As the blonde looked hastily away, Maggie was amused to note that Anthony had completely missed the brief exchange. He was so accustomed to men being the aggressors that he apparently didn't suspect women were every bit as capable of predatory behavior. Perhaps that was just as well, since Maggie had to admit she was a little shocked by her own action. Never before had she felt such a sense of possessiveness about a man, a determination to keep him exclusively for herself.

"I liked it," Anthony was saying. Teasingly, he added, "Even the romance part. If I get a chance, I'll read the book."

They went on to talk of other movies they had both seen and enjoyed. The waitress brought them a pitcher of beer, followed shortly by platters of sweet crayfish and a basket of fluffy rolls.

"I love the *Thin Man* movies," Maggie said. "Nick and Nora Charles are my idea of a terrific couple."

"They're pretty good," Anthony allowed, "but Simon Templar is my favorite. The Saint is a great character."

"He's very romantic, like a modern-day Robin Hood."

Anthony grimaced playfully. "Trust a woman to see it that way. The Saint is a loner; it's him against the bad guys."

Maggie studied Anthony for a moment, wondering if that was how he saw himself. It wouldn't be surprising, or even unrealistic. Despite the lack of officer's bars on his uniform, he was the type of man others instinctively looked to for guidance and protection. She had done that herself on the Rock, and she accepted the fact that she might well do so again.

But the desperate circumstances of Corregidor had

placed them on an equal footing, her nursing skills matching his abilities as a fighter. With their return to safety, that situation had changed. Like it or not, she had to admit that he had the distinct advantage of far greater worldliness, which enabled him naturally to take the lead in their developing relationship.

She might have fought against that, except for what she believed about him. They had gotten to know each other in surroundings that stripped away all pretense and revealed the true essence of a person's character. Anthony had proved himself to be a decent, honorable man; if she hadn't thought so, she would never have agreed to continue seeing him.

Listening to the low, slightly husky flow of his voice as he told her about Saturday afternoons at the movies with his brothers and sisters in Brooklyn, she assured herself that her faith was not misplaced. Trusting him would give her the best of both possible worlds, allowing her to be daringly romantic without placing herself in the least amount of danger. Because Anthony would protect her.

Far in the back of her mind, a small voice warned that she was putting a heavy burden on him, but Maggie didn't listen. She was running too fast from pain and doubt to worry about where her heedless trust might lead them both.

Chapter Six

ANTHONY SMOTHERED a sigh as he stared at himself in the mirror above the sink. For a man who was supposed to be on R&R, he was looking downright haggard, and not for the accepted reasons.

There were dark circles under his black eyes, his brow seemed permanently furrowed, and the lines on either side of his mouth were deeper than ever before. Not even the fact that he had just showered, shaved and put on fresh khakis seemed to make any difference in his appearance. He looked exactly like what he was, a man teetering on the sharp edge of frustration.

Worse yet, he had only himself to blame. He had realized from the beginning that Maggie was something special, different from the women he'd had relationships with before. How could he not understand that when he'd been raised with a clear understanding that there were two types of women in the world?

As his father had explained it, "There are good women, like your mother and sisters, the kind for marrying and having a family with. And then there's the other kind, for fooling around with. Don't make the mistake of confusing them."

To which Dom, always cocky, had replied, "I get it. There are two kinds of women. Good and...better." He and Anthony had laughed at that, as had

Joseph. But both sons had also accepted the basic truth of what their father had said.

Maggie was unmistakably one of the good women Anthony had always been so careful to avoid in the past. He didn't question that she was supposed to be treated with respect, and he cared far too much for her not to want to do what was right.

Except for one little problem. While his mind knew how he was supposed to behave, his body didn't seem to care. He wanted her so badly that if something didn't happen soon, he was liable to explode. It had gotten to the point that every time he looked at her, he felt guilty, if only about the fantasies he'd been having. The fact that she was so sweet and trusting just made it worse.

After that night at the movies, they had seen each other several times a week. He loved being with her; she made him forget the nearness of war and helped him concentrate on the pleasure of living. She was remarkably easy to talk with, but also comfortable with long silences. He could relax with her, let down his guard and renew his energies. Or at least he would be able to if his body didn't insist on reminding him that he had other needs to consider.

Maybe it would have been better if he'd never touched her, but that much restraint he hadn't been able to muster. Still staring into the mirror, he thought of the first time he kissed her, and stifled a groan.

They had gone to see another movie, *Wuthering Heights* with Lawrence Olivier and Merle Oberon. It was heady stuff, seething with dark passion. Anthony could identify with that all too easily. Afterward, they'd had dinner again at Digger Sam's—it had become their favorite spot—and, at his suggestion, gone for a walk near the beach.

It had been a warm moonlit evening. Maggie, in a simple white dress that set off her honeyed skin, had never looked lovelier. Her high-boned cheeks were slightly flushed, and the perfume of violets wafted from her silken hair. They were talking about England, where the film was set and which they both hoped to visit one day. The news from there was cautiously optimistic.

The terrible German air attacks of the previous year were not being repeated. With Hitler's attention turned toward Russia, the citizens of London and other cities that had suffered so brutally in the blitz were getting a much-needed respite. But how long it would last or what its aftermath might be, no one could know.

The war had seemed very far away as they strolled along the curve of white sand washed by frothing waves. Though they couldn't get close to the water— it was closed off by walls of barbed wire and signs warning of mines—they could still enjoy the sound and scent of it. Here and there they caught glimpses of other couples half-hidden by the kindly darkness.

"It's so beautiful here." Maggie sighed softly. "The war seems like nothing more than a bad dream."

Anthony's hand tightened on hers. "I wish that were true, sweetheart. When I think of all the things I used to take for granted. . ."

"Me, too. . . Little things, like being alive tomorrow."

They turned to each other as one, their eyes meeting silently for a long moment. A surge of raw need struck Anthony more forcibly than any wave that had ever pounded on a beach. She was right not to take anything for granted. Neither could he. Fate was a harsh and arbitrary mistress. Tomorrow might bring the end of all their dreams.

The shadows of an ancient eucalyptus tree sheltered them gently. Slipping an arm around her slender waist, he urged her closer, all the while murmuring to her in a soft, coaxing voice he had never heard himself use before. "Maggie...sweet Maggie...do you have any idea what you do to me? You're so innocent in some ways.... Don't be frightened.... I'll never hurt you...."

Her lips parted—to answer him? Afraid that she meant to protest, he waited no longer. Lowering his head, he claimed her mouth with all the passionate intensity she had unloosened in him, yet bridled by a depth of tenderness he had not known he possessed.

The taste of her, clean and slightly tangy with a hint of peppermint, entranced him. His arms tightened around her as he explored the edge of her teeth and the ridge of her upper mouth. The velvety moistness of her tongue, which at first darted shyly away from his, returned an instant later and, to his delight, met him in a sensual feint and parry that left them both breathless.

He was on fire for her, swept by thrashing undulations of need. His loins hardened, his manhood swelled. He wanted nothing so much as to lay her down on the sand, strip away the virginal white dress, and bury himself in her sweet mystery.

And he was perilously close to doing exactly that. It

was the realization that his hands, seemingly of their own volition, had begun to undo the buttons of her dress that brought him up short.

"I didn't mean..." he muttered hoarsely. "Sweet Lord. I'm losing control of this...."

He had to be out of his mind even to consider going all the way with her. This wasn't some two-bit whore with whom he could amuse himself. This was Maggie, a woman of rare beauty and courage, whom he needed in ways he hadn't fully begun to understand.

There was a brief but fierce struggle with his baser needs before he groaned huskily and raised his head. Lambent flames burned in his eyes as he gazed down at her with an expression that was nothing short of anguished. "Sweetheart...we can't..."

Maggie didn't seem to hear him. She tightened her arms around his neck and gave a soft, shimmering moan.

"Please...Anthony...don't stop...."

Resisting her artless invitation was far and away the most difficult thing he had ever done. Grimly, he wondered if there was any hope of freeing himself from the streak of chivalry that compelled him to put her best interests before his own.

Where was the cynicism that had served him so well in the past? If he could get over the sense of responsibility she provoked in him, he would have no reason not to take what she was so clearly offering. But he could not do it.

Regret and the sheer pressure of his need made his voice tight as he said, "Maggie...love...you deserve better than this. We both do. Please...help me stop...."

Standing away from him somewhat abashedly, she nodded, her cheeks very flushed. "You're right. I shouldn't have—"

He cut her off with a gentle kiss. "Don't regret anything. You're perfect. And so is what's happening to us."

His words that night hadn't changed the fact that he was well and truly stuck between the proverbial rock and a hard place, with only himself to blame. Because not only had he gone on seeing her, he had also taken every opportunity to kiss and caress her, despite the torment his actions inflicted on him.

Still staring at himself in the mirror, he shook his head ruefully. For both their sakes, he had to do something quickly, before the situation got completely out of hand. Maggie was on duty that night, and he had already made arrangements to get together with his Aussie buddies. Maybe in their company he would be able to come up with a solution.

The Australian marines he had met in Brisbane had wasted no time making him unofficially one of their own. They had the same irreverence for authority shared by all enlisted men, and they liked nothing better than to complain about the brass while hatching their own schemes for winning the war.

Stretched out on a patch of sand on a favorite beach near their regimental headquarters, they were dealing the cards for the latest hand in what was apparently a long game of euchre when Anthony arrived.

"Join us, mate?" Sergeant Jake Dylan asked, moving over to make room for him.

Settled down on the sand, Anthony accepted the bottle that was being passed around and took a swig before he said, "Deal me in. Anything new with you guys?"

"Not a bloody thing," Jake muttered, his eyes on the cards. He was a big, hard man with unruly red hair and a battered face that suggested he liked few things as well as a good fight. Grumbling, he added, "We keep expecting to get shipped out any day, but so far there's no word."

Anthony grinned, even as the raw whiskey burned its way down his throat. "Pretty tough, having to cool your heels like this."

Jake snorted and tossed in a card. "War's hell. We sit while the brass argues strategy. Your MacArthur wants to make an all-out push to New Guinea, but he hasn't got the go-ahead yet."

"He'll get it," Anthony said.

"How can you be so sure?"

Anthony shrugged and passed the bottle on. "Simple. He's all Washington's got down here. They can't afford to get him pissed off."

"Can't say I much like the idea of fighting over on New Guinea," another man put in. "Hell of a place, with all that bloody jungle and those mountains."

"Yeah," Anthony drawled, "it'll probably take you guys the better part of a week to finish it off."

They laughed appreciatively, even though no man was fool enough to believe him. New Guinea was a green hell, plain and simple. Even the natives had trouble surviving.

Soon enough, they all would have to face it for themselves. But in the meantime, there were pleasanter things to think about. The talk turned to how they might spend the remaining hours until they were due back on duty.

"What do you say we drop in at Madame Rosa's?"

"Not a bad idea. We haven't been there in a while."

"Any particular reason why not?" Anthony asked.

"Well, it's not exactly cheap," Jake explained. "She's got the real top-drawer girls."

"I'll say," another man chimed in, grinning in anticipation. "Worth every bloomin' penny."

"Madame Rosa's it is, then," Jake said. He showed his cards and scooped up the pot, ignoring the resigned groans of the other players. "Let's off, mates."

As they secured their broad-brimmed felt hats on their heads, Anthony murmured, "Remind me to teach you guys poker sometime."

The sergeant laughed good-naturedly. "Sure thing, mate, but in the meantime, how about coming with us?"

Anthony hesitated, torn between his first instinct to refuse and his second, which suggested he might be wise at least to consider the invitation. Hadn't he just been thinking that if he didn't do something soon, he was going to betray Maggie's trust in him?

Maybe this was the solution, not ideal certainly, but still a potential way out of his dilemma. Deciding not to reject it out of hand, he rose, brushed the sand off his khakis and, with a slightly wary grin, sauntered off with the others.

Madame Rosa's looked to be everything the Aussies had claimed. He'd been in some pretty fancy cathouses in his time, but this one beat them all. Just about every square inch of space was covered with red brocade and velvet. Ornate chandeliers hung from the ceilings, and gilt-framed paintings of naked ladies and leering satyrs helped create the proper mood. The long, marble-topped bar was doing a brisk business, serving both a military and civilian clientele.

But the star attraction was very clearly the young ladies clad in diaphanous gowns and other interesting outfits that left no doubt about exactly what a prospective customer would be getting for his money.

Anthony had barely walked in the door before he found a curvy, bright-eyed blonde at his arm. She said her name was Claudette, and she looked to be very good at what she did. With high, full breasts crowned by rosy nipples, a small waist and generously rounded hips—all visible through the sheer black lace negligee she wore—she was exactly the kind of woman Anthony had always found appealing. At least until he'd met Maggie.

Madame Rosa's was a classy place, not some wham-bam-thank-you-ma'am dive where the bedrooms had revolving doors. Etiquette called for him to spend a little time—and a healthy hunk of cash—at the bar.

Perched on a stool beside him, Claudette sipped the "champagne" he had obligingly ordered for her, even though he knew it to be plain soda water, while he downed a couple of whiskeys.

"Have you been in Brisbane long, marine?" she asked, her fingers drifting through the thick black hair at the nape of his neck.

"Long enough." He had no intention of talking about where he'd been. Running a hand up the bare expanse of her arm, he satisfied himself that her skin

was as soft as it looked. Unbidden, a memory of softer
skin lightly scented with violets came to him, and he
cursed under his breath.

At Claudette's surprised look, he shrugged apolo-
getically. "Nothing to do with you, honey. Just something I've got on my mind."

She smiled provocatively. "You say the word and I
promise to make you forget everything."

His mouth twisted slightly as he considered that. It
had been months since he'd had a woman, since before the Fourth Marines had arrived in the Philippines. Such an extended period of celibacy went
completely against the grain. He felt like a kid again,
desperately trying to figure out how to release what
was, after all, a perfectly normal biological urge. No
wonder he was perilously close to taking advantage of
Maggie.

"I'll bet you could, too," he said, stroking
Claudette's arm again. She cuddled closer, all the
while taking a careful look at him. Her profession had
taught her to be cautious, but in this case she could see
no reason to be concerned. He looked young, strong
and healthy in both mind and body.

While definitely on the lean side, Anthony still
radiated a sense of virile strength and confidence she
found appealing. Every once in a while, a customer
came along who pleased her as much as she pleased
him. Wetting her lips, Claudette wondered if this
might not be one of those times.

"I'd just love to show you my room," she murmured,
smiling lingeringly.

Anthony hesitated a moment longer. A mental picture of Maggie lying in his arms rose before him. She

was so sweet, so trusting. . . and he was so scared of hurting her. Anything would be better than that.

Abruptly making up his mind, he got to his feet and wrapped an arm around Claudette's waist, lifting her easily off her stool. Her smile widened. She liked the power she felt in him. Catching the eye of one of the other girls, she winked. The brunette cast a glance at Anthony and grinned a little enviously, recognizing the signal that meant Claudette expected to be occupied for quite some time.

"Let's not keep your motor running, honey," Claudette purred as she led Anthony up the stairs and down a dimly lit corridor. From behind the doors they passed, familiar sounds reached Anthony, but he ignored them. All his attention was focused on the woman he would soon possess.

Claudette walked slightly ahead of him, her hips swaying back and forth and her plump buttocks gleaming whitely through the diaphanous material. His pulse jumped and his breathing became more ragged as he waited for the expected surge of hot desire through his loins. When it did not develop immediately, he felt a twinge of concern, but pushed it aside and resolutely followed her through the door she'd opened.

The room was nicely furnished with a double bed, a nightstand and a dresser. Either Claudette was very neat or she lived elsewhere in the establishment, for there was no sign of personal belongings. A swift glance told him the sheets were clean—another advantage of patronizing a top-drawer place.

After undressing quickly, with Claudette's help, he lay down on the bed. She let the filmy negligee slide to her feet and kicked it away before joining him there.

As he had suspected, she was very good at her job. Her talents were such that she should have been able to get the necessary response out of a stone. But Anthony defeated her. To his initial bewilderment and then growing dismay, he discovered that he could not perform.

Claudette soothed him as best she could. "Don't worry about it," she advised gently. "It happens to everyone at some time."

"It sure as hell has never happened to me before," he growled, staring up at the ceiling and wondering what could possibly be wrong.

It was a damn good thing his Aussie pals couldn't see him now, he thought. They'd split themselves laughing. Anthony Gargano, with his flag at half-mast. He could be drummed out of the Marines for this!

"You just need to relax," Claudette suggested. "I'll give you a massage."

She did a thorough job of it, but succeeded only in making Anthony feel drowsy. Completely disgusted with himself, he paid Claudette generously, despite her insistence that it wasn't necessary, and took himself off, slipping out the back way so he wouldn't run the risk of encountering Jake or the other Aussies.

Much later that night, after putting away the better part of a bottle of scotch in a futile effort to forget, he wandered down to the beach. Flopping down on the wet sand, he gazed owlishly at the full moon and wondered again what was wrong with him.

Physically, he felt completely restored to health, so

that couldn't be the explanation. It had to lie elsewhere, in the uncharted realm of emotions. What if he kept on having the same problem? He'd heard of men who could never perform with a woman. If that happened to him, he'd just as soon slit his throat.

Sighing, he lay back with his arms folded behind his head and told himself not to be an idiot. Of course this condition wasn't permanent. He obviously wasn't completely recovered from what he'd gone through on the Rock. And then there was the whole business with Maggie, which certainly had shaken him up. . . .

A groan broke from him. At the mere thought of her, his body had instinctively hardened. What Claudette had not succeeded in achieving with all her arts was now more than amply in evidence.

Anthony shook his head ruefully, unsure whether he felt like laughing or crying. He seemed, quite unexpectedly, to have developed a conscience, when all he really wanted was a good stiff. . .

Cursing under his breath, he clambered to his feet and wandered back to the barracks in which he was temporarily lodged. Fumbling in the darkness, he somehow managed to find his bunk and fall onto it.

His last thought before plummeting into sleep was that old Mother Nature was definitely trying to tell him something.

MAGGIE CAME OFF DUTY shortly before dawn. In the solitude of the nurses' locker room, from which everyone else had long since departed, she slid out of her surgery fatigues, showered, then tugged on her uniform to make the brief trip back to her quarters.

She was bone-tired, since it was now some six hours past the time when her shift was supposed to have ended. Early in the evening, a young sailor had been carried in by his buddies after a savage barroom fight over a woman. Maggie had rarely seen worse wounds and had really thought the sailor didn't have a chance. But against all odds, he had pulled through and was on his way to the recovery ward.

That was where she felt she ought to be heading. Gathering up her bag and switching off the light, she walked slowly down the corridor, wondering how it was possible to feel close to a hundred at the tender age — as of just two weeks ago — of twenty-four.

It was very quiet outside the hospital. Brisbane was not yet stirring, except for the usual horse-drawn delivery trucks bringing milk, produce and newspapers into town. Far in the distance she could hear the whistle blast of a departing ship and wondered briefly where it might be going. The air, smelling pleasantly of the sea, was already warm with the promise of still another pleasant day.

Not that she minded. As tired as she was, nothing would keep her awake. Or so she thought. After entering the small bungalow that was about the only privilege of her rank, she put a pot of water on the hot plate and undressed swiftly. When her tea was ready, she carried a cup to bed.

With the pillows propped up behind her, she took a sip and smiled to herself. Her mother had always brought Maggie tea when she was upset or worn out. Inevitably, she continued to associate it with moments of tender, loving care. She could do with some of that now.

Life was getting very complicated. Each time she was with Anthony, she became more vividly aware of her feelings for him and more confused about what to do about them.

A small, sad smile tugged at her mouth as she remembered a conversation she and Sheila had had a few weeks after they met. Sheila had admitted frankly that she and Charlie had "gone all the way." Far from having any regrets, her only wish was that they could be together more often.

Maggie had never thought of herself as a prude, but she had still been taken aback by Sheila's revelation. By that time, she had known Sheila well enough to like and respect her, and—perhaps even more importantly—to be aware that their outlooks on life were very similar.

She couldn't believe that her friend would have done anything truly wrong, yet neither could she reconcile such behavior with the version of morality instilled in her from childhood.

Nice girls didn't. Elizabeth Lawrence had made that perfectly clear. Maggie could still hear her mother's soft, melodious voice with its slight Southern accent explaining why it was necessary for a woman to save herself for her wedding night.

"Men don't respect anything that's too easy for them. If a woman gives in before she should, she creates doubts about her future fidelity. No man wants to believe his wife will betray him, so no matter how much he claims to like good-time girls, he ends up marrying a very different sort."

"That doesn't seem fair, Momma," Maggie had ventured tentatively. "If men take advantage of those girls, they should marry them."

"I know, honey. But it doesn't work that way. A man has to respect you before he can see himself settling down with you. After all, marriage is an unnatural state for men. They'd rather be free to roam."

"Then why don't we just forget about marrying them?"

"Because a man's protection and support are necessary to the strength of each family. Without that, our civilization wouldn't exist." Elizabeth had smiled gently at her daughter. "It's really the women who create civilization, but sometimes we have to be rather subtle as to how we go about it."

Maggie had listened with a young girl's natural skepticism, but eventually she had believed. How could she not, when she saw the evidence of her mother's wisdom in the behavior of the people around her?

When she was about fourteen, the beautiful daughter of a surgeon who lived down the street from the Lawrences had gone away for several months. Rumors quickly spread that she was "in trouble" as the result of going too far with her steady boyfriend. She came back eventually, pale and very quiet, stayed only for a few months, then left again to go to an out-of-state college. But during that time Maggie noticed that the girl was excluded from the general life of the neighborhood, while the young man, who no longer had anything to do with her, continued to be well liked. No one thought badly of him, only of the girl who had gotten herself in trouble.

The lesson had not escaped Maggie: if a woman broke the rules, she paid for it on her own; a man got off scot-free. Except that it no longer seemed to be that simple. Sheila had first made her realize that, and the events of the past few months had only reconfirmed it.

Putting the half-empty teacup on the bedside table, Maggie stretched out beneath the thin covers and shut her eyes. She badly needed to rest, but her turbulent thoughts kept sleep stubbornly at bay.

The past couple of weeks had been not unlike a dream. Her work at the hospital was deeply challenging and fulfilling, but it was her off-duty hours that glittered with the promise of happiness beyond any she had ever known. Anthony was. . . She sighed softly and turned over onto her side. Words alone could not describe him. He was everything she had ever wanted in a man and more than she had guessed was possible.

Not, she reflected wryly, that he was perfect. For one thing, he seemed to have developed a disconcertingly noble streak that was proving most inconvenient.

What an odd thought, her mind whispered. Anthony was obviously keeping a strict check on his own desires, purely for her sake and at no small cost to him. She should be grateful, but instead, she was becoming increasingly annoyed.

Why? Even as she tried to shy away from the answer, it pursued her unrelentingly. Simply put, she was caught on the horns of a dilemma. On the one hand, she bore the burden of strict moral teachings whose basic soundness she really did not doubt. But on the other, she desired him intensely, with all the passion of her intrinsically sensual nature.

No wonder women liked to fantasize about being swept off their feet by a demanding male! It neatly solved such problems and freed them from having to make so difficult a choice. But it was also very unfair to place such a burden on a man.

In the quiet darkness of the small room, Maggie forced herself to confront the truth of that unnerving thought. When they were together, Anthony was unfailingly gentle, kind, considerate — all the qualities a woman could possibly want. Yet she was very aware of the signs of ever-increasing strain stamped on his proud features. Even if she hadn't truly cared for him, she wouldn't have been able to ignore his discomfort. And under these circumstances, her sense of guilt — and more, of hypocrisy — was growing daily.

"So many rules," she murmured to herself. She had lived her entire life by regulations of one kind or another, and she couldn't say she regretted that. Her parents had raised her strictly, but also with great love. Certainly they could ask nothing more of her than that she be guided by both respect for herself and genuine caring for others.

As sleep at last began to drift over her, she thought distantly that perhaps it was time to show she had achieved both.

Chapter Seven

"THAT'S A REAL NICE OUTFIT," Anthony murmured as Maggie slipped into the jeep. He'd been reading a paperback copy of a Dashiell Hammett mystery, squinting slightly in the fading light, and hadn't seen her coming down the street. It wasn't until she opened the door on the passenger side and began to get in that he'd looked up. . .and continued to look at her.

Maggie caught his startled expression and smiled a little nervously. Not for a moment did she make the mistake of believing he had noticed only her clothes; the blue silk dress, cut in the Chinese style with a high fitted collar, snug bodice and tapered skirt, was beautiful, but its primary attraction lay in the way it clung lovingly to every curve of her slender body.

She had put her hair up in a simple chignon at the nape of her neck, exposing the delicate line of her throat and jaw. Beneath a dusting of powder, her cheeks were slightly flushed. Her thick lashes could not entirely hide the half-excited, half-tremulous light in her eyes.

"Thanks," she said softly as she took her place beside him, crossing one slim leg over the other, so that the dress fell open at the side split to expose a very long length of golden thigh. Her hand reached instinctively to close the gap, but stopped as she reconsidered and left the dress as it was.

"Uh . . . that's new, isn't it?" Anthony asked, rather hoarsely.

"Hmmm . . . I went shopping this morning."

"That's nice." He fumbled for the ignition key, managing to turn it without taking his eyes from Maggie. "You . . . look different."

"I was a little tired of nurse's whites and simple little cotton things, so I thought I'd splurge." This was not completely a lie, but not the entire truth, either. In her anxiousness, she went on chattily. "Did you know that there are all sorts of wonderful little shops around here? At the same place where I found this dress, I bought a lovely red silk robe embroidered with peacocks." Almost to herself, she added, "I have to admit the robe is a little daring."

Anthony swallowed hard, his hands tightening on the steering wheel. "W-why do you say that?"

Maggie regretted her careless words and wished she could ignore the question, but a quick glance at him told her he would persist. Resignedly, she said, "The silk is so finely woven it's practically transparent." The quicksilver flare of his eyes emboldened her. With uncharacteristic provocation, she murmured, "But that's really all to the good, isn't it?"

"G-good?"

"It will be cooler that way, don't you think?"

"Th-think? Uh, yeah, sure . . . cooler. . . ."

A horn blared behind them, and an irate soldier yelled, "You gonna sit there all day, Mac?"

Anthony scowled, put his foot down hard on the gas pedal and sent the jeep lurching ahead. Maggie gripped the edge of her seat and took a deep breath. There was a tightness in her chest that had nothing whatsoever to do with the snug fit of her dress. They drove for a half-mile or so before she managed to ask calmly, "Where are we going?"

Anthony had just been trying to figure that out, hoping to come up with a quick revision of his original plan. But his mind didn't seem to be working too well, and those big blue eyes gazing expectantly at him weren't helping any.

"I...uh...borrowed a house from a friend. Actually, a friend of a friend. It's near the beach. I thought we might have a quiet dinner there." Hastily, he added, "But if you'd rather not, that's fine. We could go dancing or take in a movie or—"

"Dinner at the house sounds fine."

Anthony stifled a groan and told himself that was what he deserved for thinking he was so smart. When he'd come up with the idea of taking Maggie somewhere very private so they could really be alone together, it had seemed like a stroke of genius. In the proper surroundings, far from everyone else, perhaps they would be more open and honest with each other. If he could only discover how she truly felt about the possibility of making love with him, he would be on much firmer ground.

That, at least, had been the plan, shot to pieces the moment Maggie had got in the jeep. It would have been difficult enough for him under any circumstances to be alone with her in a romantic and secluded setting without trying to push her too fast too far. But, dressed as she was, looking sexier and more desirable than ever, she was straining his control right to the breaking point.

Yet he could hardly pull out now without drawing

attention to his predicament and risking scaring her off. Grimly, he reminded himself that he was a Marine, stronger and tougher than other men, and certainly more than capable of withstanding the torture she was so innocently inflicting.

"Okay," he muttered, "we'll stick to the plan."

Beside him, Maggie bit back a shaky laugh. She was torn between amusement and anxiety. Since having accepted in her own mind that the stalemate between them could not continue, she had been careful not to let herself dwell on the implications of her decision. They were clear enough to her, but she didn't want to think about them too much, lest she falter in her resolve.

The house Anthony had borrowed—with Jake Dylan's help—was built of white clapboard along simple yet elegant lines; its pleasantly weathered look suggested that it had withstood the elements for a comfortable length of time. It stood alone on a cliff overlooking a long, curving expanse of secluded beach that, even in the fading light, glittered as though sprinkled with flecks of gold.

Inside the house were cream-colored walls and polished wood floors, overstuffed couches and scatter rugs. This was the sort of place where people could relax and forget their cares.

Some of Maggie's nervousness eased as she looked around her. She felt a budding sense of rightness, almost of contentment as she breathed in the crisp salt air and stretched languidly. "This is really wonderful. I could stay here forever."

Anthony watched her with narrowed eyes. The motion of her body pulled the dress even more tautly over her high, firm breasts. He had suspected she wasn't wearing a bra and now he was certain. His body hardened reflexively, causing him to cast about swiftly for some distraction. "How about a glass of wine?"

She flashed him a shy smile. "Wonderful. Can I help?"

"No. . .thanks. . .I'll be right back." He retreated hastily to the kitchen with the bottle of prewar Chablis he had brought along, opened it and poured two glasses, all the while struggling to retain his rapidly eroding self-control.

When he returned to the living room, it was empty. A screen door stood open, leading to a porch overlooking the beach. Maggie was leaning against the railing, staring out at the water.

"Look," she said softly as he joined her, "the moon is rising." A pale disk had floated up out of the darkening sea. Above it, where the sky was turning from deepest blue to midnight black, a few stars could already be seen. On the opposite horizon, the last lavender and mauve traces of the sunset were slowly dissolving.

It was an instant poised between day and night, replete with a sense of natural and inevitable transition.

Maggie took one of the glasses from him and held out her other hand. Without pausing to think, he slipped his into it. Cool air scented with tropical blossoms caressed them gently. The only sound was the rush of the waves hitting the beach, which, to Anthony at least, echoed the increasingly heavy beat of his heart.

The idea, he reminded himself firmly, had been that they would relax with each other and talk honestly about what they both wanted. But nothing seemed to be going as he had planned. He took a swallow of the wine to ease his suddenly dry throat and stared into her eyes.

"Maggie. . . I think maybe it wasn't such a good idea for us to come here. . . ."

She didn't answer at once, only looked at him as though she were seeing right past all his defenses to the vulnerable man within. When she did speak, her voice was little more than a murmur on the night wind. "But we are here. . . and I'm glad." A sudden, tender smile lit her gaze. "Wouldn't you say this has been a long time coming?"

What was she telling him? Anthony wondered warily. Surely not what he wanted so desperately to hear. But why, then, was she moving closer to him until they were almost but not quite touching, the scent of her skin filling his breath and the warmth of her body reaching out to surround him?

His mind scrambled in search of some explanation. He'd spent the day drilling his men hard over a grueling obstacle course; maybe he'd stumbled at some point and hit his head. Or maybe he was simply asleep and dreaming. But whatever the explanation, he could swear that Maggie was trying to tell him that she wanted to. . .

When is he going to get the message? she asked herself. Granted, she had no experience with this sort of thing, but surely her signals weren't so inept that he couldn't interpret them! Did she have to make them even clearer?

Taking a deep breath, she murmured, "Anthony...I want you to know I've been doing a lot of thinking."

He shook his head slightly, as though not sure that he was hearing her properly. "What about?"

Infuriating man! He couldn't possibly be so obtuse. Or could he? A quick glance from the corner of her eye revealed a dull flush spreading over his face and an unnaturally bright glitter to his onyx eyes. How she loved those eyes, she thought dreamily, the mirrors to his soul that could be hard as flint one moment, soft as velvet the next.

"About us," she said gently, putting her glass down. Who needed wine when the very air itself seemed to be making her head swim? A small, soft laugh escaped from her. "You know, you really are a perfect gentleman."

He started, then cleared his throat. "...I haven't had much practice at that...thought maybe I wasn't any good at it."

"No," she assured him solemnly, "on the contrary, you've been extraordinary. So much so that I feel quite guilty about what I've put you through. I hope you realize none of that was intentional. I just... needed some time."

Her directness surprised him. He hadn't expected it, but then, there was so much he hadn't dared to hope. Putting down his glass, he raised his hands, hesitated, then brought them down gently on her shoulders. "Maggie...I don't want anything to happen that you might regret later."

"I know," she breathed out softly. "I feel the same way about you."

Such simple words, yet they told him she understood that he, too, had much at risk. His body tightened at the force of emotion washing over him. She
was so lovely, so soft and feminine, yet strong in a way
he had not anticipated. Why had he thought he was
the only one struggling to do what was right?

The silk of her dress was cool against his fingers as
he drew her to him. Through it, he could feel the
delicacy of her bones and the firm texture of her skin.
His hands slipped down, below the short sleeves,
caressing her bare arms.

Moonlight poured over them, a ribbon of liquid
silver linking them to sea and sky. Air redolent with
the perfume of fertile earth filled their lungs. Sound
narrowed down to rushing heartbeats...ragged
breath...an ancient song echoing in the recesses of
the mind. Touch overwhelmed all else. Velvet
against steel...satin and silk...impossibly soft, en-
ticingly hard...a man and a woman embarked on
the ultimate adventure.

Her lips parted eagerly beneath his, her tongue
meeting the ravenous thrust of his with matching
hunger. Against the tensile hardness of his chest, her
breasts swelled, the nipples tightening to taut buds
beneath the thin silk.

He moved slightly, planting his feet more firmly
apart and drawing her within the cradle of his thighs.
His big hands, toughened by calluses, splayed over
her back, tracing the ridge of her spine down to the
curve of her buttocks. There he hesitated an instant,
before letting his fingers spread out to cup her gently.

A soft moan broke from her. She arched closer,
twining her arms more tightly around him, raking

through the thick pelt of his hair, drowning in the taste and texture of him.

He bent over her and ran his hands farther down along her thighs, exploring through the thin silk closer and closer to the secret place of her womanhood. A tremor raced through him, shaking him to the very core. The hard urgency of his arousal pressed against her, reminding them both that they were dangerously close to the point of no return.

Anthony raised his head and rasped out, "Maggie . . . are you sure . . . ?"

She stared at him dazedly, the words not registering at first. Only when they had penetrated the fog engulfing her mind did she manage to respond. Without a thought of dissembling, she nodded and said, "Don't leave me now, Anthony. I couldn't bear it."

That was all he needed to hear. Triumphant exaltation coursed through him even as he felt a surge of tenderness so powerful as to make him tremble. Bending, he lifted her high against his chest and carried her to the wide divan hidden away in a corner of the porch.

A slight smile curved his taut mouth. He had never thought of himself as a particularly romantic man, but he wanted everything to be perfect for Maggie. He laid her down gently and straightened up to stand over her, staring at the slender length of her body, whose scant defenses he would soon strip away.

Maggie gazed back at him, her eyes bright with desire, yet also with flickerings of concern she could not quite conceal. He looked very large in the darkness, hard as tensile steel cast in a white-hot flame. She swallowed tightly, tried to glance away, and found that she could not.

A soft exclamation broke from him as he saw what was in her eyes, and he moved instantly to erase her fear. Kneeling beside her, close but not touching, he murmured, "Don't be afraid. I know this is new to you. We'll take it very slowly."

She nodded and smiled tremulously, reaching out a hand to cup the back of his head. Her expression was at odds with her action, yet the conflict did not disturb him. He understood that she truly wanted what was happening between them, but retained a natural fear of the unknown.

The awareness of her vulnerability redoubled his determination to make the experience the best it could be for her. Through his skill and his patience, he would express the full depth of his love.

The fire within them both leaped higher, flames catching at the tinder. Anthony stretched out next to her on the divan, moving his body half over hers without imposing any of his weight on her far slenderer form. He wanted her to feel completely safe, not restricted in any way.

A long, burnished finger reached out to stroke the curve of her cheek. He smiled shakily. "I've never felt like this before. Scared, excited, almost too happy to bear, all at the same time."

The admission of how deeply he was affected by what they shared eased some of her own tremulousness and allowed her to lessen the tight hold she had been keeping on her emotions. Tentatively at first, then with growing confidence, she returned his caress.

Her finger traced the square line of his jaw upward to the firmness of his chin, lingering at the slight cleft she found there before moving on to explore the hard, chiseled mouth that could wreak such havoc on all her senses. Her eyes followed the path of her touch, studying him intently as though he represented a mystery she was determined to solve.

He held himself absolutely still, giving her time to grow a little more used to him. But at length his restraint broke and he groaned huskily, moving over her with an urgency he could not conceal.

"Maggie...sweetheart...you're so beautiful. Let me show you how you make me feel." Pressing her gently back into the thick, soft cushions, he claimed her mouth once again. This time Maggie's response was even more uninhibited. She met his passion instantly, lips parting, tongues tangling, breaths mingling as they sipped and nibbled and sweetly tormented.

In the heat of passion, he lowered himself onto her, letting her feel at last his weight and power, still carefully held in check so as not to frighten or discomfort her. She moaned softly, deep in her throat, her head tossing back and forth. The chignon came loose and her gleaming hair tumbled about her shoulders.

Anthony breathed in deeply, the scent of jasmine and spice and pure woman racing like a drug through his blood. He grasped her head, his hands tangling in the silken strands, holding her still as he trailed feather-light kisses down her throat, where a pulse beat raggedly.

She was all sweet vulnerability, feminine strength, a storm in his soul that threatened to overwhelm him.

His fingers trembled as he undid the small buttons on the back of her dress, tearing at them in his urgency until at last the thin silk slipped away to bare her to the waist.

He stared at her for what seemed to Maggie like a long time. She had to fight the impulse to cover herself, finding instead that after the first feeling of strangeness had passed, she could take pleasure in his obvious appreciation of her.

"I knew"— he groaned —"that you'd be lovely, but I hadn't guessed how much. . . ."

Her eyes widened with wonder at the sincerity in his tone. Was she really so remarkable? A glance down at herself showed that her breasts were swollen, the dark pink nipples full and velvety, like the petals of a rose come gloriously into bloom. She breathed in dazedly, trying to comprehend this transformation she was undergoing and to prepare for where it would lead.

But before she could do so, Anthony had bent his head, his mouth capturing an aching nipple. His tongue bathed it with swift, wet strokes that quickly sent her head arching back as a cry of primitive delight tore from her.

His hands moved downward to grasp her slim waist, pushing the dress away. His fingers traced the fragile line of her ribs before moving farther to the flat plane of her abdomen, protected only by the lacy scrap of her panties.

There he stopped and raised his head to stare down at her. "Maggie," he whispered huskily, "if you don't want this to happen, tell me now."

Her eyes were wide and dark, glazed by passion, as

she met his fevered look. How could she possibly not want it? She was consumed with desire for him, desperate to release the terrible, coiling pressure building up inside her.

The ferocity of her hunger amazed her even as it awakened a vague sense of shame. Everything she had been taught from childhood told her that a decent woman wasn't supposed to feel this way, at least not with a man other than her husband. It was as though the marriage ceremony was somehow meant to create such feelings spontaneously while at the same time giving holy sanction to their release. Without that, great as her joy might be, she could not bring herself to take the final step of admitting out loud how much she wanted him.

Anthony watched the play of emotions across her face and felt his heart tighten in sympathy. He had no difficulty understanding what was going through her mind. After all, he came from a background that was not so very different from her own. He, too, had absorbed the idea that a good woman was somehow supposed to be above passion, even though he knew that idea was at best inaccurate and at worst destructively hypocritical.

Maggie was not about to draw away from him at this late juncture; he could see that clearly in the ardent, almost pleading look she gave him. No further acknowledgment was necessary.

He smiled tenderly and dropped a light kiss on her full, moist mouth. "Time's up. I'll just have to take your agreement for granted."

Infinitively relieved, she managed a husky laugh. "You don't hear me arguing, do you?"

"No . . . but I think I do hear the beginnings of a very different sound." He leaned forward, resting his head between her bared breasts, the rough silk of his hair teasing her nipples. "Hmm . . . there it is again . . . a definite purr. . . ."

Playfully she tugged at his ears, until he raised his head, put his palms flat down on either side of her, and said challengingly, "How about giving me a little help to get out of these clothes?"

That she could do, gladly. His tie went first, swiftly unknotted and tossed away. She went to work on the buttons of his khaki shirt, her fingers trembling slightly as they slipped inside to brush the thick pelt of hair covering his chest. The texture reminded her of rich, glossy fur. She shivered faintly and went on before she could lose her courage.

When the last button was undone, he rolled over suddenly, drawing her with him so that their positions were reversed. Her round, full breasts swayed above him as he held out a hand with his wrist turned up. "Don't forget the cuffs."

She swallowed hard and obliged, undoing first one and then the other. His shirt had fallen open, baring the full expanse of his burnished torso. She stared entranced at the rippling muscles lightly covered with tanned skin and at the thick line of hair that began just below his collarbone and covered the width of his chest before tapering down over his hard abdomen to disappear beneath the waistband of his trousers.

On Corregidor, she had seen him often in a state of partial undress and could not deny that she had been moved by the sheer male beauty of him. But not even that had prepared her for the impact he had on her now.

Perhaps it was the setting, or the knowledge of what they were about to do, but never had she been so acutely conscious of everything that made them different from, yet complementary to, each other: two parts of a whole that, since time immemorial, were meant to fit perfectly together.

He sat up slightly, tugging the shirt out of his belt, and was about to discard it when Maggie gently stopped him. Their eyes met as she took over the task, slipping the fabric from his high, wide shoulders and easing it down his steely arms and back, her fingers lingering all the while in feather-soft caresses.

A tremor began in the hard ridge of muscles that bracketed his chest, spreading quickly along the sharply defined line of his ribs. She watched, fascinated, as the taut skin rippled convulsively. Her hands slid lower, touching the slightly concave curve of his stomach, made more pronounced as he sucked in his breath.

"Maggie. . . for God's sake. . ."

She barely heard him, so absolute was her concentration. Her eyes were bright and unblinking, her lips parted. A pulse throbbed in the delicate line of her throat, echoing the potent drumbeat roaring through her blood. The small voice of caution that had been whispering in the back of her mind faltered, then faded away. Conscious thought slowed and stumbled finally to a stop. There was only feeling, sensation, need.

Her arms fell away from him as she slid from the

divan and stood up. Their gazes locked, hers alive with
a growing sense of her own power, his clouded with a
passion so intense it was barely endurable.

High, full breasts, darkened at the peaks by bud-
tight nipples, swayed slightly as she moved. The
Chinese dress was snug; she had to wiggle it down her
hips and thighs before it at last fell around her feet. In
the same graceful motion, she stepped out of her
shoes, returning to him clad only in a tiny scrap of lace
that emphasized, rather than hid, her femininity.

Anthony's bare chest rose and fell raggedly. The
corded sinews of his arms and throat stood out in sharp
detail. A tremor raced through him as the great
strength of his body and spirit coiled tighter and
tighter, heading inevitably toward explosion.

His mouth pulled back in a hard, tight line, slightly
exposing his teeth. He had wanted so badly to be gentle and patient, to prove to himself as well as to her
that he was driven by something higher than stark passion. Yet she had made that impossible and, in the
process, had taught him something about the myster-
ious, complex thing called love.

It was not the noble, tender emotion he had imagined. There was nothing gentle or selfless about the
feelings that threatened to consume him. On the contrary, he was gripped by forces that defied control,
driven by violent, primeval needs that burned straight
through his civilized veneer to free the feral male
within.

He took a deep, quivering breath—not in an attempt to deny what was happening to him, but simply
to buy himself a moment more. And in that moment,
his eyes met hers, piercing to the depths of her soul. He

held himself absolutely still, searching for some flicker of fear or doubt, anything that would cause him—even at this extreme point—to pull back.

But in her eyes there was only a steady acceptance, and something more—a glimmer of purely feminine challenge that spoke directly to his masculinity and wiped away, as though it had never been, the last traces of his restraint.

His callused hands shot out to grasp her hips at the same moment that he pulled her toward him, upsetting her balance and causing her to fall with a soft gasp into his arms. She landed on her back, with him above her, her taut nipples nestling into the thick pelt of hair covering his chest. He groaned harshly and lowered his mouth to hers, claiming it with devastating thoroughness even as he hastily undid his belt and began to unfasten his trousers.

Then he stopped, struck suddenly by the simple, physical requirements of what he was about to do. Tensely, he tore himself from her and sat up to rip off his boots and swiftly dispense with the rest of his clothes.

Maggie lay against the pillows, the silken fall of her hair tumbling about her slender shoulders. Moonlight poured over her body, silvering the rounded curves of breasts and hips and thighs.

She watched Anthony unflinchingly as the full strength of his manhood was revealed to her. He was all burnished planes and angles, chiseled bone and articulated muscle, every part of him in perfect proportion to the whole. Stunningly different from her, yet not in the least alien, and frightening only in the intensity of emotion he unleashed within her.

She raised her arms, alabaster in the pale light, a low cry breaking from her even as the waves broke against the beach below them. He was beside her in an instant, bringing her to him with convulsive strength. Then his hands and mouth were everywhere, kneading, stroking, tasting, biting, until she thought she would surely die from the wild, rushing need he unleashed. Her head tossed back and forth against the pillows, her hands clasping his shoulders tightly as her hips arched instinctively to him.

He waited only a moment longer, remembering even in the midst of the love madness that he wanted to protect her; then he moved with consummate grace to claim his place between her slender thighs and seek the dark, secret path into her body.

July 1942–December 1942
THE CANAL

Chapter Eight

STRANGE, MAGGIE THOUGHT, how so little time could make such an immense difference in one's life.

Only the night before, she had been filled with ecstatic happiness and confidence. And now, barely twenty-four hours later, she had to face the fact that a single revolution of the earth had wreaked havoc with all her hopes and dreams.

Wearily she closed her eyes, struggling against the slow oozing of tears that would not be completely denied. Stretched out on her narrow bed in the solitude of her bungalow, she could let down her guard and admit, if only to herself, how much she hurt inside. The swift plummeting from joy to despair had bruised her badly.

Anthony was gone.

She kept saying that to herself as though the repetition might bring understanding. Yet how could it? What reasonable, halfway sane person could cope with the insanity that had seized them all?

For a brief time she had managed to forget. In his arms, while they shared the joyful consummation of love, the war had been nothing more than a half-remembered nightmare, the happiness they had found together the only reality.

"What should we do today?" he had asked softly as they lay on the divan together, watching the sun rise out of the azure water, their bodies briefly quiescent in the aftermath of passion. Propped up on his elbow, he had looked down at her with an expression that made her blush, tenderness mingling with possession and utterly male knowledge.

They had slept only a few hours, rousing to make love again, finding in the joining of their bodies a source of energy as potent as it was addictive.

Memories quivered through her, dimly remembered snatches of the words they had said and the things they had done. She trembled inwardly. Never had she imagined that she could behave with such unbridled sensuality. But with him, all barriers fell, all limits were surpassed.

"Should?" she had teased gently. "I'm not sure I want to think in those terms. Not when all the things I was told I *shouldn't* do have turned out to be such fun."

He had grinned quirkily. "It was terrific, wasn't it? Not that I'm bragging, but I really didn't know I had it in me."

His frank delight had deepened her blush even as she exulted in the joy they had found together, a joy made all the more precious for being so cruelly curtailed.

The Australian night was clear and calm. A vast sea of stars sparkled overhead. Palm fronds waved lazily in the breeze. Opening her eyes, Maggie caught a glimpse through the window opposite the bed of white walls awash in silvery moonlight. The hospital was quiet, but for how much longer?

Anthony was gone.

The words drummed through her, agonizing in their implacability. She moved her head restively, listening to the muted cry of a night bird.

She and Anthony had barely returned to Brisbane, intending to have dinner together, when he had found a message informing him that his leave was canceled. Left with no choice but to report back to his base immediately, he had promised to call her as soon as possible.

But the opportunity to do so had never arrived. Instead, she had to be content with a scribbled note delivered by a sympathetic Aussie, telling her that Anthony was shipping out at once. His destination was New Zealand, where the First Marine Division had just arrived. There was no explanation for the hasty summons, but Maggie had managed to find out the reason nonetheless. The First Marines were being thrown into something big, and Anthony was apparently going with them.

One moment she and Anthony had been safe together in the haven of their love; the next, they were torn apart by the bitter reality of war.

Sighing, she straightened up in the rumpled bed, mute evidence of her troubled night. Propped up against the pillows, she unfolded the letter she had received that morning from her mother and read it again, taking comfort from the simple words.

Dearest Maggie,

Your father and I are both so relieved to know that you are safe. Rusty Osborne came by to see us yesterday and told us how you are doing. We are prouder of you than words can say. You have truly fulfilled all our hopes and more.

The apple trees in the backyard are full of fruit this year. I look at them and think how you used to climb to the highest branches and gaze out at the world. I know right now the world looks like a harsh place, but believe me, there is still much love and beauty.

Stay well, my dear daughter, and know that you are always in our thoughts.

At the bottom, her father had penned a brief note:

Kitten—don't try to rush your recovery. These things take time. The memories fade, and better things replace them. This will end someday, and we will all begin to live again.

Love, Dad

Maggie put the letter down slowly. Her cheeks were wet. She was very tired and she wanted to rest. Morning would arrive soon enough, with all the responsibilities that came with it, but sleep continued to elude her.

She thought about her parents and the home she had grown up in, where love and tenderness were as natural as the ripening of fruit on the apple trees. And she thought of Anthony, of what he had told her about his own family.

The Garganos were really not so different from the Lawrences. It was not difficult to imagine how they must be feeling as they listened to the news from the Pacific and prayed for their son.

A soft sigh escaped her as she closed her eyes. In the darkness of her room, in the quiet of the night, she prayed, too. For a continuation of life, for a chance to heal, for a time to love.

ANTHONY LEANED against the railing of the assault craft and stared out at the blue-green waters. Like the three dozen or so men crammed in around him, he was feeling nauseous. The steak sandwiches they had been fed for breakfast were not setting well with the roll and pitch of the open sea.

Several hours before, they had entered the assault craft, one of many others circling the larger transport ship that had brought the Marines from New Zealand. They would remain as close to her as possible while awaiting the command to storm the beaches lying just beyond the mine field.

The waiting was tough. Besides the rocking of the small boats and the natural tension of approaching battle, there was also the constant naval bombardment, intended to soften up the Japanese positions before the Marines attacked. The warm breeze could not disguise the rank smells of sweat and bile and fear.

"Think it'll be much longer, Sarge?" a young private asked. His face, still showing a hint of childhood softness, was pale, his eyes wide and dark.

Anthony sighed inwardly. "Take it easy, kid," he said lightly. "We don't want to deny the Navy its moment of glory."

The private managed a wan smile, then winced as a mortar shell whizzed over them. The softening-up was going well, at least as far as Anthony could see. If it went on much longer, there wouldn't be anything left to storm.

Before that could happen, the order they had been waiting for was at last barked through the bullhorns. "Land the landing force!"

He straightened up immediately. "Okay, men, it's time to earn your pay. We're gonna hit that beach, establish our perimeter, and hold it until we receive further orders. I don't want anybody getting any ideas about being a hero. Just do your jobs. Got it?"

"Got it, Sarge!" the three dozen men answered in unison, just as they'd been taught back in boot camp. Anthony looked them over and stifled a groan. Not one of them was more than eighteen. The closest any had ever come to a battle was a barroom brawl.

He practically had to wipe their noses for them, and here they were about to hurl themselves at the combined might of the Japanese army and navy. Worse yet, they were champing at the bit. Every damn one of them had visions of glory. Why not? They were Marines, weren't they?

Under ordinary circumstances, their gung-ho spirit might have been enough to carry them through. The trouble was, there was nothing ordinary about what they were going to face.

After weeks of being jammed into the steaming hold of the transport—interrupted only by two disastrous "rehearsals" of the invasion, in the Fijis—they were underweight, slack-muscled and all too aware that much of their equipment did not work as advertised. Their overburdened packs added to the problem, as did the scarcity of salt tablets, needed to offset the incredible heat and humidity.

The best Anthony could do was to order them to stick close to him as the assault craft jarred up against the white sand beach and the ramp slammed down. It hadn't quite settled into place before he jumped out, rifle held high to keep it from the water, and began wading ashore. There was nothing heroic about his speed; he just preferred to be a moving target.

His men followed instantly, their young faces self-consciously grim and their eyes wary. They knew this was for real, not some movie, but the full understanding of exactly what that meant was only beginning to sink in.

Marines from the other landing crafts joined them in rushing the beach. This was their most exposed moment. If the Japanese were in a position to attack, they'd be able to pick the troops off like clay pigeons.

But the softening-up operation had apparently worked. The enemy had withdrawn to more defensible positions. It was a straight march up the beach for the Marines.

The ease with which they established the beachhead exhilarated the less-experienced men. As the few veterans like Anthony remained watchful and quiet, the others exploded into boisterous good cheer, clapping one another on the back and talking about what a short war it was going to be.

"Hell, I don't see what all the fuss has been about," one particularly young Marine from Tuscaloosa declared. "We'll have the Japs licked and be home by Christmas!"

"Damn straight we will," another said. "Jeez, there ain't nothing to this!"

"We're not done yet," Anthony reminded them quietly. He didn't blame them for being cocky, but he couldn't share their elation. After what he had seen of the Japanese in the Philippines, he knew they weren't pushovers. They were out there somewhere beyond the beach, and they sure as hell weren't going to leave without a fight.

"Be glad you're getting a breather," he advised. "We'll be on the march again in no time."

And they were. Their objective was Mount Austen, a grassy knoll south of the airfield the Japanese had just built, the takeover of which was vital to the capture of the island.

For several hours, they continued to advance without being challenged, but other problems plagued them. The maps showed that the knoll was about two miles from the beachhead. It turned out to be closer to four.

Realizing that, Anthony cursed under his breath. He had never seen, or even imagined, anything like the jungle they were attempting to cut through. It was all but impenetrable. Even in full daylight, visibility was limited to just a few feet. In such an eerie green darkness, every alien sound sparked instant fear.

As though that weren't bad enough, the stench of rotting vegetation was such that it made him want to gag. He managed not to, only because he would not do anything to weaken his men further. They had all they could do to cope with the unrelenting heat and suffocating humidity that were quickly draining their strength. He kept them moving even as he cursed the criminal stupidity of the officers who had sent them into such a hell.

By nightfall, they had made relatively little progress toward the airfield and were in far worse shape than when they had come ashore. Dug in until morning, they all hoped to sleep, but the darkness resounded to constant gunfire as scared, trigger-happy troops shot at shadows.

Anthony's men were not among those firing. He'd settled them down with a few well-chosen words, then crawled into his own foxhole and resigned himself to a sleepless night. Sweat trickled from beneath his helmet. His utilities were soaked through, and his feet, swollen inside his boots, were numb. Vast clouds of malarial mosquitoes droned incessantly.

So much for a tropical paradise, he thought. His mind drifted back over the past week's events, and he wondered how Dom was doing.

It had been a shock to find his brother on the transport carrying the troops to Guadalcanal. In the chaos of the New Zealand port where the Marines transferred from the ships that had brought them from the States, he and Dom had remained unaware of each other. It wasn't until they'd ended up on the same grub line aboard the troop carrier that they realized they would be going into battle together.

The days on the ship had been mainly spent reminiscing. The folks were fine, Dom assured him, although they had naturally been extremely worried while he was on Corregidor and very relieved to get his letter telling them he was safe.

"So things are generally okay over there?" Anthony asked.

"Yeah...I guess..."

"You don't sound very sure. What's wrong?"

"Nothing...exactly..."

In the darkness of the blacked-out ship, Anthony wasn't able to see him very well. But he could hear the rhythmic thud of Dom's favorite baseball as his brother tossed it from one hand to the other. This was a gesture that from childhood had meant something was bothering him.

"Come on," Anthony urged quietly. "Get it off your chest."

Dom shrugged, continuing to toss the baseball back and forth. Finally, he said, "On my way through San Diego, I saw something that kinda bothered me. . . ."

"A girl you didn't get to kiss?" Anthony teased.

"I'm not kidding. It was serious. They were. . . rounding up all the Japanese and shipping them off to some kind of camps."

"So what's wrong with that? We're at war with the Japs."

"These people weren't *Jap* Japs. They either came to the States years ago, like Pop, or were born there, like us. They had homes, businesses, all the usual stuff. Paid their taxes, stayed out of trouble. Suddenly they're being treated like criminals."

"You're exaggerating. We wouldn't do that."

"We are," Dom insisted. "I saw it." He was silent for a moment, seeing again in his mind's eye the face of the young Japanese man he had noticed while riding in the bus through San Diego to the pier. The guy must have been about his own age and was wearing a sweater with the insignia of the University of California on it. He held a little girl in his arms, trying to comfort her as they were herded into the back of a truck. Police formed a cordon around the vehicle, keeping the jeering crowd from getting close and making sure none of the Japanese escaped.

The scene had shaken Dom. He knew the Japanese were the enemy, but he didn't see what that had to do with rounding up American civilians who happened to be of Japanese heritage.

"Think about it," he said to Anthony. "Pop was born an Italian and we're fighting them now. So how come he's not being shipped off to some camp? How come we aren't?"

"I don't know.... I guess people are kind of panicky after what happened at Pearl..." Anthony's voice trailed off as he frowned into the darkness, trying to reconcile what Dom had told him with his ideas about what he was fighting for.

In the past few months, he'd seen men blown to pieces, civilians terrorized, families ripped apart. He'd lost friends, learned to live with the constant threat of death, and been forced to leave the woman he loved. Only the belief that he was fighting for something far more important than himself had made him able to endure.

He still believed in what he was doing, but he was shaken by the realization that nothing was as cut-and-dried as he had thought. There were good and bad on both sides. Knowing that was going to make his job a lot tougher.

"About people panicking..." Dom ventured quietly, breaking into his thoughts, "there's something I wanted to ask you."

Anthony rubbed his face wearily as he tried to find a more comfortable position against the bulkhead. His attention still on what he had just learned, he murmured, "What's that?"

"About the fighting...I was wondering...what's it like?"

Dom's tense, faintly apologetic voice told Anthony

what was going through his brother's mind. He reached out in the darkness to touch Dom's arm lightly. "Don't worry about it. You'll do okay."

"How can you be so sure?" Embarrassment gave way to a hint of anger. Dom didn't want his fears brushed aside.

"Look," Anthony said more gently, "I'm not going to tell you it isn't bad, but when the time comes, you'll do what you have to. You won't have a chance to think—you'll just act."

Dom was silent for a moment, then he asked, "Were you ever scared?"

"Ever?" Anthony laughed shortly. "I've gotten so used to being terrified, I don't even feel it anymore. About the only good thing you can say for a battle is that it's the only time you're too busy to worry. Before, after, in between—that's when the fear comes."

"What do you do about it?"

"Nothing. What can you do? You just go with it and hope it isn't your turn. Everybody has a different way of coping." He didn't add that his was to think about Maggie, drawing from his memories of her the strength to go on.

Now, lying awake in his foxhole, he found his mind returning instinctively to her, replaying snatches of the time they had spent together. Images from their last night in Brisbane rose to torment him. He groaned in protest against the swift, heedless response of his body and tried not to think about how desperately he wanted to live.

ANTHONY ROUSED his men early the next morning. The brass had finally accepted the obvious—that the jungle surrounding them was impenetrable — and given orders to move west in an effort to take the airfield from that direction.

They finished off the last of their C rations, assured that there were more on the way, and began their advance once again. Anthony took the point himself, with his men strung out behind him. The heat was every bit as bad as on the previous day and the jungle just as unrelenting. They moved slowly, their weapons cocked at the ready. Anything might lie directly ahead, and they were determined to be prepared for it.

They had gone a few hundred yards when a movement in the brush just beyond alerted them to danger. Anthony quickly gave the order to take cover. The men did so tensely, believing they were about to encounter their first Japanese and expecting a firefight to follow.

On that score, they were half right. The six ragged men who stumbled toward them from out of the jungle were Japanese but seemed to have no intention of fighting anyone. Moving slowly, with their hands above their heads, they gave every evidence of being genuinely terrified of the Americans who watched them with wary disbelief.

The man in the lead called out something incomprehensible and waved a scrap of white material in a signal that was supposed to be universally recognized and respected.

Still, Anthony hesitated. Everything he knew about the enemy told him they didn't surrender. This might well be a trap. If it was, he sure as hell wasn't going to send any of his men to find out.

Giving orders for them to stay put, he stood up slowly and headed toward the little party, his rifle held at the ready. Behind him, his men prepared to give cover fire if necessary. The click of triggers being cocked was an unnaturally loud sound in the suddenly quiet jungle.

He was within a few yards of the Japanese when they stopped and stared at him, wide-eyed and trembling. A quick glance was enough to tell him they were unarmed and looked even worse than he felt. Their small, slight bodies shook with fever, and they seemed about to collapse.

Deciding to take a chance, he yelled to his corporal to get back to the rear lines and try to find someone who could interpret for them; then he motioned the Japanese off to the side of the bush path and indicated they could sit down but had to keep their hands up.

His men wasted no time getting a look at what their sarge had "captured." As they clustered around, the kid from Tuscaloosa whistled softly. "*That's* what we're fighting? Hell, they don't look bigger than a flea on a hound dog."

"I don't understand, Sarge," another murmured. "I thought the Japs were supposed to be the toughest things going."

"So did I," Anthony agreed, staring at the prisoners. He was pretty sure now that they weren't faking, but he was still unable to explain their presence.

"Nothing tough about these dudes," a big, red-faced private muttered. He jammed the butt of his rifle toward one of the men and laughed as the Japanese cringed.

After the time spent in the troopship and the miserable night in the jungle, the private was eager to forget his fear and lord it over the enemy. The other Marines grinned. They were ready to do the same when Anthony snapped, "Belay that!"

He took a quick step forward, putting himself between his men and the Japanese. Why he did so, he didn't know. Maybe it had something to do with the story Dom had told him, or maybe he was just sick to death of people hurting one another. But he was damned if he'd stand by and let any funny stuff go on with the prisoners.

"What's the matter, Sarge?" the private asked, not belligerently but with genuine surprise. It hadn't occurred to him that what he was doing might be wrong. "We're just getting a little of our own back."

"Hell," someone else said, "after what happened on the Rock, you oughta be glad of a chance to get even."

"Don't tell me what I oughta," Anthony snarled. "We've got rules for the treatment of prisoners, and they're damn well going to be followed. You want some action, haul ass down that road and tell me what's around the next bend."

Grudgingly, the two men did as he ordered while the others shrugged and turned away. If they weren't going to have any fun, they might as well grab a little rest.

Anthony remained on his feet, alert for any trouble. He knew the Japanese were watching him, not daring to say anything, but still clearly puzzled by what had just happened. Their scrutiny made him self-conscious. He was very relieved when the corporal finally returned with a hapless-looking local who had the dubious advantage of being able to make himself understood in both English and Japanese.

"They are laborers working on the airfield," the man explained after he had spoken briefly with the prisoners. "When the bombs started falling, they ran into the jungle. They have no weapons and they don't know how to fight, so they decided to give up."

"Smart guys," Anthony murmured. He thought for a moment, trying to decide what to do with them.

"There's a stockade going up on the beach," his corporal told him. "Major Callahan said that all prisoners could be left there until we're ready to ship them out."

That sounded all right. Anthony didn't know much about Callahan, but rumor had it he was an all-right guy, for an officer.

As the prisoners were led away, Anthony cautioned his men, "Don't be misled by what just happened. Believe me, that is not what your regular Jap soldier is like. He is bad news all the way through. I've got a feeling you're going to find that out for sure before much longer."

He was convinced he was right, but events through the rest of that day continued to suggest otherwise. The Marines reached and secured the vital airfield without incident.

Word filtered back that other Marines had found the empty camp of the construction crew. Large supplies of chopsticks, rice bowls and Japanese cigarettes were being scooped up as souvenirs.

As the men dug in for the night, only one real

problem faced them. They were out of C rations and, contrary to expectation, no new supplies had reached them from the rear. They had to content themselves with a meal of captured Japanese rice that was filled with maggots.

Anthony wrung wan grins from his troops by commenting that it was a good thing it wasn't Friday or, being Catholic and forbidden to eat meat, he would have been put to the bother of plucking the maggots out.

Settled into his foxhole after the sparse and less-than-appetizing meal, he listened to his stomach growl and wondered what the hell was happening to screw up the supplies.

Dom could have told him what had gone wrong. Everything. The original crew allotted to unload supplies had been far too small, and the beach itself simply could not accommodate all the transport boats waiting to disgorge their cargo. The Navy brass had balked at the idea of extending the unloading operation to other beaches, on the theory that the waters might be mined; but as the situation worsened steadily, they had finally agreed.

So far, the superb air cover had allowed the Americans to weather three attacks by Japanese planes without heavy damage. But the movement of vital supplies was still running more than twelve hours behind schedule. Those troops up the line that weren't already out of food would be soon enough. The situation was rapidly becoming critical and was destined to get worse.

Anthony had just managed to drift into an uneasy sleep when the deep rumble of a distant but obviously intense explosion woke him. Yelling at his men to stay down, he disobeyed his own order long enough to stick his head up and try to get some sense of what was going on.

What he saw told him that the relative ease of the island invasion so far was over. The Japanese had bided their time until they could hit back at the most strategically vulnerable part of the Allied force—its fleet.

Out over the Savo Strait, where the cruisers and destroyers were clustered, an immense barrage of salvos and flares lit the sky. The men in the foxholes could do nothing except watch and listen as the naval battle raged.

Or at least that was what any sensible man would do. Captain Beauregard Whistler had other ideas. When Anthony saw his commanding officer heading toward him, he groaned. Of all the jar heads to get stuck with, Whistler was the worst. He was a blustering braggart fresh from cushy duty on the home front. Even there he had managed to earn a well-deserved reputation as a first-class idiot, proving that on occasion even the Marines could get stuck with a turkey.

Whistler had been on combat duty only a few months, but in that brief time he had earned the most dangerous reputation an officer could have—that of being careless with the lives of his men.

Rumor had it that three Marines had died unnecessarily during the practice assaults in the Fijis because Whistler had ordered them over the side too soon and they were accidentally strafed by their own men. He had had some idea of looking good for the brass by getting to the beach first.

Anthony had been willing to give him the benefit of the doubt, but that faded the instant Whistler flung himself down beside the foxhole, his face flushed and his breathing harsh, and demanded, "What the hell are you doing in there, Gargano? This is the perfect time to attack!"

Anthony took a deep breath and forced himself to stay calm. "Attack what, sir?" he asked quietly.

"The enemy, of course! The last thing he'll expect is a direct assault while he's busy with our ships. We'll go right through him!"

"Sir, we don't even know where the enemy is. We haven't located him yet."

"Bull! He's right out there, I know it! Come on, get your men together. We're attacking."

The private crouched in the foxhole nearest to Anthony sent him a disbelieving look. He was seventeen and from a farm in Kentucky. He had yet to shoot anything bigger than a possum and couldn't claim to know the first thing about fighting a war. But even he knew that what the officer was proposing was lunacy.

Anthony tried again, patiently. "Sir, my men are exhausted. They need to rest, not to go out looking for trouble."

"Do I hear you right, Gargano?" the captain bellowed, his small eyes narrowing even further. He had never liked the smart-mouthed platoon sergeant, and now he felt that his every doubt about him was being vividly confirmed. The son of a bitch was yellow!

"Are you refusing a direct order from your superior officer?" he demanded belligerently.

Anthony sighed. He really didn't need this, not on top of everything else. Wherein was it written that he, Anthony Gargano, should have inflicted on him the biggest horse's ass in the Corps? His patience was fast running out.

"Sir, what exactly are you ordering me to do?"

"I'm telling you to take your men, go find the enemy and kill him! Now, are you going to do that or not?"

Anthony thought about it for a moment. If he refused the order, he would be running the risk of a court-martial. At the very least, he could be broken in rank; it wasn't impossible that he could end up doing a stretch in the stockade. On the other hand, if he accepted the order, he'd be as big an idiot as Whistler.

The way he figured it, any Japanese commander worth his chopsticks would have had the sense to station snipers around the American positions in the hope that the bombardment going on in the Savo Strait would flush some of the dumber troops out.

But he was damned if he or any of his men were going to be picked off like fish in a barrel.

"I'm sorry, sir," he said at length. "I just can't do that."

Whistler stared at him dumbfounded. His face turned bright red, and for several moments he seemed unable to breathe. His meaty hands clenched into fists and his jaws locked together.

"You insubordinate SOB," he said in a grating tone. "I'll make you sorry you were ever born."

"That's certainly your privilege, sir, but I suggest that for right now you climb into this foxhole with me. There are snipers all around us."

"Why you yellow belly! You're afraid of your own goddamn shadow!"

"No, sir. There are Japs out there, and I'm willing to bet they're pretty good shots."

"Don't try to make use of that excuse when you're brought up on charges," Whistler sneered. "Everybody knows the Orientals have lousy eyesight."

Anthony didn't know any such thing, but he couldn't see the point of arguing. "Sir," he said instead, "if you try to return to your position now, I really think you won't make it."

"Go to hell, dago." On that note, the captain hoisted himself up and, with a final dire warning of what lay ahead, began moving off.

The private murmured, "Jeez, Sarge, I think he really means to break you."

"Yeah, I guess so." Resignedly, Anthony raised his Browning automatic rifle, cocked the trigger, and prepared to give Whistler cover fire—provided he got the chance.

"Ain't you worried?"

"No...can't say that I am." He scanned the ground ahead, watching the captain's progress. Whistler had gone perhaps a hundred yards when his body suddenly jerked, hung suspended in the air for a moment, then crumpled to the ground.

Anthony cursed. He'd had no warning of the sniper's position until the burst of gunfire revealed it. Steadying his weapon, he aimed in the sniper's direction and squeezed off a round.

"Hey," the private exclaimed, "you got him!"

"Looks that way." The sniper tumbled from the nearby coconut tree, hit the ground and lay still, not very far from Whistler. The captain had been shot right through the front of the skull. There was no possibility that he was still alive.

Shortly afterward, the sea battle ended, and Anthony and his men were able to catch a little more sleep.

Chapter Nine

MAGGIE GLANCED UP at the clock, saw that it was
almost time for the radio news, and left the ward. Two
young nurses watched her go, then glanced at each
other. Their captain took an even greater than usual
interest in the events on Guadalcanal, and they wondered why. For themselves, they preferred not to think
about what was happening there. It was too horrible.

About to enter the lounge where the radio was
kept, Maggie hesitated, wondering if it might not be
wiser to get a breath of fresh air or a cup of coffee.
Why subject herself to more worry and pain? There
was no good reason to, except that not knowing was
worse than anything she might learn.

Resignedly, she switched on the radio and sat down
to listen. There was quite a lot of war news in
general, but very little about Guadalcanal. That
worried her. It meant that the situation had not im-
proved; if it had, the morale-conscious commen-
tators would have wasted no time in saying so.

The battle at Savo Strait had been a disaster for
the Allies. In the space of little more than an hour,
the Japanese had sunk the American cruisers *Quincy*
and *Vincennes* and so badly damaged the Australian
cruiser H.M.A.S. *Canberra* that she had to be sunk
the next morning. Another American ship, the *Asto-
ria*, also sank then. The Japanese, however, lost none
of their own.

As the sun rose, it revealed the grisly sight of more than a thousand survivors clinging to life rafts, crates, anything that would float. Many men were badly burned and bleeding. Unfortunately, the blood attracted sharks. Rescuers from the beaches managed to shoot a great number of them, but others got through. Men vanished beneath the water with a terrifying suddenness just as they were on the verge of being saved.

It was, plain and simple, a debacle. In its aftermath, the Navy, fearing yet more attacks from the obviously superior Japanese forces, had chosen to withdraw. To all intents and purposes, the Marines were abandoned on the Canal—as everyone now called it—left to await their fate as they had been left on Corregidor.

Maggie cherished no hope that Anthony would be miraculously saved a second time. If he was still alive, and she was by no means certain of that, he was trapped along with all the rest of the men.

This time reinforcements really were on the way, but before they could arrive, the Japanese would certainly attack, seeking to throw off the toehold that the Allies had gained at such a terrible cost and plunge their resources into New Guinea, where the Aussies were fighting valiantly.

When the news was over, Maggie switched off the radio and went back to work. Long, grueling hours in surgery and in the wards were her salvation. Unable to sleep more than a couple of hours at a time, she had put herself on perpetual call.

Her nurses were grateful, for they had more than they could cope with and were expecting the situation to get worse. But they sometimes wondered what drove the young captain, why she seemed so deeply sad, and how much longer she could expect to keep up so exhausting a pace.

ANTHONY PUT DOWN his chopsticks and leaned back against the trunk of a palm tree, a contented smile on his face. For the first time in days, his stomach was comfortably full. That it was thanks to tinned Japanese beef, accompanied by—of all things—seaweed, didn't bother him. Anything was an improvement over rice and maggots.

His men thought so, too. They had been extremely fortunate to liberate a store of food being kept for Japanese officers. Just as was true with the American forces, the enemy brass also ate better. Only this time the goodies were going to a troop of filthy, exhausted leathernecks. Maybe there was some justice in the world after all.

Other Marines were not nearly as lucky. They were surviving on subsistence rations, growing weaker by the day, in a vicious replay of an experience Anthony had sworn he would never go through again.

"If you get killed by a Jap," he told his men, "that's the luck of the draw. But I'll be damned if I'll see any of my men starve to death or die from some friggin' sickness."

Nobody had to ask what he meant. A particularly virulent form of dysentery was running wild throughout the American troops. One in five was estimated to have come down with it, and the doctors were practically dead on their feet. Anthony's platoon was among the few to be spared, because he insisted on the most stringent sanitary measures and made sure they were enforced.

"I don't care that there's nowhere to take a bath," he kept saying. "You can still dig fresh latrines every day and wash your hands before you eat. Hell, do I have to tell you guys what you're in for otherwise?"

He didn't. The evidence was all around, worse in its own way than the ever-present danger from the Japanese, who continually shelled the beaches and took strafing runs over the interior of the island. No one was safe from them.

The desperate, gnawing need to fight ate away at Anthony's men. They had been trained to take the offensive, not to sit by and wait to see what would happen. At last, just when they were about to give up hope, word came that they were going out on a search-and-destroy mission.

"Major Callahan wants the west bank of the river cleared of any Japs and their weapons, so get rid of them," a fresh-faced lieutenant told Anthony.

"Yes, sir!" Anthony was frankly relieved. This was a mission that not only made sense but was also doable. He had sent scouts out to survey the river and he knew the best way to approach whatever enemy forces they might find. With a little luck, they'd be able to take them by surprise.

Their luck held. In company with several other platoons, they crossed the Matanikau River and advanced on a village of thatch-roofed huts where the Japanese were believed to be holed up. That intelligence proved correct, for the platoon members immediately came under attack.

"Return fire!" Anthony shouted. He was just beginning to squeeze off rounds from the Browning automatic when his eyes beheld a sight his mind could not credit. From the thatched huts, several dozen Japanese emerged with bayonets fixed to their rifles. Despite the deadly barrage being thrown up by the Americans, they advanced steadily, hollering, "Banzai!"

It was the first time Anthony had heard that word, and he prayed it would be the last. The Browning automatics mowed the Japanese down without effort, yet still they kept coming, over the bodies of their comrades, straight into the arms of death. On and on they came, until the last of them lay unmoving on the blood-soaked ground.

The faces of Anthony's men were green as they dazedly surveyed the carnage. He suspected his was the same. As a soldier, he accepted the risk of death, but it was completely beyond him to understand the behavior of these people who had so wantonly thrown away their young lives.

"They've got a lot of guts," one of the Marines muttered later in the day as he finished the last of his beef and flopped down in the grass. He and the other men had been talking about what they'd experienced that morning, trying to make some sense of it. They hadn't succeeded and were still looking for an explanation.

"But not much sense," another Marine ventured. He glanced over toward Anthony. "Why do you think they did it, Sarge?"

"Bushido."

"How's that?"

"Bushido. It's the warrior's code of honor." Anthony reached into his shirt pocket and pulled out a precious pack of Lucky Strikes. Lighting one, he inhaled deeply before he went on. "We heard all about it on the Rock. The greatest glory for them is to die for their emperor. They're supposed to welcome any opportunity to do so."

"Sounds like suicide to me."

Anthony shrugged. "Different people see things differently. Nobody will ever convince me the Japs aren't incredibly brave fighters. We've got our hands full beating them."

"But we will, won't we, Sarge? Nobody can defeat the good ol' U.S. of A."

Anthony sighed and stretched out more comfortably. "I think we'll win. But it's gonna take awhile."

"So maybe we won't be home for Christmas," his corporal said. "But I'll bet we're back in New Zealand soon." He grinned at his buddies. "They've got some mighty good-lookin' women, and you couldn't ask for friendlier people."

"Won't be long now. We'll be sittin' on a beach somewhere with a pretty girl and a bottle of booze. Watch out, honey, the Marines are on their way!"

The young voices were raised in laughter and good-natured comments about what life would be like once they mopped up the Canal. Anthony listened to them wryly, understanding the mixture of bravado and desperation that fueled his men. Understanding, but not sharing. Only one force ruled him these days—the quiet, unrelenting determination to live so that he could return to Maggie.

He would do his duty, there was never any question

about that, but it was becoming increasingly more difficult. Each time he killed, he felt the loss within himself. And each time he avoided being killed, he wondered how much longer he could expect to survive.

His best hope—indeed, the only one he possessed— was that victory would come soon and bring with it an end to death. He believed himself willing to make any sacrifice to see that hope become a reality.

The chance to test his belief came unexpectedly a couple of days later. His men were finishing breakfast when a message arrived for him to report to Major Callahan. He left his corporal in charge, forded the river, and headed for divisional HQ.

He found it set up in a tent near the airfield, with a Marine sentry standing watch and officers coming and going as though it were the newly completed Pentagon.

James Callahan was inside, working at a desk beside his cot. He was a big, tough man from the Hell's Kitchen neighborhood of New York. Unlike most officers, he was a "mustang," having come up through the ranks as an enlisted man. For that reason only, Anthony was willing to give him a certain grudging respect.

"Platoon Sergeant Gargano reporting, sir. The major wished to see me?" he asked as he stood before the desk. His utilities, what were left of them, were badly frayed, and he couldn't remember when he had last shaved. But his shoulders were squared and his back was straight. Whatever was coming, he was ready for it.

Or so he thought. Callahan glanced up, piercing

him with crystal-blue eyes set in a craggy face that looked older than any twenty-nine-year-old's ought to. He was black Irish, with thick ebony hair much like Anthony's own. His cheeks were also unshaved, and he sported a grimy bandage on a shoulder wound taken several days before.

"You're Gargano?" he inquired in a soft, faintly raspy voice. He hadn't lain down on the cot in more than forty-eight hours and was beyond exhaustion. But he wasn't about to rest now.

"That's right, sir. Platoon Sergeant Gargano, U.S. Marines."

"Not anymore."

For once Anthony's composure failed him. His mouth dropped open and he stuttered. "S-sir. . . ?"

"You lost your commanding officer awhile back, didn't you?"

"Th-that's right. . . ."

"Whistler, wasn't it?" Callahan leaned back in his chair, rubbed a weary hand over his face and without warning grinned. "I guess even the Japs aren't all bad."

Anthony stared at him in bewilderment. He thought officers always stuck together, but here was one who apparently was expressing satisfaction that Whistler was no longer around to get their men killed. What the hell was going on?

Callahan didn't keep him in suspense any longer. He gestured to a paper on his desk and said, "You're taking over for him."

"How's that, sir?"

"I thought I was very clear. You're assuming Whistler's command."

"Sir . . . a sergeant can't do that."

"I know," Callahan said patiently. "That's why you're a lieutenant now."

A lieutenant? An officer? Him? "Uh . . . I don't understand, sir. How can you—"

"Haven't you ever heard of a battlefield commission, *Lieutenant?*"

He had, but only dimly, and he had certainly never imagined such a thing could happen to him. In a desperate effort to retrieve the situation, he murmured, "What about the ranks in between?"

Callahan shrugged. "You're skipping them." Humor danced in his light-blue eyes. "*Semper fi,* buddy." He uttered the catch-all Marine phrase that literally meant "always faithful," but in practice often boiled down to "take what life dishes out and don't complain."

Summoning all his fast-fading composure, Anthony managed to point out what he thought should have been obvious. "I don't really think I'm officer material, sir."

The harsh lines etched on either side of the major's mouth deepened as he grinned. "I don't recall asking if you wanted to volunteer."

"B-but I don't know anything about leadership or strategy or all the rest of whatever it is officers do."

Callahan stood up and stretched, ignoring the apparent pain in his shoulder. Anthony studied him from beneath half-hooded eyes. Anyone capable of creating such upheaval in his life was worthy of careful attention.

The major was a big man, in more than simply the physical sense. He exuded a palpable aura of power and determination that seemed in no way diminished by either his injury or his fatigue. Yet there was a somberness about him that was in keeping with the reality of the Marines' present circumstances.

He was clearly not one of the gung-ho brigade that saw war as a great adventure to be waged with impunity from behind a desk. Rumor had it that he cared deeply for his men and went to great lengths to protect them, often seriously endangering himself. Not for nothing had he come to be called "Cat" Callahan, as word circulated of the enormous risks he took and the ability with which he survived them.

Apparently impervious to Anthony's scrutiny, the major rubbed a weary hand through his hair and yawned. "You know enough to have kept your men in the best condition of any on this godforsaken island, while accomplishing every mission you've been given. You've taken the lowest casualties, gained the most ground, and suffered the least sickness. *That's* leadership, Lieutenant. As for strategy, I'd say you've got pretty good instincts and will pick up the refinements as you go along."

He ended on a frankly dismissive note that made it clear he considered the discussion over and done with.

Anthony thought otherwise. He felt as though he were trapped in some kind of absurd nightmare. Major James Callahan seemed like an intelligent man; how come he couldn't see that Anthony had no business being an officer?

Apparently he didn't, for minutes later Anthony found himself back outside in the tropical sun with lieutenant's bars pinned to his uniform and a sick feeling of inevitability in his stomach.

He, Anthony Gargano, who had always considered officers to be a blight on the face of the earth, had suddenly been transformed into one!

Much as he would have liked to creep back into camp, he wasn't able to. His corporal spotted him almost at once, started to say something, then broke off as his eyes fell on the insignia of Anthony's new rank.

"S-Sarge...uh...sir...?"

"Cut the crap," Anthony snarled. "It's just some HQ screw-up."

"You're a lieutenant now?" The young man was already grinning. He clearly approved, as did the other platoon members quickly gathering around them.

"I told you, it's a mistake. They'll straighten it out in a few days." Even as Anthony spoke, he knew the hopelessness of that wish. HQ *never* straightened anything out.

He was well and truly done for this time. *Lieutenant* Anthony Gargano. He'd have laughed, except that it would have hurt too much.

Later that day, when his men had finally stopped talking about how the brass had managed to do something right for a change, and after he'd had a chance to familiarize himself with the other platoons now under his command, Anthony was able to get a few moments to himself—long enough to realize that his new status had a faint silver lining.

If he managed to keep from getting killed and *if* he got back to Australia, at least he and Maggie wouldn't have to worry so much about the fraternization regulations.

Mildly comforted by this revelation, he resisted the

impulse to tear his bars off and instead began to reconcile himself to the incredible vagaries of fate and the
jokes played by the gods of war on unsuspecting men.

MAGGIE PUT the clamp in the surgeon's hand and
moved quickly to stanch the flow of blood from the
incision he had just made. It was very hot in the
operating room, but she barely noticed. They had
been working since dawn, twelve hours before, trying
to cope with the seemingly endless stream of wounded
men who were being brought off the hospital ships.

The doctors and nurses seemed to be fighting a losing battle. Maggie had lost count of the number of
operations at which she had assisted. No matter how
many were performed, there were always that many
more to follow.

"Okay, that's it," the surgeon said as he deftly
removed the shell fragments from the young soldier
and turned him over to an assistant to be stitched up.
"Who's next, Captain Lawrence?"

"Uh. . .I'm not sure, sir." She glanced around
wearily, her eyes above the white mask having trouble
focusing. Taking a deep breath, she barely managed
to clear her head.

A wounded Marine had just been brought into the
operating room on a stretcher. He was out cold, his
face turned away from her. Automatically, she
signaled the orderly to hold up his chart so that she
could read it without contaminating her surgical
gloves.

"Gargano, Dominick, private, U.S. Marine Corps,
serial number 0743987. Religion: Roman Catholic.
Blood type: O positive."

The words swam before her. For one horrible moment she thought she was going to faint. Then sanity reasserted itself, and she realized she was looking at Anthony's kid brother Dom, the young man he had spoken of with such love and protectiveness. Dom was here, in her hospital, badly wounded from the look of it and desperately in need of care.

"Over here, sir," she called to the doctor, mindful that her voice was weak and trembling, but hoping he would put that down to fatigue. "This Marine has an abdominal wound with complications."

The surgeon took a look and whistled softly. "Looks as if we'd better get him on the table."

It took more than an hour to patch Dom back together. He lost a chunk of his small intestine and needed a dozen pints of blood, but eventually he was stitched up and wheeled to the recovery room. Maggie went along with him. The flow of the wounded had finally eased up. She could afford to take a break.

"I'll keep an eye on him," she told the nurse who bustled over to take his vital signs. The woman nodded, grateful for the help, and hurried off. The ward was jammed to bursting, and she had more than enough to cope with.

Maggie remained with Dom throughout the rest of the day and into the evening. She left his side only to tend to other soldiers in the recovery room, always returning to check on Dom.

His heartbeat and pulse rate picked up as the hours wore on, and his breathing grew less ragged. By the time he was moved to the post-op ward, she was feeling a good deal more optimistic about his recovery.

Dom himself was less so. He came to shortly before dawn, with no idea of where he was and no memory of what had happened, except for a searing instant of terrible pain immediately followed by the world going dark. He figured he must have been shot and didn't discount the possibility that he was dead. Accordingly, he opened his eyes gingerly, unsure of what he would encounter.

What he saw was the delicate, lovely face of a woman peering down at him. She had large blue eyes with thick lashes, a small, upturned nose and a nicely shaped mouth.

He couldn't tell much about her figure, since she stood in the shadows, but he did make out the white cap perched on top of glossy brown waves and sighed with relief.

"You're not an angel."

Maggie smiled gently. "Far from it. I'm a nurse. You're in the hospital in Australia, Private Gargano. You've been wounded, but you're going to be okay."

"Australia? Jeez, how did I get here?"

"On board a ship."

"All the way from the Canal?"

"That's right." As she spoke, she was looking him over carefully, relieved to see that his color was good and his eyes alert. His resemblance to Anthony was really uncanny, except that Dom was not as well built and his features were a little softer, the latter undoubtedly owing to the difference in their ages. She didn't doubt that, given a few more years, Dom Gargano would turn out to be every bit as formidable as his brother. Thank God he would have those years.

"T-Tonio..." he murmured, still feeling the effects of the anesthetic and the painkillers he had been given.

"W-what's that?"

"My brother...on the Canal...so worried..."

"Maybe I can get word to him," she suggested gently.

"His name's Anthony.... Everybody called him Tonio... Long time ago.... He's a sergeant...."

Dom paused for a moment. He started to laugh, then stopped when he found out how much it hurt. "No...I heard...before I got hit...he was promoted...to lieutenant. Poor Tonio...hates officers."

Belatedly remembering to whom he was talking, he flushed. "Begging...your pardon, ma'am. Only male officers...of course."

"Of course." Her mouth twitched. Anthony, an officer? His brother was right—he must be appalled. "I'll do my best to make sure he knows you're okay," she promised.

Dom nodded weakly. He couldn't stay awake much longer, but before he slid into sleep, he murmured, "Thanks...Tonio's got enough on his mind... wouldn't want anything...distract him...."

Maggie remained beside his bed long after he'd drifted off. Fervently, if silently, she echoed his words. The knowledge that Anthony had been alive as of a few days ago did not in any way lessen her grinding fear that he might yet be killed.

Gazing down at his wounded brother, she struggled not to think about how relieved she would feel if it were Anthony lying there instead.

ANTHONY RAISED HIS HEAD from the map he had been studying and squinted into the darkness, hoping that the full extent of his anguish did not show on his face. Try as he might, he could find no way out of the trap the Japanese had sprung around them.

The night was a maelstrom of gunfire, shouted taunts and curses, screams and moans. Unlike some others, his men were standing fast, but he wondered how much longer they could hold out. If they fell, so would the vital airfield. With no way for the Americans to resupply their troops, the Japanese would be able to pick them off at leisure.

He had been wounded in the first assault and treated by a medic, then had insisted on staying where he was. The pain in his shoulder did not bother him as much as his concern for the young troops he led.

"Lieutenant," his corporal whispered urgently, "the field telephone wires have been cut. We're out of touch with HQ."

Anthony cursed softly. Without such contact, it was impossible to call in the artillery barrages that were their first line of support. The Japanese were constantly testing their defenses and would no doubt shortly discover what had happened. They would waste no time in beginning their final drive for the airfield.

"Let's send some flares up," he ordered. "I want to get a better look at what's going on."

Moments later, bursts of red and yellow lights illuminated the night sky and the jungle below. Resting his elbows on the rim of his foxhole, Anthony adjusted his binoculars and scanned the ridge immediately ahead.

Shadowy figures moved along it. Without the

sounds of artillery, it was so quiet that he could almost hear the Japanese talking among themselves; he wondered if they were as scared as his own men, whose fear rose all around him like a fetid cloud. Probably not; their almost eager acceptance of death was sometimes a tremendous advantage.

"You think they'll attack again, sir?" his corporal whispered.

"I think they'd have to be crazy not to. Pass the word to everyone to conserve what ammo he's got left. Make every bullet count."

His best marksmen were stationed in the forward foxholes near his own. They would pick off the Japanese soldiers as they came out of the jungle, but many would undoubtedly get through. Grimly, he added, "Fix all bayonets. It's going to come down to hand-to-hand combat."

The corporal blanched but nodded and relayed the message. Fortunately, their own communication lines were still intact, allowing Anthony to be in contact with his sergeants even if he couldn't reach headquarters. Cut off as they were, they had only one another to count on. It would have to be enough.

A relatively quiet half hour or so passed before the shadowy figures left the jungle rim and began moving forward. Anthony braced himself. He knew that what was about to happen would be very bad, but he was also sure that he had done everything possible to prepare his men.

Even so, it was almost not enough. The ferocity of the Japanese was all but unstoppable. Wave upon wave they came, hurling themselves against the wall of gunfire without a thought for their own lives. Hundreds died, but hundreds more made it through to attack the Americans in their foxholes.

There the faceless anonymity of war gave way to individual acts of fierce desperation, one man struggling silently with another, their bodies locked together, knives and bayonets gleaming red, until one, or both, slumped into the arms of death.

For a time it seemed as though the Japanese would keep coming forever and that the Americans would be fighting them to the very end of the world and beyond. But there were limits even to the tenacity of a banzai attack.

Slowly, inexorably, the enemy began to fall back. The fighting lessened; the screams and shouts diminished. At last, just before dawn, all was still except for the ragged moans of the wounded.

Anthony pulled himself gingerly from his foxhole and surveyed the remnants of battle through bleak eyes. His face was gray from pain and loss of blood. One arm hung uselessly at his side. A bayonet wound in his left thigh continued to ooze. He was unaware of these injuries, or of the myriad others he had sustained.

All his attention was focused on the evidence of the night's unbridled savagery. The bodies of enemy soldiers littered the ridge, lying twisted and misshapen in the final embrace of death. Closer in, where the hand-to-hand fighting had occurred, the Japanese and American dead sometimes lay together.

It was all but inconceivable that such obscene destruction could be called a victory, but he knew that it was. Against all odds, they had held the line. The airfield, the Americans' vital link to the outside, remained intact.

The battle for Guadalcanal was by no means over, but the tide had been turned. Despite what had happened at Pearl Harbor, Bataan, Corregidor and elsewhere, the Marines had proved that the Japanese were not, after all, invincible. They could die as easily as other men, and in death they looked like nothing more than puppets broken by a careless hand.

The nightmarish scene he gazed on began to blur and waver before his eyes. He blinked once, twice, only dimly aware of his corporal hurrying to him.

Loss of blood, exhaustion and an overload of horror took their toll. He never knew when his knees hit the ground or when he keeled over onto it. The blackness swallowed him whole, his last thought no more than a whisper rising above the carnage to the mocking blue sky. *Maggie. . .*

January 1943–October 1943
AUSTRALIA

Chapter Ten

"DEAR MA, POP AND EVERYBODY, They're really treating us great here in Australia. I'm getting better and hope to return to duty soon. Not fast enough to suit me, but I can't complain."

Maggie snorted indelicately. Breaking off his dictation, Dom grinned. "Okay, so maybe I do complain a little. But who listens?"

"Not me," she assured him, her pen poised above the notepaper. "Shall we get on with it?"

"What's the hurry? You're off duty, and I'm sure not going anywhere." He stared down at himself distastefully.

Clad in pajamas and a bathrobe, he looked much the same as the several dozen other recovering soldiers also out on the sunny hospital veranda. But he thought he ought to look better and couldn't figure out why it was taking him so long to recover.

"You've written to your folks only once since you got here, and that was two months ago," Maggie reminded him. "There's a mail plane leaving tonight; this letter had better be on it."

"Yes, ma'am!" He laughed at her reproving glance and grinned engagingly. "You're so pretty I keep forgetting how tough you can be."

"You're not supposed to say things like that to officers," she pointed out mildly, reconciled to the fact that her words would have no effect. Like his brother, Dom was less than awed by rank.

His smile faded, replaced by a pensive look. "Speaking of officers, I wonder how Tonio is doing."

So did Maggie, but she wasn't about to admit it. Why she hadn't told Dom that she knew his brother escaped her, but some instinct had urged her to keep silent. Perhaps it was because she couldn't bear to talk about him when she didn't know from one day to the next whether or not he was still alive.

At least her fear for him was beginning to ease a little. In the weeks immediately before Christmas, word had arrived that Guadalcanal was at last secure enough for the Marines to be withdrawn. Anthony was on his way back to Australia, but when he would arrive and in what condition he might be were unknown factors.

"I'm sure he's fine," she murmured, fully aware that she was no such thing.

Dom stared off into the middle distance, his eyes bleak. "I can't imagine anything happening to him, but—"

"Your folks are probably saying the same thing about you," she interrupted briskly. "Only they know you've been wounded and must wonder if you're really recovering."

He held up his hands in mock defeat. "Okay, okay, back to the letter. Let's see. . . ." A grin lit his eyes. "I met this really nice girl, only I'm not supposed to call her that because she's also an officer. Her name's Maggie Lawrence and she's got big blue eyes and freckles and—"

"*Dominick!*" she chided gently.

"Am I going too fast for you?"

"You've got better things to tell your folks about than me."

"I do? Like what?"

"Like yourself. How you're doing."

"I already told them I'm getting better."

Maggie put her pen down and glared at him. "You're impossible."

He grinned complacently. "Tonio always said that was my middle name."

"I can believe that. Now are we going to get on with the letter?"

An exaggerated sigh escaped him. "Okay, okay. Maybe I'd better explain why it isn't in my handwriting, and tell them a little bit more about what it's like here."

Half an hour later, Maggie dropped the letter into the mailbag, reassured that when the Garganos received it, they would be greatly comforted about the condition of their youngest son.

Like the vast majority of wounded soldiers, Dom had minimized the full degree of his injuries and glossed over the pervasive weakness that made it difficult for him to do something as simple as hold a pen. But other than that, he had been fairly forthright. The letter really sounded like him—funny, cocky, quietly courageous. Not unlike his brother.

She grimaced, wishing Anthony would stop popping into her mind. She could hardly bear to think about him, yet try as she might, she couldn't seem to avoid it. He dominated her every waking moment and haunted her dreams. Her only relief from him came while she was deeply embroiled in her work, and even then she could never be sure when the sight of a wounded soldier or the sound of a voice or even something completely unrelated would trigger memories of him.

Of course, spending so much time with Dom didn't make things any easier for her. He was just enough like his brother to vividly remind her of Anthony, but different enough—gentler, less sure of himself—to make her acutely aware of how attracted she was to Anthony and only to him.

Come what might, she was unable to change that, but the suddenness of their parting had left her wondering about his feelings. Did he regret what had happened between them? Had he perhaps lost interest in her? Her mother had warned her that once the "thrill of the chase" was over, some men tended to look elsewhere.

She shook her head wearily. Surely he wasn't capable of such callousness. Yet despite her faith in him, she couldn't deny that she both longed for and dreaded their reunion.

ANTHONY STARED OUT at the harbor of Brisbane, watching the hectic activity on the docks without really seeing it.

His mind was on other things: the gradually dawning realization that he was still alive; the dismal condition of those of his men who had also survived; the odds that they would be allowed to recover properly from their ordeal; the knowledge that he would soon be able to see both his brother and Maggie.

While still on Guadalcanal, he had learned about Dom's being wounded and evacuated to the hospital at Brisbane. Thanks to Maggie, he had also gotten a couple of reports assuring him that his brother was recovering.

Sliding a hand into his pocket, he drew out her most recent letter. It was dog-eared and tattered from repeated readings; soon it would be completely indecipherable, but that didn't matter, since he had memorized it.

Dear Anthony,

It's very late here and the ward is quiet. The night is clear, and through the window I can see a shower of meteorites in the western sky. Does it seem foolish to you to wish on a falling star? I can't help doing it, even though I'm afraid to admit all that I'm wishing for. Dom is coming along very well. He's champing at the bit to get back to the action, but that will be awhile yet. There's so much more I'd like to say, but you know as well as I do that these letters are censored. Just stay well, please.

Maggie

The letter had cheered him a little but had also left him wondering about the things she hadn't said. He tried to read between the lines in the hope that what he wanted to see was really there, but he still couldn't be sure how she felt. If she regretted what had happened between them, he had no idea what he would do.

"Lieutenant," one of his men said quietly, breaking in on his thoughts, "it looks as if the brass has turned out to welcome us back."

Anthony glanced in the direction the private was indicating and frowned. On the dock was a staff car emblazoned with four stars. A cluster of photographers and reporters—both civilian and military—stood nearby. Their attention was not on the approaching hospital ship, but on the tall, grave officer posed in profile to watch it.

General Douglas MacArthur was more familiarly known as "Dugout Doug" to the survivors of Bataan and Corregidor, who, fairly or not, had despised him for escaping to the safety of Australia and leaving them to their fate. Anthony's view of him had mellowed a bit over the past few months; he was willing to give MacArthur top points for his role in protecting Australia. But he still had no more use for the general than he had for any other officer. The lieutenant's bars he wore had not changed that.

"Just what we needed," he muttered. The idea that his men would be paraded before the cameras for the greater glorification of MacArthur sickened him, but there was no way to avoid it.

As the soldiers began to file slowly down the landing ramps, the photographers and reporters pressed forward, eager to record the moment. But when the condition of the returning troops registered on them, they began to pull back. Shock and dismay replaced the benign grins and wide-eyed stares. The sight of weak, gray-faced men in tattered utilities that hung on their fever-racked bodies brought home the full magnitude of the desperate battle they had waged. Months of inadequate food, constant danger and the rampant diseases of the pestilent jungle had drained even the strongest.

Anthony knew himself to be in worse shape than when he'd left Corregidor, but he was damned if he'd let that slow him down. Ignoring the photographers, the reporters and the brass, he led his men off the ship and straight onto the trucks sent to pick them up.

The last of the troops were getting aboard when an enterprising journalist approached him with a wary smile. "Lieutenant...if you could spare a moment..."

Anthony looked the man up and down. He was a civilian, dressed in a neatly pressed khaki shirt and trousers. His shoes were shined, and he had a fancy, silver-toned clip on his belt. His gut protruded slightly, as though he had spent a few too many hours snuggled up to the bar. His face was pale beneath his thinning hair.

But his dark brown eyes radiated intelligence. He smelled a story and wasn't about to let it get away.

"What for?" Anthony growled, hoping against hope that a little surliness would discourage him.

It didn't. "Just a few questions," the reporter said smoothly. "I'm Haley, of *The New York Times*. My readers would like to know what it was like on Guadalcanal."

Anthony raised an eyebrow skeptically. Aware that his men were listening, he asked, "What would they want to know that for?"

"Why, because they...they care, of course. Many of them have boys of their own over here." Haley gave his words a moment to sink in, then lowered his voice confidentially. "What *was* it like, Lieutenant? If you don't mind my saying so, you and your boys don't look so good."

Anthony laughed dryly. He had to admit this guy had nerve. How many civilians would willingly suggest to a Marine that he looked like something a cat wouldn't drag in?

"Haley—that's your name, isn't it?—saying we don't look so good is like saying we're sort of at war. I seem to remember the *Times* was a pretty straight-shooting paper. Isn't that true anymore?"

"Yes, of course it is. It's just that, with the war and all, there's a certain feeling that we don't want to say anything really. . .discouraging." The journalist halted, obviously embarrassed.

"Discouraging? We won this one, didn't we? There's nothing discouraging about that."

"Of course not, but. . . ." Haley glanced around at the exhausted, ill men again. "The price seems to have been rather high."

Anthony regarded him steadily for a long moment before he said softly, "You ought to see the guys who lost."

"Th-the, uh, Japs are worse off?"

"The Japs are either dead or wishing they were. They're a proud people, Mr. Haley, and damn tough fighters. We had to bleed for every inch of that god-forsaken island, but we took it in the end."

"Is that what accounts for the condition of the men, Lieutenant? The tough fighting?"

"That was the least of it," Anthony answered frankly. "What really did the damage was the jungle itself and the screw-up with supplies."

"Oh." Haley's hands tightened on his notepad, but he wisely resisted the urge to jot anything down. He wasn't about to risk losing what he suspected might be a page one story.

"It was just one of those things," Anthony said. "We ran out of everything—food, ammo, you name it. The men did the best they could, but it was rough. Under those circumstances, the people back home should be even happier that we managed to win."

"I'm sure they will be, Lieutenant...Gargano, is it? Where are you from?"

"Brooklyn."

Haley smiled. The *Times* was read nationwide, but it wouldn't hurt to have a hometown angle. "That's great, just great. Hold still a sec." Grabbing the camera he had fortuitously remembered to sling around his neck before leaving the hotel that morning, he snapped a quick picture.

Anthony barely noticed. He climbed into the truck and gave the signal to roll out. The truck hadn't even passed through the gates leading to harbor before all thoughts of the reporter faded from his mind. He had better things to think about.

Like Maggie. Throughout the long weeks after the battle on the ridge, he had clung to the memory of her, using it as a shield against the pain of his wounds. She consoled and strengthened him, helping him to resist the ever-present fear and depression, as well as the efforts of the doctors who had wanted to evacuate him along with the other seriously wounded.

That he would not do. Once before, he had left his men because of circumstances beyond his control, and those who were still alive languished in Japanese prisoner-of-war camps. He had vowed that if any more soldiers under his command suffered the same fate, he would share it.

As a sergeant, he had frequently ignored orders he thought were misguided or just plain stupid. As an officer, he didn't hesitate to do the same.

Despite the best efforts of the doctors, he'd remained on Guadalcanal and returned to duty with his men, sharing their hardships and dangers until the last remnants of the once mighty Japanese force were defeated.

Now he was glad he had done it. As he got the platoon members settled into their new quarters and assured himself that they were comfortable, he felt a deep sense of satisfaction. By the following morning, he was ready to head into town.

Brisbane was busier and more crowded than he remembered it from a few months before. So many temporary buildings had been put up to house the military and civilian bureaucrats that he had trouble finding his way through the streets. He had to step quickly to avoid being hit by speeding trucks, jeeps and the ubiquitous bicycles that had replaced most private cars.

By the time he reached the hospital, his nerves were stretched taut and his body trembled. Standing on the steps of the big stone building, he gritted his teeth and determinedly ignored the concerned look a young nurse shot him.

Inside, it was a little cooler and quieter. Ceiling fans whirled overhead. Screens kept out the worst of the mosquitoes. He wiped his forehead, got his bearings, and approached the information desk at the front of the lobby.

"Morning, ma'am," he greeted the matronly civilian ensconced there. "I'm looking for my brother, Private Dominick Gargano. I believe he's a patient here."

"Just a moment, young man." She checked the thick register, then nodded. "That's right. He's in enlisted men's post-op. That's Ward B, on the second floor."

Anthony thanked her and climbed the marble stairs as swiftly as he could. At the end of a hallway, he found the door to Ward B. Pushing through it, he stood for a moment looking at the neat rows of beds that seemed to stretch on forever.

A quick glance was enough to tell him that most of the men there seemed to be doing pretty well, though they certainly weren't recovered enough to be back on the line. Some were even wandering around in bathrobes, talking to one another or chatting with the duty nurses.

His presence was quickly noted. A pretty little thing in a white uniform approached him. "May I help you, sir?"

Anthony clenched his cap more tightly between his hands. "Uh...yeah...I'm looking for my brother, Private Gargano."

"Dom? He's on the far left, about halfway down."

He mumbled his thanks and headed in the direction she'd indicated. He hadn't gone very far before he spotted the familiar figure of his brother, sitting on the edge of a cot with his back to Anthony, chatting with a couple of other patients. They were laughing at some story he was telling them.

Anthony drank in the sight. Knowing that Dom

was all right had been a great relief, but it didn't dim the sheer pleasure he felt now at finding him alive and on the mend.

"So then I explained to the major that he had it all wrong. There was just no way any Marine would—"

"'Tention!" One of the privates gathered around the cot had spotted Anthony and automatically given the signal that an officer was on the floor. The men who could rise did so, and came as close to standing at attention as they could.

Thoroughly embarrassed, Anthony mumbled for them to be at ease. He was acutely aware of Dom staring at him and of the swift play of emotions across his brother's face. He saw chagrin at the interruption, startled recognition, wholehearted amusement at his discomfort and then shock and worry—which he had hoped to avoid.

"T-Tonio...it's you...."

"Who did you think, Santa Claus?" He didn't get any further. Dom threw his arms around him and hugged him boisterously as the other men looked on, puzzled.

"It's my brother, guys! Jeez, I heard they made you an officer but I figured you'd be busted by this time. Did you just get back? What kind of shape are you in? You don't look so good."

Anthony laughed and ruffled Dom's hair. "Give me a chance, mouth. I can only answer one question at a time."

"Oh, yeah, sure. Here, sit down. Meet the guys." Dom introduced them quickly, each man nodding respectfully to Anthony. There was great curiosity in their eyes, but they restrained it and, as soon as the

amenities were completed, took themselves off so that
the two brothers could be alone.

"I can't believe it," Dom exclaimed, grinning
widely. "You're actually here. Last time I saw you,
you were getting ready to hit the beach."

"And last time I saw you, I told you to stay out of
trouble. What the hell happened?"

Dom shrugged. "No big deal. I caught a couple of
rounds, that's all. I would have been out of here
weeks ago, except the doctors are a bunch of worry
warts."

"I'll bet. Seriously, how are you feeling?"

"I'm telling you, I'm fine. I sure as hell feel better
than you look." Dom studied his brother anxiously.
Anthony's face was gaunt. There were deep hollows
beneath his cheekbones and shadows under his eyes.
The collar of his shirt was loose. Though he still
looked powerfully built, there was an air of vulnerability about him that Dom had never sensed before.

Hesitantly, he said, "Tonio... what's happened to
you?"

"Nothing. There's a war on, you know. We're both
lucky to be in one piece."

"I know that, but—"

"But what?" Anthony demanded impatiently. He
wasn't there to talk about himself. It was understandable that his brother would be concerned about him,
but he wished Dom would just drop it.

The silence stretched out between them until at
last Anthony sighed deeply and said, "It was rough.
I'd be lying if I said otherwise. But it's over and I'm
okay, so let's forget it."

Dom swallowed hard. He was enough of a veteran now to understand what his brother was telling him. The horror went too deep for words. "You don't want to talk about it, so we won't," he said at length. "But I want you to remember that I'm here for you. If you change your mind or if you don't, either way I'll do whatever you want."

Anthony blinked hard and managed a shaky grin. "So tell me, what's it like in this place?"

"Hey, it's not bad at all. Three squares a day and plenty of pretty nurses. Speaking of which—"

"Don't tell me," Anthony teased. "You're in love. With at least a couple of them."

His brother grinned. "Close. I'm in like."

"How's that?"

"Like. I really like one of the nurses here. She's a terrific person. I don't know what I would have done without her." He shrugged abashedly. "I was kind of out of control for a while after I came to. I wanted to go right back to the fighting, and when they wouldn't let me, I sort of made an idiot out of myself, hollering and yelling and all. A couple of the doctors were ready to ship me off to the loony bin just to teach me a lesson. But Maggie made me see reason. She got me calmed down and—" He broke off, suddenly aware that beneath its weathered tan, his brother's face had paled.

"M-Maggie?"

"That's right. Captain Maggie Lawrence, the nurse I'm in like with. Don't get the wrong idea— she's a terrific looker. I'd be head over heels about her, except I've got enough brains to know she isn't my type. Which brings me to what this is all about. I think you and Maggie would really hit it off, so I thought I'd introduce the two of you. With you being an officer now, there shouldn't be any problem."

Anthony stared at him, dumbfounded. The irony of what his brother wanted to do did not escape him. Here he was, worried sick about what Maggie really thought of him, and Dom was determined to fix them up. As much to buy time as anything else, he said, "I don't know how long I'm going to be here. Besides, maybe she's already involved with someone." The mere thought of Maggie with another man made his stomach flinch, but if that was the case, he had to know it.

"If you'd been listening to the scuttlebutt," Dom said, "you'd know none of us is going anywhere for quite a while. Remember that training we were supposed to get when we first arrived here? It's finally gonna come through. Better late than never. We won't see action again for months." He grinned engagingly. "Unless we make a little of our own. As for Maggie already being taken, I gotta admit that's a possibility. She acts as if she's kind of hung up on some guy. But maybe you can beat his time."

Sweet relief flowed through Anthony, but he managed to keep his face expressionless. "What makes you think she cares about somebody?"

"Trust me, big brother. If there's one thing I know, besides the exact number of spots on the ceiling above my cot, it's when a lady's got a guy on her mind and when she doesn't. This one does, but like I said, don't let that discourage you."

It didn't. All Anthony felt was delight, until it occurred to him that there was no guarantee he was the object of Maggie's interest. Suppose there was somebody else? "Did she ever mention this guy she cares about?" he asked stiffly.

"No...not exactly. But I think he might be a Marine, on the Canal. She's always listening to the news from there."

The tightness in Anthony's stomach began to ease a little. Grinning, he asked, "Are you suggesting I should try to take a buddy's girl?"

Dom shrugged philosophically. "Hey, you know what they say—all's fair in love and war."

"Okay, but suppose she doesn't go for me?"

"Call it a hunch, a shot in the dark, but I think the two of you are meant to make beautiful music. Anyway, I'm gonna fix you up with her." Dom scanned the ward swiftly, then nudged his bemused brother. "There she is. Didn't I tell you she was a looker?"

Anthony turned around slowly, savoring the sight of the woman who had haunted his dreams waking and sleeping. His first thought was that she hadn't gained back much of the weight she had lost on Corregidor. There was an air of fragility about her that caused his throat to tighten. Her slender shoulders, small waist and slim legs made her look almost achingly delicate.

Yet she carried herself with graceful strength. The healthy glow of her chestnut hair and apricot-tinged skin told him that his first impression was deceptive. Maggie had clearly experienced hardship and deprivation, but she was too much of a fighter not to come back better than ever.

The low, melodic sound of her voice reached him as she gave instructions to one of the other nurses. He sat transfixed, studying the play of light and shadow over her face. There, too, he could see the effects of what she had been through. Her cheekbones seemed higher and her eyes looked larger. But her chin was just as firm as he remembered, and her mouth. . .

He swallowed hastily and glanced briefly away, fighting to keep himself under control. But without much success. Her slenderness emphasized the ripe curve of her breasts and hips, reminding him all too vividly of what it had felt like to hold her in his arms and possess her. Her voice felt like a caress rippling over him. Just to see her was enough to arouse him intensely.

Torn between the desire to claim her immediately as his own and the fear that any such behavior might anger her, he began to shift restlessly on the cot. Dom noticed his discomfort, opened his mouth to make a joke, then shut it abruptly. The look on his brother's face was unlike anything he had ever seen: a combination of intense joy and dread that indicated a profound emotional battle warring within him.

Maggie finished her conversation with the nurse and turned toward them. She took a step forward, caught sight of Dom, and started to smile. The smile froze on her face as the color suddenly drained from it. She swayed slightly and clutched the files she was carrying so tightly that her knuckles showed white against her tanned skin.

Dom glanced from her to his brother and back again. He was fascinated by what was happening. They seemed completely unaware of him and everyone else in the ward, as if the two of them were the only people in the world.

Maggie stood riveted by the force of her own emotions. The sheer joy she had felt the instant her eyes had lighted on Anthony was followed swiftly by a mixture of feelings so intense and contradictory as to all but overwhelm her. She was at once elated that he was alive and whole and there before her, yet appalled by how vulnerable she was to him. She was achingly aware of how tired he looked, yet acutely conscious that even in his present state he was still the most compellingly attractive man she had ever encountered.

Anthony was watching her intently. What he saw in her eyes made him tremble. There was no sign of regret or resentment, only a joy that mirrored the exultation of his own soul.

Slowly he rose and walked toward her, mindful now of the crowded ward and the many pairs of eyes that could light on them at any moment. As cautiously as though he were about to make his way through an uncharted mine field, he offered his hand. His voice was deep and heartfelt as he said, "I've missed you, Maggie."

Chapter Eleven

MAGGIE GOT OFF duty at six that evening. Anthony met her outside the hospital and they headed for Digger Sam's. A waitress who remembered them smiled when they arrived and showed them to a relatively quiet table in the back.

"The place hasn't changed any," Anthony murmured as he held out Maggie's chair for her.

"It's certainly as popular as ever," she agreed, wishing that she didn't feel quite so awkward with him. In the ward, with so many interested eyes watching them, there had been no chance to do anything except say hello and arrange to meet later.

"Do you still like it at the hospital?" he asked after the waitress had brought over a couple of mugs of beer, taken their order and left again.

She nodded, her eyes focused on the table. "It's the most satisfying nursing I've been able to do since Manila. We're not so busy that we have to cut any corners."

"I hope it stays that way."

She took a sip of beer, her hand shaking slightly, and put the mug back down with great care, as though afraid she might drop it. "Do you think things will be quiet for a while?"

"I don't know. Dom tells me the scuttlebutt is that we'll be here for months, training for a new mission. If it's true, it would be great."

Looking at him directly, she forced herself to recognize the harsh lines etched into his face and the slightly sunken look to his eyes. So quietly that he could barely hear her, she said, "It was very bad, wasn't it?"

He hunched slightly in his chair. "You don't want to hear about it."

Like Dom, she understood what that meant, but she was still a little hurt by his refusal to reveal anything of his feelings to her. That only seemed to emphasize the distance between them. "Of course," she murmured stiffly. "I didn't mean to intrude."

Anthony grimaced impatiently, at himself, not at her. They were talking at cross-purposes. "I'm not trying to shut you out, Maggie. But you've been through an awful lot yourself, and there's no sense in my adding to it."

"Maybe not," she said softly, "but some things are better if you share them."

He stared at her, thinking of how true that had been in their case.

The waitress returned before he could reply and set out steaming plates of pot roast and mashed potatoes. After making sure that they wanted nothing else, she withdrew.

They began to eat in silence. Anthony didn't taste the food. He was too busy wondering how Maggie felt about him. Did she imagine he had come back expecting to take up where they had left off? If so, that would be ironic, since in his present condition he doubted that he could.

He hated to think of what he must look like to her. Shaving that morning, he had confronted with rueful resignation the evidence of the hell he had passed through. A lot of men looked much worse. But maybe Maggie didn't see it that way.

Quietly, but with iron determination, he said, "There's no reason for you to feel sorry for me."

She laughed outright, her reaction shocking him. "I should say there isn't! You're alive, aren't you, and pretty much in one piece? My sympathy goes to the guys with more wear and tear on them."

In his relief, he let his fingers move forward and tighten gently around hers. "I'm glad we got that straight."

His touch and the warmth in his eyes made Maggie swallow tightly. She had to fight to keep her smile in place. The truth was that she was deeply affected by his condition. The stiffness with which he moved did not fool her for a moment. She knew he was in constant pain and suspected he needed further medical attention. But now was not the time to mention that. Not when he would mistake compassion for pity and be offended by it.

The moment passed, and they went on to talk of other things. Anthony teased her about Dom, asking how she was managing to put up with him.

"He's not so bad," she retorted. "He reminds me a lot of you."

Anthony pretended to wince. "Don't tell me that. Dom's still wet behind the ears."

Maggie met his gaze unflinchingly, her own becoming more serious. "Is he? It seems to me that we're all growing up fast."

Anthony nodded, thinking of the boys he had led into battle. Those who had made it back were men now, for better or for worse. He stirred slightly in his chair, only to stop abruptly as a shooting pain stabbed through his leg.

Maggie saw him whiten and looked at him questioningly. Embarrassed, he shrugged and said, "Growing old might be more like it. It was so wet on the Canal, I think I rusted."

She smiled, even though she saw nothing humorous in his condition. Sweat beaded his forehead, and the lean brown hand he reached out for his water glass shook.

"Anthony . . . have you seen a doctor?"

"What for?"

"Come on, don't be like that. We both know you're hurt."

"I *was* hurt. I'm getting over it."

The hint of frost in his voice made her back off. They finished dinner while talking determinedly of neutral things: the conditions in Australia, which both agreed were a testament to the civilian population's courage and fortitude; the outlook for peace—dim; MacArthur's strategy—obscure; the news from the home front—both encouraging and exasperating.

"Some folks back there still don't seem to understand what's going on here," Maggie said. "I had a letter from my mother last week, and she told me that some ladies in one of her charity groups were complaining about the clothing regulations. They hate having to wear narrow skirts and do without cuffs or patch pockets on their coats."

"Gosh, that's tough."

"Isn't it?" she asked ironically. "Dad nearly got

into a fight with a neighbor who was boasting about buying gasoline on the black market. When he told the guy that it was needed at the front, he looked at Dad as if he couldn't care less."

"He probably doesn't, unless he's got somebody over here or in Europe. America's the only country in this war where the action isn't right in everyone's backyard."

"Or front yard. There's still talk here that the Japanese will try to invade."

"I'm sure it's occurred to them," Anthony said dryly. "But after what happened on Guadalcanal, they'll have to think again."

"We've heard a lot, of course. But the press reports seemed pretty heavily censored. According to them — if you can believe what they said — it must have been a piece of cake."

"It wasn't."

"No. . . I can see that." She hesitated a moment before saying, "I don't want to take advantage of your hospitality. Maybe we'd better be going." That was as delicately as she could put it. What she really wanted to say was that he was looking grayer and shakier by the moment, that he clearly belonged in a hospital, and that if he had any sense he would come back with her and check himself in.

In his pain-filled state, Anthony was willing enough to end the evening. He wanted to be at his best with her, even if that meant only seeing her for short periods,until he really got his strength back. He was sure he would; it was only a matter of time.

Rising from the table with difficulty, he paid the bill and offered her his arm. Maggie took it and surreptitiously rested her fingers on his wrist. His pulse was alarmingly weak and erratic. Near the restaurant door, he stumbled, but caught himself and grinned ruefully. "Guess I don't have my land legs yet."

"Guess not," she murmured. They were only a few blocks from her quarters, and she thought he'd be able to get there all right, but what would happen after that? "Where are you staying?" she asked casually.

"We're billeted down near the Aussie barracks."

That was a good couple of miles away. No cabs were available, and the chance of getting a lift at this time of night was all but nonexistent.

By the time they reached her bungalow, Anthony's face was gray and his breathing labored. With her hand resting lightly on his forearm, she could feel the clamminess of his skin and the tremors racking him. The thought of his going off into the night was becoming more intolerable to her by the moment.

But that was clearly his intention. When she had unlocked her door and turned to face him, he said tensely, "Thanks for your company, Maggie. Okay if I call you tomorrow?"

"Yes, of course," she answered automatically, wondering how to handle the situation. Her professional commitment as well as her personal feelings made it impossible for her to let him leave. But she sensed the pride and determination that would keep him from admitting his need.

"Uh...Anthony...would you do me a favor? I know this sounds a little crazy, but we've had a couple of scares around here about Japanese infiltrators—that sort of thing. It's got me a little spooked. Could you just take a look inside for me?"

"Sure," he agreed instantly. "You're smart not to take chances."

Behind him, Maggie frowned. She was smart to worry about Japanese hiding under her bed, but it was all right for him to walk a couple of miles on a leg that was all but crippled. As soon as he stepped inside and switched on the light, she followed him and shut the door behind her.

He took a careful look around the place before nodding. "Seems okay to me. You get a good night's sleep, and I'll be in touch tomorrow." He headed for the door, about to leave. She searched frantically for some way to keep him there.

His hand was on the latch when she blurted out, "I don't think I'll be able to manage that. Sleeping, I mean. I can't remember the last time I slept through a night."

He frowned, obviously concerned. "You can't go on like that. You need your rest."

"Oh, I know. It's just been terrible." With an absolutely clear conscience, she lied through her teeth. "Why, I even talked to one of the doctors at the hospital about it. He said I was going through a phase of extreme apprehension and that what I really needed was for someone to stay with me."

Anthony's brows shot up. "Oh, he did, did he? Some nerve."

"He didn't mean anything, honest," she assured him hastily. "It was just his professional opinion. Besides, I think he's right. I really hate being alone when it's dark."

"Couldn't one of the other nurses stay with you?"

She smiled bravely. "Now that I'm a captain, I'm

supposed to set a good example. It wouldn't do to let them know how scared I feel sometimes."

His throat tightened. He knew all too well what it was like to be kept awake at night by real and imagined terrors. The thought of Maggie having to cope with such things alone hurt him.

The small bungalow where she lived seemed spacious enough. In the living room was a small kitchenette, and a neatly made up bed was visible through an open door.

After so many weeks of being crammed into troopships and foxholes with other men, Anthony was enticed by the lure of privacy. The fact that Maggie was here, and that he might actually be able to do something to help her, made it even more attractive.

Hesitantly, he said, "Don't take this the wrong way, but . . . if you wanted . . . I could stay."

"That's very nice of you."

So anxious was he for her to accept his offer that it never crossed his mind that he had been carefully maneuvered into making it. Instead, he was afraid she was going to refuse. "I'm not trying to put any pressure on you," he assured her. "I know we've been apart for a while and I wouldn't presume anything."

Maggie was barely listening. She just wanted him to finish so that she could get him to lie down before he collapsed.

"I really appreciate your willingness to do this, Anthony. Just give me a sec and I'll make up the couch."

Her ready capitulation left him a bit dazed. He sat down heavily in a chair and watched as she fussed with sheets and blankets. When she was satisfied, she straightened up and smiled at him gently.

He was so tired and in so much pain now that his vision was beginning to blur. The last thing he remembered was her helping him over to the made-up couch. Then his head hit the pillow, and he went out like a light.

Maggie watched him for a few moments before finally tiptoeing away. She undressed quickly and slipped into a light cotton nightgown. Once in bed, she lay there listening for any sounds from the living room. Anthony seemed to be resting peacefully. With that knowledge, she managed eventually to drift into sleep.

It did not last long. Before very many hours had passed, her subconscious was pierced by a harsh, strangled cry that jerked her bolt upright in bed. The sound came again, this time more clearly, from the direction of the living room.

Without pausing to think, she pushed back the sheets and jumped out of bed. The heavy night air was being torn by cries when she reached Anthony and knelt beside him. He was tangled in the coverings of his makeshift bed, his arms and legs lashing out and sweat dripping from his bare chest. Even to the most untutored eye, he was clearly in the grip of a terrifying nightmare.

"They're coming in! Oh, God, stop them, please! I've just got kids here...."

He cried out hoarsely and raised his arms. His fists closed reflexively around an imaginary weapon. *"So many of them... Have to hold the line... Can't fall back..."*

His eyes opened wide but unseeing. All the deeply etched lines of his face tightened with concentration and the fierce will to live. *"Fix bayonets!"*

He lunged forward, straight into Maggie. She fell back as he slipped off the couch and sprawled on top of her. Tears streaked her face, and instinctively she put her arms around him.

All the stories she had heard about the obscenely brutal close-quarters fighting on Guadalcanal came back to haunt her. Men had literally waded in blood and gore, never knowing when the next broken body sprawled in the mud would be their own. The worst moments she had experienced in the operating room could not equal what Anthony had lived with for months and was reliving now.

Desperately, she tried to wake him, calling his name repeatedly and holding him close, despite the struggles of his weakened body. At length, the sound and feel of her reached him. He stirred dazedly, staring down at her. "Maggie...oh, Jeez, I'm sorry..."

"You haven't done anything.... It's just a bad dream. Come on, let me help you up."

With the last of his strength drained by the nightmare, he was all but dead weight in her arms. Only by dint of great effort was she able to get them both to their feet.

A glance at the couch showed her that the covers were drenched with sweat. He couldn't sleep there. Resolutely, she steered him toward her bedroom.

"Wait a minute," he protested weakly, "I don't think I should go in there."

"You're in no condition to argue. Right now I could knock you over with a feather, and if you don't stop being such a jackass and get into that bed, I will!"

Caught off guard by her aggressiveness, he was

unable to stop her from tugging and dragging him across the room. They dropped onto the bed together. Both were breathing hard, only partly because of their physical exertion.

Anthony lay on his back with Maggie half-sprawled on top of him. Even in his exhausted, pain-racked state, the feel of her body against his had the predictable effect. He stifled a groan and prayed she would not become aware of his arousal.

Maggie's problem was a little different, but not much. She was torn between concern for his suffering and pleasure at his nearness. He was easily the most desirable man she had ever known. Sternly reminding herself that he was injured and in need of help, she tried to push aside any other consideration.

Glancing at the windows to make sure the blackout curtains were in place, she switched on the bedside lamp. A soft gasp escaped her. Its light revealed a long, livid scar running across his bare shoulder. The wound was unbandaged, even though it had only partially healed. The skin around it was hard and bore the signs of infection.

"Why hasn't this been treated properly?" she demanded. Her experienced eye told her it most likely was the result of shrapnel wounds suffered some time ago, possibly as far back as several months. The idea that it hadn't received correct medical care infuriated her.

"It was treated," Anthony said hastily in an effort to ward off the explosion he sensed was coming. For a slender little thing, she certainly didn't shy away from speaking her mind. "The doctors at the field hospital on Guadalcanal checked it out."

"And they okayed you for duty?" she exclaimed, astonished.

"Not exactly.... I okayed me for duty."

"Of all the bullheaded, asinine..." Muttering to herself, she stood up. "Take your pants off."

Anthony's mouth dropped open. He was getting used to episodes of blurred vision, but this was the first time he'd started hearing things. "Wh-what did you say?"

"You heard me. If my guess is correct, that shoulder wound is the least of it. I want to get a look at that leg."

"Forget it! My leg is fine."

"Look, Gargano, you've got two choices. Either I check you out, or I report you to the doctors and you can say good-bye to your leave. You'll be flat on your back in a hospital bed before you know what hit you. Now what's it going to be?"

Easy for her to ask. He was busy grappling with the transformation of his quiet, soft-spoken Maggie into a steely-eyed, no-nonsense nurse who clearly intended to carry out her threat if he didn't behave. No wonder they'd promoted her to captain! The way she looked right now, it wouldn't surprise him if she made general.

"Tell you what... When I get back to camp, I'll let the medics have a go at it."

"No deal! You can hardly walk as it is. If you think I'm going to let you go traipsing around here, you're nuts." Without giving him a chance to comment further, she leaned forward, grasped his belt and deftly undid it.

Maggie had been routinely stripping men for surgery for months. She thought no more of it than she did of applying a bandage or cleaning a wound. That her feelings for Anthony were very complicated and far from strictly professional did not affect her actions. Without hesitation or fumbling, she unzipped his khakis and eased them down past his hips.

"Maggie, for God's sake!"

On the edge of her mind, she registered the fact that he was becoming sexually aroused. She was relieved by that; it indicated he wasn't in quite as bad a condition as she had feared. But she didn't linger on it. All her attention was focused on the wound she had just revealed.

Her professional composure cracked a bit as she surveyed the deep, virulent injury to his thigh. Like his shoulder wound, it was only partially healed and showed signs of an ongoing infection. But that was only the beginning. She guessed there had been at least some nerve and muscle damage, which made it difficult for him to walk under the best of circumstances, let alone under the ghastly conditions on Guadalcanal.

She took a deep breath, trying to steady herself, and met his gaze. "H-how did you manage with this?"

"It's not as bad as it looks."

"Don't give me that! I'm a nurse; I've seen thousands of wounds and I know how serious this one is." As her initial shock eased slightly, anger roared through her. It was bad enough that Anthony insisted on abusing himself; why had the doctors allowed him to do so?

"You had no business remaining at the front," she snapped. "Don't you realize how much damage you may have done to yourself?"

Too tired to argue effectively, and too bemused by her attitude to want to, Anthony lay back against the pillows and shrugged. "Believe it or not, that thing is healing up. It's just taking awhile."

"What about the infection?"

"When it gets bad, I sprinkle a little sulfanilamide powder on it and that does the trick."

"You can't go on doing that. Eventually, the medication will lose its effectiveness. The infection has to be cleared up."

"And now that I'm back in Australia, it will be. I don't need any hospital for that."

Sitting down on the edge of the bed, she regarded him perplexedly. "Have you got something against hospitals?"

"No, of course not. But I wanted to stay with my men on Guadalcanal, and I still want to. It's not going to be easy for them here. Their nerves are shot, they're worn out, and they've got a long recovery ahead of them. This is no time to jump ship."

"That's not what you'd be doing and you know it," she said softly. Much as she disagreed with the choice he had made, she understood and respected it. The responsibilities of command had that effect on good men, making them willing to sacrifice themselves unflinchingly for others. "All right, I can see your point—sort of. But if you won't go into the hospital, then you're going to have to let me treat you. Agreed?"

Anthony hesitated. He would have liked nothing better than to put himself in her hands, if only because it would give him a perfect excuse to see her often. But what she was suggesting involved a certain level of intimacy he wasn't sure he could tolerate without making physical demands on her.

"Do you think that would be a good idea?" he hedged. "I'll be staying down at the barracks, which isn't very convenient for you, and—"

"You'll be staying here."

"W-what are you talking about?"

"Just what I said. There's no way I can treat you if you're miles away. The bandages will have to be checked every few hours, plus I've got to get you started on physical therapy. This place is big enough for the two of us. There shouldn't be any problem."

"Shows what you know," he muttered. It really didn't seem fair that this should be happening to him. Hadn't he been tested enough? Did he have to have temptation thrown right in his face?

But Maggie had clearly made up her mind; either he let her look after him or he checked into the hospital and risked having his men transferred to some other officer's command. That he couldn't live with. Grudgingly, he agreed to her terms.

"Good. First thing you need is some decent rest. I'm going to give you a shot that will help you sleep, all right?"

"Do I have a choice?"

She smiled gently. "Not really. Turn over."

"Just give it to me in the arm."

"It'll hurt more."

He sent her a look that made it clear what he thought about that remark. Shrugging, she got out her first-aid kit and did as he asked. The sedative was not particularly strong, but Anthony was so exhausted that it took effect almost instantly.

When he was asleep, Maggie carefully cleaned, medicated and bandaged his wounds. By the time she was finished, exhaustion was catching up with her. The couch in the living room seemed farther than her leaden feet could take her, and her own bed was so inviting, particularly with Anthony in it.

She debated only briefly before deciding that there couldn't possibly be any harm in staying with him. He would be out cold for hours and need never know where she had slept.

Switching off the light, she stretched out on the bed, careful not to disturb him. Their bodies barely touched, yet there was undeniable comfort in his nearness. Smiling, she drifted into sleep.

Sometime toward dawn, Anthony awoke. The sedative that had hit him so powerfully was going through his system just as quickly. He was still groggy but becoming more alert with each moment.

This was fortunate, if the sight that greeted his eyes was anything to go by. Maggie lay snuggled against him, her head on his chest and one slender arm resting lightly across his abdomen. Her hair flowed out over his arm and her soft breasts pressed against his side.

He drew a ragged breath and tried to tell himself he was dreaming. Things like this just didn't happen. She was some sort of beautiful, tantalizing illusion — exactly the sort of thing a wounded, drugged man could expect to experience.

Except that she was vibrantly, exquisitely real. Tentatively, hardly daring to move, he touched a feather-light finger to the curve of her cheek. Her skin was warm with sleep and soft as velvet. She smiled faintly and snuggled closer. His hand shook as he jerked it away.

What on earth was he to do? If he tried to move, she was sure to wake up. Yet if he stayed where he was, the consequences didn't bear thinking about. Long moments passed as he struggled to decide on a course of action. For a supposed leader of men who hadn't hesitated to make the toughest of choices, he was proving remarkably indecisive.

Seemingly of their own volition, his arms closed gently around her. She was wearing some sort of little cotton nightie that offered only the slightest barrier to his touch. Entranced, he stroked her back tenderly, watching her to make sure she didn't wake up.

When she remained deeply asleep, he gained confidence. Maybe this wasn't so bad after all. He could hold her close without provoking fear or resentment. A relieved sigh escaped him as he settled back into the pillows, drawing her with him.

Maggie kept her breathing slow and steady. She had awakened several minutes before, when he'd touched her cheek, but didn't want him to know that. Every feminine instinct she possessed warned her that he was extremely wary about being so close to her. She was determined to get around his scruples and convince him that what they had shared once could — and should — be theirs again.

As strategies went, playing possum wasn't bad. Though it undoubtedly wouldn't be found in any Marine order of battle, it seemed to be working well enough. She could hear the steady beat of his heart beneath her cheek and feel the renewed strength flowing through him.

The little care he had permitted her to give so far was clearly working. But he needed much more before he could fully recover. A soft smile, hidden by the darkness, curved her mouth as she reflected that she was, after all, a dedicated nurse sworn to help those in need. What greater need could any man have than to know the shared pleasure of passion fulfilled?

His hands moving lightly over her back sent a quiver of delight through her. Anthony felt her response and instantly stopped, only to resume again a moment later when she still gave no sign of waking.

She felt so incredibly good to him, soft and slender, with curves in all the right places and hair like warm silk cascading through his fingers. A faint, natural perfume rose from her skin, tantalizing him. He breathed in deeply and shuddered.

Maggie almost sighed in relief. That slight movement gave her the excuse she needed. Raising her head slowly, as if only just waking, she murmured, "Anthony. . . are you all right. . .?"

"Uh. . . yeah, I'm fine. Go back to sleep."

Instead, she nestled closer to him, a slim leg lying over his uninjured one. He closed his eyes and summoned all his self-control. The intimacy between them was becoming unbearable, yet he could not imagine ending so sweet a torment.

"Perhaps I should change your bandages," she suggested helpfully.

"No! That is—there's no need. They'll be fine till morning."

"If you say so. . . . As long as I'm awake, would you like a back rub?"

He drew a ragged breath and shook his head. "No, thanks. Go back to sleep."

His plea was becoming increasingly desperate. Maggie smiled and ignored it. Instead, as though completely unaware of what she was doing, she trailed her fingers over his broad, bare chest and down to the rim of his briefs. "Hmmm . . . you feel cooler now. Not so feverish."

Little did she know, Anthony thought. He was burning up, but not from any sickness. On the contrary, he couldn't remember the last time he had felt so vigorous. Catching her hand in his, he rasped out, "Maggie, I really don't think we should be doing this."

She glanced up at him innocently. "This what?"

"This . . . being in bed together."

"I know I could have gone back out to the couch," she murmured contritely. "But I was so tired. . . ."

"There's no reason for you to do that. I'll go." But in order to get up, he had to untangle himself from her, and she didn't seem predisposed to let that happen. "If you'd just move a little . . ."

"But I told you, it's so hard for me to sleep alone."

His senses were whirling, and he knew he had to get out of there. "I thought you meant you wanted to have someone nearby," he said thickly.

"This is nearby, isn't it?"

By any definition that he knew, it was a damn sight more. She couldn't possibly be unaware of what was happening to him. So why was she letting it go on?

"Maggie . . . if I stay here . . ."

"Yes?"

"I promised myself I wouldn't try to rush you just because we'd already made love."

The raw truth in his voice turned the little game she was playing suddenly serious. All pretense dropped away as she sat up and looked at him. "Anthony, let's get something straight once and for all. I have no regrets about what happened at the beach house. You did *not* take advantage of me in any way."

"Maybe not, but it's still my responsibility to protect you."

"Why?"

"Because I'm the man, of course."

Lying back against the pillows, she grinned challengingly. "You know, Anthony, I'm beginning to get the idea that you don't think much of women."

"Don't talk crazy."

"No, I mean it. You seem to think we're like little children who can't be held accountable for their own actions. I don't happen to feel that way about myself."

"I don't think that way at all," he protested. "But men are supposed to protect women, not take advantage of them."

"That's fine, but it doesn't have anything to do with our situation. We're both adults, and I, for one, know exactly what I want."

"Y-you do?"

"Yep." Her long, slender fingers trailed again over his chest, this time lingering at the flat nipples surrounded by whorls of dark hair. Lightly, almost absently, she caressed them with a slow, circular motion that made him gasp. Leaning closer, she let her hair spill over his chest. He could feel her breath on him, teasing the surface of his skin like the softest feather imaginable. Almost inaudibly, she murmured, "By the way, have you heard there's a war on?"

"I thought it might be. . .something like that," he said, groaning. "All those people. . .shooting at each other."

"Exactly. Dangerous, don't you think?"

"C-could be. . .Lord, but that feels good. . . ."

"Mmm. . .I'll be happy to keep on doing it. Now, what was I saying? Oh, yes, the war. It seems to me this isn't the right time to be wasting time, if you see what I mean."

"I, uh, think I'm beginning to get the message."

She smiled approvingly, her tongue darting out to taste the faintly salty elixir of his skin. "You're so smart. But I'll bet lots of people have told you that."

"Only my mother."

"Really? What did your teachers say?"

"Th-that I was im-impossible. *Maggie*. . ."

A low, contented chuckle sounded deep in her throat. "I wouldn't say that. You seem quite co-operative."

That was putting it mildly. His vigor entranced her. It seemed the most natural thing in the world for her to ease his briefs from him, careful to avoid touching his wounded thigh, and then slowly, entic-ingly, explore his body.

During their first encounter, she had been too dazed to do more than follow his lead, and that alone had been wonderful. But this time, she reveled in the opportunity to take the initiative.

Anthony endured it as long as he could. He under-stood instinctively that she needed to feel in control. That was a new experience for him; he had always presumed that the man should be the aggressor in lovemaking. But he was rapidly discovering that variety was truly the spice of life.

Maggie's soft, artless caresses were more potent than any he had ever known. Part of him wanted the delightful torment she inflicted to go on forever, but another part made it clear that was impossible. He was rigid with desire, swollen to bursting with the need for her.

"Sweetheart . . ." he murmured huskily, his hands closing on her shoulders and drawing her up to him. "I can't stand any more. . . ."

Maggie's face was flushed, her thick-fringed blue eyes bright. She breathed raggedly through slightly parted lips. Deep inside her, she was turning to molten gold. "I—I can't either . . . I want you so much. . . ."

Her innocent admission snapped Anthony's last thin hold on his self-control. Without pausing to think of what he was doing, he slid his hands down to her rounded hips and lifted her onto him.

Maggie gasped softly with mingled surprise and delight. This new position made her feel even more unrestrained, free to give full rein to the torrent of hunger racing through her.

Her response drew a deep chuckle from Anthony. She gave him the confidence to cast aside his preconceptions about how a man should behave and allow himself to be loved by her.

Their union was slow and sweet. He did not move until she had drawn him fully within her, and even then he was cautious, watching her intently for the slightest sign of discomfort or fear. Instead, he saw only delight and the dawning of even greater joy. It came to her gradually, in long, leisurely strokes that enabled her to savor fully what was happening between them. Her eyes fluttered closed, only to open wide as a rippling bolt of pleasure shot through her. Their gazes locked, his taut with passion, hers darkened by the force of the storm building within her.

"A-Anthony . . . ?"

"It's all right, sweetheart," he gasped out. "Let it happen."

She was riding the crest of an immense wave, driven higher and higher by a life force far beyond her control. The pressure built until she thought she couldn't possibly bear anything more. She cried out, her body tightening around him, ardently claiming him as her own.

Anthony groaned and grasped her to him, all restraint gone as he drove fiercely into the sanctuary she offered. Radiant bursts of light exploded within them, small at first, then increasingly more powerful, until their very souls seemed to fly apart into diamond-bright shards of pure, unbridled sensation.

Slowly, the world re-formed around them, the room becoming solid once again, the bed firm beneath their spent bodies. They lay in a tangle of arms and legs, skin slicked with perspiration and their breathing ragged.

Anthony managed to prop himself up on an elbow and gazed down at her bemusedly. He had never imagined that such pleasure existed. If he had been told it did, he would have rejected the suggestion as romantic fantasy. Sex was sex; a release of pent-up hunger, the satisfying of a natural appetite. He had never credited it with any mystical significance, but now he had to revise his thinking. What happened to him when he was with her went far beyond physical bounds to touch the very core of his being.

Could it really be the same for Maggie? Almost tremulously, he touched her cheek. "Honey...are you all right?"

She stared back at him dazedly. All right? No, she couldn't say that she was. Every cell of her body radiated fulfillment. She felt as though some giant, unseen hand had taken her apart, infused her with a completely new sort of strength and awareness, then carefully put her back together again.

"Anthony..." she murmured hesitantly, "before it was glorious. But this time... Is it often like that?"

He shot her a crooked grin. "Not by a long stretch. I think we may have achieved some kind of major breakthrough."

She laughed softly, nestling closer to him. The first stunned awareness of what had happened was beginning to pass over her, leaving a warm, languorous sense of contentment. "Maybe we can get it patented."

He chuckled and settled her more comfortably against his chest, reaching down to pull the covers over them. "Could be. But I think we probably need more practice first."

"Mmm...you're right. We wouldn't want to miss anything."

"We won't, honey," he promised as he cradled her in his arms. The darkness and despair of the past few months had dropped away from him. He felt reborn, free to share his life with the woman who had given it back to him.

"I love you, Maggie," he murmured as sleep eased over him.

"I love you," she responded, her eyes fluttering closed.

It was a pledge freely given, yet it was also a challenge. Outside the quiet room, the horizon was stained blood-red. The future remained, at best, a tenuous thing. There were no guarantees, only dreams and the ever-present knowledge that the love they had found could not shield them from death.

Chapter Twelve

"YOU KNOW, you're looking pretty good these days," Dom commented as he and Anthony strolled on the hospital veranda. "In fact, you look nearly as good as me."

"Thanks," Anthony muttered dryly. Beneath his crisp khaki shirt, he flexed his shoulder experimentally. It felt fine, as did his leg.

Three weeks of Maggie's tender and very loving care had worked wonders. He grinned as he considered that her methods might be unorthodox, but there was no arguing with success. Not a day passed that he didn't savor his great good fortune and give thanks in the privacy of his own heart that they were once more together.

"I hear you're about to be kicked out of here," Anthony said, eyeing his brother indulgently. Dom had regained much of the weight he'd lost right after surgery and no longer tired so easily. He even had a healthy tan. His growing impatience indicated that he felt strong enough to leave.

"Thank God for that," Dom replied fervently. "If I had to stay here much longer, I swear I'd crack up. I can't wait to get back on duty."

"Wait till you start training. You'll be singing a different tune then."

"Nothing can be as bad as just sitting around," Dom insisted. "I'm ready for action." He grinned boldly, then added, "And not necessarily of the military kind."

"I'll bet. Just watch yourself on that. You know some of the Aussies are starting to trickle back from North Africa, and they aren't taking too kindly to finding their women going out with Yanks."

Dom shrugged, unconcerned. "A little healthy competition won't do them any harm. Besides, if your buddy Jake Dylan is anything to go by, the Aussies can take it."

"I hope so," Anthony murmured, thinking of the last time he had seen Jake before he shipped out for the Canal. The Aussie sergeant and his unit had been fighting on New Guinea for months. The green hell was taking a savage toll on the men who challenged it. He told himself that if anybody could make it through that, Jake could, but he still worried about him.

Friends of Jake's had looked Anthony up a short time ago, on the eve of their own departure for New Guinea, and invited him to spend a farewell evening at Madame Rosa's. Anthony had declined. The diggers knew the reason, having met Maggie, and their good-natured kidding had held a pardonable hint of envy. But Anthony had felt that, even if he didn't go along, the Americans should show the flag—so to speak—and he'd wangled a twelve-hour pass from the hospital for Dom. The results had convinced the younger Gargano that he was ready for duty.

The two brothers talked awhile longer, until Anthony glanced at his watch. "I've got to go. Callahan wants to see me."

Dom grinned. "Better watch out. You know what happened the last time you had a chat with him."

Last time, he'd found himself transformed into an officer. Surely nothing that bad could happen again. Or so he thought as he made his way to the major's office in the new jerry-rigged quarters housing the overflow from MacArthur's headquarters.

Callahan was at a staff meeting when Anthony arrived. He cooled his heels for a few minutes, flipping through a copy of *Stars and Stripes* and chuckling at the Bill Mauldin cartoons. The Joe and Willie characters might be fighting in Europe, but they weren't any different from the dogfaces in the Pacific.

The major strolled in shortly before noon and gestured for Anthony to join him in his office. When they were both seated, Callahan leaned back in his chair, stuck his big booted feet up on the desk, and sighed deeply. His broad, blunt features looked weary, and his blue eyes were hooded.

"I've just had the pleasure of spending an hour with Dugout Doug himself. He was none too happy to see me."

"What's he got to gripe about?" Anthony asked. He felt at ease with James Callahan. Though they didn't know each other well, there was a current of understanding between them. Both were street fighters who had come up the hard way and both had an instinctive distrust of authority.

"This." Callahan reached into a folder he had been carrying, extracted a sheet of newsprint and tossed it across the desk to Anthony.

It was a recent front page from *The New York Times* with an article about the fighting on Guadalcanal, written by its correspondent in the Philippines. Anthony glanced at the story without any particular interest. "I met this guy Haley in Brisbane, right after we got off the ship," he commented casually.

"No kidding? Read on."

Puzzled, he did so, only to stop abruptly when his own name jumped out at him. He grimaced as he saw that he was referred to as "one of the gallant officers who led our men to victory against almost insurmountable odds."

"Oh. . .jeez. . ."

"It gets worse," Callahan drawled.

So it did. Haley went on at some length to discuss the screw-up with supplies that had caused severe deprivations for the Marines. He analyzed how the situation had occurred, pointing an unmistakable finger of blame at both the Army and the Navy. Although he didn't quote Anthony directly, the suggestion that much of his information had come from him was clear. There was even a photo of Anthony surrounded by his men that drove home the truth of how badly off they had been.

"I barely talked to this guy. . . . Why the hell did he have to go and do this?"

"Because it's a good story. If the brass didn't want it published, they should have stopped it from ever being dispatched."

"So why didn't they?"

Callahan shrugged and reached for a cigar. "It seems that the censors screwed up, too. Anyway, the story made it into print, and now MacArthur's hopping mad. He says it's bad for his image."

"He actually said that?"

"In his usual roundabout way. He kept talking about morale, keeping the support of the home front, not running down our own — that sort of stuff. But what it amounts to is that he likes to look good and this makes him look bad." Callahan's rugged features split in a grin. "He had a few choice suggestions about what ought to be done to the Marine who gave the interview."

"I'll bet," Anthony muttered. He was just getting used to being a lieutenant and realized to his surprise that he didn't mind it anywhere near as much as he'd expected. But it looked as though he could say good-bye to his bars. "I suppose you're going to bust me?"

"I did consider it," Callahan admitted. "But then I thought, what business does any Army general have to tell me who my officers should be? So what if we technically report to him? We're still Marines. You've done a damned good job and I expect you to keep right on doing it."

"But with MacArthur on my case, I don't see how you—"

"Simple. We've got to fix it so good old Dougie can't afford to throw you to the wolves. Fortunately, I'd already done something about that even before this little problem cropped up."

Grinning at Anthony's puzzled look, Callahan swung his feet off the desk and rooted around in a drawer until he found what he was looking for. "This came in from Washington a few days ago," he said, gesturing to an official-looking document. "Seems you've been awarded the Navy Cross." His grin widened. "There's a promotion that goes with it. You're a captain now."

Anthony jerked as if he'd been stung. His eyes widened in disbelief. "What the hell are you talking about?"

"That little episode on the ridge, when you and your men held off the Japs. It helped to keep us from losing the airfield, you know. I put you in for the medal and the boost in rank right afterward. Mentioned it to you when you were in the field hospital, but I guess you were scheming so hard to get out of there, it didn't register."

Anthony stared at him, aghast. He did have some vague recollection of Callahan's telling him he had acted with great courage, but he'd brushed it aside. To his way of thinking, he'd just done his job.

"There's got to be a mistake. I'm no hero."

The major shrugged and put his feet back up on the desk. "You told me you weren't officer material, either."

"B-but—"

"No buts. I pointed out to MacArthur that you are a certified grade-A Marine hero and that busting you would cause a bigger stink than any comments you made to Haley ever could. He didn't like it, but there's not a whole lot he can do."

"Oh, great! You're telling me I have to go ahead and accept that medal—and be a captain—to keep Dugout Doug off my back!"

"That's the size of it. So dust off your wash khakis and go buy yourself some captain's bars. There's going to be an awards dinner for you and a few other guys day after tomorrow."

"I don't have any wash khakis; they got left in the Philippines. And as for going to some friggin' dinner—"

"Get some," Callahan snapped. "And forget any ideas you may have about ducking out on the ceremony. That little bit of ribbon and metal they're going to pin on your chest is the only thing that's saving your ass right now. Got that, Gargano?"

Anthony sighed resignedly. He knew when he was done for. "Got it, sir."

"Good." The major stood up. "It won't be so bad. I've been through it myself. Once the speeches are over, we can relax and have a good time."

An aide stuck his head in the doorway to remind Callahan he had another meeting to go to. As the major started to leave, he stopped and turned back to Anthony. "They're really going to put the dog on at this thing, so bring a date." Grinning, he added, "Somebody with a little class. Mrs. MacArthur will be there, and we don't want to do anything to shock the general's lady."

Anthony privately thought that any woman who could survive the fall of Manila, the siege of Corregidor and a thousand-mile escape across enemy waters must be pretty much shockproof, but he agreed nonetheless. If he had to go through with the damned thing, at least he wouldn't have to do it alone.

"A FORMAL DINNER?" Maggie repeated disbelievingly. She had come off duty less than half an hour before and hadn't even had a chance to change out of her crumpled uniform before Anthony sprang his little surprise on her. The news that he was now a captain and was going to be decorated was wonderful, since he certainly deserved this recognition. It was just the dinner that threw her.

They were sitting in her bungalow, sipping a couple of cold beers and generally relaxing. Sometime in the next few weeks, Anthony's men would start their training in earnest, and then he wouldn't be free to spend all his evenings with her. But at the moment, he and all the other veterans of Guadalcanal were enjoying some hard-won R&R.

"That's right," he said. "I guess you'll need some kind of long dress. It's going to be pretty fancy."

"Fine. I'll just pull something out of my closet," she muttered, wondering frantically what on earth she was going to wear. With the exception of the Chinese-style dress and robe she had bought months before, her wardrobe consisted strictly of uniforms and a few casual clothes.

"Good," he agreed complacently. "This might not be so bad after all. Thanks to you, I'll even be able to dance." As he spoke, he edged across the couch closer to her and put an arm around her shoulders. "Anyone ever tell you you're terrific at that physical therapy stuff?" he murmured.

"Oh, sure. I hear that all the time."

"You do?"

"Absolutely. There's hardly a soldier, sailor or marine who comes through here and doesn't say that."

"Cute, really cute."

"Thanks. It's the freckles."

"Come here, woman. You're going to get yours."

"Promises, promises." Worries about the dinner were forgotten as she gave herself up to the delight of his caresses. Morning was soon enough to confront the problem of what to do about her inadequate wardrobe.

As it turned out, the problem was easier to solve

than she had expected. When she mentioned it to some of her nurses who were gathered around the coffee urn during a break, they immediately began vying to help her.

"I've got a terrific pair of gloves," Lucy Jacobs announced. She was a petite redhead from New York who somehow managed to remain in high spirits no matter how grim things became. "They're about the only souvenir I've saved from the good old days. You're welcome to borrow them."

"My pearl earrings would go perfectly with your skin," Carrie Ludlow offered. At the age of thirty-five, with more than ten years of nursing behind her before she joined the Army, she was the backbone of the team, second only to Maggie in respect and authority.

"There are a couple of Australian girls working here who used to do hair before the war," Jane Hall mentioned. Tall and slender, she was a quiet perfectionist, utterly devoted to her hardworking superior officer. "I'll bet they'd help out."

"Don't forget she's got to have shoes," Lucy reminded them.

"And an evening bag," Carrie chimed in.

"Silk stockings."

"A stole."

"Really great lingerie."

"Perfume. . . lots of perfume."

"Hold on!" Maggie exclaimed, laughing. "This is just a dinner we're talking about, not a battle plan!"

"Begging your pardon, Captain," Jane interjected, "but are you going to this affair with that Marine we keep seeing around here?"

Maggie flushed and nodded. "Lieutenant Gargano." With a hint of pardonable pride, she added, "He's being promoted to captain and awarded the Navy Cross."

When their congratulations had died down, Lucy said, "Then you've got to look really special."

"No doubt about it," Carrie insisted. "This has to be a night he'll never forget."

"I suppose..." Maggie said reluctantly.

"No 'suppose' about it."

"Don't worry, we'll take care of everything."

"Just put yourself in our hands."

Maggie nodded wanly. She didn't seem to have any choice. Her nurses had clearly taken her to their hearts. The little things she did—making sure they didn't work more than a single shift whenever it could be avoided, seeing that their quarters were comfortable, standing up for them on the occasions when overworked doctors were apt to be snappish—counted heavily with them, and now they were determined to help her indulge in a healthy bout of sheer female frippery.

Anthony had gone to get his new uniform fitted, so once Maggie got off duty, she had several hours to herself. After a long, leisurely bath replete with fragrant jasmine oil, she dried and powdered herself, then began to dress.

The Australian girls had done her hair in a soft chignon nestled at the nape of her neck. The style emphasized the line of her throat and shoulders and made her look unexpectedly regal.

Her hands, graced by newly polished nails, shook slightly as she slipped into silk panties and a lacy garter belt. Carefully rolling each precious silk stocking, she drew them up her slender legs and fastened them in place, then put on a pair of new black evening sandals with uncustomarily high heels.

The dress she had found, of yards and yards of sapphire taffeta, was vintage prewar. Its strapless bodice made wearing a bra impossible. Only a few precious drops of the perfume Joy graced her breasts as she slipped into the gown. The touch of the fabric against her skin was undeniably sensuous, and she smiled to herself as she pulled up the short zipper in the back and fastened the hooks.

Her eyes widened as she caught sight of herself in the mirror. After months of wearing only uniforms or fatigues, she could hardly believe the transformation that had taken place. The woman who stared back at her looked like something out of a fairy tale, a beautiful princess untouched by the slightest hint of ugliness or violence.

Her bare shoulders and arms shone opalescently. The boned bodice of the gown pushed her breasts up, emphasizing their fullness. Her waist looked tiny, and beneath it her hips flared ripely as the taffeta fabric spilled over them.

She moved with instinctive grace, laughing as the skirt swirled and rustled around her. She felt deliciously feminine, as if she'd been lifted out of the real world and set down in a magical place where all things good were possible. Wait until Anthony saw her!

His reaction when he did so was everything she could have hoped for and more. She had the delightful experience of seeing him momentarily at a loss for words. His mouth dropped open as he stared at her, dumbfounded.

"M-Maggie..."

Giggling, she twirled before him, showing off her gown. "Isn't it fabulous? I haven't worn anything like this since..." She paused and grinned. "Come to think of it, I've never worn a dress this lovely. Do you like it?"

"What? Oh, yeah, it's great." Actually, he was barely aware of the dress. It looked nice enough, but what really struck him was Maggie herself. She was...magnificent. There was no other word for it. He had always known she was beautiful, but he hadn't dreamed that she could look so enthrallingly feminine and delicate and—

His face darkened as his gaze fell on her rather exposed bosom. "Isn't that thing cut a little low?" he growled.

She shrugged, the motion making him even more aware of how much of her breasts he could see. "It's the style."

"It doesn't leave much to the imagination."

Surprised by the tartness in his voice, she faltered slightly. "You...don't like it?"

Anthony hesitated. He understood how much it meant to her that he appreciate the effort she had made. But he was damned if he enjoyed the thought of other men seeing her like that.

"I..." Whatever he had meant to say evaporated when he saw the shadows in her eyes. She would be deeply hurt by his disapproval. Relenting, he said, "You look fantastic...like a princess."

What the hell; he was a hero, wasn't he? Surely anyone with half a brain would think twice before trying to take any liberties with his woman.

Relieved, Maggie swept him a graceful curtsy. "Thank you, kind sir."

The sheer happiness bubbling out of her made him grin. He wrapped an arm around her waist and kissed her lingeringly before stepping back. "Here," he said, handing her a package, "maybe this will cover things up a bit."

She sent him a gently chiding look as she tore the box open, exclaiming over the lovely orchid nestled within. "How beautiful! Will you pin it on for me?"

"Sure." Laying it over the cleft of her breasts, he asked, "How about right here?"

"Don't be silly. It goes at my waist."

"Hmm... if you say so. I still think it would look better covering up your—"

"Never mind. There, that's perfect. Now just let me get my bag and stole."

As she hurried off to find them, Anthony grinned ruefully. He would just have to resign himself to a very watchful night. They left the bungalow arm in arm, under a cloudless sky lit by a full moon.

Maggie sighed contentedly. She really did feel like a princess going off to a ball. The fact that her "coach" was a jeep Anthony had borrowed from the motor pool in no way affected the romantic fantasy she was happily weaving.

When they arrived at the Brisbane hotel where the awards dinner was being held, she wafted regally up the steps, certain that Cinderella couldn't have done it better. Once inside the plush entrance hall, she was instantly glad that she hadn't let Anthony discourage her about the dress. It was perfectly in keeping with the gowns worn by every other woman there. Her natural modesty prevented her from recognizing that she filled it out considerably better than most of them could have.

"We're sitting with Major Callahan," Anthony told her as they made their way through the lobby. Several people noticed him and stopped to offer their congratulations.

Maggie listened proudly, thinking that he had never looked stronger or more attractive. The khakis were perfectly tailored to his wide shoulders, broad chest and tapered hips. His burnished skin, thick black hair and deceptively slumberous eyes gave him an undeniably sensuous look that none of the women missed.

Maggie's hand tightened on his arm, and she was pleased by the care he took to introduce her to everyone they met.

Unlike her, he was completely oblivious to the inviting smiles coming his way from a bevy of lovely ladies. All his attention was focused on the stares Maggie was getting.

A growl rose in his throat as one particularly appreciative colonel beamed at her. The officer had a gut on him that would have stopped a horse. He looked as though the only time he stirred from behind his desk was to go as far as the nearest bar. And all the while he was supposedly telling Anthony what a great job the Marines were doing, he was staring mesmerized at the curve of Maggie's breasts.

"Thanks a lot, sir," Anthony snapped, cutting the colonel off in mid-platitude. "Maybe you'd like to join us sometime."

"Huh. . .what's that?"

"Join us, sir, the next time we take an island. I bet you'd really get a kick out of the action."

"Oh, sure, son. Sure I would. It's, uh, too bad some of us have to stay behind to keep everything organized and going smoothly."

"You mean like with the supplies for Guadalcanal?"

Maggie's back stiffened. Hastily, she sent the colonel a warm smile and said, "Anthony, dear, didn't you say we had to find Major Callahan? You will excuse us, won't you, sir? Such a pleasure talking with you."

When they were safely away, her smile vanished, replaced by a very determined look. "What on earth got into you? You're in enough trouble without provoking him."

"Then he should have kept his eyes to himself. I'm getting sick and tired of watching these guys ogle your—"

"Isn't that Major Callahan over there? Come on, let's join him."

"It won't do you any good to keep changing the subject, Maggie. I think you're enjoying the looks you're getting."

"And I don't have the faintest idea what you're talking about. Good evening, Major." She held out a slim hand to James Callahan. "I'm Maggie Lawrence. It's a pleasure to meet you."

James grinned at her appreciatively. He didn't know which he was enjoying more, the lovely vision before him or Gargano's chagrined glare. Bending low, he said gallantly, "The pleasure is mine, my dear Maggie. There's a rumor going around that Anthony has the devil's own luck. I'm beginning to believe it."

"Good heavens, how charming you are!" She laughed, genuinely pleased with him. "I'll be spoiled rotten in no time." As she spoke, she studied the man, taking in the powerful set of his body and his confident stance, but also noting the shadows that never quite left his eyes. With the intuitive knowledge of a woman whose perceptiveness about one particular man had led her to understand all of them better, she sensed that beneath James Callahan's rugged exterior was a complex person it would take her a very long time to get to know.

"You're already spoiled," Anthony muttered, turning his attention to the tall, voluptuous redhead at James's side. She was more or less poured into an ivory silk dress that heightened the honey tones of her generously displayed skin. Her luxurious hair fell in waves to her shoulders, her mouth was full and inviting, and her green eyes looked as though they weren't missing a thing.

"Meet Delia Follett," James said. "She's, uh, a friend of mine."

"A good friend," Delia corrected as she nodded pleasantly to both Anthony and Maggie. She snuggled a little closer to James and said, "You told me I was going to be bored stiff, but so far it's not too bad."

Callahan laughed tolerantly. "Delia has a habit of speaking her mind. You'll get used to it."

The redhead shrugged, unabashed. "Life's too short to twiddle your thumbs. What do you say we scout up some champagne?"

"Sounds good to me," Maggie chimed in, surprising

both Anthony and James. She and Delia had sized each other up with a quick glance, deciding that each was thoroughly occupied with the man of her choice and approving of that selection. "I'm absolutely parched," she added cheerfully. "We had a full house at the hospital today."

"You're a nurse?" Delia asked as the four of them made their way toward the bar. When Maggie nodded, she said, "I'm with the USO — which is sort of surprising, since I'm hopeless at singing or dancing." Arching an eyebrow, she drawled, "I can't imagine why they picked me to help entertain the troops."

Delia's sense of humor about the effect her appearance had and her store of amusing stories of the pitfalls of being a show-business gypsy kept them laughing as they got their drinks and found their table. Maggie could easily see why she and James were so comfortable together. Delia's droll, sardonic approach to life suited him perfectly.

The awards dinner got under way shortly thereafter with the arrival of General and Mrs. MacArthur. Maggie had seen him several times before, but she was still understandably curious about the man whose decisions had such a profound impact on their lives.

Just a few days before, he had celebrated his sixty-third birthday, yet he looked better than many men twenty years his junior. Tall and well-built, he radiated a powerful sense of presence that caused attention to focus automatically on him. In profile, he resembled a watchful hawk. Seen full-face, he had a tendency to make even high-ranking, battle-hardened officers tongue-tied.

Unless they happened to be Marines. Between Mac-

Arthur and the leathernecks ran a deep current of enmity. They would not soon forgive him for what they regarded as his abysmal misuse of them in the Philippines, nor would they forget that they had been excluded from his recommendation of presidential citations for all the other units that had fought on Bataan and Corregidor. The omission had been a deliberate and, in their view, petty attempt to repay what he knew to be their poor opinion of him.

And yet, Maggie thought, he couldn't be all bad. Not if the woman at his side was anything to judge by. Jean MacArthur was a tiny, vibrant lady of Southern extraction with bright hazel eyes and a brilliant smile. Almost twenty years her husband's junior, she clearly adored him. Whatever softness and gentleness there was in his life he owed to her. She had given him a home and a family at a time when he could well have expected to have neither.

With the MacArthurs came much of the Australian and American brass, including Admiral Halsey, who was there to show the Navy's flag. They arrayed themselves on the dais as the waiters hurried forward to begin serving dinner. To the strains of an Army band playing the best of swing, the party worked its way through a dinner of steak, salad, potatoes, peas and ice cream.

Then the speeches started. Various officers got up to comment on the recent successes of the Allied forces and the important role of individual commanders who inspired their men to victory.

James and Anthony puffed on cigars and looked impassive. Their expressions didn't change when

MacArthur stood up, although they did join very briefly in the applause that greeted his appearance.

Somewhat to Maggie's surprise, the general's speech was interesting, well delivered and neither too long nor too short. She remembered hearing that he was extremely eloquent and could have had a successful career as an actor. He made a sincere and moving appeal for courage in the face of seemingly overwhelming odds and received an enthusiastic ovation, which he allowed to continue for several minutes before politely cutting it off.

It was now time for the medals. Anthony sighed and put down his cigar. When his name was called, he marched up to the podium, saluted MacArthur and Halsey, then stood erect while the Navy Cross was pinned to his chest.

Maggie was fairly breathless with pride; she wished fiercely that her father could have been there to see the moment. But in her pleasure, she did not mistake Anthony's extreme discomfort. He returned to his seat with alacrity, promptly unpinned the medal and placed it in the velvet case he had been given.

"Here," he said, handing it to her. "Would you stick this in your bag for me?"

James chuckled as she swallowed her surprise and did as Anthony asked. "You've got to understand," he said. "It's damn embarrassing to have to go through that."

His eyes lingered on her as he spoke. Maggie Lawrence was a surprise to him, being both more intelligent and more self-possessed than he had expected. He found himself able to understand why Anthony was so attracted to her, despite the fact that he nur-

tured a deeply rooted distrust of all women gained
through personal experience and had vowed never to
let another one hurt him.

"I felt like an idiot up there," Anthony was saying.

Delia giggled and raised her champagne glass in a
toast to him. Winking at Maggie, she said, "Don't
worry, honey. I'll bet you'll be feeling better before tonight's over."

The men laughed, as much at Maggie's blush as at
what the brash redhead had said. Anthony leaned
over and squeezed Maggie's hand. "Think she's
right?" he whispered slyly.

Maggie raised an eyebrow and met his gaze unflinchingly. "Wouldn't surprise me."

His startled glance was followed swiftly by a bold
grin. Rising, he held out a hand to her. "Come on, let's
dance."

Perhaps because of the purpose of the dinner and
the constant reminder of the nearness of war, there
was an ineffably romantic air about the evening. Men
and women tended to pair off, moving slowly to music
meant to be savored and concentrating on each other.
There was very little of the posturing Maggie as-
sociated with military events. Few seemed interested
in trying to make points with superior officers. They
had more important objectives in mind.

The MacArthurs' departure early in the evening
was the signal for a general relaxing of whatever re-
straints had been in place. The music became a shade
more languid; the liquor flowed a bit more freely.

On the dance floor, Maggie snuggled contentedly
against Anthony. At that moment, she couldn't have
imagined any other place she would rather be.

Until he bent closer and murmured, "What do you say we scram?"

Glancing around, she noticed that James and Delia had already taken their leave. There was no reason they couldn't do the same. "All right, let's go."

They had barely gotten into the jeep when Anthony stripped off his tie, dumped it in the backseat along with his cap, and sighed with relief. "Jeez, I'm glad that's over!"

"It was fun. Don't tell me you didn't enjoy yourself."

He shot her a teasing grin. "It wasn't all bad. There was a cute-looking dame there who liked to dance."

"Dame, huh? So that's how you think of me."

"Wait till I get you home, then I'll show you what I've been thinking."

Laughing, she wiggled down in her seat. "Major Callahan is nice, and I like Delia."

"Yeah, she's okay. He needs somebody like her."

"Any particular reason why—besides the obvious?"

Anthony shrugged, his eyes on the road. "I don't know the whole story, but I think he's had a rough time of it. Somebody who knew him Stateside said he was married to a real tramp."

"Married? But—"

"I know what you're going to say, but he's divorced now. Has been for a couple of years. Problem is, there's a kid involved. The mother's drinking herself into an early grave and Callahan's stuck over here, so there's nobody to look after the boy properly."

"Poor man. I thought there was something. . ."

"He's a great guy, even if he did make me an officer."

Maggie laughed softly. "*And* insist you show up for the awards ceremony."

"Don't remind me. From now on, I'm not doing anything that could remotely earn me a medal."

"I'm praying you won't have the opportunity," she murmured, almost to herself.

He slowed the jeep slightly and glanced over at her. "Hey, come on now, we're a couple of the lucky ones."

"I know.... It's just that—" She broke off, ashamed of her weakness and hoping he would put it down to tiredness and the effects of a very romantic night.

Instead, he leaned over and put a hand on hers reassuringly. "Let's talk about this when we get back to the bungalow."

"No, that's not necessary."

But apparently it was, for after they had parked the jeep and gone inside, he drew her to him tenderly. "Sweetheart, I'm not going to try to tell you that we're home free, far from it. It's going to be a long war, and who knows what might happen. But we've got each other and we've got right now. That's more than most people have."

She leaned into him, letting his strength support her. "I know. There are so many couples who are separated, so many women who must be afraid to answer the phone or go to the door for fear of what they'll learn. I wonder how they get through the days, let alone the nights."

"They don't have much choice. At least their husbands or boyfriends don't have to worry about something happening to them. They're home safe and sound, whereas you...."

She looked up at him. "Me, what?"

He shrugged and glanced away. "I just wish you were in a safer line of work."

"I'm a nurse. I go where there's need."

"That's what I mean. You don't think of yourself."

"Neither do you." She touched his chest lightly, her fingers lingering at the spot where Halsey had pinned on the medal. "If you did, you wouldn't have been decorated."

"It's different for me. I'm a man."

"I've noticed. But I don't see how that makes it different. We both have a job to do."

"There are hospitals Stateside where you could be working," he pointed out.

"Are you saying you're sorry I'm here?" she asked, astonished.

"No, of course not!" His hands tightened on her bare arms. "It's just that—" He broke off, suddenly aware that he was imposing an unfair burden on her. She didn't need to hear how much her work worried him. They both knew that either one of them, or both, could be sent back to the front. When that happened, if it did, they would have to face it together.

"Forget what I said, honey," he murmured against her hair. His mouth quirked in a gentle smile. "We've got better things to do than stand around talking."

"I should hope so," she sniffed. Anthony was continually surprising her. She had really thought he intended to deliver a lecture on the proper place for women during wartime, but instead he was once again proving himself unexpectedly sensitive to her feelings.

He buried his hands in her hair, removing the pins that held the chignon in place and combing through the silken strands with his fingers. His touch sent tremors of raw delight racing through her. She arched against him, her arms tightening around his taut waist.

His mouth brushed hers gently, then with increasing urgency. Maggie parted her lips willingly. She felt not the slightest urge to deny him anything. Whatever he wanted, she would gladly give.

"Do you know how I've felt?" he murmured thickly, "Watching you all evening, yearning to touch you like this..." One big, calloused hand closed around her breast, kneading gently. "And this..." The other hand grasped her hip, pulling her even more firmly against him.

She felt the hard arousal of his sex and moaned softly. "Anthony...it wasn't easy for me, either."

"What wasn't?" he demanded absently, nibbling at her neck.

"Seeing you...being with you. You're so handsome in that uniform." She giggled softly. "Or out of it. I was so jealous of the other women who kept looking at you."

"What other women?"

"You're a regular diplomat."

He leaned back and gazed down at her with a heart-tugging smile. "My mother didn't raise any stupid children."

"Wonderful woman, your mother."

"Pop's not bad, either. They'll both love you."

The presumption that she would be meeting his parents sent a wave of warmth through her. "Oh, Anthony," she murmured shakily, "I love you so much." Her hands flattened against his broad chest, her fingers setting to work on the buttons of his shirt. More firmly, she added, "And I need you . . . right now."

He laughed deep in his throat. "Let it never be said that a Marine shirked his duty." Bending, he scooped her up and, ignoring her laughing protests, carried her into the bedroom.

Setting her down gently, he deftly unzipped her gown and slid it from her. The sight of her standing bare-breasted in her silk panties, garter belt and stockings brought a dull flush to his cheeks.

Compulsively, he reached for her. "Lord, but you're a lovely thing! Come to me, sweetheart. I need you so much!"

She obeyed without hesitation. Together they fell across the bed. His hands and mouth moving over her drove her swiftly to rapture. But despite the raging hunger he provoked, she could not resist the urge to tempt him even further.

Languidly, she murmured, "I'm *so* tired. I'm afraid you'll have to help me off with the rest of my clothes."

He shot her a narrowed look. She lay stretched out on the bed, her hair spilling across the pillows and her eyes soft and luminescent, looking for all the world like an immensely tempting courtesan. Ruefully he acknowledged that he was intensely susceptible to the heady spell she wove.

"All right," he agreed thickly. As she smiled and raised a slender leg, he grasped one slim ankle and removed her evening sandal. Its mate followed swiftly.

"How do these things work?" Anthony asked huskily a moment later as he set to work on her stockings. The complexity of the garters eluded him until he finally managed to slip one free. The others were undone in the time it took to grasp them, and he carefully rolled each silken tube down her legs and over her slender feet.

"It's awfully nice of you to do this," she said, sighing. "I really do appreciate it."

"Think nothing of it," he muttered, reaching around her narrow waist to unclip the garter belt and remove it. As he did so, she sat up slightly, and the back of his hand brushed against the underside of her breasts. He paused, struggling for breath. Her nipples taunted him with their rosy fullness. He could almost feel them in his mouth, under the moist persuasion of his tongue.

"M-Maggie . . ."

"Hmm?"

"I think maybe you'd better do the rest yourself." The hard bulge in his trousers was becoming uncomfortable. Something was going to have to give, and soon!

"But you're doing such a good job," she protested mildly, lying back against the pillows. Raising her arms, she stretched luxuriantly, well aware that the movement brought her breasts into even greater prominence.

A low groan escaped him. Without taking his eyes from her, he ripped off his shirt and tossed it onto the floor. His shoes and trousers joined it within seconds, followed by his remaining garments. When he stood naked before her, resplendent in his fully aroused masculinity, she smiled at him invitingly.

"Remember what Delia said about your feeling better?"

"Yes," he murmured without moving.

Maggie laughed softly. "I think you can count on that." Slowly, as though she had all the time in the world, she rose to her knees and began inching her panties down over the rounded curve of her buttocks, gradually easing one leg out and then the other before at last tossing the silky garment onto the floor.

By the time she had finished, Anthony's massive chest was rising and falling rapidly. His big hands were clenched at his sides and a jagged pulse beat in the shadowed hollow of his lean cheek.

Maggie met his gaze serenely as she lay back down on the bed. Loving laughter danced in her eyes. "Planning on standing around all night, Marine?"

"No," he rasped out in the instant before he lowered himself onto her. "I've got something else in mind."

"That's good to h—" She broke off, moaning softly as his steely thigh eased between her legs, urging them apart. The sheer power of his virility overwhelmed her. Instinctively, her hips lifted to him. "A-Anthony. . .please. . ."

"No more teasing, sweetheart?" he asked, cupping her face between his hands and pressing his body down on her just enough so that she could feel the full strength of his urgency.

"N-no more."

"Good." He said nothing further but moved with breathtaking grace and skill to make her his. Joined in the most intimate of embraces, they soared together, finding in the loving union of their bodies a sanctuary from the turmoil of the war-torn world.

Chapter Thirteen

"This is really very interesting, dear," Elizabeth Lawrence said as she glanced up from the letter she was reading. "Maggie says the Australians couldn't be kinder or more generous. She's made several good friends and feels quite at home there now."

"That's nice," her husband murmured. He was looking out the window at the brown lawn dotted with patches of snow. Winter was holding on into late March. It was his first day off in several weeks, and he was content to spend it inside, catching up on family news.

The V-mail that morning had brought two particularly welcome letters, one from Maggie and another from Tad. He had survived the sinking of the carrier *Hornet* and been assigned to the Fifth Air Corps on New Guinea. He wrote that they were continuing to hammer away at the Japanese strongholds there and on nearby New Britain. Implicit in his comments was the suggestion—more correctly, the hope—that their efforts were in preparation for an Allied assault throughout the area.

Colonel Lawrence could have told him he was right. At the War Department, plans were being finalized for a major offensive in the Pacific, which, if it went well, would continue all the way to Japan.

Turning his back on the bleak scene outside the

window, Will said, "Maggie mentions that fellow a couple of times, doesn't she?"

His wife nodded patiently. They had already discussed this, but the colonel was having a hard time accepting it. "You mean Anthony? Yes, she does. He's the same young man she's written about before, and he sounds very nice."

"He's a Marine."

"Dear, you've said yourself that the Marines are doing a splendid job."

"That's true, but I don't see why one of them has to get involved with our daughter. I thought when they weren't actually fighting they were kept busy training."

"They are, but not nonstop. Besides, what's the harm in her seeing him?"

Will cast his wife a jaundiced look. Being no stranger to the special pressures inflicted by war, he had a pretty good idea of where Maggie's relationship with the Marine was headed, if it hadn't gotten there already. Fatherly hackles rose at the mere thought. It would have been bad enough if the object of her affections was regular Army, but a Marine?

"What's his last name, Gorgonzola?"

"That's a cheese, dear. It's Gargano."

"Italian."

"It does seem so."

Will sighed deeply. He sat back down on the couch and fumbled with his pipe, making a halfhearted effort to light it. When he didn't succeed right away, he gave up. Matches and tobacco were both in short supply; there was no point in wasting them. Staring off into the middle distance, he murmured, "Why couldn't she have stayed eight years old? Everything was so much simpler back then."

Elizabeth laid a gentle hand on his arm and smiled sympathetically. "She sounds happy. Isn't that enough?"

"I suppose...but a Marine..." He glanced up warily. "You don't think she's really serious about him, do you?"

"Well, dear, I did seem to detect a very great degree of interest."

"Perhaps it's just one of those adolescent things."

"She's almost twenty-five, Will. Hardly an adolescent."

"Be that as it may, she's too young to be serious about anyone."

Elizabeth put down the letter and picked up the wool skirt she was shortening to bring it more into line with current styles. The strict clothing rations were an excellent incentive for recycling her wardrobe.

Off in the distance she could hear the kitchen radio playing. Both she and Will winced as the sound of an increasingly familiar voice came on. It was that of a remarkably skinny young man named Frank Sinatra, who made bobby-soxers swoon and parents cringe. "The Voice," as he was so aptly called, had just started his rendition of "Fools Rush In" when the cook switched him off. Elizabeth breathed a sigh of relief and went back to her sewing.

Being a good wife, she resisted the impulse to point out to her husband that by the time she had turned twenty-five, she was a wife and a mother twice over. If she had read between the lines of her daughter's

letter correctly, there would be time enough to remind
Will of that later.

"Now DON'T THINK that just because you're getting out
of here for more than a few hours, you've got to rush
around and do everything at once," Anthony cautioned as he and Dom left the hospital.

"Hey, I'm fine," Dom insisted, pausing to glance
around in the bright sunshine. He stood with his hands
on his narrow hips, savoring his restored strength.
"Never better. Jeez, I feel as if I could move a mountain."

"Then join the Seabees. But in the meantime,
you're gonna take it easy for a while yet. Remember
what Maggie told you."

"Yes, sir, brother, sir." Dom laughed. "I'll
remember." Dutifully he recited, "Get plenty of sleep,
eat proper food, don't drink too much and try not to
set any records right away with, uh, extracurricular
activities."

Anthony grunted, satisfied that at least Dom had
been listening. They left the hospital grounds and
headed into the city. The sun was high and the air dusty; both quickly worked up a thirst.

"Come on," Anthony said, "I'll buy you a beer."

The pub was dark and cool, smelling of sawdust and
old sudsy beer. Several soldiers were drinking in the
back, but otherwise the place was empty. Anthony
and Dom settled down at a table and gave their orders
to the elderly waiter who approached them. Then they
leaned back in their chairs and surveyed each other.

Dom was the first to speak. "So how's it going these
days?"

"Pretty good. Most of my men who are ever going to be back on duty are ready for it, and we're starting to get the kinks out. The new equipment we're receiving is a big improvement over what we had at the Canal."

"What about the replacements? Any good?"

Anthony shrugged. "They're about the same as the recruits you came over with."

"That bad?"

Both men laughed. The waiter arrived with their beer and a dish of peanuts. The beer was warm, as always. Convincing the Aussies to chill it was easily the toughest job of the war.

Neither Anthony nor Dom felt a great urge to talk. It was good just to be near each other in a place where there was no shooting going on.

After a comfortable silence, Dom asked, "You're seeing a lot of Maggie, aren't you?"

An image shot through Anthony's mind of the night before, when she had lain naked beneath him, writhing in the throes of orgasm. He didn't know a sweeter sight. Smiling inwardly, he nodded. "You could say that."

"So I was right about the two of you?"

"Yeah, you were right. I suppose I'll never hear the end of it."

Dom grinned. "Heck, what are brothers for if we can't remind each other how dumb we are? Anyway, I'm glad you got together with her. Life's too short to waste it alone."

"I'll go along with that." Anthony finished his beer and signaled to the waiter. In due time, two more mugs appeared on the table. He blew the head off his and said, "Remember that girl you were dating a couple of years ago...Stella somebody?"

Dom's eyes lit up. "Stella? You bet I remember her. Jeez, she had the greatest pair of knockers and could she ever—"

"Yeah, yeah, I know. You wrote all about her. Seems to me you were even thinking about asking her to marry you."

"It crossed my mind," Dom admitted, scooping up a handful of peanuts and popping them into his mouth.

"So how come you didn't?"

Dom shrugged. "I kept looking at her and wondering what she'd be like five or ten or even twenty years from now. She'd probably put on a lot of weight like her mom and get a mouth on her like her old man. Even if she didn't—I don't know, it's hard to explain exactly—I just didn't feel there was anything to her except what I already knew, and I guess I was scared I'd end up bored."

"That makes sense. I know that feeling myself."

"You don't think it's just an excuse?"

"So what if it is? You're still a kid. You ought to have time to yourself before you take on somebody else."

Dom thought about that for a moment, then said, "There are a lot of people these days who would disagree with you. Seems as if everybody's getting married."

"Getting married isn't hard—it's staying that way that's the trick."

The door swung open as several men entered the pub. Sunlight and sounds briefly interrupted the quiet, then retreated again, leaving only little particles of dust swirling in the dim air.

"Maybe Stella would have sent me a 'Dear John' letter," Dom suggested, grinning.

"Maybe. Three guys in my outfit have gotten them."

"Yeah? How did they take it?"

"One was real broken up, but the other two were relieved."

"I guess that's about par for the course."

They drank awhile longer, then decided to get something to eat. The elderly waiter wandered over with the check. They paid it and stood up to leave.

"You ever think about getting married?" Dom asked as he pushed the door open.

"Sometimes," Anthony admitted, pausing to let his eyes adjust to the sunlight.

"More lately than before?"

"Yeah, but don't go trying to make anything out of that."

Dom laughed. He put an arm around his brother's broad shoulders, reaching up slightly to do so. "I won't say a word. But I sure as hell hope I can be there to see it."

"Seems to me you've got a little trip to take first."

Dom released him and patted the breast pocket of his shirt with something akin to wonder. "Yeah, I can hardly believe it. I figured to see Tokyo before I made it back to Brooklyn."

"JOSEPH! COME HERE!" Barely pausing for breath, Maria Gargano hurried up the walk to the house, the mail clutched in her hand. "You've got to hear this! Dominick is coming home!"

Breaking off his study of an aircraft identification chart used by Civil Defense spotters who kept watch over the skies of Brooklyn, Joseph lifted himself out of his easy chair and headed for the front door.

Maria burst in, her silver-blond hair unaccustomedly awry and her face flushed. She waved a letter at him. "Dom's coming home!"

"What're you talking about? He's in Australia."

"No, he's got leave. He's coming home!" Her eyes shone with tears. "Oh, Joseph, we'll see him soon!"

Her husband grabbed the letter and read through it swiftly, a wide smile creasing his weathered face.

Dear Ma, Pop and everybody,
   By the time you get this, I'll be on my way to San Diego. From there it's just a quick train trip across country. I can't wait to set my feet on Brooklyn soil again. Ma, start the lasagna baking. You wouldn't believe how long it's been since I had real food. Pop, tell the guys down at the factory to get the boccie balls out. I'm anxious for a game.

"You've got it," Joseph murmured, his throat tight. He could scarcely believe this news. Word was out that soldiers were getting leave wherever possible, but he hadn't had much hope that any of his boys would be among the chosen. Now it seemed that Dom's luck had really held.

"Does he say anything about Tonio?" Maria asked, peering over Joseph's shoulder. "I didn't get that far."

"Let me see... Tonio has to stay in Australia; he's so busy since he became an officer.... What's this? Tonio won a medal! The Navy Cross. Imagine that. Dom says there was an awards ceremony. General MacArthur was there, and Admiral Halsey himself pinned the medal on."

Maria clasped her hands, fairly bursting with pride. "First his picture in the paper and now this! Wait till I tell the neighborhood!" Her face darkened slightly as she murmured, "I wonder what he did to earn such a thing."

"Never mind about that. Whatever it was, it's over and done with, and he's fine. Let's see what else Dom says.... Something about a girl... Here, look at this. I can't make out his handwriting."

"It always was bad." She studied the letter for a moment. "Her name is Martha somebody...no, Maggie. Maggie Lawrence. A nurse, he says. Tonio took her to the awards dinner, and Dom says they're—oh, Joseph, he says they're in love!"

"Let me see that!" Joseph demanded. He read: *She's the girl he's*—several words were carefully crossed out—*in love with.*

"What did he cross out?" Maria asked. "I know he wrote something else first."

Joseph held the letter up to the light, scrutinizing it. Finally he made out the words *thinking about marrying.* "I can't read it," he insisted quickly. "It's enough what he says, isn't it? In love—that's serious." He snorted disparagingly. "What kind of name is Lawrence, anyway?"

"It sounds... American," Maria ventured.

"Of course it is. I want to know what kind."

"American American. You know, like those people who came over on that boat a long time ago."

"That's what I thought. Probably WASP. Wonerful; just what we needed."

"Now don't get upset. I'm sure she's a lovely girl."

"She had better be, if Tonio is really serious about her. What business does he have getting involved with someone in the middle of a war?"

"When better? You'll see, they'll be good for each other."

Joseph grunted. He had no such confidence. With all the lovely Italian girls in Brooklyn, what did his eldest son need with a WASP nurse? "Maybe," he suggested hopefully, "it's just one of those things."

"What things?"

"You know, the kind of stuff that's going on these days. People getting involved overnight, thinking they're in love—"

"Going to bed together?"

"*Maria!*"

"You think I don't know what's going on? Don't fool yourself, Joseph Gargano. If your son takes after you—and I happen to know he does—this Maggie Lawrence person had better watch herself."

"What makes you think she wants to? He's a wonderful boy. She's lucky to have him."

"That's true," his wife agreed complacently. "Now what are we standing around for? Dominick is coming home and I've got nothing cooked!"

"Dear Maggie and Tonio," Maggie read aloud. "I figured I'd save myself some trouble and write to you

together since I know that's where you both are anyway. Stop scowling, Tonio. I'm just teasing."

"How did Dom know I'd scowl?" Anthony interrupted. He and Maggie were taking advantage of an
unusually balmy day to visit the beach.

The V-mail had come in just before he'd left the
base to pick her up, so he'd stuck the letters in the
pocket of the shirt that was now waving from a piece
of driftwood. The barbed wire and the signs warning
against going near the water were familiar sights that
they barely noticed. Nor did they pay any attention
to the lookouts posted in the concrete bunkers to keep
constant watch over the approaches to the coast.
Both Maggie and Anthony could understand why the
sentries had to be there but thought it highly unlikely
that the Japanese would decide to invade, considering how bogged down their forces were in New
Guinea.

"He's your brother," Maggie pointed out reasonably. "He knows you. Let's see what else he says."

Coming home was pretty much as I imagined,
only better. I never saw Ma so excited, and even
Pop looked a little teary-eyed. Me, I bawled like a
baby and I'm not ashamed to admit it. Just being
here under the same roof with the family is like a
miracle. The only thing that would make it better is if you were here, too. Though I've got to admit I don't mind having all the girls to myself.

"I'll bet," Anthony muttered. "There's not a girl in
Brooklyn who's safe from him."

Maggie grinned archly. "You know whom he takes after."

He landed a playful swat on her bottom. "Get on with it."

Still smiling, she read on.

Of course, some things are different. Ma's practically going nuts trying to keep the ration coupons straight. With meat, butter and sugar on the point system, a lot of juggling is going on. Don't get me wrong, though—the food here is great. Ma outdid herself with the lasagna, roasted peppers, gnocchi and so on. I must have gained ten pounds easy. I know Tonio's having a fit right now, so I'll change the subject.

The rest of the family's doing okay. Sal got some kind of medal from the British for saving one of their officers, and Paulo's thinking about getting married.

Reaching for one of the beer cans he had buried in the sand, Anthony shook his head. "So Paulo might be getting married. That's really a surprise. Even more than Sal's being a hero."

"How come?" Maggie asked, munching on a grape. She watched him unabashedly, loving the play of sunlight over the rugged planes and angles of his face and the flow of muscle in his broad, burnished chest.

"He was always so shy around girls."

"Oh, yes? Not like you."

"Cute. What else does Dom say?"

"That's about it. You know you've also got a letter from your mom and dad."

"Yeah, I'll read that one later. I gotta write to them today."

"Hmm . . ." She lay back on the blanket she had brought along and smiled. "You know what else you gotta do today?"

He regarded her lazily over the rim of his beer can. "I forget. Maybe you'd better show me."

A short while later, in the privacy of her bungalow, she did just that.

As THE SHADOWS of evening fell across sunbaked streets and slanted against shuttered windows, behind which the more fortunate men and women found a brief interlude of peace, James Callahan sat slumped on his cot at the Marine base, grappling with the particularly dismaying reality of his personal war.

He had deliberately spent the day on hard, grueling duty, hoping to exhaust himself so that he would be protectively numb to any news from home. Unfortunately, his plan hadn't succeeded. Barely had he opened the letter from his lawyer than he knew that all his nerve endings were painfully alive.

The man wrote politely, the underlying note of sympathy at odds with his usual professional as he informed James that the efforts to revoke his former wife's custody of his son, Matthew, had failed. The only remaining alternative was to have Matthew declared a ward of the court and placed in an orphanage until James returned. To do this, the lawyer said, would require solid proof that Charlotte Callahan was an unfit mother.

That shouldn't be too hard, James mused bitterly.

Her heavy drinking and carousing assured that she couldn't possibly be taking proper care of Matthew.

His throat tightened as he thought of his son. Matthew had just begun to walk when they were last together, and his intelligence, curiosity and utter vulnerability had won his father's heart. More than anything in the world, James wanted to protect him. But he seemed powerless to do so.

His hands clenched, crumpling the letter. How he wished there were someone else with whom Matthew could live. But the boy's grandparents on both sides were dead, and there were no other relatives but James's brother, a gambler who drank as heavily as Charlotte.

His own isolation in the world rarely bothered James much these days; he had become used to it over the years, and the war was, after all, a great distraction. But Matthew's lack of family, other than a drunken mother and an absent father, endangered the boy's entire future, if not his life itself.

He wondered if it might be worth another try to request emergency leave so he could go back to the States and see the situation for himself. But his previous attempts had failed, his superiors citing the critical need to keep officers like him in the war theater. Considering all the sitting around he was doing these days, that attitude was especially frustrating, but bureaucracies and red tape seemed impervious to human considerations.

Wearily, he lay back on his cot and stared up at the ceiling. Tomorrow he would write to the lawyer, telling him to proceed with the investigation regardless of what it might cost. But he had little hope that it would do any good. No matter how often she drank herself into a stupor, Charlotte was too clever to risk losing the money he sent for Matthew's support.

He shook his head despairingly as memories of her flitted through his mind. It was really a shame that she hadn't decided to become an actress, since she could give some of the best performances ever. No amount of liquor had ever stopped her from getting herself dolled up, chewing half a roll of peppermints and convincing even the most discerning people that she was merely feeling ebullient and effervescent.

It was those very qualities of her personality that had first drawn him—a rather somber, serious young man—to her side, only to discover that the bright smiles and gay chatter hid a nature incapable of reform.

Repressed tears burned his eyes. As a man—and a Marine—he'd never have allowed himself to cry. He hadn't done that since he was a child. But now he felt a strong need to, if only to release the iron band around his chest that threatened to crush all the life and hope out of him.

The long, exhausting hours spent on the training field took their toll at last. He fell asleep with the letter still clutched in his hand and one arm thrown out in mute appeal.

Anthony found him like that hours later when he returned to the base and stuck his head in to say hello. Something in James's defenseless posture made him frown. He stepped into the small room and stared down at him. James's lean cheeks, with a day's growth of dark whiskers, were streaked with tears that in sleep had found release.

Anthony's eyes shifted to the letter in the major's hand. His frown deepened. He didn't have to see it to guess that it contained some word of Callahan's son. Shaking his head, he unfolded a blanket from the foot of the cot and laid it gently over James. Then he withdrew, to leave his friend to whatever healing that sleep might bring.

AFTER ANTHONY had reluctantly left her to return to the base, Maggie took a shower, changed into her uniform and headed over to the hospital to start her shift. It wasn't until much later that day, when the activity had calmed down a bit, that she opened her own mail.

Her father's letter began with assurances that he and her mother were well, as was Tad. Colonel Lawrence's continued efforts to get a combat assignment had so far been unsuccessful, but he intended to pursue it. He went on:

> In your last letter, you asked if I could find out anything about Sheila Kilpatrick. I've made inquiries, but all I've been able to come up with is that she is presumed to be interned in a camp near Manila. I'm sure I don't have to spell out for you how difficult it is to get information from such a place; suffice it to say that I believe she is still alive and as good as can be expected. Her fiancé, Charlie Fletcher, is still stationed on the *Nashville* somewhere in your area.

As she absorbed this information about her friend, Maggie's eyes continued down the page, only to stop abruptly as a wave of shock hit her.

I'm sorry to tell you that Rusty Osborne was killed in early May. He was on his way back to Australia when his plane was shot down. Our only consolation is that Rusty would have wanted to go like that, quickly and in the midst of a firefight.

It's getting late and I want to get this into to-day's mail, so I will close now. Take care of yourself, kitten. Remember that we love you and we want whatever makes you happy.

Dad

Maggie put the letter down slowly and stared off into space. Uncle Rusty dead? It didn't seem possible. He had always been so vividly alive, so full of energy and compassion.

Taking a shaky breath, she glanced around the neat rows of beds, finding some small degree of comfort in their familiarity. The men here were among the lucky ones; they were healing. So many others were dying in the jungles of New Guinea.

Each day now brought in more and more casualties; if they weren't suffering from shrapnel or other wounds, they were racked by fever, dysentery and jungle rot.

How many families had received the dreaded telegram from the War Department that began, "The Commander in Chief of the Armed Forces regrets to inform you that your..." Fill in the blank. Sons, husbands, even a few wives and daughters like herself were having their lives snuffed out almost before they'd truly begun.

She stood up and absently patted a stray hair back

into place under her neat white cap. After all the deaths she had seen, she ought to be more accustomed to the frailty of life. But somehow she wasn't. Some essential quality of humanity in her cried out against each and every destruction of what might have been.

Wearily, she shook her head. It had to stop someday. The insanity had to end and the world had to right itself. But when it did, what would it be like for those who were left? What would they go back to?

A faint smile tugged at her mouth as she considered that. What she wanted was all that was blessedly ordinary. A home; nothing fancy, just a place where there was peace and security. A husband who came home every evening and sat down to read the paper while she prepared dinner. Children; a boy and girl would be nice. With black eyes and—

Abruptly, she broke off her reverie. The man sitting on her imaginary couch reading his imaginary newspaper was most definitely Anthony. The children he smiled at indulgently were cast in his image. The dinner she was cooking even held a decided hint of oregano.

Maggie sighed and picked up a stack of files that needed updating. She had promised herself she wouldn't indulge in romantic fantasies. All they did was open the way to greater disappointments. Life was too precarious as it was without trying to build any castles in the air.

But later—when, as the song said, the lights went on again all over the world—what then? Home, family, blessed ordinariness? She wanted so badly to recapture it all that she ached inside with the need.

But it would mean little unless the man she wanted to share it with was also there.

ANTHONY LAUGHED when he read the note his father had slipped in with the letter from his mother. After a brief mention of the unhappy state of the tomatoes due to the late arrival of summer, Joseph had asked who Maggie was and said that, while love was a wonderful thing, it wasn't a good idea to rush into anything.

Anthony's grin widened. His father was a good one to talk about not rushing into anything. He seemed to remember that his parents had been married within a few months of meeting each other. It hadn't done them any harm; they were about the happiest people he knew.

He was thoughtful as he folded the letter and put it back in his pocket. Around him, his men were busy devouring their mail from home. Some read in groups, sharing certain passages. Others were off by themselves, needing privacy.

Looking them over, Anthony felt a great sense of satisfaction in the improvements achieved during the past few months. The veterans of Guadalcanal once again looked fit and ready for battle. Their principal complaint these days was that they didn't have enough to do, despite a rigorous training schedule.

As for the new recruits yet to be bloodied, they could barely restrain their eagerness. Strutting around Brisbane with pretty Aussie girls on their arms, they were the ones most likely to get into barroom fights and have to be bailed out of the

hoosegow. Anthony shook his head ruefully as he
thought of how soon they would lose their cockiness.

"Good news from home?" James Callahan asked as
he joined him near the gate to the Marine base. Both
men were waiting to go off duty. They planned on
spending an evening together with Maggie and Delia
before settling down to enjoy the weekend.

"You might say that. My pop's advising me not to
rush into anything."

James grinned wryly. "Funny thing to tell a
Marine. Aren't we always supposed to be storming
something?"

"I think he's got a different kind of combat in
mind."

"In that case, he's right."

"You think so?"

Piercing blue eyes glanced away from Anthony un-
comfortably. "Forget what I said. It's none of my
business."

"No sweat. You've got a right to an opinion."

"Yeah, but Maggie's a terrific woman. Even I can
see that."

Anthony was pleased. He liked the idea that she
was admired by a man he respected, and he knew
James well enough to be confident that the major
would never try any poaching. Glancing toward the
gate, he grinned. "Speaking of . . ."

Maggie and Delia were pulling up in the jeep they
had borrowed. With Maggie at the wheel and Delia
by her side, the contrast between the two women was
vividly apparent. Delia was all lush, ripe sensuality,
while Maggie was more subdued, more delicate. Yet
there was no mistaking the strength in her, Anthony

thought as he and James strolled toward them. For the long haul, he would pick Maggie any time.

"How you doing, hon?" he asked as she moved to the backseat and he joined her there. They exchanged a quick kiss.

"Fine, how about you?" Her bright smile could not quite mask the strain in her eyes. Just a half hour ago, a young pilot from the Army's Fifth Air Force had died on the table. She had stared down at him, thought of her brother, Tad, and come close to weeping.

Anthony studied her quietly for a moment, then put an arm around her shoulders and drew her close. He didn't need to be told what caused that look in her eyes. Even as he hurt inside for what she was going through, he set himself to comfort her. Half listening to Delia's gay chatter and James's amused replies, he nestled her head against his chest and stroked her hair gently.

They drove into Brisbane as the shift was changing in the dockyards. Maggie couldn't help but notice that the rate of activity seemed to be picking up. More ships were in port than ever before, bringing supplies and fresh replacements to augment the strength of the Allied forces. It didn't take any great military genius to see that something was in the works.

And if the pace of fighting on New Guinea was any indication, it wouldn't be much longer before the lid came off and the units being kept in reserve in Australia were thrown back into action.

Maggie couldn't bear to think about that. She closed her eyes and let the breeze thrown up by the jeep cool her flushed face. Beneath her cheek, she could feel the tensile strength in Anthony.

Some men had a look about them—vulnerability, sorrow, defeat—something that seemed to single them out for death. Anthony did not. He looked, acted and thought like a survivor.

But then so had Rusty Osborne and, in all likelihood, the young pilot she had watched die that day. No one could guess whom the capricious hand of fate would tap next.

She was still thinking about that several hours later when she said good night to James and Delia and headed for the bungalow with Anthony. Her need for him, and her fear of how vulnerable that made her, lent a heightened sense of poignancy to their lovemaking. Afterward, she slept exhausted in his arms, striving without success to hold off the dawn.

October 1943–June 1944
THE RAIN

Chapter Fourteen

THE TELEPHONE RINGING beside Delia's bed woke James in the middle of the sultry early-autumn night. He turned over reluctantly, disentangling himself from her arms, and groped past the mosquito nets for the receiver.

"What?" he grumbled.

"Major Callahan, sir?" a tentative voice inquired.

"Yeah, who's this?"

"Lieutenant Evans, sir. General Rupertus would like to see you in his office immediately."

Squinting in the darkness, James glanced at his wristwatch. He wasn't surprised by the summons; in fact, he'd been expecting it for days. The rush of adrenaline it prompted cleared his mind with alacrity.

"It's 0400, Lieutenant, and you've caught me with my pants off. I'll need half an hour."

"Fine, sir. I'll tell the general you're on the way."

"Who was that, honey?" Delia murmured, half-waking as James left the bed.

"Nothing. Go back to sleep."

"You're leaving?"

"Yeah. . .listen. . .I may be gone awhile." As he spoke, he pulled on his pants and reached for his shirt.

Sleep fell away from her. She sat up, her gleaming red hair tumbling around her bare breasts, and frowned. "Like that, is it?"

He shrugged lightly. "We both knew it would happen eventually." Stopping by the bed, he dropped a kiss on her lips. "I'll miss you, babe."

She twined an arm around his neck and drew him closer. This time their kiss was hard and fierce, but brief. When they broke apart, her voice shook slightly. "I'll miss you, too. Watch out for yourself."

"Sure." He buttoned his shirt, then sat down for a moment to lace up his boots. On his feet again, he reached into his back pocket, removed his wallet, and dropped a wad of bills on the dresser near the bed.

Delia raised her eyebrows. "It's just in case you need anything," he explained.

He picked up the small bag that held his shaving gear, flashed her a grin, and turned to leave. At the door he hesitated, throwing her a glance over his shoulder. She said nothing, but then she really didn't have to. With the sheet clasped around her, she waged a determined struggle for dignity he could not help but admire.

James strode back to the bed and stood staring down at her for a moment. The unshed tears gleaming in her green eyes made his throat tighten. He touched the back of her hand to his cheek in a gesture of great gentleness.

"Don't worry about me. I'll be okay."

Delia swallowed hard before trying to answer. "Yeah. . .me, too."

"Good. . ." He hesitated, wishing for something more, some reassurance he could not give her. Regretfully, he let his hand drop and turned away again. This time he did not look back.

For a long time after he was gone, Delia sat staring

at the screen door through which he had vanished
and listening to the sounds of the night.

IN THE DOCKYARDS, men were being routed out of
their bunks. Overhead lights were switched on.
Cranes swung into place to lift supplies onto waiting
ships. Shouted orders pierced the predawn quiet.

At the Marine base, all passes were being canceled
and everyone was put on full alert. Sergeants went
out with trucks to round up the noncoms who were
sleeping elsewhere. Corporals headed into the darkness to find their officers and alert them to what was
happening.

Two miles away, near the hospital, Anthony and
Maggie were asleep in her bungalow. They slept
naked with their arms around each other, sated by
their lovemaking.

Cicadas chirped outside the windows where gerani-
ums flowered. Maggie had planted them several
weeks before, on a day when Anthony was busy training with his men and she was left briefly on her own.
She didn't mind the times by herself, in part because
they were fairly rare but also because they gave her
the chance to fully appreciate all that they shared
together.

She stirred slightly in her sleep, her mouth curved
in a soft smile. They were both off duty tomorrow
and planned another visit to the beach. A vision of
sun-dappled sand and strong brown arms was interrupted by a sudden knock at the door.

She woke at once, accustomed as she was to sudden
summonses from the hospital. Several months before,
she had been appointed chief surgical nurse, and

whenever there was a particularly tough case, she was liable to be called.

But the young corporal who had knocked on the door was not looking for her. It was Anthony he wanted.

"Begging your pardon, ma'am," he murmured, unable to hide a faint blush. "Is the captain here?"

Resisting the impulse to smile, since she knew that would only heighten his embarrassment, she nodded. "Yes, just a moment." Her relationship with Anthony was hardly a secret, nor did she have any desire for it to be. Such alliances were commonplace among men and women living with the constant threat of war.

She turned back toward the bedroom, intending to wake him, but that proved unnecessary. Anthony was already on his feet. Wearing only a pair of slacks, he looked very large, very male and somewhat rumpled. But not at all sleepy. He rubbed a hand over his shadowed jaw and asked, "What's going on?"

"Message from Major Callahan, sir," the corporal said. "You're to report in at once."

Maggie's stomach clenched so painfully that it was all she could do not to gasp. She had known this was coming; the rumor mill had been predicting it for weeks. But that in no way made it easier to cope with.

"All right," Anthony said quietly. "I'll just be a few minutes."

The corporal nodded and went outside to wait in the jeep. When he was gone, Anthony drew her to him and stroked her head tenderly. "Hey, it's okay, sweetheart. You know we're just going on a little jungle training."

Maggie knew no such thing. She didn't believe for

a moment that the Marines were being dispatched to New Guinea simply so they could get some practice living in the jungle.

For more than a year, the combined U.S. and Australian forces had fought to drive the Japanese forces from that vital island. The enemy had responded with a tenacious ferocity that outstripped even its previous feats of military genius and fortitude. Every Allied victory had been extremely costly.

Though the Japanese had finally been neutralized on New Guinea, they remained a formidable presence elsewhere, especially on nearby New Britain. As long as that essential stepping-stone remained in enemy possession, MacArthur could not hope to fulfill his long-cherished dream of returning to the Philippines.

"I'll bet we're back here in time for Christmas," Anthony was saying. He leaned back a little way and gazed at her. "Should I write and tell Santa Claus what I want?"

"Don't bother," she murmured, managing a fragile smile. "I think I can guess."

He nodded and drew her into his arms again, his embrace tightening. They stood like that for several minutes, until the passing of time caught up with them. He stepped back reluctantly, his eyes never leaving hers.

"I have to get a few things together."

She nodded and headed for the bedroom. Without speaking, they selected what he would take. In the portion of her closet she had long since cleared for him, he left most of his uniforms and all his off-duty clothes. He packed some underwear, socks and his shaving gear in the bag, as well as a book Maggie had given him about the Marines in World War I and a photo of her he had taken on their favorite beach.

Maggie helped him zip up the case and went with him to the door. There they embraced again, silently. It was beginning to get light outside. They could make out the shape of the corporal sitting in the jeep, thoughtfully looking the other way.

"I love you," Anthony murmured. "Don't forget that."

"Never." Her voice cracked, and she had to take a deep breath before she said, "Be careful."

He nodded. "I will be, and I'll be back."

"I'll be waiting."

They shared a last kiss, passion supplanted by a yearning that went far beyond the flesh. He put her from him with great effort and picked up his bag.

Maggie watched him go down the path and get into the jeep. She raised a hand, but it trembled so much that she had to lower it at once.

Their gazes locked. His mouth was drawn in a hard, straight line, and she could see the restraint he was imposing on himself. There was no question in her mind that she could do no less.

She was still standing at the door, dry-eyed and composed, as he drove away. Just before the jeep turned a corner, he looked back, his last sight that of a slender, erect woman whose hauntingly beautiful face mirrored the pride and sorrow echoing within his own heart.

THE TROOPSHIP plying the route to New Guinea was cramped and stifling. Men moved around as best they could or simply stayed put, playing cards, sleeping, talking quietly among themselves. Lined up to eat at the slop chute, they swapped rumors and what little news filtered down to them.

Scuttlebutt and common sense both said that they would be using New Guinea as a jumping-off point to attack New Britain. On that island, one of the most awesome forces the Japanese had ever put together was located at the stronghold of Rabaul. It included vast munitions warehouses, four airfields and more than a hundred thousand troops. The soldiers, sailors and airmen of the Rising Sun knew the Allies were coming and they were confident that they could beat them.

Anthony didn't want to think the Japanese might be right. The Marines were only nineteen thousand strong, but they would be supported by the Fifth Air Force and various other Allied services. Odds of more than five to one weren't supposed to faze the leathernecks. They had a job to do and they would damn well see it done.

Nonetheless, Anthony slept little during the trip, preferring to move among his men to quiet speculation and keep them as steady as possible. This time around, most were veterans—a decided improvement over the situation he had faced at Guadalcanal. But even they were prone to the apprehension that was inevitable under such circumstances.

In the time they had been recuperating in Australia, other men had been fighting and dying to prepare the way for them. Yanks and Aussies alike had waged a savage campaign throughout the deadly jungle of New Guinea and over the spiny mountain ridge that bisected the island.

Only a few days before, the Seventh Australian Division, to which Jake Dylan belonged, had succeeded in capturing the last Japanese stronghold controlling the straits through which the Allies had to pass to reach New Britain.

Everything possible was being done to assure that the Marine assault would succeed, but in the final analysis the outcome would rest on the shoulders of the leathernecks.

"How long do you think we'll be here, sir?" a private asked Anthony as they disembarked. The day was hot and overcast, the landing craft rocked viciously, and the fetid smell of the jungle reached out to choke the troops even before they landed.

"Hard to say, kid," Anthony murmured as he surveyed their destination. It looked dismally similar to the jungles of Guadalcanal, only worse—something he wouldn't have thought possible. "With luck, not too long."

Amid the tangle of banyan and palm trees, strangling vines, giant ferns and slime stood what had been a sleepy native village. The war had transformed it into an Allied command center. Concrete bunkers vied for space with Quonset huts and tents put up to provide at least minimal shelter from the bugs, heat and rain.

Anthony had heard about the rain, but that wasn't the same as being prepared for it. The brief lull in the weather didn't last much longer than it took them to disembark. Barely had they begun to settle in when the skies opened up and a torrent of water descended on them.

By the time they'd unloaded all the equipment and

found their billets, they were soaked through to the skin. Their ponchos had proved to be scant protection. The rain seeped right through, turning them into heavy, sodden masses that weighed the men down. The ground—if a sea of mud could be called that—oozed and bubbled beneath their boots, finding its way through every crack.

The rain was so heavy that visibility was limited to a few yards. Saturated with moisture, bugs and the stench of rotting vegetation, the air was all but unbreathable.

Men who a short time before had been looking relatively confident began to have second thoughts. All the stories they had heard about the green hell were apparently true. It had come perilously close to defeating the best that the Aussies and Americans could throw at it. Now it was their turn.

"When I get back to the States," James said as he and Anthony hunkered down in the officers' tent that night, "I think maybe I'll move to the desert."

"Sounds good to me. Arizona...maybe New Mexico. Sand, beautiful sand."

"I don't know what those guys in North Africa were complaining about. What could be worse than this?"

Jake Dylan took a slug from the bottle they were passing around and grunted. "Bloody awful, it's been. Let me tell you, mates, you're going to have your work cut out for you over on New Britain."

"So we hear," Anthony said. "The sooner we hit the beach there, the better." When his Aussie friend had dropped by to visit shortly after their arrival, Anthony had hardly recognized him. Jake was about thirty pounds leaner than when they'd last seen each other. His face was gaunt, his eyes were bleak, and his body was racked by the familiar tremors of malaria.

Yet compared with many of the other veterans of New Guinea, he was in relatively good shape. Certainly his condition was not being allowed to get in the way of his drinking.

"Good stuff, this," he commented appreciatively as he passed the bottle of twelve-year old whiskey.

"Thanks," James said after a swallow. "A guy I know in the Navy keeps a stockpile. It's expensive, but worth it."

"Better than what they've got back in the States," Anthony commented. "Dom said they've had a whiskey drought there since last fall." His brother had returned to Australia a few weeks before, full of stories about the home front. He was somewhere nearby in one of the hundreds of tents, probably also sharing a bottle with his buddies. For the immediate future, there wasn't much else to do.

James grunted unsympathetically. "Too damn bad. They've got it easy enough as it is."

"Ain't it the truth," James muttered. "Civilians, they're the same everywhere."

Anthony grinned and lifted the bottle. "Here's to 'em, and to the day we rejoin their ranks."

"Amen," his friends murmured. They were silent for several minutes, listening to the rain falling heavily through the palm leaves.

"I hear the fly-boys have been doing a good job over here," James said.

"That's true," Jake admitted. Like most foot soldiers, he didn't have much use for any air force, but this time around, it did seem to be doing some good.

"They'll be needing a new base if they're going to hit Rabaul really hard before you chaps go in."

"My guess is Halsey will take Bougainville," James said, naming the last of the islands in the Solomons chain whose capture would put their flyers within easy reach of the Japanese citadel.

"I wonder if the Fifth Air Force will be transferred there," Anthony speculated. "Maggie's brother, Tad, is with them."

"Who's Maggie?" Jake asked.

"She's, uh, a friend of mine."

James laughed. "To quote the lovely Delia, 'a *good* friend.'"

Anthony flushed slightly, wringing a hoarse chuckle from Jake. "Ain't love wonderful? A man can survive the worst on God's green earth and then willingly put his head in a noose, all because a pretty young thing wiggles her arse at him."

"It's not like that," Anthony protested. "Maggie's. . . special."

Jake gave him a gently tolerant look. "Lord, you really do have it bad. When's the great day?"

"Gimme a break. We've never even talked about marriage."

"Take it from me," James said, "there's never much talking. You just wake up one day and find yourself shackled."

"That's how it was with my ex," Jake recalled. "I never did figure out how she got me to the altar, but once she did, I was done for. Until she traded me in for a colonel."

"Did you mind?" Anthony asked, not really wanting to pry, but still curious. The truth was, ever since he began to think seriously about marriage, he wondered what other people thought of it. Apparently not much, at least as far as his buddies went.

"Hell, no," the Aussie said. "I could have kissed the guy, except he really wasn't my type. She went through him in about a year, and last thing I heard, had worked her way up to a major general."

"You were lucky," James said. "Between paying alimony and worrying about my kid, I swear I'd hire somebody to take my ex-wife off my hands. It'd be cheap at any price."

Anthony frowned and shook his head. "I don't know about all this. Some people must have good marriages."

"Our parents had the last of 'em," James claimed. "Back when they were getting hitched, you knew where you stood. There were rules, and people more or less followed them. That's all over with now." He sighed. "It was the Depression what did it. Threw everything out the window."

"But the Depression's over," Anthony said. "And the war will end eventually. I've got a feeling that someday our kids won't have the slightest idea what it was all about. They'll think they're the first ones to have any doubts."

"God love the little buggers." Jake laughed. "They'll have to live in this world we're making, however it turns out."

"I wonder about that sometimes," James admitted a bit blearily. They had started drinking on empty stomachs and were near the bottom of the bottle. He was beginning to feel it a little. "My son, Matthew, is going on four. I'd like to give him something better than what I've managed so far."

Was there a more fundamentally human wish? Anthony wondered as they finished off the whiskey in silence. Greater even than the desire for personal survival was the need to build for the next generation.

He had seen it with his own parents as they struggled to overcome poverty and prejudice in order to give their children a better life. Lately he had felt it in himself; a faint yet growing need to perpetuate himself, not just physically, but also in the fullest spiritual sense. He wanted to sire a child and to father it. And he wanted the child's mother to be a very special woman. Maggie.

Lying back on his cot, he shut his eyes tiredly. Soon he would be in battle again. Death could reach out for him at any moment. If he let himself think about how truly precious life had become to him, he might hesitate at some crucial instant. A split-second slowness in reflexes could make the difference between survival and death. Paradoxically, it was those who put aside thoughts of their own safety and immersed themselves in the tide of battle who tended to survive.

For Maggie, and for the child or children they might someday have, he could not allow his desperate desire to live distract him once he stood again on the killing ground.

SEATED AT THE SMALL TABLE in the front room of the bungalow, Maggie began her weekly letter to her parents.

Dear Mom and Dad,

It's relatively quiet here at the hospital. The calm before the storm, I suspect. With luck, this letter will reach you by Christmas. I hope it finds you both well.

Anthony has been on New Guinea several weeks now. He writes that he's fine. Considering how strong and determined he is, perhaps it's true. The capture of Bougainville was a great morale booster. I understand Tad may be based there now. It's hard to tell for sure, since security is so tight, but the letter I got from him a few days ago indicated that he's okay.

There's a strong feeling here that the "big push" is really getting under way. It seems as though we've been waiting so long—almost two years since Pearl Harbor, eighteen months since Corregidor—but at last it's beginning.

Lately, I can't even remember what peace feels like. When we get back, we'll have to start creating it all over again. I wonder how good a job we'll do.

Please excuse any note of depression in the last paragraph. Probably the best thing I can do is get off to bed. I'll write again soon. In the meantime, my love to you both.

ELIZABETH LAWRENCE STARED pensively out the living-room window. A sparrow was feeding nearby where she had cleared a patch of snow and put down crumbs. The panes of glass reflected his small, bobbing head, as well as the glittering Christmas tree behind her.

They hadn't really planned to put up the tree this

year, but Will had finally received his long-awaited combat assignment, so they'd decided to celebrate the holiday in style. Immediately after the new year, he would be heading for the Pacific.

It was going to be very quiet in the house. She would have to make a special effort to keep herself busy. The Red Cross received most of her attention these days, and she intended to increase her work there.

Particularly because of how little time they had left together, Will had been very apologetic about having to be at the office all day. The fact that it was Christmas Eve made no difference to the war effort, not when something major was in the works.

That it was, she could not doubt. Maggie had mentioned a "big push" in her most recent letter. Elizabeth suspected that it might be getting under way at that very moment.

The sparrow pecked up a few more crumbs and flew off. Elizabeth remained at the window, thinking about her son and daughter and wondering what each was doing. Eventually the light faded, her thoughts became unbearable, and she went up to bed.

JOSEPH AND MARIA GARGANO WENT to midnight mass at St. Ignatius Church with Vita and her children, then walked home, pausing along the way to chat with neighbors. It was a cloudy night with a hint of snow in the air, but not too cold. At the corner, right before they got to their house, they paused at an all-night newsstand to pick up a paper.

Once back in the living room, with a fire going and

the tree lit, they put a record on the Victrola and sat down to open their presents while sipping mulled wine and nibbling on almond cookies.

When they had heard Bing Crosby sing "White Christmas" for the fourth time, Joseph announced he was turning in. Maria followed a short time later, after helping her daughter settle the children for the night and checking to make sure that the key was under the mat for Sophia, who had opted to spend Christmas at the USO with the boys far from home.

The neighborhood traditionally slept late on Christmas, people not stirring until the afternoon, when it was time to start the festive dinner. Joseph was in bed reading the *Times* when Maria joined him.

"So what's new today?" she asked as she carefully removed her black wool dress and hung it up.

"The president named General Eisenhower to head the invasion of Europe. Seems like a good choice."

"Is there a picture of him?"

"Right here on the front page."

Maria glanced at it as she rolled down her stockings. "He has a nice face."

"Looks okay to me. You see where our planes hit Berlin?"

"They should bomb Mr. Hitler to hell and back. Is there anything about Italy?"

"Let me see. . . Yeah, here, they're still trying to take Ortona. It says they found a German cemetery nearby with at least a hundred new graves."

She shook her head sadly. "I know this isn't a popular thing to say, but I feel for those boys' families."

Joseph raised an eyebrow. "Have you forgotten who started this mess?"

"Politicians started it. Hitler, Mussolini, Tojo— little men with evil dreams."

"They wouldn't have gotten very far if people hadn't supported them."

They had argued about the same subject before, with Maria always contending that the ordinary people in the Axis countries had never had any real sense of freedom. They automatically followed a strong leader who told them what they wanted to hear. After the war, it would be up to the Allies to change that.

Joseph was less tolerant. He believed that all people were responsible for their own actions no matter what their background was. If they took part in aggression against others, they had to pay the price.

Yet even he admitted that the women, children and old people in the enemy nations really had very little to do with the conflict, but were likely in the end to suffer the most from it.

Maria didn't want to think about such things right then. The mass she had just attended gave her a lingering sense of serenity she hoped to preserve as long as possible.

She turned away to remove the rest of her garments and slip into a nightgown. When she glanced back at her husband, he was unabashedly regarding her with a gleam in his ebony eyes she had no trouble interpreting.

Maria shot him a chiding look. "Joseph Gargano, have you forgotten it's a holy day?"

"Of course not. I went to mass, didn't I?" He smiled innocently. "What more do you want?"

"Well. . ." She hesitated before climbing into the high four-poster bed in which all six of their children had been conceived. "You really don't have anything else on your mind?"

"A man my age? I'm flattered." Under the covers, his hand gently stroked her thigh. She met his gaze and laughed. They turned to each other lovingly.

A while later, just before he fell asleep, Joseph glanced at the clock. It was getting on to early morning in Brooklyn. In the Pacific, where Anthony and Dom were, Christmas Eve would just be giving way to Christmas Day.

He closed his eyes, wondering what his sons were doing. Several possibilities occurred to him. He picked the least unattractive and imagined them sitting in some quiet place, listening to Christmas music and thinking about the peace the new year might bring.

As it happened, Joseph was almost right about that. But not in any way he would have wished.

Chapter Fifteen

PEACE WAS THE FURTHEST THING from Anthony's mind as he listened to the strains of "Silent Night" falter and die away. Somebody had gotten the idea that Christmas carols would cheer the men up. They hadn't. There was no room on the transports for thoughts of anything but the coming battle.

It was not yet dawn on Christmas morning. They were moving in a convoy, their destination a beach six miles east of Cape Gloucester on the northwestern tip of New Britain island.

The Japanese knew they were coming. Radio Tokyo had announced that the jungles would run red with the blood of the butchers of Guadalcanal. When Anthony heard that, he'd merely shrugged. It was all a matter of perspective. The Marines were making similar promises.

Christmas Day passed quietly. The weather was decent, the sea not too rough, and the mood of the men relatively optimistic.

Coast watchers on New Britain, left behind to keep an eye on things when the Japanese took over, were reporting that the enemy wasn't in such good shape. Apparently even its forces were not immune to the destructive effects of the green hell. Malaria was rampant, along with dysentery, jungle rot and a few other diseases for which nobody had yet come up with a name.

To add to these problems, General Matsuda, the Japanese commander, didn't exactly see himself as one of the boys. He was hidden away in a well-concealed headquarters from which he planned to "lead" the battle in relative safety.

The brass wasn't all that different from one side to the other, Anthony thought as he whiled away the time studying his maps and rechecking equipment. The maps worried him a little. He remembered the experience on Guadalcanal, when they had turned out to be so inaccurate, and wondered if these were any better.

"What's this 'damp flat' shown here, sir?" one of his lieutenants asked, pointing to a broad region immediately adjacent to the beach where they would be landing.

"Some kind of marsh maybe," Anthony speculated.

"I guess if it were really bad, we'd know by now," the lieutenant said, thereby revealing a touching degree of faith that under other circumstances might have amused his captain.

As it was, Anthony merely shrugged. "We'll find out soon enough." Privately, he recalled that the area they were going into was reported to be only lightly defended, and he wondered if there might not be a good reason for that.

A few hours later, in the predawn light of the day after Christmas, he found out that the mapmakers were batting a thousand. Their "damp flat" was a cross between a pestilent swamp and an open sewer.

The first men ashore fell into sinkholes as high as their armpits. Casualties were taken not from enemy snipers but from huge banyan and coconut trees whose hold on the water-soaked soil was weakened by the preassault bombardment. Toppling to the ground without warning, they crushed men beneath them.

Anthony gritted his teeth, cursed under his breath, and urged his men on. It was the toughest going he had ever encountered. Equipment he could have sworn would work malfunctioned in the intense humidity and dampness. Flamethrowers failed. Amtracs became stuck in the mud, making them easy targets for snipers. Bazookas were useless, their rockets colliding harmlessly with the spongy earth heaped up around the Japanese bunkers.

About the only things that worked properly were their trusty Browning automatics and their grenades, which they made heavy use of. Finally, after much effort, the Marines were able to secure their perimeter.

Back down on the ribbon-wide strip of marshy sand laughably called a beach, Dom was helping to unload supplies. At least this part of the invasion worked better than it had at the Canal. The first items off the boats were the most vital: food, drinkable water, ammunition.

In midafternoon, Anthony ordered his men to dig in. They had gone as far as they could that day. Out over the Bismarck Sea, the sky was turning gray. The trunks of palm trees bent in the ever-increasing wind.

An uneasy feeling ran down Anthony's spine. Once, years before, he had been in a hurricane in China. This was beginning to look like more of the same. Telling himself he was just tired and hungry, he ate his way through a can of K rations and managed to catch a nap. But his rest didn't last long.

Barely had the sun set when the wind increased even more. Sticking his head out of his foxhole, he had to hold on to his helmet to keep it from being blown away. Silently cursing the meteorologists who, as far as he knew, had failed to predict this turn in the weather, he shouted to his men to hold their positions and hunkered down.

Staying put proved more difficult than any of them could have imagined. The wind drove waves up across the shore clear to their positions. Cold, salt-laden water sloshed into the foxholes, all but drowning many of the men. Before dawn there wasn't a single leatherneck who wasn't soaked, shivering and damn mad. Their only consolation was that not even the Japanese could counterattack under such conditions. They were at least as badly off as the Marines.

With the first light, James Callahan showed up, wearing mud-encrusted utilities and a few days' growth of beard. He carried a Browning automatic and had a pistol tucked in his belt. A couple of lieutenants slogged ahead of him, looking as though they would rather have stayed where they were.

"Hell of a place," James muttered as he and Anthony shared a tepid pot of coffee in the water-logged foxhole. To complicate matters further, it had started to rain again. James pulled his poncho closer and shook his head. "It's even worse than your pal Jake said it would be."

"Jake's an eternal optimist," Anthony muttered, spitting out a mouthful of grounds. "How's it going?"

"Not too bad. The Fifty-third Infantry ran into a problem last night—took a banzai attack and lost some good men. They hit the Japs back hard, but I

don't expect them to make any progress until our
tanks reach them, and right now the tanks are bogged
down in this friggin' mud."

"What about Target Hill?" Anthony asked, naming
an objective he knew they had to secure if the invasion
was to have a hope of succeeding.

"It's ours. The Japs tried to take it back, but we
threw them off."

"So we go on to the airfield."

"That's right, old buddy. You ought to be a pro at
that by now."

"Sure," Anthony muttered. "It'll be a piece of cake."

If the Japanese had needed any lesson about the im-
portance of holding on to landing strips, they had gotten it on Guadalcanal. They weren't about to make
the same mistake twice.

Twelve concrete bunkers ringed the airport. By the
time Anthony, his men and the other Marines chosen
for the mission approached, the tanks had worked
their way out of the mud and — with a little help from
the miracle-working Seabees, who spun roads as a
spider spun webs — were back in commission.

So far so good. What followed seemed almost routine. The tanks fired, the bunkers blew up, and the infantry went after those of the enemy who tried to escape, mowing them down remorselessly. Anthony
took it as a sign of his own sad state when he found the
sight of a Japanese soldier trapped in a trench only
mildly disconcerting.

The man was buried up to his neck and unable to
move, either to flee or to kill himself as honor demanded. He had to watch helplessly as the Americans
dug him out.

Whatever he was expecting then, it wasn't the rations and cigarette he was offered. While he was just beginning to take in the fact that he was going to live, a civilian interpreter fluent in both English and Japanese came slogging along. The prisoner obligingly told him everything he knew about General Matsuda's deployments.

Anthony was flabbergasted when he realized what was going on. Over the past year or so he had developed a grudging but nonetheless powerful admiration for the enemy. The idea that one of them would give away information so freely struck him as preposterous, until the interpreter explained the situation.

"He was never told what to do if captured. It was always just presumed that he'd do the right thing and go out in glory. Nobody ever said, 'If the Yanks get you, don't talk.' So he talked. Hell, he figured he didn't know anything worthwhile, anyway."

"He was wrong, though, wasn't he?" Anthony asked.

"Yeah." The interpreter glanced back at the Japanese man, who still looked barely able to believe his luck. "Poor bastard, he was wrong about a lot of things."

Maybe so, but he was also alive and headed for the relative safety of captivity. Chances were he would survive the war, whereas the rest of them had no such guarantees.

Anthony smothered a sigh and gave the signal to his men to move out. By the following day, they and the other Americans had successfully surrounded and taken the airport. The news was radioed back to New Guinea as a belated Christmas present.

MAGGIE HEARD of it as she was coming out of surgery, after helping to patch up the lung of a private who had been among the first to be wounded on New Britain.

Lucy Jacobs, the little red-haired nurse, hurried up to tell her the news. "There's an updated casualty list posted, Captain," she added. "I've checked it already, and Captain Gargano's name isn't there."

Maggie nodded, hoping that her face wasn't revealing too much. It was fine that her nurses knew how concerned she was; it wouldn't do to let them see her fear.

"Thanks," she murmured. "Is the list very long?"

Lucy's smile faded. "I'm afraid so. Our boys are taking a real beating." On a brighter note, she added, "But they're giving more than their own back."

Maggie went off to change into her regulation whites, then returned to the ward. She stopped on the way to take a quick look at the list herself, noting as she did so that, while it did run to too many pages, Dom's name wasn't there, either.

So far so good. But she had no illusions that such luck would necessarily hold. For many men, it had already run out.

The ward was more crowded now than it had been in a while. It was also quieter. Anyone strong enough to sit up and talk, let alone move around, had been transferred elsewhere. The ones who remained were the gravely wounded recovering from surgery. And they already took up almost every bed.

A few moaned fitfully, but most lay silent and grim-faced, reliving the hell they had survived and wondering what was ahead for them. For some, the answer was obvious. Missing limbs and blinded eyes meant a lifetime of disability.

The fate of others was not so clear. As Maggie moved up and down the rows of beds, she saw men whose blank, inward-looking gaze suggested that it would be a long time before they could cope with the world again, if they ever did.

Against one wall of the ward stood a rather forlorn Christmas tree. Maggie and her nurses had put it up and decorated it, then gathered around to sing carols to the men on Christmas Eve. They had done that, knowing the invasion of New Britain was about to be launched. The songs of joy and exaltation had held some comfort, but not much.

Sighing, she returned to her desk and put on the soft cardigan sweater that was a gift from her parents. The ward wasn't the least bit cold, but she was shivering nonetheless. A recent inability to eat or sleep probably had something to do with it.

She missed Anthony terribly. His absence was bad enough by itself, but combined with her fear for his safety, it was all but intolerable. Looking at herself in the mirror at night, she saw a woman whose haunted expression made her seem far older than her years.

Only on duty did she continue to function smoothly; at all other times her nerves were strained to the breaking point. Tiredly, she admitted to herself that something would have to give soon, or else she was liable to.

ANTHONY FINISHED the letter he was writing to the parents of a dead Marine in his command. He read it over once, then signed it and gave it to a corporal to be mailed. Of all the duties he performed, he considered what he had just done to be the toughest.

Platitudes wouldn't do, but neither would too much truth. He always wrote that the dead man had served with distinction and been well liked and admired by his buddies; with very rare exceptions, this was invariably the case. But he never hinted at the full horror the son or husband had endured, nor did he ever suggest that death might not have been instantaneous and painless.

The recent lull in the fighting gave him an opportunity to take care of such chores, but it also left him needing a distraction.

Wandering over to the other side of the base where Dom was housed, he found his brother stretched out in a hammock with a baseball cap over his eyes and a can of beer in his hand.

Surveying the scene, Anthony shook his head ruefully. Not exactly the popular image of a Marine at the front—but he was glad to see that nothing seemed to faze Dom. He had been through some tough fighting lately, but this time he had managed to emerge unscathed.

Pushing back the cap, his brother opened one eye and glanced at him. "How you doin', Tonio?"

"Okay. Got another beer?"

"Sure." Swinging his legs over the side of the hammock, Dom rooted around in a pool of stagnant water and pulled out a can of Japanese beer, taken from

General Matsuda's former headquarters after the enemy brass had withdrawn.

Anthony cracked it open and took a long, appreciative sip as he sat down next to his brother. "Not bad."

Dom shrugged. "Schlitz has nothin' to worry about."

A scrawny dog, a canine deserted from the other side, sniffed at Anthony's boots. He petted him absently as he said, "Bet the beer in Germany is good."

"Maybe Sal will get a chance to try it soon."

The brothers looked at each other and grinned. "Poor guy, he's really in the thick of it," Anthony grunted.

"From North Africa to Italy. He sure can pick 'em."

"Should have come out here, where it's nice and peaceful."

"I was thinking about that." Dom put down his beer long enough to open a can of K rations and feed it to the dog. "We've about wrapped it up here, haven't we?"

"Seems that way to me. The Japs who are still alive are doing their damnedest to get the hell off this island."

"They're heading into Rabaul?"

Anthony shrugged and took another swallow of beer. "Guess so. It's their biggest fortress in this area."

"So how come we aren't doing anything to take it?"

That was a pretty good question, Anthony thought. He'd been wondering the same thing himself for some time, and he just might have come up with an answer.

"I was looking at a map the other day," he said, "and I noticed something. We've got Rabaul surrounded; there's no way for the Japs to resupply it. The Fifth Air Force is using the field here to bomb the hell out of that place. So why should we bother to take it?"

Dom shot him a startled look. "Why? Because it's gotta be taken before we can go on to the Philippines."

His brother shook his head. "No, it's gotta be neutralized, that's all." With commendable understatement, he added, "You know I'm not exactly a big MacArthur fan, but I've got to give the guy credit. If that is what he's up to, he's pulled off a real fast one. The Japs must be going nuts."

Dom considered the idea as he finished his beer, then whistled softly. "Jeez, those poor bastards. They must be sitting over there waiting to die for their emperor and wondering when the hell we're coming."

"Yep...only we aren't. Not if we take an end run around them."

"If you're right...what do you think will happen next?"

Anthony shrugged. He was scheduled for a staff meeting with James in half an hour and had to get going. Standing up, he said, "My guess is we won't be here much longer. They'll move us back to New Guinea."

Dom rolled his eyes and settled back in the hammock. "Great. I can only think of about a million other places where I'd rather be."

Anthony laughed and headed off toward the headquarters tent. He, too, had no desire to return to New Guinea. Australia would have been a lot better.

He thought of Maggie there alone and felt the familiar sense of yearning well up in him. It would be so good to see her again, let alone touch her. Their reunion couldn't come soon enough.

IN HER BUNGALOW near the hospital, Maggie was thinking the same thing as she pulled clothes from her closet and bureau and hurriedly packed. The transfer she had requested to Port Moresby had at last come through just hours earlier.

Among the items she put in her duffel bag was the packet of letters from her folks and Tad. Her father had written recently from Pearl Harbor. He was on his way through there to his new assignment. For security reasons, he said nothing of its exact nature, but she had heard through the grapevine that he was to act as a liaison officer between General MacArthur and Admiral Nimitz.

Tad had also written recently, his letter sounding an unusually somber note. He'd seemed tired and depressed, not at all his cheerful self.

One of Maggie's patients currently in the ward was a young fighter pilot who'd been shot down over New Britain. He knew Tad and had told her a great deal about her brother's outstanding record.

"Tad's an ace—a real hotshot flyer," the pilot had said. "The Japs are on the lookout for him all the time, but he always outsmarts them."

She was very proud of him, of course, but she was also very concerned. With luck, she might be able to see him soon and decide for herself how he was really doing.

Lucy, Jane and Carrie—the three nurses who had turned out to be the core of her staff—had requested transfers along with her. They made the trip over with her on the same ship and arrived eager to see their new home.

"Would you look at this place?" Carrie murmured as they stood on the dock. "I thought it was supposed to be a hellhole, but it doesn't seem bad at all."

In fact, it didn't. After all the stories they had heard about the green hell, New Guinea appeared surprisingly benign. From where they stood, they could make out beaches of black and blue-green sand framed by lush hills. On closer inspection, Port Morseby itself looked neat and orderly, as did the field hospital to which they were assigned.

The recently constructed frame building boasted a tin roof and screen wire sides, with head-high paper partitions separating the interior into single rooms. Raised off the marshy ground on stilts, the plank floor admitted light through its many cracks and knotholes.

The nurses' accommodations were quite comfortable, given the circumstances. Besides canvas cots, there were two empty ammunition crates pressed into service as bedside tables, an ample supply of mosquito nets and even a woven rush rug for the floor.

It might not be a palace, but it was considerably better than any of them had expected.

"I get the feeling the men here have gone to a lot of trouble for us," Maggie remarked.

"Who's more deserving?" Jane teased in a rare burst of humor. Maggie laughed and finished putting her belongings away in the wood-and-paper wardrobe.

"A regular home away from home," the nurses agreed as they took a quick tour of the facilities and settled down to work.

Duty was relatively light, thanks to MacArthur's decision not to take Rabaul. Maggie had always had mixed feelings about the general, but when she heard how brilliantly he had avoided the need to shed more American—and for that matter, Japanese—blood, her opinion of him rose considerably.

With so few new casualties coming in, she had ample opportunity to explore her surroundings. Quickly she discovered that there was excellent swimming to be had from a beach near the hospital and began working on a tan to mask the yellowing effects of the Atabrine she swallowed daily to prevent malaria.

Actually, little discoloration showed outside the jungle uniform she wore, which consisted of a high-necked blouse with long sleeves, a pair of slacks and high boots. The outfit was intended to keep the ubiquitous mosquitoes at bay. Not even regular spraying with the new "miracle" pesticide, DDT, could hold them off entirely.

Some of the orderlies had started a small garden near the hospital, and for the first time in years Maggie found herself pulling up weeds and hoeing around neat patches of beans, lettuce and melons. Most of the rest of the food was canned or dehydrated, but still good. Perhaps because she knew she was closer to Anthony, she began eating more and gradually gained a few pounds that suited her.

She was just heading toward the mess hall early one afternoon when the sight of several nurses standing around in a circle and chatting with a tall young man brought her up short. With so many men vying for the attention of the few women on the island, it was rare indeed to see any one of them receive special notice. But the rugged, blond airman with the cocky grin was definitely getting more than his share. He was—

She stopped in midstep, her mouth dropping open. It couldn't be! *Tad?* Had the skinny, shy brother she'd left behind in Virginia four years ago turned into this gorgeous blond giant with the rippling muscles and virile stance?

"T-Tad. . .?"

At the sound of her voice, he turned, glancing around as though he wasn't sure who had spoken his name. His startled gaze brushed past her, only to return rapidly as he realized who she was.

"Maggie!" A broad grin split his face. Sprinting across the compound, he scooped her up in his arms and hugged her so tightly that her ribs threatened to crack.

Not that she minded. Oblivious to anything except the sheer joy of his presence, she hugged him back, laughing and crying at the same time.

"Oh, Tad, it really is you! My Lord, how you've changed! You're all. . ." She managed to draw away from him a little and gazed at him ruefully. "You're all grown up!"

His white teeth gleamed against burnished skin as he laughed. "I can say the same about you, Sis. Boy, are you ever a sight for sore eyes!"

"Thanks—I think! Where did you come from? Are you staying long? Can we have dinner together? I've got so much to tell you and I want to hear everything about what you've been doing."

"Whoa, one at a time!" Ticking her questions off one by one on his fingers, he said, "Cape Gloucester; I'm flying out of there now. Don't know for sure. And I should hope so."

"Great! Come on, I'll introduce you to everyone." Grinning, she added silently, *Or they'll never forgive me.*

Her nurses made no secret of the fact that they were delighted to meet Tad. They clustered around him as he and Maggie started through the chow line, dumped their mess kits in boiling water and shook them dry. Then the group went on to help themselves to plentiful portions of dehydrated potatoes, dried peaches, pork chops and fresh peas, washed down by reconstituted lemonade.

Sharing a table with his sister and the nurses, Tad was plied with questions and smiles until Maggie almost choked on her own laughter. She was seeing her brother for the first time in a completely new role, as a strong, desirable man. And, she had to admit, she liked what she saw. Tad had developed into a very special person. To know that they shared a common bond made her very proud.

After the meal, the nurses exercised great restraint and withdrew to give them some time alone. She and Tad sat up late, talking about their experiences of the past few years. Each realized the other was giving a somewhat truncated account, but it was still good to exchange thoughts and feelings.

Tad walked her back to the nurses' quarters a little after ten o'clock. His arm was wrapped around her waist, and her head rested on his shoulder. They were still talking and laughing quietly.

Neither noticed the man watching them until he stepped out of the shadows, his big hands clenched into fists and a very angry glare in his ebony eyes.

Chapter Sixteen

TAD SIZED UP the situation with a single glance. He dropped his arm from around Maggie's waist and took a quick step forward, holding out his hand.

"Hi, you must be Anthony. My sister's just been telling me all about you. I'm Tad Lawrence."

Sister? Anthony's frown deepened. A dull flush crept over his lean, shadowed cheeks. The resemblance between the two was slight, but still evident enough once he took the trouble to notice it.

He felt like a damn fool. For a second there, he'd been willing to commit mayhem, and both he and Tad knew it. Uncoiling his fists, he offered a hand to Maggie's brother. They shook while candidly assessing each other.

Anthony took note of the quiet strength in the young pilot, the eyes that were so much like Maggie's, and the decisiveness with which he had moved to protect her. The man he had thought was a fly-boy bozo trying to double-time him turned out to be okay after all.

Tad thought the Marine captain looked pretty damn tough, but there was nothing wrong with that. The times called for tough men. Besides, his sister would never have gone for a marshmallow.

While the silent exchange went on between the two men, Maggie stood frozen in place. The shock of seeing Anthony, and the simultaneous realization of how angry he was, momentarily numbed her. Seconds passed before she was able to respond.

Without a word, heedless of Tad's presence, she went to him. He hesitated an instant, clearly thinking that she might be angry at him; then he saw the glowing light of love in her eyes and knew it was all right.

His arms closed around her tightly, nestling her against the hard strength of his body. Ever since he'd learned from a buddy who had seen her that she was on the island, he had thought of nothing but this moment. It had kept him going through the grinding clean-up operation on New Britain during which the remaining Japanese had to be hunted down in bunkers and trenches. They had refused to surrender, preferring death to what they regarded as dishonor.

A low sigh of infinite relief escaped Anthony as he put all that from his mind. Breathing in the familiar scent of her — Ivory soap and violet-scented cologne, sun-warmed skin and pure, lovely woman — he murmured, "Maggie. . . I've missed you so much."

"Me, too," she whispered into his grimy shirt. The heavy growth of whiskers on his firm jaw, the shadows beneath his eyes, and the mud-stained condition of his utilities indicated that he had come straight from the front. He smelled of sweat, insect repellent and cordite. His beard scratched her tender skin, and the fierceness of his embrace hurt a little.

But none of that mattered in the least. He might have stepped pristine from the pages of *Gentleman's Quarterly* for all she cared. No sight, no touch could possibly have been more welcome. Shakily, she said, "I — it's been so long."

It hadn't been really, as such things went in war-time. But being so close, relatively, without being able to see each other had put a severe strain on them both. They desperately needed to be assured that the other was alive and well.

For long moments they were oblivious to anything except themselves, until Tad coughed discreetly. At their abashed looks, he grinned. "I've got to be going. Maggie, take care of yourself. I'll be in touch again soon."

Shaking hands once more with Anthony, he looked him directly in the eye as he said, "Nice to meet you, Captain. I hope we'll be seeing each other again."

Their gazes met and held in silent communication. Tad didn't shirk from the question he was implicitly asking; as a brother and the only Lawrence male on the scene, he figured he had the right to look after Maggie.

For his part, Anthony had no qualms about the commitment he knew himself to be making. Maggie was his life; it was that simple and that final. Steadily, he replied, "I'm sure we will be."

After a long moment, Tad nodded. "I'll be going, then." He hugged his sister and grinned at Anthony. "Maybe with you here, she won't be so inclined to get out of line."

Her affronted groan made both men laugh. "I'll do my best," Anthony promised. He and Maggie waved to Tad as he hopped in the jeep he had commandeered earlier that day and headed back to the airstrip for the quick flight to Cape Gloucester.

"It's great that you got to see him," Anthony said when they were alone.

Maggie pulled a tissue out of her pocket and blew her nose. "He's grown up so much."

A tender smile lit Anthony's eyes. He knew exactly what she meant; he had the same reaction to Dom these days. Drawing her back into his arms, he murmured, "Hey, it's okay. He looks like an all-right guy. I'll bet he knows all about watching out for himself."

"I hope so. He takes such terrible chances."

"You mean 'cause he's a pilot?"

"Not just that. He's an ace. The Japs know his name and everything. They're gunning for him now every time he flies."

Anthony frowned into the gathering darkness, thinking of the young man who had just left them. "Did he tell you that?"

"No, he wouldn't. I heard it from another pilot in his squadron, back at the hospital in Brisbane."

Anthony sighed, wishing he could tell her the other guy was exaggerating. In fact, he knew that wasn't likely to be the case. "Look," he said at length, "Tad's made it this far. He'll come through the rest of the way okay."

Maggie blew her nose again and got a grip on herself. Over the past few months, she had fantasized many times about her reunion with Anthony. None of those dreams had involved her standing around in heavy slacks and a shirt, her hair unwashed and her face bare of makeup, talking about her brother.

A little shyly, she glanced toward the nurses' quarters and said, "I wish I could invite you in, but . . ."

He took note of the sentry on duty in front of the wooden building and grinned wryly. "I've heard this place is referred to as the New Guinea Seminary for Young Women."

Maggie giggled. "That's pretty accurate. The regulations are tighter here than at the sorority house where I used to live."

"Oh, well, they say abstinence is good for the soul."

"*Who* says that?"

He didn't answer at once; he was too busy studying the ripe curve of her mouth and the slender line of her throat visible above the bulky shirt. A low groan broke from him as he reached for her. "Some saints...which I definitely am not."

Drawing her into the shadow of a coconut tree, he kissed her long and thoroughly. Maggie clung to him, loving the taste and feel of him. Their tongues traced fiery patterns around each other while their lips sipped and savored.

When at last they broke away, both were flushed and shaken. "That may not have been such a good idea," Anthony muttered. "I was sort of hoping to sleep tonight."

She cast him an indulgent glance. "Are you regretting it?"

"No way! Listen, when can I see you? What kind of duty are you pulling?"

"Light," she assured him quickly. "What about you?"

"Nothing, basically. A little training, weapons checks, that kind of thing. I'll probably be tied up a couple of hours a day. Other than that..."

Her smile said it all. "Then at least we can be together, even if there isn't much privacy around here."

He grinned ruefully. "No, there isn't. I guess I'd better pray we're not here long. But in the meantime. . ." Tender passion danced in his eyes as he reached for her again.

You and me both, Maggie thought later that night when she finally crept inside the nurses' quarters and lay down on her cot. Sleep proved impossible. The sheer joy of being near Anthony again had her so excited that she could barely close her eyes.

Sighing, she turned away, seeking a more comfortable spot on the thin mattress. There was none. Not that it really mattered. Hugging her happiness to her, she at last managed to drift off as a thin rim of light began to creep over the eastern horizon, bringing with it a new day.

TEN TIME ZONES to the east, Elizabeth Lawrence was going about the routine she had established since her husband had left for the front. Mornings were spent at the Red Cross headquarters, followed almost invariably by some luncheon function. On this particular day, she hosted a meeting of women officers in the WAACs and WAVES and their civilian counterparts.

That afternoon, she was scheduled to help out at the USO, one of her favorite activities. She spent a few pleasant hours chatting with young men who were shipping out soon for Europe, where General Eisenhower's "big push" was expected any day.

As she returned home, she hoped there might be a letter from Will waiting for her. He wrote as frequently as he could, but his duties kept him more or less constantly on the move, with the result that she had to be content with only sporadic news of him. And today proved to be no exception.

That, however, did not stop her from sitting down to pen her daily letter to him, as well as letters to Maggie and Tad. When she had finished, she ate a light supper on a tray in her room, took a bath, and retired to bed.

Sleep proved as elusive as ever. Midnight found her still sitting up with a Daphne du Maurier mystery.

IN BROOKLYN, Joseph woke suddenly from an uneasy sleep. He was covered with sweat and breathing hard. Staring into the darkness, he tried to recapture whatever nightmare had so affected him, but it had faded beyond recall.

Careful not to wake Maria, he slipped out of bed and padded down to the kitchen. It was a pleasantly warm night. The windows had been left open, and the curtains billowed gently in the breeze.

After getting himself a glass of milk, he sat down at the table and, on impulse, switched on the radio, keeping the sound low so as not to disturb anyone. One of the few all-night stations was playing some kind of soothing music.

He was just rising to refill his glass when the music broke off and a bulletin came on. The announcer's voice was tense with excitement as he said, "The Supreme Headquarters of the Allied Expeditionary Force has just issued the following communiqué. Under the command of General Eisenhower, Allied naval forces, supported by strong air forces, began landing armies this morning on the northern coast of France."

Joseph sat down heavily. Automatically, he glanced at the clock. 3:30 A.M. He closed his eyes and breathed deeply. A few minutes passed. Outside, in the direction of St. Ignatius Church, a bell began to ring, its voice high and sweet on the clear night air.

Off in the distance, another bell rang, then another. The sounds seemed to take on a life of their own, reaching out across vast distances in a single, simple call to prayer.

Joseph listened for a little while. Then he heard Maria moving around upstairs and he went to get dressed.

"ALMIGHTY GOD," the padre said quietly, "we beseech you to protect our sons and brothers fighting on a distant shore. Strengthen them to your service and shield them from the blows of our enemies. They struggle to free a suffering humanity, as do we."

Maggie bent her head, praying silently along with the rest of the congregation that was crammed into the small church near the hospital. There wasn't room for everyone who wanted to be there; the overflow spilled down the wooden steps across the dirt road. Many could not hear the priest's words, but no one seemed to mind.

News of the D-day invasion had reached them late in the afternoon. She and Anthony had just returned from the beach, where they had spent a very happy interlude swimming, sunning and talking.

There was so much they needed to say to each other that neither really knew where to begin. By tacit agreement, they did not speak of Anthony's experiences on New Britain. Maggie had heard enough about what had gone on there to understand why he chose not to relive it. Instead, they concentrated on more pleasant things, sharing reminiscences and confiding their hopes for the future.

"I guess I'll go back to Brooklyn when this is over," Anthony had said, casting her a cautious glance. "You ever been to Brooklyn?"

Maggie shook her head. "No, but I've heard a lot about it."

"It's a wonderful place. You'd love it. Great people, nice neighborhoods. We've got Prospect Park, the Dodgers, Sheepshead Bay—lots of terrific stuff."

She smiled at him a little shyly. "It sounds wonderful."

"It is! But, uh, that doesn't necessarily mean I'd want to live there all my life. I've been thinking maybe someplace more open would be nice. With all the pay I've been saving, I'll bet I wouldn't have any problem getting a house, maybe out on Long Island, with a lawn, in case I should end up having, uh, kids. You know?"

"Yes," she said softly, "I know. I think about the same thing myself."

"Really?"

"Of course. I can't imagine anyone coming through this war without wanting a life such as you've just described."

"Yeah," he admitted, "I guess a lot of other guys have the same idea."

"There's nothing wrong with that. As far as I'm concerned, the more ordinary everything is after the war, the better."

"Would you—that is, after the war—do you think you'll keep on nursing?"

"I'd stop for a while if I have children," she said,

not seeing any reason to be coy about it. "But I love my work and I can't imagine giving it up forever."

Anthony breathed a sigh of relief. That was more than he had hoped for.

"What about you?" she asked after a moment. "Do you have some kind of work in mind to do after the war?"

"Sort of." A rueful laugh escaped him. "Knowing how to toss a grenade and fire a Browning automatic probably won't be in great demand once we're at peace."

"No...but you've learned a lot of other things, like leading men, making plans, getting things done."

"Yeah, I suppose. Anyway, I've got a few possibilities." A little self-consciously, he added, "I always liked fooling around with radios. For a while I had a ham set. Paulo took it over when I joined up."

"Then you think you might do something in radio?"

"No...not exactly." He hesitated a moment before confiding, "What I'm really interested in is television."

Maggie looked at him blankly. She could vaguely remember having heard of television, but didn't know much about it except that it involved transmitting pictures. She thought it sounded like something H.G. Wells might have written about.

"Do you really think there's anything to it?" she asked.

He nodded firmly. "You're going to see things in the next few years that right now you can't imagine. And I hope to be in the middle of it. Not only that, but you know who else is interested in this? James. We've talked about it, and when we get back to the States, we're going into business together."

Maggie was frankly astonished. She hadn't imagined that he had such carefully thought out plans for his future, let alone that they were so ambitious. Apparently he had been working it out for quite some time.

Meeting his gaze, she knew without having to be told that she was definitely a part of the life he wanted to make for himself. That he hadn't yet asked her outright did not distress her. They both would know when the time was right.

In the meanwhile, she could only pray that the war would end before the chance for any future at all was ripped from them.

THE PRAYERS ENDED and Maggie lifted her head. Beside her, Anthony reached for her hand and squeezed it gently. They began to file slowly out of the church.

Outside, under the perpetually rain-laden sky, they met James. He was about to put on a fresh pot of coffee in his tent and invited them to join him.

"I was over at HQ," he said when they were seated, Maggie and Anthony on the cot and James in a rickety camp chair facing them. "There's a little more news from France. Our men on Omaha Beach are up against a crack German infantry troop. We're taking a hell of a beating."

"I've got a feeling Paulo's there," Anthony said quietly, staring down into his coffee mug. "I don't know why exactly, but I just do."

James looked at him sympathetically. "Maybe not.

There's another landing beach, Utah, where everything's going great. Plus we got a real break, since the *Luftwaffe* isn't in sight. I guess there's nothing left of the Nazi air force."

"If that's so," Maggie ventured, "it's going to be much easier to wrap things up over there than it would have been otherwise."

James nodded. "That's right. But it's still going to take a while. I figure a year; with some breaks, maybe a little less."

"And then?" she murmured.

"An occupation force will be left, and everybody else will be packed up and shipped over here pronto."

Maggie didn't need any explanation of why that would be the case. With the way opened to the Philippines and to the island chains that were in effect stepping-stones through the Pacific, it was only a matter of time before the invasion of Japan itself began.

Prime Minister Churchill had said that the British would fight to defend their homeland on the beaches and in the hills. They would never surrender. The Japanese could be expected to do the same.

Whatever was happening in Europe, the final invasion in the Pacific would be infinitely worse. She shivered as she thought of it and moved closer to Anthony. Their time together was so short; already rumors were circulating that the First Marine Division would be shipping out soon.

James eyed them tolerantly. A grin slashed his darkly tanned features as he said, "You know, I'm beginning to think there may be something to that old chestnut about its being an ill wind that blows nobody any good."

"What do you mean by that?" Anthony asked.

His friend and superior officer sighed deeply and pointed a finger at a typed document sitting on his desk. With no attempt to hide his disgust, he said, "I've been transferred to the Fifth Amphibious Corps."

Anthony's eyes opened wide. "The unit that's staying with MacArthur after the rest of us go back to Halsey's command?"

"That's right."

Anthony shook his head sympathetically. "Jeez, that's really tough. I know how much you were looking forward to saying so long to Dugout Doug."

"I swear, there's no justice in this world. Of all the officers he could have picked, why me?"

Anthony shrugged and took another sip of the beer he was working on. "Not because you're such a big fan of his, that's for sure. Anyway, it looks like you're stuck, so you might as well admit it."

"Your sympathy overwhelms me." James cast a look at Maggie and added, "You know, it really doesn't seem right that I should have to go through this alone."

"I don't think even MacArthur expects you to invade the Philippines single-handed," Anthony suggested reassuringly.

James ignored him and continued thinking out loud. "We've fought together now for quite a while, haven't we? And we're going to be partners after the war, isn't that right?"

"Yes, it is. So try to stay out of trouble when you're on your own."

"Mmm . . . you know, there's every possibility Maggie may be sent to the Philippines as soon as we get the situation sewed up there."

"Sure is," she chimed in. Again her eyes met the major's piercing blue gaze. They shared a smile. "I expect to be transferred pretty soon. New Guinea was always intended as a temporary posting."

"If that happens," Anthony told his friend, "I'd really appreciate it if you'd keep an eye on her for me."

James was about the only man in the world, besides his father and brothers, whom he would have trusted with such a request. Properly mindful of that, the major nodded, while Maggie did her best to restrain a giggle. She had a definite idea where the conversation was going and she was delighted by it.

"Sure, sure," James agreed genially. "But don't you think it'd be better if you could look out for her yourself?"

"Certainly, but how—" Anthony broke off, his eyes darkening as a very nasty suspicion began to form in his mind. Callahan couldn't be thinking of— He started up from his chair. *"Oh, no! There's no way you're doing that to me!"*

James chuckled, pleased with his own ingenuity. "I think," he said firmly, "that I need an adjunct, somebody I can really rely on. You're the perfect man for the job."

Anthony was on his feet, shaking his head fiercely. "Like hell! If there's anybody who despises MacArthur more than you, it's me! You can't do this!"

"Sure he can," Maggie informed him blandly. She was completely on James's side in this instance and didn't care who knew it.

"It's so simple, I don't know why I didn't think of it right off the bat," his erstwhile friend chortled. "If Dugout Doug can request transfer, I can certainly request yours."

Leaning back in his chair, James grinned broadly. "Congratulations, Gargano. You are soon to be a proud member of the Fifth Amphibious Corps. Next stop, the Philippines."

March 1945–August 1945
THE RETURN

Chapter Seventeen

Maggie stood on the deck of the hospital ship, looking out over Manila Bay. A short time earlier, they had sailed past the stark, crater-pocked rock that was all that was left of Corregidor. Relentless bombardment had changed its very topography. What the Japanese had started in 1942, the Americans had finished a few days before.

Over the Rock, near the southern entrance to the Malinta Tunnel, the Stars and Stripes flew once more. The ship's whistle had blown in proud but mournful salute, forcing Maggie to turn away lest the nurses she was with see her tears.

And now ahead lay the harbor from which she and Sheila had departed so long ago on the *Don Esteban*. In her mind's eye, she could see them both scrambling over the docks...Sheila insisting on finding some way to mail her letters to Charlie, then rushing to make the ship...herself stumbling and being caught by a pair of strong hands and ebony eyes that had looked at her so feelingly....

So much time, so many memories, so many deaths. She had been very young then, and she knew she was no longer young. Youth lost so brutally could never be recaptured. But in its place she had gained a steady maturity and the knowledge of a true love that gave her the strength to face what lay ahead.

Lists were still being compiled of the freed American prisoners of war. Maggie had scanned the names repeatedly, searching for Sheila's. So far she had not found it. But she refused to give up hope. Saying a silent prayer that her friend was still alive and whole in mind and body, she went off to gather her nurses for disembarkment.

From the dock where their baggage and equipment were still being unloaded, they were sent immediately by truck to a staging area. Each nurse was permitted to take only a single piece of hand luggage; the rest would catch up with them eventually.

Before the truck left, a group of newly arrived doctors was added to their party. Talking with them as the vehicle sped along the dusty roads, Maggie noted that almost every medical specialty was represented, including obstetrics and pediatrics. Whoever had put the team together had had more in mind than simply treating military casualties.

As they approached the outskirts of Manila, the talk died away. Of the people in the truck, only Maggie and one other person had seen the city before the war. But they had all heard of its beauty.

Not even a hint of that remained in the sight confronting the Americans. Hardly a stone stood on top of stone. Almost every neighborhood, factory and school had been razed to the ground. In their ferocious determination not to surrender, the Japanese had unleashed a bloodbath that had left as its memorial a forest of charred timbers standing starkly against the sky. Maggie could not find a single landmark to tell her where she was.

And yet, in the midst of such devastation, some people had managed against all odds to survive. Peering from the truck, she saw the gaunt figures of Filipino men, women and children emerging slowly from their hiding places. A few were already on the move, pushing all their belongings in baby carriages or carts as they headed for the refugee camps being swiftly set up.

Others simply stood and watched impassively, until they realized that there were women in the truck. Nurses. Then they cheered, weakly but still valiantly. The Americans, they knew, would not bring their women to the city unless they were certain the fighting was really over.

The fighting was done with, but not the suffering. Up ahead, Maggie finally caught sight of a place she could recognize, the old school of Santo Tomás. Once it had been a gracious enclave encompassing more than fifty acres. Now it was a forbidding symbol of what it had stood for and what its present inhabitants had endured.

The truck pulled up to the entrance of a building and everybody got out. The doctors went off together as Maggie and the nurses stood for a moment blinking in the sun.

Several things impressed themselves at once on her mind: the evidence of recent shellfire in the stone walls, the row of neat white crosses off to one side and the quiet. Above all, the quiet.

Not a bird sang; not a leaf rustled in a tree; not a voice was loud enough to be heard. Santo Tomás was as silent as the grave it had all but become.

There was a movement near the door of the building. Maggie straightened up and took a deep breath. As ranking officer among the arriving nurses, she had a simple duty to perform, one so routine that she had done it automatically uncounted times in the past. But this time, in this place, she would need all her strength to do it well.

A woman appeared at the open door, with several more behind her. She was extremely thin, with short gray hair and gaunt features. The frayed khaki slacks and shirt she wore hung on her. She moved slowly, but with dignity.

Maggie swallowed, took a step forward and saluted smartly. "Captain Lawrence reporting, ma'am. I'm here to relieve you."

Kay Broderick drew herself up erectly and returned the salute, then smiled. "It's very nice to see you, Captain Lawrence."

Maggie gestured to her nurses. "Find your quarters and get your gear stowed. Until further notice, you're all on duty around the clock."

They nodded, their eyes bleak as they took in the condition of the women who had spent almost three years in captivity, living on starvation rations, coping with virulent disease and shadowed always by the threat of death. Yet who had managed to survive with pride and honor intact.

After a brief glance, the newly arrived nurses moved away. Stamped on each face was an unspoken knowledge: *It could have been me.*

"Come inside," Kay said quietly to Maggie, "and I'll brief you on the situation here."

Maggie followed her up the steps. As she did, her eyes were scanning the group of nurses in the doorway. Almost unaware that she spoke, she murmured, "Captain Davies?"

Kay stopped and turned back to her. Gently, she said, "Jean died about a year ago of malaria."

So, apparently, had many others, of that disease or other causes. There were faces missing, women Maggie had served with in Manila and on Corregidor. Girls, really, some of them. Gone forever, but never to be forgotten.

One face above all she sought and feared most not to find. But at last, inside the shadowed hallway, the familiar features came within sight.

Sheila had hung back from the rest, waiting until she could greet Maggie with some degree of privacy. They met near the little cubicle Major Broderick used as an office. Kay discreetly disappeared inside, giving them some time alone.

For a long moment neither spoke. They simply stared at each other. Pain welled up in Maggie as she took in the mute evidence of Sheila's suffering.

Her friend had been slender enough during the final days on Corregidor, but now she was emaciated. Like Major Broderick and all the other nurses who had survived, Sheila couldn't hide the effects of what she had been through.

And yet her hazel eyes were still warm and alive. Her smile was still tender, filled with a poignant happiness that said more than words ever could. Taking a step forward, Sheila held out her arms.

The two women embraced silently. The tears of each fell on the other's cheeks. At length, Maggie raised her head and managed a damp smile. "You said we'd meet again."

"I considered it a promise," Sheila said softly. Her

gaze was loving as it ran over her friend. Delightedly, she exclaimed, "You're a captain!"

"So are you! Promotions for all of you came through several days ago." Lowering her voice slightly, Maggie murmured, "Broderick made colonel."

Sheila rolled her eyes and giggled. "Oh, God, the Army's really in for it now!"

They hugged again, laughing. Not until they broke apart did Maggie remember what she most wanted to tell Sheila. "Charlie's here—or almost, anyway. He's on the carrier *Nashville*, MacArthur's flagship. I'll bet he's doing his damnedest to get leave so he can come find you."

Color flooded Sheila's face. She clasped her arms around herself as her thin body trembled. "I can hardly believe it. Not a day passed in this place that I didn't pray he'd be safe and we'd be together again. But to know he's so near..." Her dazed smile vanished as a purely feminine thought struck her. "Oh, Maggie, I can't let him see me like this! I need time to get myself back together!"

"But Charlie loves you. He has for years. You don't really want him to have to wait, do you?"

"How can you be sure he still loves me?" Sheila asked brokenly. "He had every reason to think I might have been killed. How long can a man hold on to a dream?"

Maggie was about to answer, to try in some way to calm her friend's obviously genuine distress, but she heard the front door open and looked quickly around. Down the long, shadowed corridor, a tall male figure stood silhouetted against the light. A smile spread across her face and she turned back to

Sheila. Very softly, she said, "As long as he has to, I think."

Before Sheila could respond, Maggie gave her a gentle pat on the arm and walked into Colonel Broderick's office. Behind her, she heard a soft gasp, then the sound of rushing footsteps and a man's broken cry.

Quietly, Maggie shut the door, leaving the two of them to the precious moment of rediscovery.

WITHIN HOURS of arrival at Santo Tomás, Maggie had discovered that she had her work cut out for her. There were almost four thousand internees in the camp, including both formerly captured American troops and most of what had been the foreign civilian population of Manila before the Japanese takeover. Or at least those who had survived.

Without exception, everyone was malnourished, fever-ridden and plagued by a host of illnesses. Drinking water was scarce, but almost the opposite problem existed with rations. Care had to be taken not to overfeed the newly released prisoners, whose shrunken stomachs rebelled at ingesting anything more than a small quantity of food.

Barely had Santo Tomás been liberated than Filipino refugees began arriving. Maggie struggled unsuccessfully to become inured to the sight of children without limbs, old men and women wounded by mortar rounds and young girls suffering the aftereffects of gang rapes. Each day was a long, brutalizing litany of pain and misery, made endurable only by the relentless courage of the people she was there to help.

In another section of the city, where he and other

Marines were involved in the mop-up operations, Anthony felt much the same way.

He was worn out in mind and body, yet he persisted in clearing rubble from the streets, replacing water pipes, getting the electricity turned back on again—all because of the people around him. Whatever he had endured, he realized that they had suffered much worse.

Throughout it all, he longed for Maggie. He knew she had arrived in Manila during the middle of March and was only a few miles away from him. But he held off going to her, understanding the desperate situation she was facing and accepting that it was not yet the time for them to be together again.

So he kept on working, day after day and night after night, until at last some faint sign of progress began to appear. It came slowly at first, almost imperceptibly.

The snipers holed up in the city diminished in number, until the day arrived when there were no more. Fewer children with swollen bellies and bleak faces wandered up to him in the streets. There were no more bodies to be seen; they had all been collected and buried.

One day, several weeks after the fighting had stopped, he looked out the window of the building in which he was billeted and saw a young Filipino overseeing the clearing of rubble from a large corner lot. Making his way downstairs, he inquired as to what was going on and was told that a new school would be built on the site.

His reaction upon hearing this news must have puzzled the young man. Anthony smiled broadly, nodded his head and said, "I guess it must be time, then."

That afternoon he went in search of Maggie.

She was in surgery when he arrived at Santo Tomás, and he had to wait for a while; this gave him a chance to get his thoughts together. So much had happened lately he wasn't sure what to expect next.

As the battle had raged for the Philippines, other conflicts had occurred throughout the Pacific. He had listened with dread to the terrible news from Peleliu, the island the First Marine Division had been sent to take. The battle there had turned into one of the bloodiest of the war. One out of every five of the men who'd fought there had either been killed or wounded. But Dom had survived and, since Easter, had been fighting on Okinawa, with Iwo Jima—which had fallen in February—the last link in the chain before Japan itself.

Since late the previous year, the enemy's homeland had been relentlessly bombed in what was intended as a classic softening-up operation. Tad Lawrence was one of the pilots taking part in it, flying fighter protection for the B-29s based on a little island called Tinian.

He and Anthony had exchanged letters; in his, Tad made oblique references to what it felt like to be attacking civilians. He hated it but didn't think he had much choice, since all the pilots figured they were going to have to fight the Japanese eventually anyway.

There'd be time enough to think about that later, Anthony decided; just then he wanted to concentrate on exactly what he was going to say to Maggie. He was still working on it when she got out of surgery and came over to join him.

In her droopy OR fatigues, she looked not unlike a little girl dressed up in somebody else's clothes. Except that no little girl would choose to walk around splattered with blood, or have such a tired look in her eyes.

Maybe this wasn't the right time, after all, he thought as he stood up to greet her. But having come this far, he wasn't about to retreat. Smiling a little uncertainly, he said, "Hi. How are you doing?"

"All right," Maggie told him. She was startled by his sudden appearance, but only for a moment. Going over to the coffee urn, she filled two cups, then carried them back to the bench where he'd been waiting and sat down.

Anthony joined her, taking a sip from the cup she handed him before he said, "I would have been here sooner, but things have been busy."

"I knew you'd come when it was right." Somehow, she had never doubted that. During other battles she had feared for his safety, but she had been certain he would survive this one. It was what was coming at them that worried her.

Quietly, she said, "The news from Okinawa is good."

"Yeah, I guess Dom must have gotten the hang of things by now."

Maggie laughed softly. She and Anthony had been separated for almost six months, yet they were able to pick up again as easily as if they had been apart scant hours. She thought that boded well for their future.

The same idea flitted through his mind. He took a

deep breath, reminded himself that he was a Marine and therefore honor-bound to behave courageously, and said, "Looks like we're going to be here awhile."

"Seems that way to me," Maggie agreed.

So far so good. "I was thinking . . . as long as we've got the opportunity . . . maybe you'd like to get married."

Maggie lowered her cup and looked at him steadily. As proposals went, it was pretty low on the romance scale. On the other hand, he would have looked silly down on his knees.

"W-when were you thinking of doing this?" she asked.

"Let's see . . . there must be forms we'll have to fill out . . . and a padre to line up . . . find a church . . . invite a few people. . . . I guess you'll want to get some kind of dress." He thought for a moment, then said, "How about a week from today?"

Maggie considered. A week, seven days, before she pledged her heart to this man for all eternity. It seemed long enough. "That will be fine," she told him, smiling at his look of infinite relief. "Sheila and Charlie will be back from their honeymoon by then. She can stand up for me."

"They got married? That's great." He remembered Sheila well from the time they had all shared on Corregidor, and Maggie had told him of her friend's great love. Its fulfillment seemed very much a vindication of the suffering that had gone before.

"Not only can Sheila be there," Maggie went on, "but in a week —" She glanced up at him through the thick fringe of her lashes, bright blue eyes dancing. "In a week, my dad will have arrived. He can give me away."

"Y-your dad. . . ?"

"That's right. He's doing liaison duty between MacArthur and Nimitz, and he's due here on Monday. How's that for luck?"

"Oh, it's great. . . ."

Maggie watched the color fade from beneath his tan and grinned. "Surely you're not nervous about meeting my father?"

"Who, me? Of course not." Recovering at least some of his equanimity, Anthony added, "Heck, he'll probably thank me for taking you off his hands."

Several young nurses coming out of OR paused to wonder why their captain was hitting a Marine over the head with her surgery cap. At least he didn't seem to mind, if his laughter was any indication. Shrugging, they went on their way.

"Colonel Lawrence," an aide said, "your daughter and Captain Gargano are here."

Will looked up from the pile of papers he was sifting through and nodded. "Thanks. I'll be right there." He took a moment to collect his thoughts and straighten his tie, then rose and strode out of the room.

Maggie and Anthony were standing close together, looking out a window at the busy street scene. In the bustle of the hectic outer office, they didn't see him at once, and he was able to observe them for a moment unnoticed.

The sight of his daughter brought a lump to his throat. It had been so damn long—almost five years since he and Elizabeth had seen her off for San Diego and the ship to the Philippines. None of them could have imagined on that day what would happen to them all before they would be together again.

His last glimpse of her had been as a smiling, excited twenty-two-year-old with no concerns except that she do a good job and fully enjoy the adventure she was embarking on.

Now, even at first glance, he could see how much she had changed. Five years had brought the beauty she had inherited from her mother to its full potential. She was no longer a sweet young girl with slight vestiges of adolescent softness clinging to her. Instead, her features were honed to the purity they would undoubtedly have all the rest of her life. Her expression was somewhat grave, as certainly befitted the occasion. But a smile danced in her eyes as she gazed at the man at her side.

Will frowned slightly. So this was Anthony Gargano. Tad had written about the Marine and made no secret of the fact that he liked and approved of him. The colonel had preferred to withhold judgment. In was all very well for this leatherneck to think he was good enough for Maggie, but that remained to be seen.

At least he looked fit enough, in the overly large way most Marines seemed to favor. He was quite tall; Maggie only came to his shoulders, which were very broad. Whatever hardships he had suffered in battle—and Will admitted they were likely to have been immense—he showed no evidence of them now.

Unless one counted the hint of vulnerability in the dark eyes watching Maggie so closely, or the tenderness about the firm mouth set in a rough-hewn face.

Will sighed inwardly. Elizabeth had been right;

they were serious about each other. He had only to see the silent look that passed between them and the way they seemed to be touching without doing so to know it was true.

Perhaps it was just as well that he had arrived on the scene when he had. Taking a step forward, he cleared his throat and said softly, "Maggie. . ."

She turned instantly. "Dad!"

They were in each other's arms in no more time than it took to cross the narrow room. Will held her close, uncaring of whoever might be watching. This was his firstborn child, his little girl, the source of immense love and pride. His vision blurred slightly, and he knew that if he had tried to speak at that moment, he would not have been able to.

Maggie struggled to blink back tears. She had absolutely promised herself that she would not cry, and she was perilously close to doing so. After such great hardship, happiness this intense threatened to overwhelm her.

Anthony watched them with a deep sense of pleasure. He was poignantly glad for Maggie and grateful to Will Lawrence simply for giving her this moment. However the colonel reacted to him, Anthony was determined to like his future father-in-law. Taking a deep breath, he mentally rehearsed what he planned to say and waited until at last father and daughter moved slightly apart.

"Well, now," Will murmured huskily, "you certainly have grown up. Last time I saw you, you were a pretty young girl. Now you're a lovely woman."

The simple tribute brought fresh tears to Maggie's blue eyes, but she smiled through them. "You haven't changed at all." This wasn't quite true; there were lines in her father's weathered face, and he looked undeniably weary. Yet the solid, constant strength she remembered from her childhood was still there. As were the firm sense of purpose and the certainty that he could always be counted on to do what was right.

Turning, she held out a hand to Anthony. "Dad, there's someone I want you to meet."

Anthony met the older man's calm gray eyes unwaveringly. He and the colonel shook hands as Maggie introduced them.

"It's a pleasure, sir. I've been looking forward to this."

Will continued to study him for a moment before a broad grin split his face. Laughing softly, he said, "I'll just bet you have, son. Come on, let's go into my office and get acquainted."

Maggie squeezed Anthony's arm to let him know everything was going well. He wasn't so sure. Seated on the couch across from the colonel, he was keenly aware of the older man's scrutiny.

Will Lawrence had not been trusted with his present sensitive position simply because he had a lot of years under his belt. He positively radiated intelligence and perception; Anthony did not need to be told that very little got past Maggie's father.

Trying not to think about exactly how much the colonel had already figured out about their relationship, Anthony said, "Maggie may have mentioned that we met in the Philippines almost three and a half years ago. Despite everything that's happened since then, we've managed to, uh, spend a fair amount of time together."

"That's good." Will leaned back in his chair, crossed one perfectly tailored leg over the other and added, "When's the wedding?"

With those words, all of Anthony's careful mental preparations went flying out the window. He had lain awake throughout the previous night, planning what he would say and trying to anticipate the objections the colonel would undoubtedly raise.

He had intended to lead into the whole subject of marriage carefully, stressing his deep love and respect for Maggie, and the good life they would be able to build together once the war was over.

Her father would undoubtedly point out the uncertainty under which they lived, but Anthony had an answer to that: It was better, wasn't it, to know at least a little happiness than none at all? Besides, he and Maggie loved each other and wanted to make the commitment implicit in marriage.

What about the possibility that they were not really in love, but simply reacting to the pressures of war? the colonel would surely ask. Anthony was ready for that one, too. They had had more than three years to discover their true feelings and were convinced they were the kind that would last forever.

All very moving and, he was certain, quite persuasive arguments. But it seemed now that he wasn't going to get a chance to use any of them.

It was the hallmark of a good Marine that he could react quickly to changing circumstances. Anthony reached over and took Maggie's hand in his. "Day after tomorrow, sir. If that's all right with you."

Will looked at his daughter. She had said nothing so far, merely sat listening to them both. The Maggie he remembered had been something of a chatterbox; now she had the quiet self-possession of a fully mature woman. A woman more than capable of deciding her future for herself.

"And what do you think of all this?" he asked her gently.

Without hesitation, she said, "I think it's wonderful luck that you're here to give me away."

That was enough for Colonel Lawrence. He paid his daughter the compliment of believing she knew what was best for herself. If, far in the back of his mind, he knew a moment's pain at this final end to her childhood, he showed no sign of it. Standing up, he nodded briskly. "Just tell me when and where. It may not be the fancy wedding your mother would have wanted, but I'm sure we'll do it up right."

Maggie hugged him. Over her head, the two men regarded each other. The colonel's thoughts were very clear; he was going along with this because he could come up with no good reason not to, but that didn't change the fact that if Anthony didn't do right by his little girl, he would personally turn him into fish bait.

Anthony met the gaze of his future father-in-law unflinchingly. His utter confidence in what he was about to do shone clearly in his eyes. Never had he been more certain of anything in his life.

However, that did not prevent him from getting more and more nervous as the day of the wedding drew nearer. During the last forty-eight hours before they were to become man and wife, he and Maggie saw little of each other. She was off with her nurses, finalizing preparations for the ceremony and the small party that would follow. He was scouting up a place for their brief honeymoon and trying to keep his knees from knocking together.

James, whom he had asked to be his best man, found the whole thing highly amusing. "I've seen you face a banzai attack with more composure than you're showing right now."

"Why not?" Anthony shot back. "That was just a matter of life or death. This is a hell of a lot more."

His friend grinned and took a swallow of scotch. "I suppose.... But seriously, you do know, don't you, that you're getting a terrific woman."

They were sitting at the bar of the officers' club, having a couple of drinks before going on to the stag dinner James had arranged for Anthony. It was early yet, and the club was quiet. The bulk of the crowd wouldn't arrive for a few hours, and then the place would get downright rowdy.

"I know," Anthony said softly. "Frankly, I'm still a little surprised she agreed to this."

"That's no way for a Marine to talk! Hell, you're probably saving her from marrying some regular Army stiff."

Anthony flinched and gestured for the bartender to refill his glass. "Don't forget, the good colonel is regular Army. I'll bet he's about as thrilled with me as he would be by a carbuncle on his—"

"He seems okay to me," James interjected. "When I invited him to come along this evening, he was real pleased."

"I'll bet. Probably thinks he'll get something on me that'll convince Maggie to call it off."

James grinned, with a total lack of sympathy.

"Then I guess you'll just have to behave yourself, pal. It'll be good practice for the rest of your life."

Anthony reflected silently that he had no problem with that; he simply wasn't tempted to do otherwise. Realizing this brought home to him how much he had changed over the years. While he'd never been one to collect notches on his bedpost, he hadn't been adverse to upholding the reputation of young American manhood, either, and had probably had more than his fair share of pretty young things.

But none of them could hold a candle to Maggie. Her beauty was far more than skin deep; it went clear to the bone and sinew of her. He had seen her under the most brutal of circumstances, when all pretense was stripped away and the essence of a person stood revealed.

His love for her was such that it would have existed even if she had sometimes disappointed him. But she never had. He knew that he could trust her completely, and he wanted to spend the rest of his life making sure that she felt the same way about him.

That thought was uppermost in his mind as he and James went on to the bachelor party, which was being held at a recently reopened Filipino restaurant. It was quickly clear that no expense had been spared. An endless stream of dishes appeared, the liquor flowed freely, and several pretty girls provided very pleasant company.

Anthony enjoyed himself hugely. There were nearly two dozen friends in attendance, some of whom he hadn't seen in quite a while. They caught up on old times, swapped jokes, which got progressively worse as the evening wore on, and generally let their hair down.

Colonel Lawrence fitted in with remarkable ease. He held the group spellbound with his description of the battle at Château-Thierry, the decisive American action of World War I, then led the men in a rousing rendition of "Mademoiselle from Armentières" that had the Filipinos in stitches.

Anthony did his part to deplete the liquor supply, but was careful to keep a relatively clear head. He had absolutely no intention of being hung over at his wedding.

The party was still going on when he and Maggie's father left, the colonel dropping his future son-in-law off at his quarters before proceeding on to his own. Anthony was still lying awake on his cot sometime later when James came back.

He heard his friend stumbling around a little in the next room and grinned when James cursed loudly. A few moments later all was silent; shortly afterward, Anthony drifted into a sleep filled with dreams that made him smile.

Maggie also slept well that night, contrary to her expectations. She had spent the day with her friends, completing her preparations and later having dinner with them. They had all chipped in to buy her a gift, a silk-and-lace peignoir that took her breath away.

Sheila had added a special gift of her own. She'd gone to the same merchant from whom Maggie had bought Sheila's wedding present and selected a delicate pair of hand-carved jade statues meant to symbolize the eternal strength of love.

The statues sat on the table beside her bed as Maggie slept. The peignoir was packed away in her small suitcase, and the dress she would wear to be married in was hanging in her closet.

Finding the dress had turned out to be quite a problem. In the devastation of Manila, there were no little shops still stocked with prewar goodies. On the contrary, the people were hard pressed to keep clothes on their backs.

Maggie had happened to mention the difficulty she was having to one of her nurses, and was overheard by a Filipino matron whose child she had just cared for. The woman had promptly offered Maggie the use of her own wedding dress, which had been handed down from mother to daughter and packed lovingly away for the next generation.

At first Maggie had tried to decline, but her new friend had insisted, saying it would do them all a great honor if she would wear the dress. Hearing it put that way, Maggie had agreed with delight. Almost no alterations were needed for the lovely wedding gown to fit her perfectly.

Barely had she awakened shortly after dawn on the morning of her wedding than she was out of bed to check on the dress. She stood in her pajamas, smothering a yawn with one hand, as she gazed at it in awe. If her mother had slaved for months to find her exactly the right thing to wear, she could not have done any better. Forever grateful to the generous Filipino woman, Maggie touched the ivory silk reverently, then let it drop from between her fingers and went to begin getting herself ready.

Sheila arrived soon after Maggie had gotten out of the shower. The bride-to-be was bundled into an old bathrobe, her face bare of makeup and her chestnut hair falling in damp waves around her shoulders. Sheila stared at Maggie and grinned. "You look about the same as I did on the morning of the great day."

"Thanks," Maggie murmured, her attention on the flask of coffee Sheila had thoughtfully brought along. "That gives me hope. Maybe by the time we're due at the chapel, I'll somehow look as good as you did."

Sheila had been a radiantly beautiful bride, despite all the deprivations she had endured. As she had walked down the aisle to Charlie, she had glowed with a deep inner beauty and faith that moved everyone privileged to be at that ceremony.

Many of the same people would be in attendance at Anthony and Maggie's wedding. She didn't want to let any of them down by appearing the least bit inelegant.

"You're going to look great," Sheila insisted as she bustled about, laying out makeup and lingerie and setting up the ironing board to give the wedding dress a final going-over. "Now drink your coffee and try to relax."

"Sure. . . sure. . . I do this sort of thing every day. Why should I be nervous?"

"Beats me. You're marrying a wonderful man."

Some of Maggie's anxiety fled. She smiled warmly. "I know. I love him so much, sometimes I'm afraid I'll burst from it."

Sheila laughed gently. "I have it on excellent authority that that has never yet happened to a bride." As she spoke, she urged her friend over to the dressing table. Once she had Maggie seated, she lost no time in going to work on her hair.

A few minutes later, Maggie glanced at herself in

the mirror and blinked with surprise. Sheila had dried and brushed the chestnut tresses until they gleamed, then used tortoise-shell combs to draw the hair away from Maggie's face, revealing the full purity of her features.

"That looks lovely! Maybe there's hope for me after all."

"Are you kidding? You'll knock them dead. Come on now, we don't have a lot of time to waste."

A bit dazedly, Maggie stood up, gathered her lingerie together and headed for the bathroom. By the time she returned, she was clad in silk stockings, a garter belt, lacy panties and a half-bra. Remembering how Anthony had reacted to seeing her similarly attired, she blushed.

Sheila noted her friend's self-consciousness and politely refrained from commenting on it. Instead, she took the just-ironed gown from its hanger and held it up to help Maggie into it. "Careful now, don't muss your hair."

Maggie obeyed, listening to the rustle of the exquisite material as it slid over her body, falling in ivory waves to her silk-shod feet.

Stepping back, Sheila smiled admiringly. "Didn't I tell you? You look fabulous."

Maggie surveyed herself in the small dressing-table mirror. She could see little more than her face, but that was enough. The scant amount of makeup she had applied only enhanced her appearance, which was already radiant with the joy that was growing more powerful within her.

"Do you remember thinking about whom you might marry and wondering what it would be like?" she asked.

"Of course. That was a favorite topic all through school."

"Same with me." Maggie laughed softly. "The man was always tall, dark and handsome, with a really nice car and plenty of money. After I decided I wanted to be a nurse, Mr. Right became a doctor. We were going to have four kids and live in a neighborhood with good schools."

Grinning, Sheila considered what she had just heard. "Let's see, now. . . . Anthony is definitely tall, dark and handsome. He's not a doctor, but when you think about it, that's all to the good. He won't be getting up in the middle of the night to make house calls. And as for the kids. . ." She batted her eyelashes innocently. "I'll just leave that to the two of you, but with the understanding that I fully expect to be a godmother not too long after this stupid war ends."

"I'll keep that in mind," Maggie murmured. The mention of children had made her look ahead to the coming night. She and Anthony hadn't been together in months; her hunger for him was intense. She counted the intervening hours and smothered a groan.

And yet, for all her impatience, she would not have wished her wedding to be a moment shorter. The chapel they had chosen was one of the few left standing in Manila. It was decorated with white lilies and orchids, and crowded with their friends, both American and Filipino.

It was amazing, Maggie thought as she peeked from the room in which she was waiting, that so many people wanted to share this moment. She could see soldiers she had cared for some years before, who, finding themselves in Manila and hearing of the wedding, hadn't hesitated to ask for invitations. With them stood newly released prisoners of war whom she had helped treat, as well as entire Filipino families who had found their way to the refugee camp.

Colonel Broderick was there with all her nurses. They would be starting for home soon, taking the trip in easy stages. Charlie Fletcher would be going with them. His situation had come to MacArthur's attention and, in a gesture that highlighted the noble side of his complex nature, the general had ordered him reassigned to the States.

Near the flower-draped altar stood a small field organ. One of the men from Anthony's company took his place there. Moments later the sounds of the wedding march from *Lohengrin* filled the chapel.

Sheila gave Maggie a quick smile, picked up her bouquet, and in the measured step they had practiced, started down the aisle. From a seat near the front, Charlie watched her with frank adoration in his eyes.

Maggie trembled slightly as she took her father's arm. He touched her hand reassuringly, smiled at her, then looked straight ahead as he began to escort her to her about-to-be husband.

Maggie kept her eyes on Anthony. The sight of him calmed her. A deep sense of contentment spread through her, wiping out her nervousness. By the time she had reached the altar and placed her hand in his, she was completely serene.

The ancient Latin of the wedding mass was uttered with great reverence by the young priest as he prayed for God's blessing on their union. James passed the ring to Anthony, who placed it on Maggie's finger. The organ struck up again, a full, joyous sound announcing to the world that one more man and woman had joined together in matrimony.

Maggie walked down the aisle beside Anthony, both of them radiant with happiness. Outside, an honor guard of Marines presented arms. They were all men who had fought with Anthony and James and who expected to do so again.

For some, the day was a reminder of what they had left at home. For others, it was a glimpse of what might yet lie ahead, if they somehow managed to survive the great struggle looming on the horizon.

For Maggie and Anthony, it was an expression of the love born amid destruction and nurtured in the shadow of death. The feelings they had for each other were intensely personal, yet for a short time they were happy to share them with others.

It was, very simply, a rare moment stolen from the brutality of war and dedicated to the hope—however tenuous—of a future at peace.

Chapter Eighteen

ELIZABETH LAWRENCE RECEIVED the cable from her husband, telling her of their daughter's wedding, late in the afternoon. The ceremony had taken place the day before. She read the cable at the door, immediately after taking it from the hand of a sympathetic young woman, a Western Union employee who was undoubtedly accustomed by now to delivering bad news.

This news was anything but. Elizabeth was delighted for Maggie. Whatever regret she felt at missing the ceremony was wiped out by the certainty that her daughter had made the right choice.

Though she had never met Anthony, she read between the lines of Will's announcement to deduce correctly that he had no objection to the Marine. That, coupled with what she had garnered from Maggie's letters over the years, told her how right it was.

But there was no denying that it felt very strange to be receiving such good news at such a dark moment. Off in the kitchen, she could hear the cook crying softly. Upstairs, the woman who came in twice a week to clean was doing the same.

Elizabeth had tried to send them both home, but they had refused, saying that they preferred to keep busy. Perhaps so, but it didn't seem possible that any amount of work could wipe out the all-pervasive sadness that had settled over the country barely an hour ago.

Franklin Delano Roosevelt was dead. He had passed away at his home in Warm Springs at about three-thirty. To Elizabeth, it was all but inconceivable that he was gone.

He had been president for more than twelve years. She had voted for him herself four times, most recently the previous November, when he had run for reelection with Harry Truman in the vice-presidential spot.

Harry Truman? Returning to the living room, Elizabeth sat down heavily and tried to come to terms with the extraordinary fact that the former haberdasher from Missouri would be president of the United States.

Sighing softly, she began to pen a response to Will's telegram, to be followed by a letter to Maggie and Anthony. In both she would speak of her happiness on this day but would not mention the president's death. If they did not know it already, they would soon enough, and would be sharing in the pain and shock that gripped the grieving nation.

IN BROOKLYN, Joseph Gargano turned off the radio to which he had been listening for hours and leaned back heavily in his chair. His face was grim and his eyes red. He still could not really believe the news. It didn't seem possible that the man who had given them hope in the midst of the Depression and courage in the midst of war could be suddenly taken from them.

Standing at the stove, stirring a pot of tomato

sauce, Maria looked at him compassionately. He had eaten nothing all day, and she was worried about him.

"Joseph," she said softly, "have a piece of bread. . . something. . . ."

He didn't seem to hear her. Almost to himself, he murmured, "What can God be thinking of to do such a terrible thing to us?"

Maria had long ago reconciled herself to the fact that her husband did not share her deep religious belief. He went to mass only a couple of times a year—at Christmas and Easter—and hadn't been to confession in ages. Yet in his own way he was a religious man, profoundly committed to a vision of a better world that had at its root the belief that all people should learn to live together in peace. For him to speak of God with such anguish brought home to her the full depth of his suffering.

Setting down the wooden spoon, she went to him and put her arms around his broad chest. Almost as though she were comforting one of their children, she said, "It will be all right, you'll see. We'll come through this like we have everything else."

He shook his head bleakly. "I don't know about that. We've lost so much. . . hundreds of thousands of our young men. . . our future. And for what? Peace is still years away."

"You can't know that for sure," she protested gently. "Maybe something will happen—some miracle." Lowering herself into the chair beside him, she took his hand in hers.

They sat like that as the warm April afternoon

faded into night and the church bells, which had rung with such strength and hopefulness on D-Day, tolled out their mournful dirge.

ANTHONY AND MAGGIE HEARD the news the morning after their wedding, when they emerged briefly from their borrowed bungalow to take a stroll on the beach. They had slept little the previous night, preferring to spend it recapturing the ecstasy they had known together in the past.

Perhaps it was the fact that they were now married, or maybe it had something to do with the terrible shadow hanging over them, but their lovemaking had an added poignancy they had never experienced before. It drove them to hitherto unattained heights of rapture, leaving them both drained yet exhilarated.

But not, incredibly enough, satiated. They spent only a short time on the beach before a shared glance was enough to send them heading back toward their bed.

They had reached the bungalow and gone inside when Anthony said, "I want to turn on the radio for a minute. Just to make sure everything's okay."

Maggie smiled at his conscientiousness. She knew perfectly well that if anything urgent had come up, he would have been called back from leave. But she was willing enough to indulge him while she brushed the sand from her hair and slipped into the silky peignoir she had worn so briefly the night before.

Twisting the dial, Anthony started to go right by the frequency over which Radio Tokyo beamed its English-language broadcasts, which were designed to taunt the Allied troops. But something caught his attention and he paused.

A translator was relaying a statement by the premier, Admiral Kantaro Suzuki, one of the most feared Japanese warlords. "I must admit," the slightly accented voice intoned, "that Roosevelt's leadership has been very effective and has been responsible for the Americans' advantageous position today. For that reason, I can easily understand the great loss his passing means to the American people, and my profound sympathy goes to them." Quietly, the translator added, "We now introduce a few minutes of special music in honor of the passing of the great man."

Slowly, Anthony turned to look at Maggie. She was sitting at the dressing table, her hairbrush frozen in her hand.

"Did you hear?" he began.

White-faced, she shook her head. "I—it's some kind of trick. It must be."

"No...it sounded real. My God, if it is..."

"But...why would they offer their sympathy? Wouldn't they be gloating?"

"I don't know," he admitted, sitting down heavily on the rumpled bed. "They believe so much in honor and duty...and they're always so incredibly polite, even when they're wreaking the worst havoc..."

He paused, thinking about the implications of what he was saying. If Roosevelt was really dead, then what he had just heard was a genuine expression of understanding and compassion.

But how could that be, considering all that had happened between the two nations? As though the horror of the past few years were not enough, just last month the Allies had unleashed a bombing raid on Tokyo that turned the ancient city into an inferno and killed at least a hundred thousand civilians.

Recently he had learned from an intelligence officer that the Japanese had an expression that was the equivalent of "It never rains but it pours." They said, "Stung by a bee while crying."

They were certainly crying now, and everybody knew that the bee getting ready to sting them was going to pack a hell of a wallop. Yet they could still reach out across the vast chasm carved by the war and offer their sympathy for a fallen leader.

That said something—Anthony wasn't sure what—about the insanity of fighting each other and, even more, about what the future might hold. Maybe—just maybe—there was a chance for them all on both sides if, by some incredible miracle, the war could be brought to an end without devastating the entire Japanese homeland.

You're dreaming, he told himself. Hadn't what he had just heard proved there was no miracle in the works? On the contrary, things were looking darker than ever.

His face was grim and his eyes bleak as he rose and went to Maggie, who had begun to cry brokenly.

OTHER TEARS FELL in the days that followed, a seeming ocean of tears flowing for a man whose once vocal enemies were drowned out in a torrent of loving tribute from both the great and the small.

At the funeral in Washington the dignitaries held center stage, but ordinary people also found a way to take part. Joseph had come home from the factory early; all businesses were closed for the afternoon. At four o'clock, he and Maria went into the living room and sat down.

There was no way for them to follow what was happening in the East Room of the White House, where the funeral service was being held. The radio stations had gone off the air. Every bus, trolley and subway stopped where it was. Even the telephone had no dial tone.

Not that it mattered. The Garganos didn't need to know exactly what was going on in order to participate.

It was a time to sit quietly and think about all that had gone before; to remember the droll voice and the cocky grin, the wave and the bright smile; to hear again in the chords of memory the sprightly notes of "Happy Days Are Here Again" and savor the echo of a strong voice that came to a suffering people in their darkest hour to tell them there was hope.

"He gave us so much," Joseph murmured under his breath.

"He was a good man," Maria said softly. "God rest his soul."

For most, that was the final good-bye. But for Joseph, there was one more chance to pay his respects to the man he had admired so greatly.

Later that evening, he gathered up his grandchildren. Little Salvatore, Jr., and his sister, Philomena, were unaccustomed to being out so late, but Joseph was determined that they, too, would know what had happened that day.

Vita and Maria satisfied themselves that the children were dressed warmly, then stood aside. They understood that Joseph needed this time alone with the youngsters amid the memories he wanted to pass on to them.

The trains had begun to run again shortly after the funeral service ended. They took one all the way up to the Bronx, along with a silent crowd of other people — men, women, children, even babies held in their mothers' arms. Near the Mott Haven train yard, they disembarked and trooped to a siding by the railroad tracks. It was cold and everyone shivered a little, but no one minded.

After a half hour or so, a train went by, carrying the dignitaries who would watch the president being lowered into his final resting place in Hyde Park. Then came the funeral train itself, moving slowly, a plume of white smoke rising behind it.

Joseph took off his hat, then lifted Philomena in his arms and placed a hand on Salvatore's shoulder. "Look," he said, "the president is coming."

The last car of the train was ablaze with light, and all the window shades were raised. A casket lay inside on a simple catafalque covered by green Marine-issue blankets. The coffin was draped with the American flag. An honor guard stood at attention.

"Where is he?" little Philomena asked.

"Under the flag," her brother explained importantly.

"Did you see?" Joseph asked when the train had passed. Both children nodded somberly. "Good. Then remember, and when you grow up and have children of your own, you tell them about this. All right?"

Again both nodded. Satisfied, he took their hands and headed for home.

"HEY, LAWRENCE, the old man wants to see you."

Tad frowned impatiently. He had just come back from flying escort for another bombing run over Japan and was looking forward to a hot meal and a few hours of shut-eye. Like most of his fellow pilots, he was in no mood to talk to anyone, let alone the commanding officer. It wasn't that Tad didn't think highly of him—he did. But the way things were these days, meetings with the colonel tended to produce very little good news.

Leaving his leather jacket and cap in the wardroom, Tad walked wearily down the corridor to the C.O.'s office. It was late in the day and relatively quiet. Only a few orderlies were still busy filling out the ubiquitous requisition forms needed for everything from toilet paper to bombs.

Colonel Reeves was at his desk. He glanced up as Tad entered and waved him into a chair. "How did it go, Lawrence?"

"Fine, sir. No problems."

Reeves nodded, his blunt features relaxing slightly. He was a middle-aged, sandy-haired man with narrow gray eyes that didn't miss much and a reputation among his men for being tough but fair. He never asked his fliers to do something he hadn't done already, and he never wasted lives.

"Good," Reeves said. "Glad to hear it. Make sure you get some rest tonight; you're flying escort duty again tomorrow."

That was a surprise; as far as Tad knew, there were no bombing raids scheduled for the next day.

The C.O. leaned back in his chair, lit a large black cigar, and pulled for several moments before he went on. "A B-29 is going to make a run. It will be dropping only one bomb, so there shouldn't be anything to it."

Tad's eyebrows rose. "One plane, sir? One bomb?"

"That's right. You'll get the flight plan right before you leave. Also . . ." Reeves rummaged around in a drawer, found what he was looking for, and tossed a small object across the desk. "Put these on when you get near the target."

Tad stared for a moment before he realized what he was holding. "Welder's goggles, sir?"

Reeves nodded. "That's right."

"Is this some kind of . . . test?" Tad thought it likely. The desk jockeys back in Washington were always coming up with bright ideas for improving the pilots' flying. Most of the ideas were no better than this one appeared to be.

The colonel shrugged. "Who knows? Just make sure you wear those things."

Figuring it would do him no good to argue, Tad stuck the goggles in his pocket and stood up. "Will there be anything else, sir?"

Reeve hesitated an instant, long enough for Tad to notice and to think it was unusual; the colonel was normally very decisive. "No . . ." he said at length. "Just . . . look out for yourself."

A short time later, back in the Quonset hut that was home to him and about a dozen other pilots, Tad mulled over Reeves's words. The C.O. was not exactly the sentimental type. He cared about his men and did everything he could for them, but he never went in for any hearts and flowers.

Tad couldn't ever remember his telling a pilot to be careful; you did what you had to do to get the job done, and that was all there was to it.

Turning over onto his side, he stared at the blank wall near his head and considered the mission he would fly the next day.

There were several squads of bombers stationed on Tinian, the small island within easy flying reach of the Japanese mainland. They flew regular bombing runs, and he'd done his share of escort duty for them. But he'd never heard of a single-plane mission.

What the hell did it matter, anyway? It was just one more job to do. Except that...He couldn't quite pin it down, but it seemed to him that this might have something to do with the peculiar flying missions of the 509th Composite. Their pilots would go out someplace really remote and practice strange maneuvers, releasing dummy bombs and then banking and pulling away fast in a flight sequence that seemed to have no purpose. But they kept doing it, over and over, because the brass told them to.

Apparently, the 509th's fliers had no idea what all that training was supposed to result in. They hated the situation and wanted out, so that they could join their buddies flying the real missions over Japan. With the fall of Berlin and the celebration of V-E day, the Pacific was where all the action was. Unless you were with the 509th.

Just before he drifted off to sleep, Tad thought

that it would be interesting to see if tomorrow's B-29 was one of theirs.

ANTHONY AND MAGGIE were also in bed, but with no interest in sleeping. The bungalow she had been assigned near Sternberg Hospital wasn't far from those she had shared with the other junior nurses on duty in Manila at the outbreak of the war. Not a day went by that something did not jar her memory and make her recall that earlier time.

She was living with one foot in the past, the other in the present, and doing her best not to think of the future at all.

"Mmm," she murmured, her voice muffled by the pillow, "that feels so good."

Anthony chuckled and gazed down at her admiringly. He was kneeling on the bed, straddling her buttocks, as his big hands gently massaged the contours of her bare back. In the dim light of predawn, her skin gleamed like honeyed cream.

They had made love several times the night before and were about to do so again. No matter how many times they came together in ecstatic union, they could not sate their thirst for each other. The knowledge that they were soon to be separated made true assuagement impossible.

Even beyond the loneliness each would feel was the awareness that this parting might be final. So far they had both been very lucky, but such good fortune would not necessarily continue, especially once the invasion of Japan began.

The night before, when Anthony had reached for

the box beside the bed, as he always did, intending to protect Maggie, she had stopped him. Wordlessly they had stared at each other.

The need to leave something of himself behind had been growing stronger and stronger within him as the time of his departure neared. Yet he had scrupulously avoided making any mention of it, believing that to do so would be to place an unfair burden on her.

Maggie understood that, but in the privacy of her own mind she had forced herself to face the possibility that he might be killed, and she knew that to be left with nothing of him except memories would be far worse than to bear and raise a child of theirs alone.

So her hand had reached out to stop him and her arms had drawn him back to her, her body welcoming his with tender strength. . . as it had several more times during the night, as it did now.

Turning over, she smiled up at him, her eyes slumberous with passion. In the predawn shadows, he looked even larger than usual, all burnished skin and bulging muscle. Running her hands over his powerful arms, she wondered how he could seem so indestructible yet be so vulnerable.

He hovered motionless above her, letting her hands roam over him at will, as though she sought to memorize the very shape and form of him. Her expression was taut with concentration, her lips slightly parted and her eyes dark with need.

When he had endured all he could, a husky groan broke from him and he parted her thighs. Maggie reached out, cupping him gently, and brought him to her. Joined, they moved as one toward a peak of fulfillment that was at once a reaffirmation of life and a prayer for the future so long awaited, yet still so far away.

TAD WOKE before sunrise, swung out of bed, then showered and shaved quickly. Dressed in his usual jumpsuit, with his heavy leather jacket tossed over his arm, he headed for the mess and breakfast.

It was very quiet at the air base. Only a few fuel trucks and mechanics were about. He got his food, sat down and began to eat without actually tasting what he put in his mouth. His mind was on the coming mission.

In his pocket were the goggles Colonel Reeves had given him. He had stuck them in reluctantly, not just because he thought the idea of wearing them was stupid, but because something about them really bothered him. He couldn't put his finger on it, but the goggles themselves and Reeves's insistence that he make use of them caused little pinpricks of unease that he was unable to ignore.

He was just finishing a stack of pancakes when the old man himself strode into the mess. Tad looked up, surprised. Reeves worked hard enough; there was no reason for him to be stirring at this ungodly hour.

The C.O. apparently felt differently. He got himself a cup of coffee, grimaced at the stuff in the steam trays, and came over to join Tad. "Sleep okay?" he asked.

"Yes, sir, fine. Mission still on?"

"Sure is. Meteorology reports the weather is good all the way in. Ought to be a milk run."

"That's fine, sir.... Uh, just where are we headed?"

"Hiroshima."

Tad frowned. He'd seen the city marked on maps, but didn't know anything about it. "We haven't hit that one before, have we?"

"No, even though the Japanese Second Army is headquartered there." The colonel started to take another sip of coffee, then changed his mind and put the cup down. Almost to himself, he said, "I understand they've evacuated a lot of the civilians."

Tad hesitated a moment, not wanting to be too hopeful. Finally, he asked, "Most of them, sir?"

Reeves's eyes darkened. "No... not most." He sat a moment longer, then rose abruptly, wished Tad good luck, and strode out.

The remains of the pancakes no longer looked very appealing. Tad dumped his tray and headed for the field.

Once there, he discovered that he was only one of two pilots flying escort. The other man had also been informed of the mission in private by Reeves, given a pair of goggles, and told to look out for himself.

"It's the damnedest thing," he said. "For one lousy mission, they sure are making a hell of a fuss."

Tad shrugged and glanced at his watch. Time to go. He hoisted himself into his plane, fastened his helmet, and began running down his preflight checklist.

Minutes later the planes were airborne. It was a beautiful morning, the weather everything that meteorology had promised, with nothing but high, thin cirrus clouds against a sky that turned dark blue

with the approach of dawn. Not a single enemy aircraft was in sight. Heading northwest, the fliers were
soon on their way toward the Japanese mainland.

Tad checked his flight plan again. In it he had
found orders stating that immediately following the
release of the bomb by the *Enola Gay*, he was to pull
away hard. He'd done that often enough in dog-
fights, but he sure couldn't see the sense of it now.
There was also another reminder to wear the goggles.
Tad shook his head disgustedly. All this fuss for one
bomb. What the hell was the point?

Shortly before 0900, he pulled the goggles from a
pocket of his flight jacket and stared at them for a
moment. That strange talk with Reeves over coffee
came back to him. Shrugging, he put them on.

Hiroshima loomed in the near distance, a beautiful city of some 350,000 people. He remembered
what the colonel had said about evacuations and
hoped they had been more effective than the C.O.
thought.

Not that those people down there could have all
that much to worry about. Reminding himself that
the *Enola Gay* was carrying only a single bomb, Tad
relaxed slightly. This flight was probably intended as
some sort of demonstration; they might even be carrying propaganda leaflets urging surrender.

The run in was straight and clear—still no enemy
aircraft, no indication that the planes had even been
noticed. At 0915 they were directly over the center of
the city. The B-29's bomb bays opened, and a single
long, black missile plummeted earthward.

Obedient to his orders, Tad immediately threw his

plane into a hard turn and pulled up steeply. He concentrated strictly on completing the maneuver, giving it all his attention until, in a split second of infinity, something incomprehensible appeared on the edge of his vision.

A flash of purplish light—no, that was gone already, transformed into a fireball—so big... how could it be?... rising on a pillar of smoke, higher and higher, until at about ten thousand feet, it began to spread out, forming something... a cloud that looked like a... mushroom.

Tad shook his head dazedly. He'd never seen any bomb have that effect. Already another cloud was forming above the first, the whole monstrous thing reaching to at least fifty thousand feet. As it entered the stratosphere, it flashed the entire spectrum of color, like some hideously distorted rainbow.

From the recesses of Tad's mind, a memory surfaced: he and Maggie in school, the nuns telling them that God had set His bow in the sky as a token of His covenant with man, and that He had promised that the bow would not be hidden by any cloud He brought over the earth.

But He had not brought this one; man had. It was almost... beautiful... except that the sweat prickling Tad's spine and the sickness in his stomach told him it was not.

Not unless death was beautiful, for this, he had no doubt, was the very incarnation of death, held in check since the beginning of time and now unleashed on the world.

Beneath the goggles, whose purpose he at last understood, his eyes were filled with horror. Automatically, he turned his plane onto the proper course and headed away, knowing even as he did so that there could be no escape from the new world they had all so abruptly entered.

MAGGIE WOKE UP FIRST the next morning. She lingered in bed for a few minutes, gazing at Anthony, who was still asleep. Her eyes were somber and her mood dark. In place of the joy they had shared during the night, morning had brought sadness and a swiftly growing sense of apprehension. All too soon he would be leaving for Okinawa.

Knowing that he needed his rest, she slid from the bed without disturbing him, put on a robe and padded out to the small kitchen to start the coffee.

While it brewed, she went to the front door and retrieved a copy of the daily Philippine newspaper, left there a short time before. On her way back to the kitchen, she glanced at the headlines.

ATOMIC BOMB DROPPED ON HIROSHIMA.
TRUMAN WARNS OF A "RAIN OF RUIN."

The coffee was forgotten as she read quickly through the stories blanketing the front page. By the time she had finished, she knew she ought to be glad about what had happened, if only from a strictly personal perspective. But she was not.

Instead, she thought of the people whose lives had been snuffed out in an instant. This was a new kind of destruction, far beyond anything she had ever known. Surely no one, no matter how fanatical or how desperate, would continue to fight under such circumstances. The peace they had all prayed for was finally at hand, but not in any way they could have imagined.

Her face was pale when she went back to the bedroom. Anthony was awake. His smile was full of tender recollection as he murmured, "Mornin', angel... Jeez, I wish we weren't on duty today." Raising his arms over his head, he stretched languidly. "I'd like to spend it—"

"It doesn't matter," Maggie said softly. At his surprised look, she added, "We won't be on duty much longer." Going over to the bed, she held the paper out to him.

Epilogue

"WE'LL NEVER find them!" Maria exclaimed, clinging to her husband's arm as they tried to make their way through the milling crowd packed into New York's Pennsylvania Station.

A huge wreath above the main doors sported a banner that wished everyone "Peace on earth and goodwill among men." The trombones of a Salvation Army band soared on the crisp winter air, mingling with the excited voices of men, women and children about to receive what was surely the best possible Christmas gift.

Joseph squeezed her hand reassuringly. He was tall enough to be able to see over the heads of most of the people, and big enough to encourage them to open a path for him and Maria.

It was slow going, but eventually they reached the barrier stretched across the entrance to the track on which the train from Washington had just arrived. Ahead was a sea of khaki; servicemen swarmed off the train, duffel bags balanced on their shoulders, their faces tense with anticipation.

"Joy to the world," the carolers sang, and joy there was in the hundreds of tiny, personal scenes being played out around Joseph and Maria. An aged mother wept in the arms of her son; an elderly man stood stiffly with pride; a wife comforted a shy child as her husband tenderly ruffled the boy's hair. Simple, ordinary events had become, at that moment and in that place, a testament to the power of miracles.

A young blond woman standing next to the Garganos suddenly gave a cry and ran forward, ignoring the pained look of the guard, who was trying to maintain some semblance of order. She was caught up in the arms of a sailor who whirled her around deliriously before delivering a kiss that had their audience grinning.

A family group—parents, a young wife, a toddler in her arms—waited nearby. They, too, were concerned about being able to find one person out of so many; but as the stream of servicemen moved past them, joyful recognition flashed across their faces. Moments later, a young Army officer was meeting the son he had never before seen.

"Oh, Joseph," Maria moaned, "what if they missed the train? What if they couldn't get on? It's so crowded."

"They're here," he assured her, his calm words masking his own anxiousness. "We have to be patient."

She nodded and tried to distract herself with thoughts of the celebration to come. The girls would be busy putting the final touches on dinner. She frowned slightly, hoping that Vita wouldn't put too much oregano in the spaghetti sauce, then remembered that Sal was on hand to stop her.

Maria and Joseph had gone to the Brooklyn dockyards the previous week to welcome Sal home, accompanied by Paulo and his English bride, who had arrived a few days earlier. Barely had Sal settled in than it was Dom's turn; he brought with him the news that Anthony and Maggie were stopping off in Virginia for several days to visit her mother and would arrive in New York on Christmas Eve.

Maggie and Anthony had sat up all night on the train, lucky to have two seats together, but they weren't the least bit tired. There was too much excitement for that.

"I can hardly believe it!" she cried, glancing around as Anthony helped her off the train. "All these people—just like us!"

He grinned down at her, keeping a protective arm around her waist as they made their way up the platform. "Not quite. Nobody else has such a good-looking girl."

She laughed softly. "I think you're a little prejudiced." Her smile faded as she added, "I hope your parents will like me."

"Sweetheart, they'll love you. They can't help but." Teasingly, he reminded her, "Your mom seems to think I'm okay."

"She's crazy about you and you know it." Elizabeth Lawrence had made no secret of her affection for her son-in-law. The days Maggie and Anthony had spent with her in the Virginia house were filled with happiness, if a bit hectic. Elizabeth was busy packing to join Will on his new assignment in Japan. With luck, she would be able to see Tad when they both passed through San Diego.

Thinking of her parents' forthcoming reunion made Maggie all the more anxious to meet her in-laws. She strained her neck trying to see over the crowd, but could make out little except a seemingly endless stream of khaki.

Joseph had the same impression. Though he wasn't about to admit it, he was getting a little worried that something might have gone wrong. Stopping a young man who was hurrying by, he asked, "Any Marines on the train, soldier?"

"Yes, sir, a whole bunch. Ought to be coming through any minute now."

Maria stood on tiptoe, almost bouncing up and down in her eagerness. Joseph spied an upturned wooden box lying to one side and quickly lifted her onto it.

"Take a good look. They've got to be here somewhere."

"No... I don't see them.... Wait—" A flash of a man's ebony head caught her eye... beneath it, a vibrant smile... directed at the girl in white next to the tall Marine officer.... Maria's throat tightened as a quick rush of tears threatened to blur her vision. "T-tonio! It's Tonio! Joseph, they're here!"

Above the din of shouts and laughter, the familiar voice of his mother reached Anthony. His eyes darted quickly toward its source. "Ma...? Hey, there's Ma...and Pop!" Almost scooping Maggie off her feet, he plowed through the crowd until at last they reached the man and woman waiting with outstretched arms.

"Let me look at you!" Maria cried, even as she seized Anthony in a heartfelt hug. His face was leaner and harder than she remembered, and his body had the taut muscularity of a man rather than a youth. She choked back a sob, hardly daring to believe that he was real.

Joseph threw an arm around his son's shoulders, grinning wildly. "You're looking great, really great!"

It didn't seem possible that the tall, powerful man in the captain's uniform was actually his child, yet it was true. He swallowed hastily, fighting for control while he uttered a silent prayer of thanks for the manifold mercy of another son returned and a family once again complete.

Anthony gazed from one parent to the other, delighted to see that the intervening years had wrought so few changes. His father's dark hair was shot through with a little more silver, and his mother's gently rounded figure was a shade plumper. But other than that, they were just as he remembered them, wonderfully familiar and dearly loved.

Maggie stood a little to one side, trying not to feel out of place. She wasn't quite sure what she should say or do, until Joseph solved the problem for her.

"And this must be Maggie!" He gave her a smile as riveting as his son's. "You're as beautiful as Dom said!"

She blushed fiercely, though she could not contain a laugh of pleasure. "Dom spins such a line of blarney, I can't help but wonder if he isn't a tiny bit Irish."

"Wouldn't surprise me at all," Joseph assured her with an embrace. "The Garganos always did get around pretty good."

"Welcome to the family," Maria said warmly as she hugged Maggie. She instantly liked the look of the lovely girl, but even more, she liked the look of utter contentment she could see on her son's face. "Tonio did himself proud."

"Sure did," he agreed as he reclaimed his bride. "She's much too good for me."

They laughed together as they slowly made their way through the station. Maria kept a tight hold on Anthony's arm, and her husband followed with Maggie.

A line of cabs waited outside. Joseph summoned one, causing his son to raise an eyebrow.

"Since when did you get so fancy?" Anthony asked.

His father turned to him. Their eyes met. "You're going home in style," he said firmly.

Anthony laughed, a deep, full sound. They all squeezed into the backseat, and the cab took off with a lurch, threading its way through traffic. Maggie stared out the window, entranced by her first sight of New York City. It was so big, and crowded with the tallest buildings she had ever seen. Everyone appeared to be in a great hurry.

She shook her head a little dazedly, wondering how she would ever learn to cope with this place, yet knowing that somehow she would manage. There was so much to look forward to.

In a few weeks, Anthony and James would be getting together to start their business. They had talked about little else during the final months in the Philippines and were all set to get moving. James had been mustered out a few weeks earlier and was even now scouting locations for their pioneer television station.

Maggie was absolutely certain they would be successful, but that was only the beginning of all that the future promised. Already she was imagining how she would furnish a home, which she and Anthony would need soon if what she suspected about herself was true. She hoped that this child would be the first of many in their family.

Above all, she could look forward to the life they would build together, founded on the love and trust that had survived so much. Snuggling against Anthony, she met his tender gaze with a smile. Whatever lay ahead, they would face it together. For both of them — and for all the millions who had passed safely through the storm — it was the beginning.

Maura Seger continues to chronicle America's recent history in *Echo of Thunder*, the enthralling story of James Callahan's tumultuous love affair with the beautiful, willful Alexis Brockton, heiress to a communications empire. Set against the backdrop of the burgeoning television industry, *Echo of Thunder* gives an insider's view of events from the turbulent postwar era to the glamour and intrigue of the "Camelot" years.

Available in September.

Author's Note

With the exception of clearly identified historical personages, all the characters in *Eye of the Storm* are purely the products of my own imagination. The story, however, adheres very closely to the actual events that occurred in the Pacific war theater and on the home front from December 1941 to V-J Day. As the men and women who lived through that time can certainly attest, it was a period in which fact was far more dramatic than fiction ever could be.

M.S.

ANNE MATHER

Anne Mather, one of Harlequin's leading romance authors, has published more than 100 million copies worldwide, including **Wild Concerto**, a *New York Times* best-seller.

Catherine Loring was an innocent in a South American country beset by civil war. Doctor Armand Alvares was arrogant yet compassionate. They could not ignore the flame of love igniting within them...whatever the cost.

HIDDEN IN THE FLAME

Available at your favorite bookstore in June, or send your name, address and zip or postal code, along with a check or money order for $4.25 (includes 75¢ for postage and handling) payable to Worldwide Library Reader Service to:

Worldwide Library Reader Service

In the U.S.
Box 52040
Phoenix, AZ
85072-2040

In Canada
5170 Yonge Street, P.O. Box 2800,
Postal Station A
Willowdale, Ont. M2N 6J3

HIF-A-I